Sisters of Vellangoose

ELAINE SINGER

Grosvenor House
Publishing Limited

This book is published by
Grosvenor House Publishing Ltd
Link House
140 The Broadway, Tolworth, Surrey, KT6 7HT.
www.grosvenorhousepublishing.co.uk

This book is a work of fiction. Any resemblance to
people or events, past or present, is purely coincidental.

A CIP record for this book
is available from the British Library

ISBN 978-1-80381-297-7
eBook ISBN 978-1-80381-298-4

For Adrian xx

Elaine lives in Cornwall with her husband, Adrian, and two Labrador dogs.

Sisters of Vellangoose

1

Becky's kitchen door crashed open.

Natalie bounded in on a gust of cold air, flung her car keys onto the oak worktop and reached for the biscuit jar.

"Have you heard the news? Everyone was talking about it at the school drop-off."

"Heard what?" Becky opened the Aga door and the aroma of chocolate sponge cake flooded the room. Delicious. A perfect start to what was going to be her perfect day.

She reached inside the oven for two cake tins, lifted them out, placed them on the oven top and waited for her younger sister to dispense the latest piece of gossip.

"Henry Williams is dead."

Becky pulled off her oven gloves slowly.

"Dead?"

"Killed by his horse."

Natalie flicked the kettle switch and moved to the dining table. Becky winced as her sister dragged a cream Laura Ashley chair along the tiled floor.

"Maybe it didn't actually kill him, but that big white stallion of his almost galloped headlong into a car near Boswyn. The driver caught the brute and walked it back along the road to find the rider. He turned a corner and … wham-bam, there he was." Natalie flicked her long, chestnut hair with her fingers. "Henry Williams. Flat out in the middle of the road. Stone dead."

"That's dreadful." An involuntary shiver ran over Becky's body. To die alone in the middle of nowhere, it didn't bear thinking about. Not even Henry Williams deserved that. She plucked two mugs from the wooden tree, dropped an Earl Grey tea bag into one and spooned coffee granules into the other. "Does Dad know?"

Natalie shrugged. "What is it with him and the Williams family, anyway? Mum was even worse; she never used to let us talk about them. The whole situation was so weird. Remember that time when all my mates went flower picking at Boswyn Manor and I wasn't allowed to go? I had to take a holiday job in that fish and chip shop. Ugh, I can still smell that fat."

An image shot through Becky's mind of her mother's red face: 'You'll have nothing to do with that family, do you hear me?' Both her parents had worked for Henry Williams before Becky was born, but something had happened. She didn't know what.

Tears came to her eyes. It surprised her how raw her grief for her mother still was, even though it had been eighteen months now since she died. She grabbed a pencil and a notepad from the table, turned to her 'to do' list for the day and took a deep, calming breath. Clean the bathroom. Tick. Change the beds. Tick. Washing. She glanced out of the window. Crisp white sheets drifted in the light breeze. Tick. Bake Red Velvet Cake. Her pencil hovered over the paper.

She looked sideways at Natalie. With her designer clothes, expensive haircut and high maintenance nails, nobody would take her sister for a stay-at-home mother. By contrast, Becky was aware of how she herself appeared: a woman in her late thirties, housewife, mother, tall and slim but not super glossy like Natalie. There were only four years between them, but anybody looking at them would think Natalie was a good ten years younger.

"That bitchy wife of his will probably get the lot, as if Veronica Williams isn't rich enough already. Blimey, she'll be the sole owner of Williams Estates and Haulage. That'll worry a few people." Natalie paused to apply a coat of lipstick and press her lips together. "Enough of that lot. Happy Anniversary. Blooming heck, twenty-one years. You and John going out to celebrate?"

Becky reached for a glass mixing bowl, then bent down and removed butter and cream cheese from the fridge. Her hair fell across her face. She made no attempt to push it back.

"John wants to stay in, so I'm cooking steak in a peppercorn sauce, new potatoes, and green beans."

"John's favourite." Natalie stood up and dropped her mug into the sink. "Must go. I've got to get to Truro and Waitrose before I pick up Lily from the nursery." She leaned towards Becky and hugged her. "You know, you really should consider having some highlights in your hair. Have a fun evening."

Becky's hand flew to her shoulder-length curls. Before she could reply, the kitchen door banged shut and Natalie had gone, only a hint of her perfume remaining.

In the hallway, the letterbox rattled.

Wiping her hands on her apron, Becky walked across the tiled floor and picked up the assorted post. Back in the kitchen, she chucked the junk mail, unopened, into the recycling bin and placed several envelopes addressed to John Farrow on the dresser. The top envelope – from their electricity supplier – felt thicker than normal. Tempted to open it, she turned it over a couple of times before she dropped it with the others. Her husband would deal with them all, like he always did.

Absentmindedly, she beat the butter and cream cheese, round and round the bowl until the mixture grew soft and fluffy. She added vanilla extract and icing sugar, then picked up the spoon again.

Outside the window, blue tits, chaffinches, and a robin fluttered around the bird feeders. A blackbird pecked at the ground underneath. The earlier sunshine had been replaced by a grey mist, typical of a Cornish day in January. Her sheets hung limp on the line.

She looked up at the clock on the wall. Goodness, the day was flying by. She needed to ring Jess.

Smiling, she picked up the phone.

"Hello, darling. Just wanted to check what time you'll be back this evening."

"What?"

"Our wedding anniversary dinner? You said you'd eat with us? I've made your favourite, Red Velvet Cake. It's so moist and … you'll love it." She knew her voice had adopted a sing-song rhythm, but she couldn't help herself.

"I only said I might get there. I've got something else on. Anyway, it should be just you and Dad."

"But, darling, you prom–"

"Sorry, Mum. Got to go."

A continuous ring tone pulsed through Becky's head.

She scrabbled in the drawer for a knife, then reached for one of the sponge tins on the worktop. What had happened to the days when she and Jess would cuddle up together on the sofa with a box of chocolates and watch some soppy film? Her daughter was hardly home these days.

A single tear trickled down Becky's cheek. She brushed it away and picked up one of the sponge tins. Oh dear, she should've turned it out earlier, before it got cold. She rapped furiously on the bottom of the tin. The cake tumbled out. A jagged chunk of blood-red mixture remained stuck to the inside.

The flickering candles cast dappled shadows across the wall, adding a touch of romance. Becky loved the hint of honeysuckle that the melted wax threw off. A stray curl fell over her eye. She pushed it back behind her ear. Perhaps she should've gone to the hairdressers that afternoon? Blast you, Natalie.

The headlights of a car flashed across the window.

She rushed to the door to welcome John. He breezed into the kitchen, gave her a brief kiss on the cheek and made straight to the pile of post.

"Put the kettle on, love. I'm dying for a cup of tea and a sandwich."

"Sandwich? You'll ruin your meal."

John swivelled around and looked at her, a frown on his face. "Ah. Our anniversary dinner." He shoved the envelopes into his jacket pocket. "Problem, I'm afraid. I've got a meeting with a work associate in Truro. He's only in Cornwall for this evening. You understand, love. It'll be good for the business."

Becky's shoulders sagged. Not John as well? Not on their wedding anniversary?

John hesitated, then reached over and pulled her into his arms. "Sorry, love. You know if I could get out of it, I would."

The feel of John's arms comforted her. She rested her head on his chest and his heart thumped against her ear. He gave her a brief hug and stepped away.

"We'll celebrate tomorrow evening. I could take you somewhere fancy. Treat ourselves to a slap-up meal, that's what we'll do."

The car keys jangled in his hand. "Don't worry about that cuppa; I'll grab something in Truro. Don't wait up."

Before she could reply, John had picked up his wallet and was gone.

The raw steak and prepared vegetables mocked her. No point in cooking just for her. She methodically placed the ingredients into plastic bags and put them into the freezer. In the silence, she blew out the candles and cut herself a piece of Red Velvet Cake. For a long time, she stared unseeing at the plate, then abruptly stood up, walked across the kitchen, flicked the uneaten cake into the rubbish bin and wiped the plate clean with a serviette.

2

Abi lay on her back in the semi-darkness. Eyes wide open, she waited as Nick slept beside her. He would be dead to the world until morning; the extra-large Domino's pepperoni and sausage pizza, washed down with several beers, had done its job. His steady, rhythmic snores competed with the tick-tock of the bedside clock. 12:45 a.m. It was time.

She slowly lifted the muscular arm draped across her stomach and placed it against Nick's side. He spluttered and the rank odour of stale alcohol wafted into her face.

She stiffened. Waited.

The snoring resumed.

Bit by bit, she lifted the duvet, eased herself out of the bed and tip-toed from the room.

In the kitchen-living area, she swiftly pulled on jeans, a sweater and a well-worn jacket. Buddy bounced around her feet, his brown and white body wriggling from side to side. She calmed him, clipped on his lead, and retrieved a bulging black plastic bag from behind the sofa. Noiselessly, she opened the front door, ran to a camper van parked on the other side of the road, and stuffed the bag into the back on top of others she'd packed earlier in the day. She opened the passenger door and Buddy jumped inside. A piece of litter lifted from the pavement and fluttered around her legs. She kicked it aside.

"Stay, Buddy. I won't be long."

Back in the flat, she opened the door to the cramped second bedroom, hurriedly reached up to the top bunk bed and gently shook Jacob's shoulder.

His face crumpled with sleep as he rubbed his eyes. "Mum?"

"Shush. Put these on. We're leaving." She pushed trainers and warm clothes into his arms. "Over your pyjamas, it's quicker. I'll wake Eve."

Without asking any questions, Jacob climbed down, picked up a row of toy cars from the window ledge and shoved them into his coat pocket.

Eve grizzled through a mop of long, curly hair. "Mummy, I don't want–"

"Be good, sweetheart. We're going on a little adventure." She scooped the tangled hair away from her daughter's face and spoke in an urgent whisper. "It'll be fun, but you must be extra quiet or you'll spoil everything."

She turned from Eve, lifted a still-sleeping Grace from her cot and wrapped her in a warm blanket. With her free hand, Abi deftly pushed Eve's arm into her coat, then grabbed her hand in a tight hold and nodded to Jacob. They were ready.

Jacob slowly opened the door and they stepped quietly from the room.

In the camper van, Abi secured Jacob and Eve into their child seats and Grace into her toddler seat. One more trip inside would do it. She glanced at the flat then back at her three kids. It would only take her a few minutes to dismantle the cot.

"Buddy, watch them for me," she whispered.

In her rush to take apart the cot, the screwdriver fell from her hand and dropped to the floor with a clang. She froze.

In the other room, Nick's snores stopped.

He coughed.

Shit, he'd need to take a leak before he'd fall asleep again.

She looked at the partly dismantled cot, swept the duvets from the kids' beds and crept out of the flat.

The keys jangled as she fumbled with the ignition key. Please start. Please.

The engine rumbled, backfired, and died. The sound hung like a gunshot in the night air.

A light in the flat flashed on. Abi's heart raced. She twisted the key again. Please.

The engine turned, spluttered once, then roared into life.

She released the handbrake, and without a backward glance, accelerated away.

"Is Uncle Nick coming with us?" Eve wriggled in her seat.

Jacob poked his sister's thigh. "Don't be silly, you won't see him again."

"Will too. I will, won't I, Mummy?"

"That's enough from the pair of you. We've got a long drive. Go to sleep."

Abi gripped the steering wheel, her eyes fixed on the road ahead. She was a rubbish mother. What was she thinking, dragging the kids out of their beds in the middle of the night and uprooting them again? Nick wasn't such a bad man; lazy and fierce tempered when crossed – something she'd experienced first-hand more than once – but to be fair to him, she'd stayed with worse. In the six months they'd lived together, he'd been kind enough to the kids, especially considering none of them were his. But this moment was always going to happen, and the telephone call the previous day had only hastened her departure, not caused it.

Something about that call still bothered her. The words on their own had shocked her, but not so much as that cold, flat voice. She knew that tone; it hid a well of conflicting emotions. A few minutes after she hung up, Abi had made the decision to leave.

The lights of Portsmouth had disappeared by the time Abi eased the camper van onto the trunk road and headed west. A few other cars rushed past them. Occasionally, a car horn tooted in the distance.

"Mummy, I need a wee-wee." Eve's voice broke into Abi's thoughts.

She had hoped to get to a service station of some sort before the kids woke up, but that was kids for you, and she had been driving for what seemed like forever. A break would do her good as well.

In the next lay-by, she turned off the engine, rubbed her eyes and glanced at her watch. 4:00 a.m.

She pushed open the driver's door, and before she could stop him, Buddy sprang over Jacob's shoulder and shot past her. He slithered under a field gate and disappeared into the darkness.

Abi ran after him.

"Buddy, come here."

Ten minutes later, with still no sign of Buddy, Eve and Jacob were back in their seats, munching on chocolate biscuits. Grace cried non-stop despite Abi rocking her to and fro until her arms ached. At fifteen months, she was getting quite a lump to hold for long. Abi filled Grace's bottle again with warm milk from a flask. Her daughter took a few sips before her eyes fluttered, then closed.

Abi picked up Grace's dirty nappy and looked for a bin. Not seeing one, she chucked it into the ditch and called again to the wayward spaniel. "Buddy, please come. Time to go."

Overhead, the branches of the trees moaned and flapped in the wind.

She needed to move now to avoid the rush hour. Stuck in work traffic in a dodgy camper van with three fretful kids and an overexcited dog didn't sound much of a plan.

An owl hooted nearby.

Abi got into the van and switched on the ignition. The engine started the first time. A few raindrops blew onto the windscreen.

"Mum, you can't leave Buddy." Jacob clutched the sleeve of her jacket. "You can't."

Eve started to cry.

Abi twisted around and reached for her son's hand. "Don't be silly. Of course I won't leave him." She swung back in her seat, thumped the horn several times, and flicked on the headlights.

"Buddy!" Jacob yelled.

In the beam, Buddy stood, tongue lolling, his tail wagging at half-mast.

Abi leapt out and waved the dog inside. She couldn't have left that silly animal behind. At twelve months, he was like her youngest child.

"Let's get going. How about I put a CD on? Is *The Gruffalo* okay?"

The rain came in waves. The miles slipped by in an endless swish-swish of windscreen wipers and the soft rumble of wheels on the tarmac. She eased one hand off the steering wheel and flexed her fingers, yawned, then did the same to the other.

That phone call continued to churn round and round in her head. Was she doing the right thing?

A signpost came into view: Cornwall.

An unexpected feeling of contentment ran through her. Home, even though she'd not been back for seven years.

The road dipped and weaved. Familiar and beautiful, the landscape calmed her. The dual carriageway gave way to country roads, and she drove on, under canopies of trees and through twisty lanes, until she came to her childhood town: Penryn.

In a narrow street of small, terraced houses, she pulled the camper van partly onto the pavement and switched off the engine. This was it.

She took a deep breath and stepped out into a fine drizzle.

"Stay, Buddy." Abi stroked the dog's silky ears, shrugged her rucksack over her shoulder and scooped Grace into her arms.

Outside a muddy-brown door, she reached out, hesitated, then rang the bell. The noise echoed through the darkness. Abi tightened her grip on Grace's sleeping body. Jacob and Eve stood on either side of her.

A minute later, she pushed the bell again.

A light appeared in the window above. Eve pressed her face into Abi's leg.

The door opened. A woman in a faded dressing gown stood in front of her. She looked middle-aged. How did that happen?

Abi's heart raced. "Hello, Mum."

3

After lunch together, Becky sank into the passenger seat of Natalie's new four-by-four as her sister sped along the narrow roads from the Pandora Inn to Truro and pulled into the car park at Waitrose.

She followed her sister and smiled as several male shoppers turned and watched Natalie sashay across the car park and into the supermarket. Grabbing a trolley, Becky rushed to catch up. The automatic doors swished open, then closed behind her.

Natalie tossed a bag of ready-washed spinach, a pack of baby leeks and another of carrot batons into her wire basket.

"Don't you do any food preparation yourself?" Becky asked.

"Too busy doing the things I like. I'd never fit it all in if I spent the day chained to the kitchen. Ugh, the whole peeling and chopping thing would ruin my hands." Natalie chucked more packs of pre-prepared vegetables and fruit into her basket without so much as a glance at the cost or use-by date. "You should've got a basket. Less hassle than a trolley. And quicker."

"What's the rush?" Becky picked up a carton of fresh strawberries. Not English but, just for once, she had to give in and buy out of season.

"I've got a yoga class later," Natalie said over her shoulder as she marched off down the aisle. "You need to get a wiggle on if you want a lift back."

Charming.

Becky hurried towards the meat section. Natalie was so bossy sometimes, and so self-righteous with her exercise classes and so-called healthy diet, neither of which seemed to stop her from eating cake and biscuits whenever she visited Rose Cottage. Hypocrite.

To be truthful, if Natalie wasn't her sister, she probably wouldn't even like her.

Becky glanced at her list. Tonight, she was going to cook Pollo Allo Spumante followed by Zabaglione. She already had most of the ingredients in her larder, but she needed to buy chicken quarters, a bottle of Marsala, and a few other bits.

"What's the theme tonight?" Natalie caught up with her in the home-baking section. The faint smell of a freshly cut wedge of Cornish Brie rose from her basket.

"Italian. Chicken in sparkling wine, followed by egg custard with strawberries marinated in brandy.

Natalie snorted. "What? All that for I-only-eat-pizza-Jess and her father, Junk-food-John? You must be joking."

Becky put a hand to her neck. She knew the tell-tale blotches would soon appear. Natalie was right. The almond macaroons and paradise cake she planned to bake would go down well, but her family would probably turn their noses up at everything else.

"Don't sulk, frowning will give you more wrinkles." No longer seeming to be in any hurry, Natalie fiddled in her handbag and pulled out her lipstick. "I meant to ask you over lunch, how did the anniversary dinner go?"

Natalie had spent the entire time going on and on about her new kitchen, so no wonder she'd forgotten to ask about the fiasco of an anniversary dinner. Becky reached for a packet of almonds. Several packs of assorted nuts fell to the floor, and she busied herself picking them up.

"You seemed a bit off, earlier." Natalie touched up her already glossy lips and dropped the lipstick back into her bag. "Did Jess manage to join you both?"

Why couldn't Natalie just shut up?

"She had a last-minute engagement with friends," Becky mumbled.

"Oh well, what did you expect? She's nineteen. Probably had a hot date." Natalie giggled. "Or maybe she's got herself a boyfriend and she's not ready to bring him home yet to meet dear Mummy and Daddy?"

Becky frowned and shoved a handful of the packets back onto the shelf. Surely Jess would tell her if she had a serious boyfriend?

"Presumably John enjoyed the peppercorn steak?"

Becky's eyes stung with tears. "He didn't make it either."

"What?"

"He had a last-minute business meeting in Truro." She blinked and plastered a smile onto her face. "But you should see the wonderful bouquet of roses he bought me."

"You're kidding?"

"Well, he does have a business to run. You know what it's like to have a workaholic for a husband." Becky ran the end of her pencil down the list, and hurriedly put ticks against several items.

"If Pete did that to me, I'd strangle him."

"I'm not you." Becky jerked the trolley forward and made for the drinks section. "You'll miss your yoga class if you wait for me, Natalie. I'll make my own way home. I'll ring you later, okay?"

Becky's handbag, hooked on the metal handle, banged against her thigh as she hurried into the next aisle. A hard knot formed in her stomach. She had no idea how she'd manage to get back to Mawnan Smith from Truro without it involving a very expensive taxi trip, but if it stopped Natalie nosing into her business, it would be worth it.

A child screamed in the adjoining lane. Becky's head throbbed. She let out a deep breath and reached for a bottle of Marsala. Her hand trembled and the bottle clunked against its neighbours. She steadied it before resting her head against the shelf.

Someone touched her shoulder.

Becky jerked around.

Natalie.

Blast her, why couldn't her sister ever do as she was told?

"What's up with John?"

"Nothing. He's fine."

"He's a jerk."

Becky opened her mouth but nothing came out. Uncontrollable tears rolled down her cheeks.

"Oh dear, everyone's looking at me."

Natalie glared at a passing customer. "Who cares?" She stepped closer. "Tell me what's up."

Trapped.

Becky bowed her head. "We ... we keep getting these telephone calls. I've asked John about them, but he tells me not to worry." She pulled a tissue from her sleeve and blew her nose. "Then there's the mountain of mail and some of the letters I've had to sign for. Something's wrong, I just know it."

"What sort of letters?"

"I don't know. John deals with it all."

Natalie arched an eyebrow. "Does he now?"

"He's always managed everything to do with our finances and the household."

Natalie turned to face the exit. "Come on, we need to go."

"But I've still got things to get."

"You've got enough." Natalie grabbed Becky's trolley and steered it towards the checkout.

Natalie banged her purchases onto the conveyor belt and glared at Becky until she followed suit.

In the kitchen at Rose Cottage, Becky slumped back against her chair and let the letter in her hand flutter onto the pile of torn envelopes that littered the tiled floor. Another final demand. Various pieces of correspondence dotted the dining table.

"This is just today's post, where does John keep the rest?" Natalie's voice was hard and businesslike. "The bank statements and your mortgage paperwork? Becky? Come on, we need to do this."

"Everything's in the filing cabinet, but John keeps it locked."

"We'll see about that."

In John's study, Natalie pushed a meat cleaver into the gap between the cabinet drawer and its casing. A loud crack filled the air.

Fifteen minutes later, John's files lay open, and beads of sweat ran down Becky's face. The stacks of final statements exposed debt, after debt, after debt.

Oh my God. How could she have been so stupid? Why hadn't she intervened before?

She shoved a clenched fist into her mouth. Oh John, what have you done?

Becky sat in the darkness and forced herself to remain calm. A hydrangea branch tapped intermittently against the windowpane.

After Natalie had left, Becky had stacked all the papers and files into subject and date order. Now, the neat piles on the kitchen table mocked her. Please let there be a simple explanation for all this; let John have a solution that will make this mess go away. Uncontrollable tremors ran over her body. She pressed her hands between her thighs. John hated it when she got emotional or made a scene. He'd be absolutely furious at what she and Natalie had done.

Becky glanced at the digital clock on the cooker. 11:00 p.m. Just as well she hadn't cooked the Italian meal.

A car pulled up outside.

She stiffened.

Footsteps crunched across the gravel. The back door opened, then closed.

She got to her feet and stood in front of the table. A switch clicked. Light flooded the room.

Head down, John tossed his car keys onto the worktop, reached for a glass from one of the cupboards, and filled it from the cold water tap.

She steeled herself to speak.

"John."

Water sloshed over his hand. "Bloody hell. You scared me half to death. I thought you'd be in bed with your nose in a book by now." He raised the glass partway to his lips. "Why were you sitting in the dark?"

The smell of stale beer and cigarette smoke reached her.

"I was waiting for you."

He placed the tumbler onto the worktop. "Ah. Sorry about dinner. Stuff I had to sort at the office. Should've rung, but you know how these things go."

"We need to talk."

"Bit late, isn't it, love? I'm tired." His gaze moved to the dresser. "No post?"

All her instincts told her to run. She couldn't do this. But … She stepped aside.

John's eyes widened. He barged past her and clawed at the piles of correspondence and files.

"What the hell have you done?"

"I had to know." She wrung her hands. "All those phone calls. And the registered mail I've had to sign for …"

"I've already told you, there's nothing to worry about."

"But …" She glanced at the heap of papers, then looked away.

"It's okay." He swept a hand over his hair. "I'm sorting it."

Relief shot through her. She'd known John since she was seventeen; he wouldn't let her down.

She bent over and picked up the outstanding electric bill.

"I'll help you."

He let out a harsh snort. "What can *you* do? Bake a cake? Kiss it better?" Scowling, he grabbed an armful of files. "Go to bed."

"I won't be able to sleep. Please, I've got to know what's wrong. Whatever it is, I can help you put it right."

"For Christ's sake, just leave it. Take it from me, there's nothing you can do."

"That's not true. I can help with telephone calls, and reply to letters. You know I'm a good organiser." She rushed to the dresser and pulled out a notepad and pencil from one of the drawers. "I'll ring the electricity company first thing in the morning, so we don't get cut off. Then I'll set up a meeting with Lloyds Bank. I'm sure they'll have a package whereby we can roll all the debts and overdrafts into one long-term loan." She scribbled on the pad. "Same with the mortgage, we–"

"Stop. You're wasting your time."

"Don't be silly. We've only got three years left to pay on the mortgage. We could extend it and get a lump sum to clear the more pressing debts."

John returned the files to the table and gripped the back of one of the chairs. "I've already re-mortgaged Rose Cottage."

Becky's heart raced. "You can't have. Not without asking me."

"You forget, I'm the sole owner. Your consent wasn't necessary."

Images flashed through her mind like some old black and white newsreel: John's parents giving them the deposit on Rose Cottage as a wedding present; his father ensuring that the property was in John's name only – just in case the hastily arranged marriage didn't last. She and John had intended to get the property details changed into their joint names. Except, they never did.

Her eyes brimmed. "Oh my God, what have you done?" She pulled a piece of kitchen towel from the holder on the wall. "How could you?"

"Because I could."

"But it's our family home. What about Jess?"

"Jess is nineteen. She doesn't need *us* anymore, let alone Rose Cottage."

Becky slumped against the dresser. "What ... what happened?"

John yanked his coat off and flung it across the room. "I thought I'd made good investments. How was I to know it would all turn to dust?"

"No. No. No." Becky put her hands over her ears.

"Go on, hide from the grown-up world if you want, but it's all gone. Finished. Kaput. Everything's gone down the tube."

Water dripped from the tap and landed in the sink with a splat.

"Damn it all," John growled. He left the room and charged upstairs.

Becky ran to the downstairs toilet and retched into the bowl.

She splashed her face with cold water. Overhead she could hear cupboards and drawers being opened and slammed shut. She couldn't go up to bed while John was in such a bad mood. She'd wait until he was asleep.

In the kitchen again, she picked up the files. It wouldn't take long to put them back in order and complete her action list.

John's footsteps thudded down the stairs. He came into the room; a holdall clasped in one hand.

"What are you doing?" she whispered. "You can't be going out again. Not at this time of night."

"It's best that I leave now."

"Leave?" Dread swept over her. "What do you mean?"

He wouldn't look at her. Why wouldn't her husband of twenty-one years look at her?

"I should've done this a long time ago," he muttered.

A mix of fear and panic swamped Becky. She grabbed his bag. "This is so silly. You're not thinking straight." She dug her nails into the flesh of his hand and pulled at the familiar fingers. If only she could get the holdall away from him, everything else could be fixed.

He let the piece of luggage go and stepped back a couple of paces.

Her heart soared. "Everything will look better in the morning. A good night's sleep, that's what we both need." She reached for his hand.

"Don't."

She dropped the bag and rushed up to him, pressed her head into his chest, and wrapped her arms tight around his torso. His wonderful heart thumped against her ear.

"I love you," she said.

John gripped her by the elbows and held her at arms' length. "You know we've only been friends for a long time now."

She shook her head violently.

He picked up his coat and holdall and reached for his car keys. "I'll be staying with a friend."

The sudden gentle tone of his voice took her by surprise. Then it hit her. A single tear rolled down her cheek.

"A woman?"

"Sorry." He turned away.

"Damn you, John Farrow. Damn you."

She watched his retreating back, then ran after him. Too late. The door slammed in her face. She leaned her head against the cool wood.

"Oh, John," she whispered.

A few minutes later, she returned to the kitchen. The bright spotlights illuminated the shiny surfaces and neat rows of glass jars and beautiful cake tins. Her lovely home, re-mortgaged?

How much?

She flung open the dishwasher, grabbed the meat cleaver – the same one Natalie had used earlier to force open John's filing cabinet – and headed for the office again; the hefty blade would make mincemeat of the drawers in John's antique desk.

4

Abi knelt on the floor and yanked another handful of unwashed items out of the washing machine and onto the black and white tiles. She should've switched the machine on last night but she'd been too weary to think. A sore back from sleeping on her mum's sofa for over four weeks and a crap job stacking shelves didn't help. She'd had no luck in finding a place of her own.

She twisted her mass of dark-brown hair into a ponytail, picked up a child's lacy, pink sock and sniffed it. It would have to do. Now she just needed the other one.

"Hey, Jacob. Come and give me a hand."

"I haven't finished yet." A couple of coco pops flew from his mouth and plopped onto the old pine tabletop. His legs swung to and fro against the wooden chair with a rhythmic thump.

Abi stiffened, but she checked herself. "Be a good boy. You're seven now. Old enough to help me when I ask."

Jacob slurped the last of his milk, dropped the spoon into the bowl, and pushed his chair back. He marched with exaggerated strides towards her.

"Mark has clean socks every day."

Abi gritted her teeth. Mark's fresh face, in his newly laundered clothes and un-scuffed shoes, filled her mind. His rosy-faced mum arriving at the school gates in her new BMW completed the image. The familiar ball of anger mixed with shame curled in her stomach.

"That's nice."

Eve got down from the table and began cramming the clothes back into the washing machine.

"Eve, don't do that."

"I'm helping you, Mummy."

Abi let out a sigh. Her mum's two-up two-down, terraced house was fine when Abi was a child, but two adults, three kids, and Buddy, pretty much pushed it beyond limits. She'd done her usual thing: upped sticks and headed back home without a thought to what that would mean. Living back in Penryn was so much harder than she'd expected.

For starters, the town had changed. These days, properties were either full of students, and therefore expensive, or the landlords didn't take pets. Nor had the locals forgotten that she was the daughter of Fran Pascoe and Henry Williams. A few had even offered her their condolences. For God's sake, why would they think she cared; they all knew he'd had nothing to do with her when he was alive.

"Grace is giving her breakfast to Buddy." Eve pointed towards her sister.

On cue, her youngest daughter burst into a giggly laugh and threw a biscuit. Buddy caught it in mid-air, sniffed around the base of the highchair for the last crumbs, then sat, his brown eyes fixed once more onto Grace.

"No, Grace. That's for you, not for Buddy."

She needed to get a move on. Jacob had to be dropped off at school, and Eve and Grace needed taking over to Kate's house. Thank goodness she and her best friend from her school days still hit it off.

Jacob waved a pink sock in the air.

She grabbed it, pulled him into a bear hug, and blew big raspberries into his neck.

"I bet Mark doesn't get bear hugs and loads of kisses before school, does he?"

Jacob squealed.

Eve ran to join in. "Me, Mummy, me. I want one."

Under their combined weight, Abi collapsed back against the kitchen unit, tears of laughter in her eyes.

"Okay. Enough."

She pushed the dirty clothes back into the washing machine, grabbed a paper towel from the worktop and wiped Grace's face. She planted a kiss on her daughter's button nose. The smell of fresh shampoo filled her nostrils. Love rushed her senses. She lifted Grace from the highchair and hugged her. Yep, she was so lucky in the things that mattered.

A full shift and then some later, Abi stood outside her mum's front door for a few moments, took a deep breath, then let herself in.

"I'm home."

"We're in the kitchen," her mum called.

"Mum, Mummy," yelled the kids.

After giving each of them a hug and a kiss, Abi took off her coat and sank into a chair.

Her mum glanced up from feeding Grace. "You look worn out."

"I was late again this morning, so I worked on. Got to keep them sweet. Thanks for picking up the kids."

"I was hardly going to leave them, was I?"

Abi rubbed her temple. Had her mum always been so sharp? They hadn't lived together for seven years, and they must clearly have been on their best behaviour during their once-a-year catch ups at some spot mid-way between Cornwall and wherever Abi lived at the time. How much more could either of them take of this?

"The children have nearly finished eating. There's a plate for you in the oven."

"Later. First, I'll bathe the kids and get them into bed."

"Thanks for fixing the doors. I've been meaning to get them repaired for ages."

"Sorry. What?"

"My wardrobe. Thanks." Her mum wiped Grace's mouth.

"That's okay. I appreciate your help." Abi slowly got to her feet and picked up Grace. "Are you staying in tonight?"

Her mum stacked the dirty plates. "Now where would I be going, for goodness sake?"

Abi smiled and closed the door behind her.

An hour later, she placed the last item of clothing on the plastic air dryer and lifted it closer to the radiator. She liked this part of the day when the kids were asleep; the only time she had a few minutes of peace. Taking a can of lager from the fridge, she flipped the top and took a glug of the cold liquid. She then poured a good measure of red wine into a glass and put it on the tray next to a plate of lukewarm cottage pie and wrinkled peas.

In the lounge, her mum sat in her favourite brown-cord armchair, her feet on a stool, watching EastEnders.

"Wine?"

"Thanks, love."

Her mum's gaze remained fixed on the screen. Finally, the credits began to roll. She flicked the television off, took a sip of wine and glanced at Abi.

"What was the flat like?"

"Rubbish."

"Oh?"

"Couldn't afford it anyway."

"You should apply for some financial help. You don't want to miss out on any more places. There aren't many rentals around at this time of year."

"You think I don't know that?" Abi sucked in air and counted to ten. She was in no position to upset her mum. "Is there any chance Buddy could stay with you for a while? I'd probably get somewhere a lot quicker, and we'd be out of your hair."

"You should get rid of that animal. Make life easier for yourself. Three children are more than enough to be going on with."

"Buddy's part of the family. Eve and Grace's dad won him in some drunken bet at the pub."

"Pity he didn't keep him when he scarpered."

"Tommy couldn't look after himself, let alone a puppy."

"Well, you always knew how to pick 'em." Her mum grabbed a magazine and flipped through the pages. "Like that Nick fella you just left," she mumbled.

Abi took a deep breath. "Can we talk?"

"What about?"

With a start, Abi realised how tired her mum looked. Her shifts at the nursing home were always hard. Perhaps she should leave it for now? But, if not now, when?

"Henry Williams."

"He's dead and buried. There's nothing to say."

"He was my father. You never spoke about him when he was alive. I thought you would, now he's gone."

Her mum rose to her feet, bent down and picked up Abi's tray.

Abi followed her into the kitchen. She wasn't ready to give up yet.

"A couple of people at work today talked about Henry Williams having numerous affairs. Is that true?"

The plate slipped from her mum's hand and crashed onto the floor. Abi got up and bent to help pick up the pieces. Her mum shooed her hand away.

"Mum. Please."

Her mum chucked the bits of crockery into the pedal bin and glared at her.

"He was a rat. That's all you need to know. I never want his name mentioned in this house again. Do you hear me?" She snatched a tea towel from the worktop.

"How can he hurt you now? Don't turn away. Talk to me."

"Death doesn't stop the likes of him." Her mum slammed a saucepan down onto the cooker top. "The subject's closed."

Abi knew from experience it was best to leave well alone. But she still needed help with Buddy. She tried again.

"It would really help if you could look after Buddy until I get myself sorted." She opened the fridge and took out Grace's food and a pack of sliced ham.

Her mum clutched the edge of the worktop and stared out of the window into the darkness.

"Mum?" Abi pulled a bag of white bread and packets of crisps from the cupboard.

"I can't."

"Can't what?"

Her mum turned back to the room. Words rushed from her. "I've been meaning to find the right time to tell you. There's no easy way to say this, but … I'm going back to Australia to see your grandmother. She's not well."

"Oh. How long will you be gone for?"

"I've bought a single ticket. For now."

"What about your job? Surely you can't go, just like that?"

"I'm going."

"But the kids need you. They've got used to having their grandmother around all the time." She heard the panic in her voice. "Please don't go."

"Your Uncle Frank says she's getting quite frail. I've not been back in years. I don't want any regrets."

Abi's heart quickened. "Is this the same mother who told you not to come home towing that little bastard with you?"

"Don't talk about your grandmother in that tone. Besides, she got over that a long time ago."

Abi slapped a slice of ham onto the bread and reached for the ketchup bottle.

The grandmother who'd never sent her presents for Christmas or birthdays had got over it? When?

She rammed the sandwiches into separate plastic tubs, added packs of crisps, and reached for the fruit bowl. Empty. A couple of chocolate bars would have to do. If Jacob's teacher said anything about his unbalanced diet, she'd give her what for.

"Can't you ask the children's fathers for help? Tommy? Or that other one?"

Abi's eyes welled. She brushed a tear away with her hand. Buddy got up from his bed and padded over to her. His warm, faithful presence calmed her. Something permeated the thoughts that filled her mind.

She whirled around to face her mum.

"We could stay here. I could pay the rent and look after the place for you." Her voice bubbled with excitement. "I'll make sure Buddy doesn't go upstairs, or on the chairs."

Yes. This would solve all her problems. Somewhere permanent for the kids to live. Not far from work.

"It's not possible." Her mum's voice quivered.

"Why not?"

Her mum buried her head in the tea towel. "I've been given notice to quit."

"What? Your landlord can't do that. You've lived here since before I was born. That's twenty-eight years and more. You've got rights."

Abi felt on safer ground now. Stroppy landlords and tenant rights were her speciality.

"I never had a formal agreement. The new owner wants me out."

"What new owner? Give me his name and I'll give him what for."

Her mum paled. "It's Veronica Williams."

Abi stood rooted to the spot. "What has Henry Williams's wife got to do with it?" she asked, stating each word slowly and clearly.

"I should've told you years ago." Her mum lifted her chin and nodded. "Your father bought this house for me."

"My ...? What? I don't understand."

"No rent. No formal agreement. I always thought ..." She chucked the tea towel into the washing machine. "No point in thinking. What's done is done. He's dead and Veronica Williams wants me out."

Slowly, realisation came to Abi. Why her mum would never consider moving from Cornwall, or even from Penryn.

"Are you telling me that Henry Williams bought this house for us?" She shook her head. "If that's the case, it makes even less sense why he never wanted to see me."

"He said it would be simpler that way."

A cold shiver ran down Abi's spine. "He didn't buy this place for us, did he? He bought it for you. God, I've been so stupid."

"Abi, I–"

"It's not like I didn't know you had a man around sometimes. I found a half-smoked cigar once. I was sixteen, and thought it was pretty cool that you had someone." Abi waved the bread knife in the air. "I can't believe you and my father carried on under my nose and you never said a word."

"Please try and understand. I was young and pregnant. He offered and ..." Her mum's arms dropped to her sides. "I couldn't go home."

Abi rubbed her eyes. "I approached him once when Jacob was only a few weeks old. Saw him walking down the High Street in Falmouth."

"Oh."

"He told me to get lost. Made it quite clear he didn't want to know me or his grandson. He said that if I stayed around, he'd make life difficult for me."

Her mum clamped a hand over her mouth.

"That's why I left soon afterwards. So many people were scared of him, it would've been impossible for me to get a job." She chucked the knife into the washing-up bowl. "The stuff I put up with at school ... and to think, all that time, you and he were still seeing each other."

Her mum poured herself another glass of wine. "I loved him. He loved me."

Abi snorted. "Not enough to leave his wife or give you the house." She struggled to make eye contact with her mum. How could her mother have kept this a secret from her for all these years, knowing how she felt about her father? Not that anything was secret in a town like Penryn. The neighbours would've known. Pity none of them told her.

Abi slammed the plastic sandwich boxes onto the table. "When are you leaving?"

"At the weekend. There's nothing for me here."

"Thanks, Mum. Thanks a lot."

"You know what I mean. The furniture came with the house, and I've only a few bits to pack."

"How long have I got?"

"Until the end of March."

"Four weeks?" Her voice rose to a shout. "Tell me you're joking."

"I so hoped you'd get the flat today. I'm so sorry."

"Sorry?" The word bounced around the room. "My kids will be homeless in four weeks and all you can say is sorry."

"Mum, why are you and Gran shouting?" Jacob stood in the doorway.

Abi rushed over to him. "Sweetheart, there's nothing to worry about. Gran and I were just having a little disagreement." She kissed the top of his head. "Let's get you back to bed."

She leaned in close to her mum as she left the room and whispered, "I'll never forgive you for this."

5

Becky woke with a start. She lay on her side for several minutes and stared into the darkness. Strands of damp hair clung to her forehead. She didn't attempt to turn over; she could pretend for a little while longer, couldn't she?

With a sigh, she flicked on the bedside lamp and rolled onto her other side. Next to her, John's pillow remained plump and crease-free. It had been nearly three weeks since he'd left, but she still hoped that his familiar body would be there when she woke, his soft snores bringing purpose to her life once again.

She hauled herself out of bed and trudged across the wooden floor to the bathroom. Washing her hands, she caught sight of her reflection in the mirror. With soapy fingers, she touched her face in the glass and traced the outline of cheekbones jutting through translucent skin, the black pouches beneath her eyes. She looked so haggard and old. Had she let herself go? Was that why John had left her?

With a fierce twist, she turned the tap. Cold water surged into the basin. Droplets splattered across the front of her silk nightdress. She caught the water in her cupped hands and threw it over her face. Rivulets ran down her neck.

On the way back to her bedroom, she peered into Jess's room. Her daughter's bed remained untouched. Jess must have stayed over at a friend's place again, not that she'd bothered to tell Becky.

The bedside clock flickered: 3:05 a.m. There was no way she would go back to sleep. She plucked a large navy sweater from the bedroom chair, held it to her face, and took a deep breath. John's smell lingered in the fibres.

In the kitchen, she flicked the kettle on, opened the door to one of the cupboards and ran her finger along the neat row of herbal tea boxes. Camomile might help her to sleep. She dropped the tea bag into a mug and topped it up with hot water.

Her mind was full of mixed thoughts and emotions, the same old stuff going round and round. If only John had confided in her when he first got into debt. How could she stop this nightmare? If he would just talk to her, they could put everything right and begin again. She took a sip of tea. Bitter. She poured it into the sink, wiped the mug, and put it back in its place. Most of all, how had she been such a fool? Why hadn't she realised sooner that something was wrong? It took Natalie to charge in and rip those envelopes and files open before anything happened.

Becky stared at the stack of flat cardboard boxes piled in the corner. John had brought them over one morning when she was out. At the same time, he'd taken away all the paperwork: the files, correspondence, even the filing cabinet. Much worse, he'd left a message on her notepad saying that the mortgage company would be repossessing Rose Cottage shortly; exact date to be advised. A stark, cold note from the man she'd known and loved for decades.

A dry, ugly sob burst from her mouth.

Deep down, she knew John wouldn't be coming back; that their marriage was over. But what would she do? Looking after this place was what she did. What other life was there for her?

Jess breezed into the kitchen and dropped her coat and bag in a crumpled heap onto the table.

"Darling. What a wonderful surprise." Becky beamed at her daughter and for a moment it was like nothing had changed.

"Those look good." Jess's hand reached for a batch of cupcakes cooling on a wire tray.

"One only. They're for Aunt Natalie's school fete." She handed her daughter a tea plate. "I thought you were working this afternoon?"

"I had some time owing."

Jess flopped onto the kitchen sofa, switched the television on and flickered swiftly through the channels. "What's with the cardboard boxes?"

"Your dad left them ten days ago when I was out."

"He did say something about the furniture being auctioned soon. Guess stuff needs to be packed."

"Don't be silly. The furniture is our personal stuff." Cold fear clawed at Becky's throat. "It's got nothing to do with the business."

Jess shrugged, her gaze fixed on the screen. "Just repeating what he said."

"You've seen your dad then?" Becky grabbed a ceramic bowl from the cupboard, chucked in cubes of butter and sieved icing sugar.

"He *is* my dad." Jess popped the rest of the cupcake into her mouth. "Seeing him with his new girlfriend was seriously weird though."

Becky beat the buttercream with fierce movements. The bowl rocked to and fro against the worktop, drowning out further conversation. She didn't want to hear any more about John and his so-called new life. What she didn't know, she wouldn't have to dwell over when he returned.

"When are you starting your new job at Jack's Bakery?" Jess asked.

Becky dripped pink food colouring into the soft mixture. Blast. Too much. Now it would be a dreadful fluorescent pink rather than the soft blush she intended.

Jack and Liz Mitchell were old friends of the family. Over the years, Becky had occasionally made celebration and birthday cakes for their shop. Soon after John had left, and the gossips had done their work, Liz called around and offered her a job, together with the use of the flat above the shop. Becky hadn't given her an answer yet.

"It's lucky the flat goes with the job," Jess said.

"Why?" Becky snapped. "I won't need it."

Jess sat upright. "You need to get real, Mum. Dad cocked up and this place will be gone soon."

Becky took a deep breath. Her daughter didn't seem in any hurry to leave, and she needed to be careful not to drive her away with her snappiness.

"Oh, I almost forgot." Jess put the plate onto the table and reached for her bag. "Dad gave me these ages ago. He said they got mixed up in the post he picked up, when he came over, or something. Hope they're not important."

Becky wiped her hands on her apron and took the two envelopes. John had scrawled her name on the front of the plain brown one. Inside was a copy of a letter from the mortgage company. It stated in legal terms that the company would take ownership of Rose Cottage on the last day of March.

She reached for the edge of the sink and clung to the cold metal.

"What's up?" Jess flicked to another channel. Gunfire filled the room.

Becky's head thumped. She handed the letter to Jess.

"Seriously, you've got to take the flat now. Where else can you go? If you moved in with Grandad or Aunt Natalie, you'd kill each other after a few days."

"Living with your Grandad isn't possible. The Housing Association has restrictions on people staying permanently. Besides, you know, it's only a one-bedroomed bungalow. And Natalie ..." She shrugged.

"All the more reason to accept Liz's offer."

Becky closed her eyes. Maybe Jess was right.

"What day is good for you to see the flat?" she asked her daughter.

"Why would I need to see it?" Jess tossed the mortgage letter onto the table. "You can decide whether you like it or not, can't you?"

"But what if you don't like it? You'll be living there as well."

"Don't worry about me." Jess walked to the hallway door and grasped the handle. "I've already made other plans."

"Not with your dad?" Becky's voice was a whisper.

"Trust me. I won't be living with either of you. I'm moving in with a friend."

Becky's heart raced as she thought about all those nights Jess hadn't come home. "A boyfriend?"

Jess nodded.

On the verge of tears, Becky said, "Can I meet him?"

"Not yet." Her daughter opened the door, then hesitated. "He's important to me. I want to make everything perfect for him first before you and Dad grill him."

"Oh, Jess. I worry about you."

"Don't."

That single, sharp word ended any further discussion. Just like her father.

Becky changed the subject. "How about us both doing something special this afternoon? We could go shopping?"

"Can't."

Becky stared out the window into the garden. A kestrel swooped across the lawn in pursuit of a blue tit.

"Please, Jess. I'd love it if–"

"I need to shower. Get rid of the stink of grilled bacon and sausages."

Sudden anger rushed through Becky. "What do you expect, working in that awful beach cafe? You should've gone to university like we planned."

"Get over it. I'm doing what I want." Jess turned and ran up the stairs.

Becky rubbed her temple. How she longed for her daughter to be ten again when they watched silly children's TV together or played endless board games in front of the blazing fire.

She scraped the last dollop of icing onto the cupcakes, then added multi-coloured sprinkles to the top of some and chocolate chips to the rest. She looked up and smiled when Jess came back into the room. The fresh smell of shower gel and shampoo drifted through the air.

"Can I make you a coffee? Or cook you something?" Becky knew her voice had adopted a begging tone.

"Don't bother."

"You must eat something. What about a cheese and tomato omelette? You love cheese and–"

A car horn sounded several times in the lane outside.

Jess quickly pulled on her coat and picked up her bag.

Panic gripped Becky. She couldn't bear to be alone again. Words rushed from her. Wrong words. Words she couldn't stop.

"What sort of man is he to honk his horn at a woman? Doesn't he have the manners to come in and introduce himself?"

Jess glared at her. "You sound just like Nan."

The words hit Becky to the core, just as her daughter meant them too. "That's hurtful. I'm nothing like my mother."

"I'm out of here."

A few moments later, the door slammed and silence filled the room.

Becky burst into tears.

As she wiped her face with the end of her apron, she saw the unopened envelope; white and expensive looking. She picked it up. 'Private and confidential' was stamped across the front, next to the logo of Penna, Truscott and Wallace, a prominent firm of local solicitors. Solicitors? Why would she be getting correspondence from a solicitor when John was dealing with everything?

She slid her fingernail under the flap, faltered, then stopped. The post date was over two weeks ago. No one had chased her for a reply, so it couldn't be that urgent. John hadn't opened it. Did he already know what was inside? If it wasn't about business stuff, what could it be about? She flinched. Divorce papers? No. John wouldn't be that heartless, would he?

She laughed at her own naivety. How would she know? The husband she'd once known was now a mystery to her.

She stared at the envelope. Whatever lay inside it was only going to be more trouble. And she'd had enough trouble for one day. Before she knew what she was doing, she ripped the envelope into several pieces, flipped the bin open and dropped the bits inside. The lid slammed shut with a satisfying crash.

6

Abi dropped the plastic bag of shopping onto the kitchen table and tugged off her parka jacket. Keeping her woolly beanie hat and scarf on, she shoved a few coins into the electric meter. The place had to be warm for when Jacob, Eve and Grace got home.

She pulled out two tins of mushy peas, a box of fish fingers, and a pack of frozen chips from the shopping bag. Yesterday, they'd had chicken nuggets and spaghetti hoops. Junk food, but cheap. With her mum no longer around to help look after the kids, Abi had been forced to reduce her hours at Asda, and fewer hours meant less money, less food, less everything.

With her sweater sleeves pulled over her hands, she looked about the kitchen. When her mum had left for Australia three weeks ago, she'd taken the essence of what made the place home with her. Gaps on the wall where family photos had hung added to the feeling of abandonment. Even when the kids were around, with all their noise and laughter, the atmosphere was grim.

Her mum had sent a text when she arrived in Sydney, saying she'd landed safely. Abi hadn't replied. She thought she'd known everything there was to know about her mum but it turned out she hadn't. Abi's eyes unexpectedly filled with tears, and for once she gave in to her misery and sobbed into her hands. It didn't help that she was so tired all the time, and she still hadn't found somewhere to rent.

On the other hand, she'd heard nothing from Veronica Williams yet. Until her father's widow forced her out, Abi would be staying put.

Buddy stretched, padded over to her and rested his head on her knee. Was her mum right when she said he was just a dog and another mouth to feed? Was she being stupid keeping him? He looked up at her with chocolate-brown eyes and lifted one paw. She took it, bent down, and kissed the top of his soft head. His warm earthy scent soothed her. Get rid of him? Over her dead body.

She stood and wiped her eyes. God, she needed to pull herself together. She'd get by somehow. She always did.

A long ring on the doorbell jolted her from her thoughts. If that was nosy Meg from next door again, she might just throttle her.

A tall man in an expensive suit stood on the step: a very handsome man with lovely broad shoulders to boot.

"Good afternoon. I'd like to speak to Miss Fran Pascoe. Is she in?" His voice was strong and authoritative.

She tugged off her beanie hat and ran a hand through her hair. "She's not here. Can I help? I'm her daughter."

The man stood back a pace and looked her up and down. "Are you now?"

She sucked in her cheeks. Arrogant git. On any other day, she would have spat back at him with whatever swear word came to her lips, but instinct stopped her. She crossed her arms and waited.

"I'm Steven Hodges, Estates Manager acting for Mrs Veronica Williams, owner of this property." He leaned towards her. "I suggest we have this conversation inside."

Her stomach lurched as she turned and walked down the narrow hallway.

His presence in the kitchen seemed to suck all the air from the small space. His gaze flicked from one object to another. "I'm here to ensure this property is vacated on the thirty-first of March, in accordance with the notice issued to your mother."

His voice was formal and self-important.

Pompous dick.

She counted to ten. "I've got three kids, and–"

He raised his hand. "I hardly think Mrs Williams would be concerned about that under the circumstances."

A mix of shame and anger rolled over Abi. Did everyone know about her mum and Henry Williams? Of course they did. This was Cornwall.

"My mother has lived here for nearly thirty years."

"Quite. The free ride is over."

Abi clenched her fists. "I live with her. You can't just evict me. Legally I'm entitled to–"

"Pull the other one. You've not shown your face around here for years. You've only come scuttling back because …" He stopped and sucked his teeth. "You've got ten days. Make the most of the time."

"What if I don't leave? What could that woman do?"

He leaned in close. His hot breath brushed her cheek.

She stepped backwards. The cold metal of the fridge pressed into her back.

"It's what I might do that you should be more worried about," he whispered in her ear, and with that he turned and strolled out of the kitchen. "Have a good day."

She ran down the hallway, locked the door behind him and leaned against it. Her heart raced.

The doorbell rang again. She hesitated then took a deep breath. She wasn't going to be afraid of Veronica Williams's lackey. She swung around and pulled the door open, ready to give Steven Hodges a mouthful.

A postman beamed at her from under a thatch of grey hair. "Hello, Miss. Thought I'd hand this one to you. Looks like it's done the rounds."

He deposited a tattered envelope into her hand. "Hope it's worth the wait." He tipped his head at her and walked off, whistling, down the street.

Abi stared at the once white envelope, now ripped and smeared with who knew what. Initially, it had been sent to where she'd lived several years ago. It was a good job she and her then-boyfriend had split up on good terms because he'd scrawled the address of another friend on the front. The friend had re-addressed it to: Abi Pascoe's Mum, Penryn, Cornwall.

Thank God for local postmen.

Abi stared at the logo on the envelope. Solicitors? For a moment, she racked her brains trying to figure out who would be setting a firm of solicitors onto her. Veronica Williams had already made her get-out message perfectly clear, so it wouldn't be about this place. Damn, it was probably some former landlord chasing her for back rent. She ripped the envelope open. No, the solicitors were based in Falmouth, so it couldn't be someone chasing a debt.

A name highlighted in bold print leapt out at her: Henry Charles Williams.

Her hand shook as she read the rest of the letter. Did it mean what she thought it did?

She picked up her mobile. Only one way to find out.

7

Becky's head throbbed and her eyes itched. Her shift at Jack's Bakery had started at 4:00 a.m. It was now lunchtime, and the shop was crowded with hungry customers. Liz, who'd begged her to stay on for a few extra hours to cover staff sickness, worked at speed next to her, putting pasties, saffron buns and various sweet and savoury items into paper bags. Jack, Liz's husband, toiled at the far end of the glass counter. Every inch the shop-owner, he smiled and joked with each customer.

It had been three weeks since Becky had started working at the bakery and she couldn't remember when she'd ever felt so exhausted. Was it any wonder? She hadn't been employed since Jess had been born. Over the years, when she'd baked cakes for friends and, on occasions for Jack's Bakery, it had only been for fun and to pass the time while Jess was at school. Thank goodness she'd been inclined to also attend various classes on catering, baking, and that very dreary health and safety course.

Being part of the night shift team suited her. She couldn't sleep anyway and the tight deadlines to ensure the hundreds of pasties, loaves of bread and pastries were ready for the 8:00 a.m. opening left little time for her to socialise with colleagues, or for them to ask her unwelcome questions.

"Becky?"

She looked up from the till. Oh dear. Mrs Dawes, the local gossip.

"Fancy seeing you here." Mrs Dawes pointed to a large white bloomer. "How's the lovely Mr Farrow? Such a charmer, that husband of yours."

Out the corner of her eye, Becky saw a woman in the queue turn quickly and stare at her. Becky stiffened as she recognised who it was.

Veronica Williams, the widow of the late Henry Williams, stood with her back ramrod straight and scowled directly at her.

Becky bowed her head and picked up the loaf of bread.

"I heard John's business is having difficulties." Mrs Dawes rambled on. "Is that why you're here? To take your mind off things, my dear?"

Becky struggled to fit the bloomer into a paper bag. She was aware that Veronica Williams was still watching her, but why? Her mother might have had a problem with the Williams family, but Becky had never had anything to do with them, good or bad. As far as she could remember, she'd never spoken to Veronica Williams, or even been near her. Until now.

Mrs Dawes coughed. Becky looked up. Mrs Dawes had moved to one side and Veronica Williams stood in her place.

The woman leaned forward. "Mrs Rebecca Farrow?"

Becky's heart thumped. She nodded.

Veronica Williams's lips moved, but Becky could only see the subtle blend of her lipstick and her flawless eye makeup. A hint of peppermint wafted into Becky's face. A few of the words Veronica Williams uttered finally pierced Becky's consciousness but they failed to make any sense. "Pardon? I don't–"

"You will never have what is rightfully mine." Veronica Williams hissed into Becky's face. "You will be hearing from my solicitor."

Becky's nylon overall stuck to the base of her back. She put her hand to her neck; it would be covered in red blotches.

"I ... I think you need to speak to John, my husband. He's dealing with everything relating to the–"

A hand touched her shoulder.

"Thank you, Becky. You can go now, your shift's finished." Jack smiled and gave her a gentle nudge towards the staff entrance.

She stepped away on heavy legs, looking back over her shoulder as she headed for the rear of the shop.

"Good afternoon, Mrs Williams. How can I help you?" Jack's cheerful voice filled the shop.

Veronica Williams turned and headed for the exit. Customers moved hastily to one side to let her pass.

At the small table in the staff room, Liz dropped two sugars into a large mug of strong tea. She placed it in front of Becky and flopped into a chair opposite her.

"My goodness, Becky, what was all that about?"

Becky took a deep breath to calm her racing heart. "I've no idea. I couldn't take in what she said. She scared me half to death."

"She scares most people around here. The woman owns half the High Street." Liz touched Becky's hand. "Sounded like you've got something she wants."

A bitter laugh rolled from Becky's throat. "Someone had better tell her she's wasting her time. I don't have anything."

"I know John's dealing with all the business stuff, and you don't have to tell me the mess he's dragged you into, but have you considered getting a solicitor of your own?"

Becky frowned, the mug partway to her lips. Another expensive white envelope had arrived that morning, exactly

46

like the one she'd previously ripped up. It had the same logo as before: Penna, Truscott and Wallace, Solicitors, based in Falmouth. The firm had also left several messages on her telephone, which she'd ignored. The latest envelope lay unopened at the bottom of her handbag.

She gently put the mug back onto the table and rose to her feet. "I need to go. I've still got the garden shed to clear." She gave Liz a brief hug. "Thanks for being such a good friend."

At Rose Cottage, the faint aroma of nutmeg and cinnamon still lingered in the air, the only trace left of the many cakes and meals Becky had happily prepared in the kitchen. A memory rushed into her mind of John kissing the nape of her neck while she washed up, his arms wrapped around her body in a tight hug. She groaned. He must have loved her once, surely?

With a sigh, she looked around. Her beautiful cream dining table and chairs had gone, replaced with an old, tatty garden table and chairs that neither John nor the bailiffs wanted. The dresser had also been sold. The unlit Aga stood devoid of tea towels and saucepans.

Absentmindedly, she wandered through the hallway and into the lounge. Her high heeled boots click-clacked on the tiled floor. There was no longer a need to remove them at the door. There was nothing left to protect.

In a few days, she would leave Rose Cottage forever. She still couldn't comprehend how it had all come about. John had loved this place as much as she did.

"Hello."

Becky jerked around. Dear God, John's voice.

She automatically patted her hair. She hadn't seen him since he'd left on the ninth of February; a date forever etched in her memory. She rushed back through the hallway.

He stood in the kitchen inspecting several boxes stacked along the wall. Her heart lurched. She moved towards him, a smile on her face, her arms half raised.

"Thought this might be a good time to pick up the rest of my stuff and sort the logistics for the handover of Rose Cottage." John's voice was businesslike. All the time he talked, his gaze flicked over the boxes and black plastic bags. "Which ones are mine?"

Her arms dropped to her side. What a fool she was. When would she get it into her head that he didn't want her anymore? For a moment, a wave of anger rose in her. He'd caused all this. He'd taken everything from her. Then her shoulders sagged. It would be better if she remained calm and didn't upset him.

She took a deep breath. "The boxes, bags, and two suitcases by the door belong to you. Your suits and best shirts are in your wardrobe. You can take the hangers as well. That way you can hang them in the car and they won't get creased."

She groaned inwardly. What did she care if his shirts got creased? She wouldn't have to iron them.

She walked over to a plastic storage box on the worktop and pulled out two mugs. "Coffee?"

John nodded, then grabbed one of the suitcases. "I'll load these into the car while the kettle boils."

A few minutes later, Becky pushed a steaming mug towards John and reached for the sugar.

He raised his hand. "Not for me. Leanne ..."

No sugar? A stab of jealousy dug into her chest. Her replacement had already changed him.

She forced herself to say the name. "Leanne?"

"Leanne Hawke. From 'The Lamb and Flag'."

She winced. She'd been traded in for a barmaid, a barmaid she'd even spoken to once or twice. From memory, she was pretty, and nice. Blast.

"Leanne's my partner now. Even if it's just for Jess's sake, we should all make the effort to get on." John gulped his coffee. "I'm sorry everything happened as it did, but you should see it as an opportunity to move on. To start a new life."

"I don't want a new life," she spat back. "I liked the one I had."

"Come on, Becky. Be honest. We weren't much of a couple."

How could he say that? He was lying to justify his actions, his adultery with that woman. Wasn't he?

"Did you ever love me?" Becky whispered.

He glanced at her. "Of course I did."

"So why did you leave me?" Her voice broke into a sob.

John placed his mug on the worktop and gave her a watery smile. "Try to understand. We had good times, and we had fun, but we changed. You changed, like when you were depressed, and–"

"That was so long ago." Becky glared at him. "We'd lost our baby, for goodness sake. I was upset."

"For six months? I needed some comfort as well. Then when Jess was born, you didn't seem to need me at all."

"That's so unfair. You were everything to me. I looked after you, didn't I? I made a lovely home. I cooked and cleaned."

"That was looking after the house, that wasn't looking after me." He pointed at his chest with his thumb, then shrugged. "Look, we grew apart. We didn't care enough to make the effort, or whatever. Who the hell knows?"

Becky snatched up the dishcloth. and wiped the worktop with fierce strokes. "How long have you been seeing this ... Leanne?"

John picked up a cardboard box and made for the door. "Eighteen months. Maybe a bit longer. What does it matter?"

Her eyes stung. Why hadn't she realised? Maybe because during all that time he'd still shared the marital bed with her?

John stepped back into the kitchen and peered at the label on another box.

She rubbed the tears away with the back of her hand. "Would you have married me if I wasn't pregnant?"

"Who knows?"

The permanent knot in her stomach tightened. "Oh," she gasped.

John straightened and rubbed the base of his back. "Look, perhaps I should accept some blame for the breakup. The business took all my energy, and I didn't spend as much time at home as I should have. But like I said, these things happen. Can't we just leave it at that?"

Becky stared at him. Had he always been so self-centred and arrogant? Had those harsh lines around his mouth been there all the time?

"Your desire to be only a housewife and mother didn't help. A few bloody cakes baked now and then didn't earn any real money. How the hell did you think all this was paid for?"

"I didn't ask you to borrow against the business or Rose Cottage," she retorted. "It was you who took the bad investment advice from someone you hardly knew."

He took a step towards her. "What makes you so clever suddenly?" A blob of spittle landed on his chin. "The bloke said he was a financial adviser. He said it was a sure thing, with loads of quick returns."

This was the first time in their married life that she had squared up to John. She bowed her head, hesitated, then said. "How could you have been so naïve?"

John grunted. "I've had enough of this. I'll come back another time for my shirts and suits."

Becky watched through the window as her husband stomped towards his car. Silently, she urged him to turn around. He didn't.

She went upstairs and opened the wardrobe door. White, beautifully pressed shirts hung on wooden hangers, alongside several suits. Polished shoes stood in neat rows on the floor. She fingered the material in John's new grey suit. It cost more than any item of clothing she owned.

Her stomach contracted. A scream burst from her in one long howl.

Frenzied, she tore the shirts and suits from the rail. Hangers rattled together and crashed to the ground. A button flew across the room. She stepped onto the heap of clothes. Her heels digging into the material, she reached down and grabbed the sleeve of one of the now dirty shirts and pulled. The sound of ripping fabric filled the room. Abruptly, she stopped. John would be so angry.

She turned and fled downstairs to the kitchen. She grabbed her handbag and pulled out the pristine white envelope. If John wanted a divorce, maybe she should give him one.

She scanned the letter.

Her heart thumped.

She read it again: 'Re: Estate of the late Henry Charles Williams'.

Veronica Williams's stony face from earlier in the day swam in front of Becky's eyes. Was this what she'd been on about?

The missive went on: 'Further to my letter of the seventeenth of February, I would be grateful if you would contact this office to arrange a mutually convenient date to discuss the above."

She clutched the document to her chest and remembered the withering look on John's face before he slammed the door on her for the last time. There could be no more putting matters off.

She picked up her mobile and punched in the number on the top of the letter. A person with an efficient voice answered.

Becky pushed her shoulders back. She could do this.

"Good afternoon. I'm Mrs Rebecca Farrow. Please may I speak to Mr David Penna."

8

21 March

With one hand on Grace's stroller, Abi stood in the middle of the pavement and squinted at the directions she'd scribbled on the back of the crumpled letter from David Penna.

Fifty yards further on, she spotted the brass plate with 'Penna, Truscott and Wallace, Solicitors' etched into the shiny surface. The granite building towered above her, one of a long line of terraced houses, businesses and shops that lined Killigrew Street in Falmouth. Its brilliant white entrance door shone in the early morning light. A glass vase of daffodils stood in the window.

She took a deep breath. Please let this meeting be worth her while; she needed some sort of miracle to help her and the kids. A glance at her watch told her it was way too early for her appointment. On autopilot, she removed Grace's blanket, shook it, and tucked it back around her warm body. Her daughter giggled. A fierce swell of love rushed through Abi. She kissed her forefinger and pressed it against Grace's nose.

A group of students sauntered along the pavement, divided, and walked either side of her and Grace. One of them bumped into the stroller. With barely a break in his excited chatter, he apologised and moved on. So what if she was early, at least she and Grace would be inside and out of the cold. She dragged the buggy up the granite step and pushed the door open with her back.

Terracotta and cream mosaic tiles covered the floor of the long corridor. At the end, a curved, mahogany staircase twisted its way to the next level. Prints of old yachts and ships hung in ornate gold frames on the cream walls. A musty smell of old offices and files permeated the air. The ping-ping of someone using their email came from one of the rooms.

A door slammed. The loud noise ricocheted throughout the building.

Grace jerked and let out a small cry.

Footsteps clattered down the wooden staircase. A tall, fair-haired woman ran wide-eyed down the hallway. She knocked against Abi, rushed past and headed for the door.

"Watch where you're going, Lady, I've got a baby here," Abi yelled.

Without looking back, let alone apologising, the woman fumbled for the handle, found it, and hurtled into the street. A car horn hooted.

"A sorry wouldn't have hurt," Abi shouted at the open door.

"Hello. Can I help you?"

Abi swung around.

A middle-aged woman peered out of a doorway at the end of the corridor, pink rimmed glasses perched on the end of her nose, one eyebrow arched.

"I'm Abi Pascoe. I've–"

"Ah, yes, Mr Penna's 10:30 appointment. Please come through, but first, be a dear and shut that door."

Abi manoeuvred the stroller into the reception-cum-waiting area: more wall art, the obligatory coffee table with neat piles of magazines, another vase of daffodils. A toy box stood in the corner.

"Please take a seat, Miss Pascoe. You're early, but Mr Penna's previous appointment was ... em ... shorter than scheduled. I'll let him know you're here."

Abi lifted Grace out of the stroller and placed her on the carpeted floor along with several toys and plastic blocks from the box. A sign stated in large capital letters that the toys were cleaned regularly.

"You're in luck, Miss Pascoe. Mr Penna will be down in five minutes." The receptionist peered at the stroller. "His office is on the first floor. I could keep an eye on your little girl down here if you like?"

Abi hesitated.

"I've raised four of my own. I promise to take good care of her."

"Thank you. Her name's Grace."

Abi took off her parka jacket, slung it over a chair, and rummaged in her rucksack for a mint. A clock ticked somewhere behind the reception desk.

"Good morning, Miss Pascoe."

Abi looked up. A man in his mid-forties with light-brown hair held out his hand to her. Suited, clean-shaven with neat short hair, a crisp blue shirt and striped tie, he was way too coordinated and polished for her liking.

"I'm David Penna. Thank you for coming."

She shook his hand. It was strong, with well cared for, evenly-cut nails. Her own, she realised, were bitten and misshapen.

His gaze turned towards Grace, who was happily chucking a variety of plastic animals into a large, red Noah's Ark.

"It's all under control, Mr Penna. Little Grace is staying with me." The receptionist took off her glasses and dropped them on the desk. "It'll be good practice for when I become a grandmother later this year."

"Thank you, Margaret. That's very kind of you. Any chance of organising a pot of tea for two?"

"Already on its way."

Grace giggled at Margaret, who was now on her knees marching a pair of giraffes along the carpet.

Abi smiled. She was so lucky her daughter was such a happy and contented baby.

As they climbed the stairs, she mechanically answered David Penna's questions about the heavy traffic and the recent spell of wet weather.

In the office, he directed her to a leather chair next to his desk. A young man came in with a tray of tea and biscuits.

She munched on a digestive and gazed around the room while she waited for David Penna to start speaking. Did people really keep such tidy desks? Only two files lay side-by-side on the shiny surface. Various law books and magazines stood in neat rows on a bookshelf in the corner.

David Penna rummaged in a grey, metal cabinet. While his back was turned, Abi swiftly grabbed three biscuits and stuffed them into her jacket pocket.

Finally, he sat opposite her, rested his clasped hands on the desk and looked straight at her. "Do you have any prior knowledge of what's in Henry Williams's Will?" he asked.

Biscuit crumbs stuck to the roof of her mouth. She picked up her cup and took a gulp of tea.

"I only know what you told me over the phone. He's left me something, but I don't know what."

He tapped a large, white envelope he'd pulled from the cabinet. "Copies of all the documents for you. For now, it's probably best I provide you with a summary of the main points." He cleared his throat and settled back into his chair. "Apart from some nominal bequests, Henry Williams left the majority of his holdings and monies to his beloved wife, Mrs Veronica Williams."

So, the old witch got his money. Abi swallowed. No miracle for her then.

David Penna picked up a pair of reading glasses and glanced at the papers in front of him. "In addition, your late father bequeathed to you a half share of the property known as Vellangoose. Interesting name, don't you think? I believe it's Cornish for *a mill in the wood.*"

A wave of emotions hit her. Her father – that cheat and liar – hadn't left her mum the house in Penryn she'd entertained him in for nearly thirty years, but now it looked like he wasn't such a slimeball after all. He'd left them a half share each in another property. If her mum had known sooner, she wouldn't have fled to Australia. What sort of heartless man played games with people's lives like that? Huh. The same heartless man who'd never had anything to do with her. But she'd known he was a shit before she pitched up today, so why had she come?

For money, that was why. For her kids.

"Miss Pascoe? Are you alright? You've gone quite pale." David Penna stood. "I'll open the window, let in some fresh air." He fumbled with the window lock. "I know this must be very upsetting for you. Your father dying so suddenly and …" He stopped, plainly uncertain how to continue.

"I'm okay." She forced a weak smile onto her face. "Please go on. You said something about a mill?"

He returned to his chair. "Yes, there's an old mill, along with several other buildings, situated in approximately fifty acres of land. As I understand it, Vellangoose was last occupied about thirty years ago. Most of the–"

"What's it worth?"

She held her breath. Just for once, please let something good happen. Tendrils of hair clung to her damp forehead.

"I'm led to believe that Vellangoose is in a terrible state of disrepair."

She slumped back against the chair.

He hurried on. "Vellangoose Mill, or The Mill as it is commonly called, and the other buildings, could probably be renovated. No doubt a developer would consider it worthwhile, given the right price. In due course, that is."

"I want to sell it. Can you arrange it?"

David Penna shifted in his seat. "I'm sorry, I should've stated at the beginning of our meeting that Mr Williams added certain conditions to the bequest."

Of course he did. There had to be a sting in the tail with him. It would have been too good to be true for that man to leave her anything worthwhile. She just needed a bit of money to get by, that was all she'd hoped for. It wasn't that much to ask for, was it?

"As I said earlier, everything's detailed in the Will and the Trust documents." David Penna paused and cleared his throat again. "However, there are two matters I need to make you aware of." He placed his finger onto the middle of an official-looking document. "Firstly, you have been jointly and equally bequeathed Vellangoose. The other party, or joint beneficiary, is a Mrs Rebecca Ann Farrow–"

"Who?" Abi stared at him. What about her mother? "Who the hell is Mrs Rebecca Ann Farrow? What kind of name is that anyway?"

"I understand Mrs Farrow is also Mr Williams's daughter." David Penna fixed his blue eyes onto her face. "She was here earlier."

She had a sister? This day just got better and better.

"I'm sorry if all this is a shock to you. I know it was to Mrs Farrow. She was very upset and, unfortunately, left before I could give her all the information."

So, the scared, wild-eyed woman in the corridor had been her sister? Abi hardened her heart. She couldn't concern herself one bit about a sister she'd never met, or even known about until five minutes ago. Her children were all she had the strength to care about right now. And Buddy, of course. They needed her.

"Miss Pascoe?"

Abi forced herself to pay attention. "Yes, right. Okay. And, what's the second thing I need to know?"

A wail sounded from downstairs. Grace. It was time for her morning snack. Abi had to fight to focus on what else David Penna was saying.

"As I said, I'm afraid there are conditions to the bequest. Vellangoose, or anything on it, cannot be sold or used to secure funds for five years from the date of Henry Williams's death. It also prohibits you or your sister from raising any money from Vellangoose. Should you or Mrs Farrow fail to meet these conditions, the property will revert to Mrs Veronica Williams."

Downstairs, Grace's cries reached a thunderous level. Footsteps thumped up the stairs.

Five years. No money for five years.

The words bounced round and round inside her head. Her father had tied his so-called gift up in knots. She was a fool to have expected anything from that lowlife.

"You also need to know that you are joint owners of Apollo and Dolly."

There was a sharp rap on the door. Margaret rushed in and handed Grace to Abi. "Sorry, my dear, but she wants her mummy." A few seconds later, Margaret was gone.

"What? I didn't catch that." Abi shifted Grace in her lap and rubbed her back. "Shush, sweetheart."

"Apollo and Dolly. A stallion and goat respectively. He's left them to you both." David Penna smiled. "I'm led to believe it's quite common for goats to be companions to horses. Interesting, don't you think?" He closed the files and stacked them one on top of the other.

"What am I supposed to do with a bloody horse and a stinking goat? Surely I must be able to sell them?"

"I'm afraid not. Henry Williams was quite emphatic in his Will that if neither you nor Mrs Farrow wanted the animals, they would be gifted to Veronica Williams." He fiddled with the papers in front of him. "I'm led to believe she would have them destroyed immediately if you both choose that course of action."

Abi snorted. More mouths to feed? Not her. She had more than enough to be going on with to care what happened to some nag and its companion. A sob half-formed in her throat, but before she could stop herself, she burst into hysterical laughter.

David Penna pushed the white envelope across the desk towards her.

Reluctantly, she took it.

9

Becky threw an empty tin of paint into the wheelbarrow. It clanked against several others already in the pile for the rubbish tip, along with dried-up paintbrushes, mouldy rags, and odd bits of timber. Why had John kept such junk? The garden shed was his domain and by rights, he should be the one clearing it out, but she hadn't chased him. He didn't know yet that she'd ruined his shirts and suits, and she wasn't in any rush for him to find out.

Next to her car, she added a trowel to a mound of old gardening implements and plant pots. At some point, she'd take them to her dad's garage for storage, together with boxes of her well-used bakeware and other kitchen bits and pieces. She wasn't sure why she was bothering with storing anything because the likelihood she'd ever have her own house or garden again was remote. She shook herself. At least she had the job and flat at Jack's Bakery.

At the thought of her dad, images from the past twenty-four hours crowded the edges of her mind. She pushed them away. Keep busy, that's what she needed to do.

She picked up a garden hose tied with string and chucked it onto the lawn. The string broke, and the cracked hose uncoiled and twisted across the grass. No wonder John hadn't wanted it when he took the new lawnmower and strimmer.

Condensation puffed from her mouth as she stuffed the hose into an empty compost bag, then rubbed her gloved hands together and stamped her feet. Her gaze flitted around the large garden – her domain. The borders were crammed with daffodils, primroses and camellias; the wonderful mix of yellows and pinks herald the coming of spring. Birds flitted to and from the feeders, and a thrush hopped across the lawn. Her eyes filled with tears. Would the new owners care for this place and the wildlife like she did?

She let out a deep sigh and let the events of yesterday morning roll over her.

She'd found the offices of Penna, Truscott and Wallace easily enough, and David Penna had been so courteous when he showed her to his office and poured her a cup of tea. She smiled politely at him, even though her stomach churned, and her heart raced. A nice man, until he began to talk and terrible words flowed from his mouth. Words that would haunt her forever.

Henry Williams was her father.

She had another sister.

The lies were unbearable. She shoved the chair to one side and ran.

Back at Rose Cottage, she found that David Penna had left her a couple of telephone messages, which she ignored. This morning, a large white envelope arrived in the post. Fortified by two cups of strong black coffee, she had forced herself to read the unwelcome contents.

The neighbour's cat burst from beneath the camellia shrub and pounced on a blackbird. In a flurry of feathers, the ginger tom immediately turned and fled over the hedge with the poor creature in its mouth. Becky shivered. The triumphant look in the cat's eyes reminded her of Veronica Williams.

Becky forced herself back to work. She picked up John's toolbox. The handle came off in her hand and the box crashed to the ground. She gave it a hefty kick.

There was no putting it off any longer.

She clenched the steering wheel and let out a long breath. Her dad hadn't seen her arrive. She could swiftly reverse the car out of the communal parking area and he wouldn't even know she'd been there.

Her dad appeared at the lounge window. Too late. She returned his wave. He looked so happy to see her, like he always did when she dropped in unexpectedly.

She pushed the car door open and made her way along the concrete footpath to the last bungalow in a terrace of one-bedroom properties. The residence was festooned with assorted containers and terracotta pots filled with hellebores, azaleas and narcissi. She hesitated by the door, then stepped inside.

The small, busy kitchen, with its black and white tiled floor, tired wood units and old-fashioned cooker, momentarily calmed her. On the end of the laminated worktop, three seed trays full of potting compost rested on sheets of the *West Briton* newspaper.

Her dad stood pouring hot water into the teapot. "Hello, love. Some nice surprise to see you."

She kissed him on the cheek. The familiar smell of boiled sweets filled her nostrils. Her eyes prickled. *This* man was her father, her dad. A tuft of compost clung to the sleeve of his old gardening sweater.

She brushed it off. "Have you been to the allotment?"

He nodded. "Too cold to be outside for long, but I thought I'd make the most of this dry weather. I've dug a small area for Thomas and Lily to sow a few lettuce and carrot seeds. Like you and Natalie did. Remember?" His Cornish burr was soft and comforting.

She forced a brief smile. His face glowed. She couldn't do this. She'd drink her tea and, after a few minutes, make her excuses and leave.

"Thought I'd plant some sunflower seeds when it's a bit warmer. The kids will love 'em."

"Dad?"

He looked up from stirring the tea bags in the pot. "What's up, love?"

Oh my God, how could she start this conversation? She fiddled with a strand of hair and pushed it back behind her ear.

"Come and sit with me. I need to talk with you about something."

He ambled over to the little table and placed a tray on the red and white spotted oilcloth. "I'm all ears. Fire away." He sat opposite her.

This was it.

"I had a meeting yesterday with a solicitor." The words came out in a rush.

"Suppose there must be divorce stuff to be sorted?"

"A Mr David Penna contacted me." She dropped a sugar cube into her tea, picked up a spoon and stirred the hot liquid. "I'm a beneficiary in someone's Will."

Her dad pushed a packet of custard creams towards her. "Who's that then? I don't remember anybody we know dying."

Becky ceased stirring and looked directly at him.

"Henry Williams."

Dear God, she'd said it.

His head jerked back as if she'd punched him. All the colour drained from his face.

She reached for his hands. The rough, gardener's hands she'd always loved. "Talk to me."

He wrenched free from her grasp and ran his fingers roughly through his grey hair. "Why? Why would he do such a thing?"

The hum of the fridge filled the silence.

"Dad. Please."

For a moment she thought he was about to feign ignorance, but then his shoulders sagged and he spoke in a whisper. "When I heard Henry Williams was dead, I was overjoyed. I thought the secret had died with him." He let out a harsh grunt. "Trust that good-for-nothing to have the last word."

So, it was true. With all her heart she'd hoped he would deny it all, and she could tell David Penna he'd got it wrong.

Her dad rubbed his eyes. "I said to your mother we needed to tell you, but … well, you know how stubborn she was."

Becky placed her palms onto the cold, waxy oilcloth. "I need you to tell me everything."

"Can't we just forget about it? He's dead. What's the point now, after all these years?"

Becky held his gaze and tried not to flinch from the pain in his eyes. "Dad, please, I don't want the local busybodies telling me their version of the truth. And they will. You know they will."

He stared at her for a moment, then nodded, picked up a handful of seed packets stacked on the table and began to sort them into order.

"I'm not much good with words, but I'll do me best to tell you what happened."

Becky pulled her hands into her lap and waited.

He cleared his throat. "When we were first married, I worked for the Council, driving and undertaking general maintenance work. Your mother was the secretary at Williams Estates and Haulage. Henry Williams had not long started the haulage side of the firm. Made it what it is today."

Her dad pulled a pencil from behind his ear and bent over to write on the back of one of the packets, then shook his head. The pencil slipped from his hand.

"We wanted a baby, but the years went by, and nothing happened. Then 'twas the recession. The interest rates scat our plans to buy a house to smithereens, so I took another job ..." He shifted in his seat. "Another job with the Williams's. Drove a lorry every weekend, up-country and back. You know, with cauliflowers and the like."

Becky wasn't sure she wanted to hear any of this. She rose, picked up her cold mug of tea and poured it down the sink. Maybe some things should stay secret?

"Our marriage hit a bad patch. To cut a long story short, the next thing I knew, your mother was pregnant." He thrust the seed packets to one side. "We both knew it wasn't mine."

Becky stood with the dirty mug in her hand. Her temple throbbed. "How did Mum explain it?"

"We only talked about it the once, but I can remember the conversation like it was just yesterday." He cleared his throat. "Henry Williams loved horses and women, and what he wanted, he got. Seems like he took a fancy to her and wore her down with that charm of his." He glanced at her. "Your mother was quite a looker in her young days, and Henry Williams was a handsome man. He knew it as well. Had an aura of power about him. Money does that. Gives a person a certain swagger." Her dad slammed his fist onto the table. "Your mother fell for his claptrap. Not that I knew anything of this at the time."

Becky gripped the edge of the sink.

"'Twas tough between us for a while, but everything changed when you came along."

"Why didn't mum get rid of me?"

"We wanted a baby so desperately. You were our miracle, and nobody knew you weren't mine."

"Except Henry Williams."

Her dad's chair scraped across the tiled floor. "The jerk guessed when your mother handed in her resignation. I think she'd been sick a few times while she was at work. He laughed when she denied it."

"How could you forgive Mum? How could you accept me?" She snatched up the tea towel. "How ...?"

"I loved your mother. And you were the best thing that ever happened to me. I loved you from the moment I saw you. You were our dream baby. And then, when we eventually had your sister, our family was complete."

"Except, mum didn't love me."

His hand, reaching for the biscuit tin, paused in mid-air. "Why ever would you think that? I know your mother was a little cold at times but she loved you dearly."

"Not like she did Natalie. Oh .... it makes sense now. Natalie was your daughter, not his."

He flinched.

"You know she treated me differently, Dad. I always felt second-best."

He removed the lid of the tin and slowly placed the untouched custard creams back inside.

She didn't need him to reply. Everything she had wanted to know had been said.

He turned towards her. "You mentioned that Henry Williams has left you something in his Will?"

"Vellangoose."

"Vellangoose! No, that's not–"

The door swung open, cutting him off in mid-sentence. Natalie flounced into the room with a bag of doughnuts clutched in her hand.

"Saw your car, Sis, and thought we'd share these with a cup of coffee." She rushed on without pausing for breath. "Hey, Dad, would you be able to pick up Lily later? I've arranged to meet with a friend for the afternoon." She spooned coffee granules into a bright yellow mug, reached for the kettle, then stopped to look at them. "What's with the long faces?" She let out a carefree laugh. "Cheer up. It's not as if anyone's died."

Head bent, their dad shuffled out of the kitchen and made his way down the short hallway to his bedroom. He'd aged ten years in little more than ten minutes.

Her sister flopped into the chair he'd vacated.

"What's up with him?"

Becky scrunched the tea towel into a ball and moved to the kettle. She wiped the chrome surface with vigorous strokes and told her little sister about Henry Williams.

Natalie sat upright. "You've got to be joking?"

"I wish."

"Are you honestly telling me that man's your father? Not Dad?" She grabbed a doughnut and bit off a big piece. "How did this all come about? Who told you? What did Dad say?"

"Dad said it was true."

"Blimey. That explains why he and Mum hated the Williams family so much." Natalie rubbed sugar off her hands. "I always thought it was something petty, like Mum had got drunk at the office Christmas party, but this is something else, for sure." She licked her lips. "A bit rough for you, with everything else that's going on with John and Rose Cottage."

Tears welled in Becky's eyes. "It's unbearable. That man can't be my father. He can't. I feel so ashamed. So dirty."

Natalie swiftly got to her feet and pulled Becky into her arms. "What are you like? It's not your fault. Anyway, nobody will know. What difference will it make? The man's dead." Her sister stepped away. "How did you get to know about it?"

"He left me something in his Will"

"What?"

"Vellangoose. It's a smallholding near Penhellick Vill–"

"I know where the place is. It's a dump." Natalie glared at her. A deep furrow had formed between her eyes. "You can't accept it."

"But ..."

"No buts about it. Veronica Williams must be beyond furious."

Becky blinked. "Why are you worried about Veronica Williams? I thought we were talking about me?"

"Are you stupid? Don't you realise what this means to Lloyd Accountancy?"

"Realise what?"

Natalie chucked the remains of her doughnut into the bin.

"Dah! Our accountancy business, you know, the one that Pete works his fingers to the bone for. It relies on work from the Williams family, like most of our clients do." She grabbed her bag. "I've got to tell Pete. I can't believe you got mixed up with this."

"This isn't my fault. Remember?"

"Tell Dad not to bother picking up Lily. I'll do it now. What an afternoon this is turning out to be."

"Think your afternoon's bad? Try mine."

"Don't be flippant. It doesn't suit you." Natalie reached for the door handle.

Becky raised her eyebrows. "There's more."

"What?"

"Apparently, Henry Williams had another daughter. He left her the other half of Vellangoose."

"Well, that's just wonderful." The door crashed shut behind Natalie, then just as quickly opened again. "Jess must be pretty hacked off with the news?"

Becky's heart thumped. "What do you mean? Is Jess okay? Have you seen her recently?"

"My God, you don't know?"

"Know what?"

"Jess is living with Steve Hodges. Remember him? Veronica Williams's nephew."

That said, Natalie slammed the door shut for a second time.

Becky parked her car in the drive at Rose Cottage and dragged herself out of the driver's seat. She locked the door and leaned against the vehicle. What a day. She'd managed to upset both her dad and her sister, and, without even knowing it, Jess. Anxiety shot through her. She rested her hand on her chest. How could her daughter be with Steve Hodges? He was nearly twice her age. Becky's head jerked up. Jess must already know about Vellangoose if she was living with the Williams family at Boswyn. Was that why her daughter hadn't rung her?

Liz Mitchell stepped onto the drive.

Becky rubbed her forehead. If Liz expected her to work extra hours tomorrow to cover lunch, she had another think coming.

Before Becky could open her mouth, Liz began to cry. "I'm so sorry, and Jack's so angry he could kill the woman. I told him you'd understand. You do understand, don't you?" Liz raised her hands, then dropped them. "The job and the flat, we can't ..."

Becky froze. This couldn't be happening.

"Veronica Williams is one of our biggest customers, and our Jimmy ... our boy Jimmy, and his family, live in a rented cottage at Boswyn Manor." Liz gripped Becky's arm. "I said to our Jack that you must stay in our spare bedroom for a few weeks. Told him she can't stop us having a friend to stay, but Jack said–"

"I understand." Becky cut Liz off with a quick nod of the head. "Don't worry, I'll be fine."

A few minutes later, Liz's car roared up the road.

A wave of fear engulfed Becky. She'd lost everything.

She looked at the wheelbarrow, full of useless, unwanted stuff. She grabbed the handles, pushed it up the ramp and shoved it inside the shed with a loud crash. Somebody else could sort that mess. She had more than enough of her own to deal with.

10

Abi gripped the steering wheel and urged the camper van along the winding country lane. She'd not long driven through the village of Penhellick, and if she'd correctly read the map that David Penna had given her, the route she now travelled would bring her to the rear entrance of Vellangoose. The main entrance to the property was on the Falmouth to Helston road but entering via the old farm track would do just fine. She wanted to suss out Vellangoose and salvage everything she could before that woman, her so-called sister, knew anything about it.

Manoeuvring the van around another bend, Abi braked suddenly, wrenched the vehicle off the road and stopped inches from a rusty gate. There was nothing to indicate this was Vellangoose, but this had to be it. The gate hung at an angle, held in place by ancient chains and padlocks. She got out and gave them a couple of swift kicks. One of the thin links broke. Specks of rust spun in the air. She yanked the gate to one side, drove into the lane, then ran back to the gate and pulled it shut.

Once more behind the wheel, she inched her way through the scrub and undergrowth. Behind her, Buddy moved from paw to paw and whined with excitement. Grace giggled as brambles and branches dragged across the windscreen. The vehicle swayed and rattled its way in and out of large potholes and ancient tractor ruts. Abi's knuckles grew white. She swallowed hard. What the hell was she doing? If she damaged the van, she had no money to repair it. This couldn't be Vellangoose. The track didn't look that long and twisty on the map.

Not able to stop or go back, she pressed harder on the accelerator to urge the van over a deep rut. The foliage parted and the vehicle pitched forward. Early spring sunlight flashed into her eyes. She braked, fumbled with the door, and climbed out.

Vellangoose.

A thrill ran through her body. She twirled in a slow circle. This place was something else. Nothing but a load of old derelict buildings and rubble, but they were her derelict buildings and rubble. She, Abi Pascoe, owned them. A smile spread across her face.

Directly ahead, the monster of all buildings stood with gaping black holes where once windows and a giant door had been. Must be The Mill David Penna talked about. In several spots, the roof had fallen in and gorse grew from the granite walls. Incredibly, yellow heads of daffodils bobbed amongst the broken tiles and other debris stacked around its base.

Several more farm dwellings surrounded the yard to form a rough square. Rusted machinery and heaps of rotten manure were piled in amongst clumps of coarse grass and weeds. Some of the buildings looked in slightly better condition than the others, but that didn't say much. To the left of The Mill, a lane snaked up a gentle incline, presumably towards the Falmouth to Helston road.

She returned to the van, moved it out of sight behind one of the old dwellings, and let Buddy out. Seeing Grace was fast asleep with a thumb in her mouth, Abi pulled on a woolly hat, locked the vehicle, and moved to peer inside one of the buildings. Mouldy hay bales and rubbish filled what looked like an old cow shed or stable. Nothing of value. Shit. She needed money; fast. She'd viewed several more properties for rent since Steve Hodges's visit but no luck. Buddy was the problem. She wouldn't get anywhere with him in tow. As if on cue, his brown and white body snaked out of one building into another: doggie heaven.

Why couldn't Henry Williams have left her some money instead of the ruin that was Vellangoose and some run-down old nag and a scrawny goat?

Her eyes flooded with tears. For a moment she longed for her mum. Since she'd left for Australia, it had been hard coping alone with the kids. Maybe she should ring her? They'd hardly said a word to each other after that evening when her mum dropped the bombshell that she'd stayed in contact with Henry Williams ever since before Abi was born. Her mum had kept so many secrets from her. A knot of anger gripped her body. Her mother should make the first contact.

Grace's cries pierced the silence. Abi rushed back to her. Five minutes later, she slung her rucksack on her back, lifted her daughter into her arms and wrapped a blanket around her, tucking in the edges to keep out the cold.

Outside The Mill, Abi hesitated for a moment, then peered through one of the gaping holes. Inside, heaps of furniture, old machinery and used fertiliser bags stuffed with who knew what, were stacked to the ceiling. It wasn't safe to explore with Grace.

She opened the gate next to the lane and ambled into the field, then came to an abrupt halt. A patchwork of small meadows dipped and rolled to the horizon. The Penhellick Church tower was visible in the distance. Other farms dotted the area. She could hear running water and guessed that the carpet of shrubs and gorse that meandered across the bottom of the field and into the next, hid a stream or river. Probably one used by The Mill many years ago. Far off in the distance, a thin sliver of sea glinted in the sun.

Abi moved over to the hedge and sat on the grass, her back against the far side of a large granite boulder that protruded into the field. The spot was warm and sheltered in the sun. Best of all, they were safely hidden from prying eyes or anyone coming into the yard or field. She settled Grace onto the blanket and pulled out a sandwich, baby food and a flask from her rucksack. Buddy leapt over the hedge and sat in front of her, his coat full of burrs.

A duck flew overhead, swooped down and landed on what Abi could now see was a series of ponds. She leaned her head back on the smooth rock and closed her eyes. This place was amazing. Why would anyone want to abandon it?

Buddy let out a low growl. She jerked upright, grabbed his collar and pulled him behind her before peeking around the edge of the boulder.

A Land Rover towing a horsebox ambled down the lane and into the yard. A lanky young man leapt from the passenger seat and walked to the gate. He dragged it wide open and beckoned to the driver.

The vehicle came to a halt in the meadow and a big man with long straggly grey hair got out, dressed in a high-viz yellow jacket with the Williams's trading logo printed on the back. His shabby, navy boiler suit was tucked inside dirt-encrusted wellington boots.

"Look at the state of this place," he said. "It were something to see when I was a nipper."

The younger man swung his gaze around the yard. "Looks like a pile of old junk to me."

"It were a thriving farm back then, part of the Williams's estate. The boss's old man escaped from Boswyn Manor most days to work on the farm or in the walled garden. Them daughters of his often came with him." He let out a hearty laugh. "Boy, you should've seen Miss Veronica and Miss Constance then. Right crackers." He laughed again. "Me and the village boys used to sneak up to the garden wall to get a glimpse of them sun-bathing. Got a clip round the ear a few times when their old man caught us."

"When was that? The Stone Age?" The young lad chuckled at his own joke.

"Don't be so cheeky, Charlie me boy." Drops of rain spotted the Land Rover bonnet. "Come on, we'd best get this 'ere job done."

Grace began to fidget. Abi picked her up and held her close. "Shush, sweetheart."

Young Charlie surveyed the old farm implements and barbed wire jutting out of the tufted grass and clumps of dock leaves. "This doesn't feel right."

"It's what Mrs Williams wants."

"Can't we put them somewhere else?"

"Not if you want to keep your job, or any job in Cornwall come to that. Upset the boss and you've had your chips."

Abi shifted a fraction to ease the cramp in her calf.

"We could at least clear some of the bits of wire. What about that farm shelter over against the hedge? It looks a wreck but–"

"Stop your fretting. The jackass will probably break his leg before the day's out." The big man spat on the ground. "Useless thing."

"But it's March. A pampered horse like him should be indoors. He's not even got his rug on."

"Shut your trap and get on with the job."

Charlie glared at the older man, then made his way slowly to the horsebox. Thuds and the clank of metal could be heard coming from inside. A plaintive bleat fractured the air.

A few minutes later, he led a large white horse down the ramp. A mottled brown and black goat trotted behind him, its long droopy ears flapping in the breeze.

Abi stared at the animals. They must be Dolly and Polly or whatever their names were? Surely the men weren't leaving the animals here?

Charlie led the horse away from the vehicle and stood rubbing its nose. The animal snorted and shifted from one foot to another. Its ears flicked to and fro. Charlie unclipped the rope.

The big man slapped the animal hard across the rump, then stood back and grinned. "Don't want to be late for me tea."

The horse bucked and galloped off across the field. The goat followed, bleating as it ran to keep up.

Charlie shook his head.

Abi held an increasingly fretful Grace tighter and whispered into her warm neck. Her other hand remained tucked into Buddy's collar.

The doors of the Land Rover slammed shut, and the vehicle roared back up the lane.

Abi stood and let out a long breath. Buddy raced away across the field. She called after him but he didn't stop. Even she had to admit he was a liability at times.

With Grace on her hip, she walked to the middle of the field. In the far corner, the horse pawed the ground; puffs of condensation gusted from his nostrils. Abi clenched her teeth and hardened her heart. She had enough trouble looking after the kids, let alone two animals she neither wanted nor asked for. They would have to take their chances. There was water and grass after all. They could shelter by the old building, couldn't they?

She turned away before she could change her mind but couldn't stop herself from looking back when she got to the gate. Her eyes swam with tears at the unfairness of it all.

In the camper van, she strapped Grace into her child seat, then stood to take one last look, the sleeves of her coat pulled down over her hands.

For the first time, she noticed a single storey building; an L-shaped barn of some sorts with boarded-up windows and doors. Weeds and grass grew from the guttering, and the walls were grey and patchy with green algae, but the roof looked sound. No holes or ridges of slipped tiles. What was this place? She could have kicked herself for not reading all the legal papers that David Penna had sent her.

There was a chimney, so it must have been some sort of residence? Her heart quickened. Only one way to find out.

She turned back to the camper van and rummaged under the front seat, pulled out a crowbar, a claw hammer and a teddy bear. With a smile, she placed the fluffy toy into Grace's outstretched arms. Blowing her a kiss, Abi turned and moved quickly to the door in the main body of the property.

The old wooden boards came away with a few tugs, but the door underneath was heavily bolted and padlocked. Not a job for today, Jacob and Eve needed to be picked up from school soon.

She turned to study the L-shaped wing to her left. It looked like it could be entered by another smaller door. She yanked it free of rotten panels. More bolts, but this time the padlock snapped easily.

Inside, stale air filled her nostrils. She coughed and automatically put a hand over her mouth. Dust motes drifted in the light from the open doorway. She'd entered at one end of what was a long, large room. French doors led into a garden. The interior had once been white with exposed granite around the windows. Large pieces of render and ceiling plaster lay on the floor.

Her boots crunched on debris and rubbish as she stepped further into the room. It was then she saw it. A huge granite fireplace filled half of the wall at the far end. Reaching from floor to ceiling, it jutted into the room. A few shelves remained in the recesses on either side. One large piece of granite formed the mantel. The grate was full of leaves and soot but who cared? It was magnificent. She walked to the fireplace and touched the cold granite, then scanned the room. Despite all the rubble on the floor, the stained walls and damaged ceiling, the space was surprisingly dry.

There was an internal door to the main part of the building, presumably to the bedrooms and the bathroom?

She opened the door. Broken furniture and other household detritus blocked her way. She was going nowhere. Damn. She kicked a rotting, stained mattress directly in front of her. Several mice ran from the loose stuffing. She slammed the door shut.

Only a few more minutes and she'd have to leave. She rushed outside, ran around the end of the protruding wing, scrambled over a granite wall and into what had been the garden. Shrubs and brambles clawed at her jacket as she pushed past the outside of the French doors to the other end of the L-shaped wing.

A window remained uncovered. She rubbed a patch of green algae away from the glass and peered in. An old Belfast sink caught her eye. The kitchen, or rather what was left of it? The sink might make some money. She tried the door. It was barred from the inside. What was this place? Fort Knox?

This building might have been a lovely home once, maybe even a beautiful one, but what difference did it make? It was a dump now.

Back at the camper van, she took a final look around. Mist rolled down the valley and the earlier drops of rain had turned to a fine drizzle. A wet Buddy settled into the passenger well. Grace sucked her thumb and blinked with sleepy eyes. Abi kissed her finger and pressed it to her daughter's warm cheek.

It had been a lovely dream to think that this place could've solved her problems, but she had to face it, Vellangoose was one big wreck. She'd wasted her time. Her only option now was to crawl to the authorities for help.

In the driver's seat, she released the handbrake. The grey clouds parted. A few weak rays pushed through the drizzle and bathed the building in a warm, welcoming light. A germ of an idea flashed into Abi's head. Maybe she could clear that big living room? She had the camper van, a primus stove, and all their camping stuff. They could live there for a while. It would give her time to recce the place properly, find something to sell. Wood? Bricks? That old stuff in The Mill?

She rammed her foot down on the accelerator and the van rattled back up the track. What a fool she was, dreaming again. It was winter. No one in their right mind would put their kids at such risk.

The hedges flashed by as she drove towards Penryn, but she didn't notice. All she could see was that big room, and a huge log fire burning in the granite fireplace.

11

28 March

Wind blasted icy daggers of rain into Becky's face and whipped soggy tendrils of hair around her head, but she made no effort to zip her anorak or pull up the hood. So, this was Vellangoose, this sad collection of grey, ramshackle buildings. Was this truly what all the fuss was about?

She stared at The Mill, its grey slate roof, battered by years of Cornish storms and neglect, punctured with holes. The remaining slates, covered in moss, clung on in ramshackle lines. Others lay broken in piles at the base of the building. Windows, devoid of glass, gawped out of the granite façade.

What she'd seen in her mind's eye after scrutinising the Trust documents and plans that David Penna had sent to her, most certainly wasn't what she saw in front of her. What did she expect? Did she think that Vellangoose would solve all her problems? A strangled laugh escaped from her mouth. No, it looked like she'd need to spend a shed load of money before Vellangoose could be off-loaded. Not that she had to worry about that for five years.

She sighed and moved to peer into The Mill. The dwelling had obviously been used as a store-cum-dump for years. The rank smell of rats filled her nostrils and she stepped away. A slate crashed to the floor a few feet from her. She jumped. What she needed was a hard hat, but who would care if she was injured or killed? She didn't, for one.

"Bring it on."

Her words echoed around the buildings.

Rain swept in waves across the yard. A sheet of grey murk obscured the fields and the wonderful view beyond. At least, she assumed there was a wonderful view. She'd entered Vellangoose from the Falmouth to Helston main road from which, on a clear day, she'd often seen the sea in the distance and, on the horizon, the tiny saucers that were the satellite dishes at Goonhilly Earth Station. The lane from the road to the yard twisted and turned as it dropped into the valley.

Now, all she wanted to see was the river that meandered onto Vellangoose land, then flowed into three connecting ponds in the middle of the property, before it crossed onto neighbouring farmland. At least, that's what it looked like on the map David Penna had also enclosed with the legal documents.

She moved towards the gate, leading into one of the small meadows, and grabbed the top bar. Rust fragments bit into her hands. She climbed over, jumped, and landed on the other side with a squelch. Good grief, would the heavy rains of the last few days ever stop? Head bent, she pushed on towards the ponds. The ground was uneven and potted with deep ruts filled with dirty water. Large clumps of grass and weeds pockmarked the surface. A boggy, organic odour wafted from the ground. She stumbled, righted herself, then stopped.

Through the gloom, she could make out a tall Cornish hedge. Covered still in grey winter foliage and savage-looking bramble stalks, stunted thorn bushes clung to its top.

The gate leading to the ponds was not where she thought it was. Maybe the undergrowth had claimed it long ago? The ponds had probably been drained anyway. Lots of farmers had done that, she remembered her dad telling her that it was something to do with grant monies or some government ruling.

The rain plastered strands of wet hair to her cheeks. Time to go. There was nothing for her here. She headed back to the yard, sticking close to the perimeter of the meadow for cover. It was then she saw it; an old animal shelter or food store of some sort tucked alongside the hedgerow in front of her. Another squall lashed her body. The building was a lot nearer than her car. She hesitated, then ran and tucked herself into a corner; the Cornish hedge on one side and the outside wall of the stone shelter on the other. There was no way she could even think about going inside the dilapidated building. It was bound to be full of rats.

An uneven piece of granite dug into her shoulder. She shifted, found a comfortable spot and let out a deep breath. Water dripped from what was left of the galvanised roof and ran down her neck.

"Oh, for goodness sake," she yelled.

For a few minutes, she peered through the drizzly rain, then frowned. The meadows closest to the yard were overgrown and uncared for, but the ones she'd passed on the way down the lane were clearly being farmed. Presumably, someone was renting them? Or maybe the Williams family used them?

If the fields were rented out, surely there would be rent money? That would help if she could get her hands on it. In three days, Rose Cottage, her home for over twenty years, would be gone. It would be wonderful if there was enough income to put down a deposit on a flat. Suddenly, she remembered reading that the conditions of the Trust prevented Vellangoose from being rented out. Blast. The same would apply to the fields.

A deep thud-thud shook the ground. Dirty white flashed before her eyes.

A horse towered above her.

A scream tore from her throat and she shrank further into the corner, arms over her head for protection, eyes scrunched shut.

Warm air exploded over the top of her head. Her eyes flew open. Pink nostrils flared inches from her face.

She screamed again.

The great white beast leapt away, spun in a circle and returned to stare at her. It tossed its head, snorted and pawed the ground. The stink of wet horse made her retch.

Dear God. Here in the rain and the mud, in a field left to her by a stranger – her hitherto unknown father – this was how she was going to die.

The horse stopped, stood still, his head to one side. One big brown eye fixed on her. Her gaze darted from the animal to the gate, and back again. Could she outrun it? No chance. Could she get into the shelter? A shudder ran through her body.

She moved one foot, then the other. The horse's ears flicked back and forth but it made no attempt to stop her. She shuffled further along the wall. Finally, she reached the corner, peered around it to see the front of the shelter. The mottled brown-black head of a goat poked out of a jagged hole in the door. A yellow eye focused on her. The animal bleated, then threw itself against the wooden structure, presumably attempting to escape into the meadow, but the door remained shut.

She looked from the horse to the goat, from brown eyes to yellow eyes. The horse bobbed its head. Fear galvanised her into action. She ran to the door, grabbed the rough wood. Splinters pierced her skin. Yanking the door open, she prayed the goat would run outside. Instead, the horse charged past her into the shelter, giving her a glancing blow as it passed.

She toppled to the ground. Pain shot through her chest. Winded, she struggled to breathe. The pain grew worse, then air surged into her lungs. Curled in a ball, she waited for the horse's hoofs to fall. Nothing. Gingerly she rolled onto her knees and stared in through the open doorway.

Both animals stood in the corner eating mouthfuls of hay. Steam rose from the horse's coat. The goat snuggled alongside him, bleating softly.

She staggered to her feet. The animals took no notice of her. The place looked reasonably dry. A piece of tarpaulin had been nailed underneath the almost non-existent roof, giving them some shelter. Somebody was looking after them. Who?

The horse turned its head towards her.

She stiffened, slammed the door shut and ran. Her feet sank into the mud. She tipped forward. One foot came out of its boot and dropped into the slime. She righted herself and tore across the meadow, snatching glances over her shoulder until she reached the yard.

Back at the car, she ripped off her remaining muddy boot and socks, and dropped them into a plastic shopping bag. Water dripped into the vehicle as she sat and wiped her hands with tissues. She would have to drive in bare feet; there was no way she was going back for the missing footwear.

She flopped into the car and turned the ignition key. The engine moaned and died. She fumbled with the key and turned it again and again. No. It had to start. A mix of rain and hail lashed the windscreen. Dear God, she couldn't be stuck in this awful place. She tried the ignition one more time. Nothing. Hunched down in her seat, she attempted to get the Penhellick Garage on her mobile phone. No signal. She thumped the steering wheel. Bloody Vellangoose. Once the storm passed, she would have to walk to the village.

A shiver ran through her body. She needed to get warm, or she'd catch pneumonia or die of the cold.

Through the windscreen, she saw a single-storey L-shaped building. Labelled *The Barn,* if she remembered correctly, on the plans attached to the Trust documents. One of the doors wasn't boarded up. Maybe she could shelter inside for a while? Without stopping to think, she got out of the car and ran. Stones dug into her feet but she didn't stop.

Inside, she stood motionless at the end of a large room. It wasn't the mess she'd expected. Huge holes dotted the walls and ceiling, but the floor was clean and clear of rubble. The windows and French doors, although smeared with dirt and algae, looked out over shrubs and brambles. The smell of freshly cut logs, stacked in one of the recesses next to the wonderful fireplace, filled the air. In the other recess, three tins of baked beans, tea bags, and a chipped mug, sat on a shelf next to a battered saucepan, a box of matches, and a small primus stove.

Black plastic bags were piled in the corner, along with a long-handled broom, and a cardboard box from which a quilted sleeping bag poked out.

A tremor ran over her. Was somebody living here? Maybe local kids were using it as a hidey-hole? Or perhaps a vagrant? Becky turned to run but stopped herself. The rain still lashed outside and she was going nowhere.

She took a deep breath, moved to the fireside, and ran her fingers over the smooth, cool mantel. A pang of hurt dashed through her as she thought of Rose Cottage, her log burner and comfy sofas.

On the hearth, newspaper and twigs poked out of an Asda bag. She looked at the empty grate, knelt, screwed the newspaper into balls, and dropped them into the fireplace. It took several attempts before one of the matches flared and the paper caught alight. She added the twigs and then a couple of logs. The burgeoning warmth brought back colour to her fingers, but her bare feet were white and numb.

She stood and removed her jeans and wet coat, quickly grabbed the end of the sleeping bag and lifted it out of the box. Who would know she'd used it? She would be gone soon. She slipped inside the bag and pulled it tight under her chin. A fresh smell of washing powder filled her nose.

The fire crackled. Becky rolled onto her side, face towards the flames, and yawned. Her eyes fluttered, then closed.

A loud crash punctured her sleep. Her body jerked. Where was she? She shook her head. Vellangoose. Her heart raced as she struggled to free herself from the sleeping bag and attempted to stand.

A tall, dark shape filled the doorway. Head down, it came towards her. Bulky black plastic bags swung from its hands.

Becky let out a feeble cry.

The dark figure stopped, looming over her.

"What the fuck are you doing here?" a loud, harsh, female voice said.

12

Abi dropped the plastic bags onto the floor and pushed back the hood of her parka jacket. Her heart sank. She knew immediately who it was, even though the wreck in front of her looked nothing like the well-dressed person who'd bumped into her that day at the solicitors. Damn it, the last thing Abi needed was for that woman to stick her nose in where it wasn't wanted.

She glared at the intruder as she struggled to her feet and kicked herself free from a sleeping bag.

"I'm so sorry. I shouldn't have …" the woman's hand fluttered. "I would've asked but …"

Abi opened her mouth to speak, but before she could say anything, the woman rushed on.

"My car broke down. I was so cold I had to come inside. The fire … I lit the fire." Her breath came in gasps. "I'm sorry, I …" Smoke billowed into the room. "Oh dear."

Abi's fist clenched. "I said, what the fuck are you doing here?"

The woman recoiled as if Abi had slapped her. "I'm Rebecca Farrow, I–"

"I know who you are," Abi snapped.

"Oh," she said. "It's Becky actually. Everyone calls me Becky. And I just … I wanted to see Vellangoose."

Water dripped from Abi's hair and ran down her face.

"Well then, *Becky*, you should've asked me first," she said, then could've happily bitten her tongue off. This woman owned half of Vellangoose and had every right to visit without asking permission.

Becky frowned, bent down and picked up the sleeping bag. She folded it, placed it neatly on top of a cardboard box and cleared her throat.

"I didn't think I needed to ask," she said, "considering this is my property as well as yours. Presuming you're Abi Pascoe, that is?"

Abi took a deep breath. She had to play this carefully. There was too much at stake. She needed to think it through before she truly put her foot in it.

"You'd better get dressed." She nodded at a pair of steaming jeans hanging from the broom at the side of the fireplace, then spun about and marched outside.

Teeth gritted, she fumbled to open the passenger door of the camper van. Buddy shot past her, cocked his leg against a bush, then rushed through the door leading into The Barn.

Frantic pleas carried through the air. "Oh! Down. Nice dog. Down."

Tension eased from Abi's body. That Becky woman would never stick the roughness of country life. Or Vellangoose. She'd poke her little rich nose in today and then that would be it. All Abi had to do was to play it cool and all would be well. They'd never have to see each other again.

She picked up the biggest cardboard box and made her way back into The Barn. Stamping mud from her boots, she put the box by the wall, ignoring the figure struggling into the damp jeans. Over the next few minutes, she brought in several more bags and another box. Finally, she hung up her dripping coat on a nail behind the door.

Becky stood with her back to the fireplace, face taut, arms wrapped tight across her chest. Abi stared at her icy-white, bare feet, then forced herself to look away.

"I'll go as soon as the rain stops." Becky's voice held a tremor." My car …"

"Yes, you said." Abi turned away and said over her shoulder, "Well, don't mind me. I've got stuff to sort."

She ripped open one of the black bags, dug out a carton of UHT milk, an extra-large box of coco pops and a packet of biscuits, and put them on the shelf next to the cans of baked beans. Prodding further, she drew out two mugs, a plastic beaker and a jar of coffee. All the time she worked, she sensed Becky's eyes following her every move.

Becky inched towards her. "What's with all the stuff?"

"It's only a few bits for when I drop in now and then to check the place. You know, to protect my investment."

"What's this place like?" Becky touched a damp patch on the wall. "Bit of a dump, I suppose. Like the buildings outside."

Abi counted to ten, then pasted a smile onto her face. "I haven't got beyond this room yet. Everything's nailed shut, and the hallway's blocked up with all sorts of rubbish."

Becky wiped her hand on her jeans. "Probably just as well."

Irritation overwhelmed Abi. She swung around to tell Becky where she could stick her opinions, but the words died on her lips. The woman's eyes were the same electric-blue colour as her kids' were. It had to be some sort of joke. But, no, Henry Williams had left his mark on them all.

With a sigh, Abi walked over to the shelf, picked up a mug and waved it. "Coffee?"

Becky nodded.

From one of the boxes, Abi drew out a bottle of tap water, then reached for the saucepan next to the small gas camping stove on the shelf. She worked in silence until the water boiled, then pulled the sleeve of her sweater down over her hand, lifted the saucepan off the stove, and poured the hot liquid into the mugs. The rich aroma of coffee filled the air.

Becky spoke first. "The plan for The Barn shows three bedrooms, a bathroom, and a kitchen."

Before she could stop herself, Abi blurted out, "The kitchen's a really good size. No units, but there's a Belfast sink, and ..."

Becky gazed at her, then looked from the boxes and bags to the items on the shelves. "My God, you're thinking of moving in, aren't you?"

Abi's heart raced. She shook her head several times, but those blue eyes fixed on her again.

"When?"

Abi sucked in air. "At the weekend."

"Oh."

"The roof's sound. This room's fine for now."

A few drops of coffee splashed over Abi's fingers. She took a sip from her mug and forced herself to remain calm. What could it possibly matter to Becky whether Abi lived here or not? She would still get her share of Vellangoose when the Trust expired.

"But ..." Becky shuddered. "It's all so ... bleak."

Before Abi knew what she was doing, she delved into the bag next to her and yanked out a pair of socks and a thick sweater. "Here, have these."

Becky hesitated, then quickly tugged the sweater and socks on. "Thanks." A brief smile flashed across her face. "I see you've been feeding the animals?"

Guilt shot through Abi, but she pushed it away. "Not me."

"But there's food in the shelter. I thought–"

"I said, it's not me."

"Oh. Maybe Veronica Williams has arranged for them to be fed?"

"That old witch? Never."

A few days ago, Abi had caught a glimpse of a short older man carrying bales of hay into the field, but the less this woman knew the better.

"I had a bit of an encounter with him," Becky said.

Abi shot her a look. "Who? Who's been snooping around?"

"Not a person. The horse. It scared me. It ... I fell." Becky looked at her dirty feet and muddy jeans. "I lost my boot in the mud."

The corners of Abi's lips twitched. She reached for a packet of chocolate digestive biscuits.

"Want one?"

Becky twisted a strand of hair round and round her finger, then shook her head.

Abi shoved a broken piece of biscuit into her mouth. "Do you have a family?"

"A daughter. Jessica. She's nineteen."

Crumbs flew from Abi's mouth and dropped to the floor. What was she doing? She didn't care about this woman or what family she had. She wiped her lips roughly with the back of her hand. Keep up the pretence of interest for a little while longer, that's all she had to do.

She forced the smile back onto her face, reached over, and returned the packet to the shelf.

"Always got a permanent supply. It's the kids. They've got pits for stomachs."

"Kids?"

"Three. Boy and two girls."

Becky stepped back a pace. "You're bringing your children to live here? But there's no heating or electric." She put a hand to her mouth. "No plumbing. How could you?"

Abi slammed her mug onto the mantlepiece. Her cheeks burned. The damn woman was right. What sort of mother was she? But what else could she do? What did Mrs Rebecca whatsit Farrow know about her circumstances?

She drew herself up to her full height. "I don't have any choice. In three days, I've nowhere else to live." Her words tumbled out. "Besides, there's loads of wood and stuff on Vellangoose. I'll use some for the fire and sell the rest."

Becky stared at her. "You can't sell anything. The Trust conditions state—"

"Fuck the conditions. My kids come first."

Becky flinched. "Oh. There must be somewhere you can go. Somewhere to rent?"

"Tell me where? The whole of Cornwall's getting ready for the holiday season. The likes of me have no chance of finding a place."

Becky's hand flapped once, then rested on her neck. "Could the Council help? What about asking Social Services or the benefits people?"

"Do you have any idea what that's like? Have you ever had to beg for money? No, of course, you haven't. You, with your perfect family and your perfect house, what would you know about it? Well, I know." Spittle flew from Abi's mouth. "And I'm not doing it again." She swallowed. So much for playing it cool.

Squally rain lashed against the door.

Becky hunched over and seemed to shrink before Abi's eyes. "John … John, my husband, hit problems with his business. He made some bad financial decisions. We lost Rose Cottage, our home, and … everything's gone."

"Bloody hell."

Becky's shoulder blades stuck out of the oversized sweater. "He left me for someone else," she whispered.

Abi picked up one of the boxes and placed it on top of another. "Join the club. My kids' fathers did the same."

"Fathers?"

Abi stifled a laugh. "Two. Neither of them was worth a fart. I've never found a good man. Looks like we've something in common after all."

"I wouldn't say that." Becky patted her hair. "I was married for twenty-one years. It was a wonderful life. He ..."

Abi snatched up Becky's empty mug and finished the sentence for her. "He left you in the shit."

Becky grabbed her wet anorak and walked stiffly to the door. "I think it's time I left."

Relief shot through Abi.

Abruptly, Becky stopped, head bowed. "I can't. My car."

An unexpected rush of something primitive shot through Abi at the note of defeat in Becky's voice. It wasn't just sympathy for another person who'd hit rock bottom, but something else entirely unexpected. Whether she liked it or not, Abi realised she and this Becky were linked by blood and circumstance. The woman was family.

Abi stood still. What now? Where did they go from here?

She sighed.

"Look, there's stuff we need to discuss. You know, this place, the animals. And," her heart pounded in her chest, "what you will do if I move into The Barn with the kids?"

Becky raised her hands and rubbed her temples with her forefingers. "I don't know ... I ..."

Her half-sister – that sounded so weird even just in her head – walked to the window and peered through the dirty pane. Abi moved to stand beside her. The rain had finally stopped. Streaks of watery sun poked through the dark clouds and threw light onto what must once have been a proper garden. A piece of old plastic, snagged on brambles, flapped in the breeze. Patches of primroses poked through the weeds.

"Why did you really come here today?"

Her sister continued to stare out of the window. "I have to be out of Rose Cottage at the end of this week," she said.

Panic shot through Abi. Not just some random visit after all then? She turned away from the window and scanned the room. It seemed very small suddenly.

Abi turned back to Becky. She had to ask the question, even though she knew already what the answer would be.

"Do you want to move in here?"

Becky spun around. "Never. I couldn't ..." Her arms rose, then dropped to her sides. "Maybe."

Briefly, Abi closed her eyes. This couldn't be happening. The last thing she needed was another person to look after. For a moment, everything seemed to close in around her, then she pushed her shoulders back.

"I'll look at your car if you would like? My camper van breaks down all the time. Cars are easy to fix." Even to her own ears, her voice sounded high pitched. "We need to have a proper talk. How about tomorrow afternoon?"

Becky nodded.

Abi opened the door. Leaves swirled around her feet.

"Okay then. Show me to your car."

Becky zipped up her anorak, pulled on her hood and tightened the strings. Her tiny, pinched face peered out at Abi, whose heart sank.

This was never going to work.

13

Becky rubbed her temple. It was only 7:30 a.m., but the noise in the living room at Vellangoose was already unbearable. She popped two paracetamols into her mouth, picked up a bottle of water, unscrewed the top and took a big gulp. The tell-tale zigzag lights that hailed the start of a migraine flashed in one eye.

For the last three nights, she'd slept on an old inflatable mattress, tucked in the corner near to the exit. At the foot of the bed, she'd arranged her clothes and containers of food into neat piles against the wall. A red storage box, positioned on its side, acted as a bedside table. On the top, an alarm clock ticked.

At the other end of the room, by the fireplace, Jacob, Eve and Grace jumped and crawled over clothes and toys strewn across assorted air beds, sleeping bags and duvets. Against the wall, Abi had laid a long, thick plank of wood on top of several breeze blocks, which served as both seating and a table.

Grace's plastic beaker rolled across the floor and came to a halt next to the battered fireguard. Buddy got to his feet and sniffed it. Abi, standing at the shelves filling bowls with coco pops and milk, made no effort to pick the bottle up.

Becky shook her head. How could a family live in such chaos?

Pulling on John's old sweater, she pushed her feet into muddy wellies and stepped towards the door. She didn't speak to Abi, nor did Abi ask her where she was going. During the past week, since their fateful first meeting, they'd cleaned and scrubbed the living room, washed years of dirt off the windows and French doors, and fixed up crude bathroom facilities outside. They'd also moved in. All of which had been completed with the minimum of conversation and without any exchange of personal information. This suited Becky. No attachments. She'd made it clear to Abi that she'd use her time at Vellangoose to get back on her feet, then she'd be off, and this terrible episode in her life would be just a bad memory.

Becky stepped outside, leaned against the wall of The Barn, and sucked in the clean, fresh air. Two crows rose from the yard in a medley of squawks and caws. A tear ran down her cheek. What would her dad and Natalie think of her now?

The last time she'd visited her dad, she'd stood at his front door and taken a deep breath before stepping inside. A fug of stale air and fried food had blasted her senses. It was the middle of the morning, but her dad sat hunched over the table, unshaven and wearing crumpled pyjamas. A hacking cough answered her cry of concern. He pooh-poohed her wanting to call the doctor, saying he'd got antibiotics and they were doing the trick.

Guilt shot through her as she watched him shuffle down the hallway to the bathroom. He was nearly seventy-four with a heart condition, and she'd forced him to lay bare all the things he thought he'd buried forever. On top of that, Natalie hadn't been over to see him either. How could her sister be so unthinking?

Becky grabbed her bag, found her phone and punched the quick dial number for Natalie. It went direct to voicemail.

"Why can't you answer your bloody phone? Dad's ill. Everything's a mess. Get over here. Now."

In a short time, Becky had the curtains drawn back, her dad's bed stripped and remade, and his clothes tidied away. The washing machine hummed and the tang of lemon washing-up detergent mingled with the sweet aroma of warm toast.

Freshly shaven and showered, her dad walked into the kitchen and flopped into his chair. She put a plate of poached eggs and toast in front of him.

He wrapped his hand over hers. "Thanks. You're a good girl. 'Tis more than I deserve."

She sat opposite him, a mug of Earl Grey in her hand. "I've something to tell you."

His fork stopped halfway to his mouth. "Not more bad news."

She took a sip of tea. "I'm moving into Vellangoose. Tomorrow."

"Why would you do that? You've got the flat above the bakery."

"Not anymore. I lost it. And the job. Veronica Williams made sure of that."

His fork clattered onto the plate. "That woman. I could swing for her. How–" Another coughing fit stopped him talking.

She jumped up and patted him on the back. "Dad. I'll be okay. Please don't worry."

"You'll regret it. That place is poison. Always has been, always will be." He stood and moved towards the hallway door. "I'm going to lie down for a bit."

Becky unlocked her dad's garage and stepped inside. She eyed the paltry hoard of belongings she'd saved from Rose Cottage; items too old or unfashionable to sell. Not much to show for twenty-one years of marriage.

She worked methodically, searching one container after another until she had a meagre pile of essential items: a single set of cutlery and crockery, a radio, bedding, and a couple of large towels. She reached for a small photo album, flicked through the pages before pausing at a photo of Jess as a baby in John's arms. She touched the print with her fingertip, sighed, then tucked the album into her jacket pocket.

The last box she opened contained her baking equipment and scales. She tenderly stroked the surface of one of the shiny tins. For a moment, she was transported back to her kitchen at Rose Cottage and the smell of fresh-baked cakes. With a vigorous shake of her head, she stuffed the tin back into the box, rammed the lid down and straightened up.

"So, you're going to live at Vellangoose?"

Becky slowly turned around, then nodded.

Natalie burst out laughing. "You'll never live in that dump on your own. You hate the dark and you're scared of spiders."

Becky's heart raced. "I won't be on my own. I'm moving in with Abi and her children."

"Abi?" Her sister's eyes widened. "Not the other illegitimate daughter? Have you gone completely crazy?"

"It's a business arrangement, that's all. We both needed somewhere to live." She chewed her bottom lip. "It just makes sense. After all, we do own Vellangoose."

"Leave the place alone. The money will still be there when you sell it in five years. Find somewhere else to live, for goodness sake."

Becky raised an eyebrow. "Where would that be? Your spare bedroom?"

Natalie pursed her lips. "I'll have you know I spent the whole of last week on a Veronica Williams damage limitation exercise, and–"

"Oh, I get it. Lloyd Accountancy comes before me?"

"Don't be flippant. Pete and I can't afford to upset Veronica Williams, that's all I'm saying. Hopefully, I've stopped any fallout from the mess you've got mixed up in, but you know how it is with that woman."

Becky knelt on the floor. Her hand shook as she packed an empty box with items from the pile. "It'll be a temporary thing until we get some money and can go our separate ways."

"Well, don't expect me to be all pally-pally with this Abi person. You won't see me in that place."

Becky turned away, pulled a large water carrier and a portable toilet from under a tarpaulin. "Tell Dad I'm borrowing the camping equipment and some of his tools. I'll bring them back."

"Make sure you do. And, don't let that woman near them. I might want to use the portaloo in the summer when we take Thomas and Lily away on holiday."

For the first time in a long while, Becky laughed. "You? Camping? Now that I would like to see."

Fifteen minutes later, she'd started the car, released the handbrake and roared away. In the rear-view mirror, she'd seen Natalie standing on the path, arms crossed.

Becky flinched as the two crows cawed and flapped at each other just above her head, before disappearing in a flurry of beating wings over the roof of The Barn. She pushed herself away from the wall, walked across the rutted yard and stopped at the gate to the meadow.

Early morning sun danced across the horizon. The sea, a silver streak in the distance, sparkled like a diamond. Apollo stood nearby with one foot resting idly on his hoof tip. His tail swished in a lazy sweep from side to side.

"Beautiful here, isn't it?" a man's voice said behind her. She spun around, tripping on a stone as she did so.

David Penna grabbed her elbow. "Mrs Farrow, I'm so sorry. I didn't mean to startle you."

"Mr Penna." She scanned the yard. "I didn't hear a car."

"I parked it in the gateway on the road from Penhellick." He grinned, causing the small lines around his blue eyes to crinkle. "I had a good idea what the back lane to Vellangoose would be like, so I walked." The trousers of his expensive suit were tucked inside green wellington boots. She detected the faint whiff of shower gel. Oh, what she'd give for a shower at that moment.

With a jolt, she glanced down. Oh dear. She was still in her pyjamas. She put her hand to her head, then her neck. What a dreadful sight she must be, with red blotches and uncombed hair. She pushed aside the urge to run, and instead pulled the oversized sweater tight around herself.

"I hope it isn't too early to call by. I got your telephone message to say you were now living at Vellangoose." He flashed another perfect smile. "I was on my way to work and thought I'd see the old place for myself."

He turned and scrutinised The Mill, then grimaced.

"We're living in The Barn," she blurted out. "Over there."

"With Miss Pascoe and her children?"

She nodded.

"How's it going?"

Laughter and yells came from The Barn. She stared in the direction of the noise. "There's such a lot to do … and … to get used to." Her hands fluttered, then dropped to her sides.

He nodded. "Presumably, you've managed to connect the water supply and sort the plumbing?"

She pinched the bridge of her nose. It was all so embarrassing.

"It's complicated. There's a well, but the water pump doesn't work." She screwed up her face. "We're using camping equipment to boil water for now, and … for other things."

"Ah."

Abi appeared in the doorway. Hand over her eyes, she waved in their direction. David Penna raised his arm and waved back. Her sister beckoned him to come inside.

Becky winced. "The place is in a bit of a mess, I'm afraid."

"I understand," he replied softly.

Indoors, Abi immediately began chatting to David Penna and Becky took her chance to grab an armful of clothes and run across the yard into the old piggery. She and Abi had cleared a couple of the enclosed pens to create two so-called bathroom areas. In Becky's section stood her dad's portable toilet and a plastic washing-up bowl. She hadn't the courage to check what Abi and her family were using.

Becky hurriedly washed in cold water from the plastic carrier, then tugged on her jeans and a clean sweater. With brisk strokes, she brushed her hair and pulled it back into a ponytail. Finally, she reached for a bottle of perfume from her wash bag, squirted a puff into the air and walked through the fine mist.

Back in The Barn, David Penna sat on the wooden plank, drinking coffee. Abi handed a mug to her. Becky nodded her thanks and sat next to him.

Abi turned back to David Penna. "As I was saying, I want to know who's been renting the fields?"

"That would be Ben Vincent. He owns the farm on the other side of the Vellangoose woods." He placed his mug on the floor and drew out a piece of paper from inside his jacket. "The payment of farm rents is all rather interesting. Did you know that traditionally they're paid on what is known as Quarter Days?"

"What?"

"The first is Lady Day, which falls on the twenty-fifth of March. Then there's Midsummer Day on the twenty-fourth of June. Michaelmas is the twenty-ninth of September, and the final quarter is paid on Christmas Day."

"Twenty-fifth of March?" Abi grinned. "So, we're owed some money?"

David Penna stroked his jaw. "I'm sorry. It's not as simple as that."

"Haven't you read the Trust documents?" Becky took a sip of coffee. "We can't rent anything to Mr Vincent."

Abi frowned. "What's the problem? Doesn't he want the land anymore?"

"On the contrary, he's desperate for it." David loosened his tie. "You already know you can't sell the place for five years, and during that time you don't have to live here. Nor do you have to maintain the property." He looked at the paper in his hand. "Unfortunately, the Trust also stipulates that you're unable to rent out any section of the property, or use any part of it, in exchange for money. Not even to Ben Vincent."

"Who the hell would know?" Abi glared at him.

"At the time the Will and Trust documents were drawn up, Penna, Truscott and Wallace were commissioned to undertake random audits. I'm afraid we must do–"

"Couldn't we get a loan using Vellangoose as collateral?" Abi butted in. Her voice was hard and sharp.

He shook his head. "I'm afraid it's watertight."

Becky slumped against the wall. How could they go on with no money, no nothing?

"I'm sorry I couldn't have been of more help." David Penna stood. "Thank you, for the coffee. If you need any further clarification, please call me again. I can always drop in."

Becky got to her feet.

He paused in the doorway. "My sister, Lisa Webber, lives in Penhellick. If you want someone to look after the children while you're at work, she could help. She's a registered childminder."

"Got no money." Abi roughly pushed her hair from her eyes.

"Oh, I'm sure she could be persuaded to consider other forms of payment." He nodded towards the pile of logs in the recess. "She has a wood-burner. Would you like me to ask her?"

Becky straightened up. "Yes, please. That would be great. Wouldn't it, Abi?"

Abi nodded.

Becky followed him outside. "Thank you for calling in, Mr Penna."

"Please, call me David."

"I'm Becky." She pushed a stray curl behind her ear.

"If anyone's interested, you can call me Abi," an amused voice chimed through the doorway.

David coughed. "Of course, Abi. Lovely meeting you both. No doubt we'll meet again."

In the distance, a rook flew erratically towards the woods, its wings dipping from side to side. A large twig hung from its beak. Becky tracked its progress, then turned back to David.

"It's very kind of you to think about Abi's children." She paused and stroked her temple. "It's not a problem then, to use logs from Vellangoose in exchange for childcare? Nothing to prevent that in the Trust?"

David tilted his head to one side.

She continued. "Perhaps there's nothing to stop us from doing the same in other circumstances?"

A smile flashed onto his face. "I don't believe there is."

"A legal loophole, perhaps?"

"You could be right, but you didn't hear that from me."
He straightened his tie. "What are you thinking?"

She looked towards the woods.

"I'm thinking I might pay Ben Vincent a visit," she said.

14

Abi dipped a small paintbrush into an old tin can and with easy strokes applied honey-coloured oil to a piece of wood propped up on bricks. Another coat would be ideal if only she had the money. What must it be like to have enough dosh to finish jobs properly? She straightened, pressed her hands into the base of her back and smiled to herself. The three kitchen worktops in front of her made her heart soar. She ran her hand over the dry, glossy surface of the large piece she'd finished yesterday, and traced the knots and intricate designs in the wood with her fingertips.

She'd found the pieces of hardwood in The Mill, covered in dust and cobwebs. Over many back-breaking hours, she'd sawn, cleaned and sanded the timber in the workspace she'd cleared in The Mill. Cold, smelly, and full of rubbish, the area would have to do until she could sort something better in one of the other buildings.

She picked up her sander, took out the battery and reached for the charger. She would discretely plug it into an electric socket at work tomorrow.

The deep throb of a tractor engine broke the silence.

She glanced through the doorway. Ben Vincent hurtled past, radio blaring, and parked near to The Barn. He jumped out of the tractor cab, and with purposeful down-to-earth strides made his way towards Becky's car, which had followed him down the lane.

Abi ran her fingers through her hair. Ben was certainly easy on the eye with his hazel-brown eyes, short curly brown hair and broad shoulders. Strong jawed and square-faced, he had the healthy complexion of a man who spent most of his life outdoors. Another time, another place, and she might've made a play for him, but not now. She couldn't be distracted. Vellangoose came first.

Neither Becky nor Ben had seen her, and she was happy to remain unnoticed. She grabbed a piece of fine sandpaper. One final check for any rough bits and the worktop would be ready.

The mumble of voices floated across the yard, peppered now and then with a little laugh from Becky. Abi realised it was the first time she'd heard that sound. It was a good one.

What an odd mix her sister was. So jumpy and uncertain most of the time, huddled in the far corner of the living room, surrounded by her stacks of containers and folded clothes. Every night she pulled the duvet tight under her chin and read a book by torchlight before eventually falling to sleep.

And yet, it was this same Becky who had pulled off that brilliant barter deal with Ben, and he didn't look like a pushover to Abi. Apparently, he'd jumped at the chance to have the land back and agreed to provide a variety of goods and services in exchange for the equivalent of a year's rent. Abi hoped that he knew what he was letting himself in for; Becky had already drawn up a hand-written spreadsheet complete with an action tick list.

Abi had to admit she'd been surprised by how hard her sister had worked since moving in. Together they'd removed the boards and padlocks from the windows and doors and hauled all the useless clutter from the hallway out into the yard. Since then, they'd fallen into a daily routine. Abi, after the school run and her Asda shift, would return to Vellangoose each day at lunchtime. Her sister did the same. The afternoon would be spent working together to make the place liveable.

Thank goodness David Penna had mentioned that his sister was a childminder. Lisa now looked after Grace most days, collected the kids after school, and gave them all a snack. She didn't know how long Lisa would be happy for her childminding fees to be paid in logs, but for now, the set-up was a miracle.

She glanced up again as Ben drove the tractor back up the lane.

A short while later, Becky made her way across the yard carrying a tray with two mugs and a biscuit tin. She came to an abrupt halt near the gate to the meadow, then turned and rushed through the door into The Mill.

"Have you seen what's got in with Apollo and Dolly? Looks like a stray pony." Her sister put the tray on the window ledge. "Oh dear. Do you think we should call the police?"

"No need. It's only Podge."

"Podge?"

"Some woman rolled up at lunchtime towing a horsebox. Heard from a friend of a friend that we had loads of land and wouldn't mind having another animal. She begged me to give him a home."

"You're kidding?" Becky stared at her.

Abi took a sip of coffee. "Divorce or something. Most of their animals have had to go." She took a biscuit from the tin and bit into it. Tasty. She wondered if Becky had baked it. Was that what she did for a living? "What could I do? The woman said she couldn't find anyone who could afford to look after him."

"And we can?"

"Podge's next stop was the knacker man if I didn't have him. You must admit, he's kind of cute, like a fluffy brown bear. The kids will love him."

Becky shook her head.

"What's the problem? He won't cost anything. There's plenty of grass now the weather's warmer." Abi gave a silent thank you for the coming of spring; the bales of hay the old bloke had stored in the field shelter had all been eaten. She'd glimpsed that man only on that one occasion, and still had no idea why he'd taken it upon himself to look after Apollo and Dolly. Since moving into The Barn, Abi had found herself taking a daily stroll into the meadow to check on them, often with slices of apple or carrot in her pocket.

"Don't fret." Abi rubbed the biscuits crumbs from her hands. "The woman said she'd be back later with Podge's rug, horse nuts, and a mineral block, whatever that is."

"Really? Do you have a name for her? Any contact details?"

"You should be more trusting," Abi said. "She's bringing a dozen or so chickens and, I think she said, bantams. Their houses and runs as well. We'll have fresh eggs. Who doesn't love fresh eggs?" Abi put her mug back onto the tray and grinned at Becky. "Don't worry. She promised."

"Well, it'll be your problem in the long run. Like I said before, I'll be gone soon." Becky picked up the tray. "What do you want me to do this afternoon?"

"I need help to get the worktop inside?"

After several stops in the yard to catch their breath, Abi eventually leaned the wood against the kitchen wall, pulled a tape measure from her pocket and double-checked the measurements. With a sigh of relief, she nodded to Becky. "On the count of three, lift your end and place it on the battens. Don't let go until I tell you. I need to screw the worktop safely into position."

"Battens?"

"The blocks of woods I've screwed along the walls. I'll also fix some struts in the front to give extra support. Ready?"

Becky nodded.

"One. Two. Three."

Abi hurriedly screwed several brackets joining the underside of the worktop to the battens and struts. "Okay. You can leave go now."

Becky stepped back a couple of paces. "Wow. That's brilliant."

A shot of pride rolled over Abi. Stupid, but Becky's praise of her work meant much more than she cared to analyse.

"I'll fit the other worktops when the wood's dry. It'll give us a run of counter space up to the Belfast sink, and a bit on the other side. I've left enough room at the end for either a cooker or a fridge."

"You wish."

In Abi's mind's eye she could see the kitchen she dreamed of, or rather the one she could afford, with cupboards, shelves, and brightly coloured walls. Slate tiles for the floor, not some cheap artificial covering. Mind you, anything would be better than the rough concrete she and Becky had uncovered a few days ago. The final touch would be the kids' paintings stuck all over the fridge door.

For now, she'd settle for a functioning kitchen; the first step towards the longed-for home she desired for her kids. Bedrooms were also on her wish list, but they were in such terrible condition, she'd decided to abandon the idea of renovating them for the time being. The living room would have to do for now. She'd slept in worse places.

Becky's voice broke into her thoughts. "What about the worktop? Won't the surface get water and heat stained?"

Abi shrugged. "Maybe. I would like to have sealed it with a coat of polyurethane, but it doesn't matter. It's wood, so it's easy to sand again when I've more time and some money." She picked up her screwdriver. "Hopefully, there's more wood in The Mill for shelves and a couple of cabinets underneath."

"You're so clever at this stuff. How come?"

"Matter of necessity. Mum was hopeless when it came to DIY, couldn't even change a light bulb, so I had to learn fast when I was a kid. One or two of my blokes were handy around the place. I learned a few things from them, and I worked on a building site for six months before Jacob was born."

Becky ran her hand through her hair. "I don't understand you. You're so skilled and sensible on one hand, and then you do something rash, like letting a stranger dump Podge on you."

Abi chuckled. "That's me."

Becky shifted from one foot to the other. "I've got something in the car that I think you might like."

Ten minutes later, Abi stood next to her sister and stared at the wooden garden table and four chairs. Battered and weathered-stained, the items fitted into the space against the kitchen wall perfectly.

"I know it's not much to look at, but I thought it might make things a bit more comfortable for all of us. It's one of the worthless items that John let me keep."

"I love it. I'll paint it if you like. Cheer it up a bit."

"Dad's got loads of half-used tins of paint in the garage. All sorts of colours he'll never use. I'll bring some back next time I visit."

"Does your dad live nearby?"

"Falmouth. He's been a bit poorly but he's getting better. I see him most mornings."

"I thought you were working?"

Becky looked down at her feet. "I use his cooker to bake a bit for friends. Nothing much, and strictly on a private basis." She turned away, closing the conversation.

Still, it was the most her sister had said about her personal life.

Abi knelt under the worktop to tighten the brackets once more. "Did Ben have any news?"

"He's putting cows in the fields near the road tomorrow. They're all about to have calves." Becky picked up a cloth and wiped one of the chairs. "The other fields will be used to make silage and hay."

Abi sat back on her heels. "So, the chickens can go into the meadow behind The Mill?"

Becky mumbled something which sounded suspiciously like 'what chickens?'

"What's that?" Abi asked.

Becky's mouth twitched. "Fittings," she said, her face the picture of innocence. "Ben will be over first thing on Monday with his men to check the water fittings and supply."

Abi ducked back under the worktop briefly to hide the smile forming on her lips. So, her sister had a sense of humour. Who knew? She stood up and laid down the screwdriver.

"The sooner we get water inside the better," she said.

"I've agreed with Ben that he should clear the well of debris, check and replace any broken water pipes, and get the old water pump working. I said we would clean out the water holding tank."

Abi nodded. "You and I should work on the bathroom next. Get the toilet and bath cleaned and ready for use." Her head whirled with what needed to be done. "I can't wait to see the back of our bloody portaloos."

Becky turned the table on its side and began to clean the underside. "When the water's plumbed inside, we'll need to boil the drinking water until we can get it properly tested. I'll add that task to my list of jobs to do."

Christ, did Becky have an action list and tick box for everything? Maybe that was why her husband had done a runner?

"I reckon the next thing on the list is electricity," Becky said. "What do you think?"

A knot of anger and unfairness squeezed at Abi's stomach. "Damn Henry Williams. It'll cost thousands of pounds to get the place rewired and the electricity reconnected. Why couldn't he have left us some money?"

Becky balled the cloth in her hands. "Ben said–"

"Ben said what? That he'd do it all for free?"

Her sister raised a hand to her neck.

"I'm sorry," Abi said. "Sorry for being so shitty. This bartering thing is great, but ..." She dropped her arms to her side.

"Ben knows a good electrician, and he's happy to have an initial chat with him about what needs to be done as part of the barter deal." Becky pulled the table upright and rubbed the cloth along the top. "I might be able to help with some cash."

Abi stared at her. Why would she help with money when she'd no intention of staying?

"A couple of friends have asked me to cater for a dinner party for twenty people. I'd use their kitchen, and they'd provide everything. I haven't agreed yet, but if I did, I could charge quite a bit for my time."

Abi rubbed a non-existent spot on the worktop. What could she say? She had diddly squat to offer on the money front. She stopped rubbing. Maybe Becky was beginning to like the place? With amazement, Abi realised she would be pleased if Becky wanted to stay. Her help over the last few weeks had felt good.

"I saw David Penna in Penhellick earlier." Becky talked as she followed Abi into the living room. "Veronica Williams is telling everyone she's challenging the Will and the Trust, and that she'll have us out of Vellangoose soon. He reassured me she wouldn't be successful."

"Let's hope he's right."

"She has so much property already, why would she bother with Vellangoose?"

Abi snorted. "She's a miserable old cow, that's why."

They made their way back into the kitchen and placed several items onto the worktop: Abi's faithful primus stove, the battered saucepan, and, in the corner, three of Becky's Laura Ashley cake tins.

Becky clapped her hands and elation surged through Abi. She had a kitchen.

Outside, a car horn tooted.

Hands on her hips, Abi grinned at her sister. "Well, would you look at that, the woman's come back with the chickens. I said you should be more trusting, didn't I?"

She marched outside, rubbing her hands together and muttering, "Eggs, eggs, lovely eggs," just loud enough for Becky to hear.

It occurred to Abi that she was in serious danger of beginning to enjoy herself. If Veronica Williams wanted them out, well, the miserable old bat could just go take a hike, couldn't she?

15

An acrid mix of bleach, lemon and vinegar filled the air. During the last two days, Becky had scrubbed the toilet, hand basin and bath free from years of mould and grime. Despite the odd chip and a couple of rust stains under the taps, which no amount of cleaning would dislodge, the ancient bathroom fixtures now looked amazing.

Her knees and back hurt, but she was triumphant. It was the first time she had completed such a mammoth task without John or her dad telling her what to do.

A few feet away, Abi pulled off her goggles. Becky caught her breath. Her sister looked so tired. No matter how hard Becky worked, Abi worked harder: up as soon as daylight streamed into The Barn, and only finishing when darkness closed in and made it impossible for her to carry on.

Abi carefully placed an unbroken tile on top of others in a cardboard box. Pieces of ruined tiles and lumps of plaster lay scattered around her feet.

"I'll get the loose tiles off today," she said. "The room won't be pretty, but it'll be useable and safe for the kids."

Becky stared at the scarred wall covered with lumps of grey adhesive and damaged plaster. Over the years, many of the tiles had fallen off, but enough had remained to give a hint of the elegant bathroom it must have once been, and what it could possibly look like again.

"Ben's scheduled to start the plumbing work tomorrow." Becky rubbed a water spot on the tap with the sleeve of her sweater. "Do you think we'll have plumbing indoors within a day or two?"

"Not a chance. The water system hasn't been used for decades. Everything will need to be checked, repaired, and cleaned, including the water holding tank. God alone knows if the pump will even work."

Becky studied her hands: pockmarked with dry skin and partly healed blisters. She winged off a silent prayer that the ancient diesel-run pump could be fixed. Otherwise, she'd have to continue lugging drinking water from her dad's, and she wasn't sure how much longer she could cope with the lack of basic facilities that she used to take for granted.

"We've got such a lot done without the kids under our feet today, but I feel awful for palming them off with Kate on a Sunday." Abi sighed. "I couldn't ask Lisa again. Truth is, I should be spending time with my kids."

"It won't be forever, and they love your friend's place in Penryn."

Abi snorted. "They love her TV more like."

"What I wouldn't give to put my feet up and watch a rom-com with a very large glass of wine and a packet of pistachios." Becky rubbed her shoulder. "How about a piece of walnut cake and a coffee, instead?"

Abi nodded and flicked on the radio.

Becky automatically looked out the kitchen window as she filled the kettle. A lone magpie pecked at the moss on The Mill roof. What was that old superstition? One for sorrow, two for joy, three for … She shook herself. Only fools believed in such things. Nevertheless, she pursed her lips ready to spit, but the magpie took flight, its rapid, high-pitched warning cackle ricocheting through the air.

A sports car powered into the yard and came to a halt in a flash of red brake lights. The engine revved, then fell silent.

The passenger door opened and a long leg, encased in spike-heeled leather boots and skin-tight black jeans, eased from the vehicle. The woman stood, her expensive cream coat incongruous against the derelict buildings and shabby surroundings.

Becky shielded her eyes with her hand against the late afternoon sun and squinted. Someone had obviously got themselves lost. The person was half in the shadow, and her long, impossibly shiny hair covered her face. A breeze suddenly blew the woman's coat open, exposing a pale pink mohair jumper. At the same time, her hair lifted in the wind.

Jess.

Becky yanked the door open and ran. Jess was here. Everything would be okay now.

Stopping in front of her daughter, she hesitated, then flung her arms wide and wrapped her in a big hug. Love hit Becky with the force of a punch. Tears burned the back of her eyes at her daughter's familiar scent and touch.

Still holding Jess's hands, she took a step back. "Darling, you've come. I was so worried. You didn't answer my texts or phone messages." She hugged her again. "None of that matters. You're here now."

Jess wriggled free from her grasp. "Oh, Mum. Don't be so embarrassing."

"I've missed you. I just …" She stopped and stared at the cream coat. "Oh dear. I've got dirt on your beautiful coat. I'm so sorry." She rubbed the sleeve but the dust smear only deepened.

"Leave it. You're making it worse." Jess shoved Becky's hands away. "Steve will be so …" She glanced towards the car.

A man eased himself out of the vehicle and turned towards Becky with what looked like a smirk on his face.

She caught her breath. Steve Hodges.

On occasions, she'd glimpsed grainy black and white photos of him in the *West Briton*, but it was only seeing him in the flesh that his resemblance to Veronica Williams became so apparent.

Steve stared at The Mill, then glanced around the yard. Tiny slivers of light sparked from his dark sunglasses as he studied each of the buildings. Finally, he took off his shades and held out his hand to Becky.

"Mrs Farrow, I presume." His sugary, sweet voice sent a cold shiver down her spine. "What a pleasure to meet you. We were passing when I thought what a lovely surprise it would be if Jess popped in to see her mum." His smile, which displayed perfect teeth, didn't reach his eyes.

Jess clutched Steve's arm. "Thank you, darling. You're always so thoughtful."

Becky stared at his still outstretched hand. A knot twisted in her stomach. It took all her willpower not to tear Jess away from him. Not only was he old enough to be her father, but it seemed like he'd already moulded her feisty daughter into someone she no longer recognised.

She glanced at Jess, the most important person in her life. When she saw the obvious adoration for Steve in the nineteen-year-old's eyes, Becky's shoulders slumped and she shook Steve's hand.

Steve towered over her. "Jess would love to see inside. Wouldn't you, Babe?"

Becky flinched. What would Abi say? She'd only spoken briefly to her sister about Jess, and she'd never mentioned Steve Hodges or his connection to Veronica Williams.

"Please, Mum."

Becky's stomach churned as she made her way along the crude garden path that she and Abi had cut through the undergrowth. Jess would not see the potential of this place. She'd only see the scruffy garden, the sorrowful kitchen with its concrete floor, and the pock-marked walls. Becky lowered her head and looked at her shabby clothes and dirty hands. Shame shot through her. If only she was a better, more worthy mother for Jess to show off to her new boyfriend.

She stepped into the kitchen. Music blared from the radio in the bathroom.

"Abi?" Becky shouted. "Abi, we've got visitors."

The music stopped. Abi ambled into the kitchen. The big smile on her face disappeared when she saw them all standing there.

"What the hell are you doing here?" she said.

"Nice to see you again, Miss Pascoe." Steve tilted his head towards Abi.

"Oh dear," Becky gasped. "Oh dear. I didn't know you'd both met before."

"Once," Abi sneered. "That was more than enough."

Desperate for the encounter to go well for Jess's sake, Becky reached out and touched Abi's arm. "Please, Abi. This is my daughter, Jess."

Her sister didn't take her gaze away from Steve. "Got it, but what's he doing here?"

"Steve is Jess's ... boyfriend."

Abi swung around to face Becky. "You've got to be joking."

Becky's hand flew to her chest. "I'm sorry. I should've ..."

"You know who he is, don't you?" Abi narrowed her eyes at Becky. "Of course you do."

Becky looked from Abi to Jess to Steve. In the silence, stupid, unplanned words tumbled from her. "Abi and I are so excited. We're getting the bathroom ready for when Ben comes tomorrow to connect the water."

Steve locked his eyes onto hers. "Ben? Would that be Ben Vincent?"

She nodded several times. "He's been so helpful, and we've struck a–"

Abi dug an elbow into her ribs. "I don't think Veronica Williams's nephew needs to know our business."

Steve grabbed Jess's hand and moved swiftly out of the kitchen and into the hallway. "Come, Babe. You wanted to see where I used to live."

Becky hurried after them. "You used to live here?"

"Seriously, Mum. Over thirty years ago when he was a child. Now you're living here. That's so weird, isn't it?"

Abi swore and shoved past Steve and Jess to block their view into the living room. "Well, he doesn't live here now," she said.

"That's not very friendly considering we're almost neighbours given how you've moved up in the world." Steve peered over Abi's shoulder. "Just as I thought, there's nothing much to see. The place is still a dump."

"Piss off," Abi snapped.

Steve grinned. "I assume they're Ben's cows in the fields. My aunt will be extremely interested to know he's renting the place again."

"Tell your aunt to keep her nose out of Vellangoose. It's none of her business."

"We're just doing a favour for a friend, that's all," Becky rushed in. "For free."

"Glad to hear that. It'll put my aunt's mind at rest." Steve turned and strode towards the kitchen door. "Have a nice day."

Becky grabbed Jess's arm. They hadn't had a chance to talk. She couldn't bear for her to go so soon. "Apollo. You love horses. You must see him."

"Oh, Steve, can I?"

Steve stopped in his tracks. "You kept that useless animal then? It would be dog food if my aunt had her way." He sucked on his teeth and resumed walking.

Jess tottered after him. Becky overtook her. "Please see Apollo. He's beautiful."

She would do anything for Jess to stay, even touch that fearful animal if necessary. Whatever it took, she would do it.

"I don't think we've got the time, Mum." Jess's eyes flicked towards Steve's departing back.

"Babe, are you coming or what?"

The hateful man jangled his car keys.

"Sorry, Mum." Jess lurched away, got into the car's passenger seat and sat with her head bowed. A few seconds later, Steve revved the engine and her daughter was gone.

"I love you," Becky whispered into the wind.

Abi came and stood next to her. "Nice car. Pity about the driver."

"He'll ruin that engine." Becky attempted to recover their earlier friendliness. "John always said new cars must be treated with care for the first few months."

"Must be right then, if John said it."

Irritation mixed with tiredness swept over Becky. "I was only making a comment. There's no need to be so rude."

"That's rich." Abi glared at her. "Why didn't you tell me your daughter just happened to be shacked up with Veronica Williams's nephew?" She shook her head. "I thought I could trust you. My mistake."

"That's not fair. Today was the first time I met him. I didn't know they were coming."

"You knew who he was though, didn't you?"

Tears pricked the back of Becky's eyes. "She's my daughter, what was I to do? I've been praying that she'd come to see me, and she came."

"You think she had a choice in the matter? Jess came because she does what that man wants. They didn't come here to see you. They came here to report back to Veronica Williams."

"Jess wouldn't be a party to anything like that." Becky sniffed. "I thought Steve acted quite gentlemanly, considering his family used to live at Vellangoose and this place probably should've been his inheritance."

"He had my mum evicted and threatened me and my kids." Abi grunted. "Sorry, but your Jess is living with a controlling bully."

"Don't you think I know that? But ..." Fear enveloped Becky and prevented her from saying anything more.

"She needs to get out of his clutches before she gets hurt. Doesn't she have a brain?"

"Don't talk about my daughter like that. She's a–"

"Whatever." Abi flapped her hand, then turned and went back inside.

Becky wrapped her arms tight across her chest. What a mess. She'd lost Jess all over again. And now, just when she was feeling more secure about being at Vellangoose, Abi didn't trust her. Again.

Dad was right. The Williams family and everything associated with them was toxic. Just as well her stay at Vellangoose was only temporary. The sooner she was out of here, the better.

16

Abi scrambled out of the water tank through the hatchway, then dropped down onto the ground. Sunshine burst through the clouds. She tilted her head back, closed her eyes and took a long, deep breath. The warmth on her face felt so good after hours encased inside what amounted to a smelly, damp concrete box, with only a small patch of sky visible above her head.

In the last four and half days, she and Becky had worked their butts off to get the tank ready, dragging buckets of debris and muck through the hatchway and scrubbing the inside walls, floor and ceiling. Although their earlier bond had cooled a little after the argument over Steve Hodges's visit, Abi was pleased that her sister continued to help.

At the same time, Ben and his men had dug up and replaced the pipes from the pump to the water tank, and then on into The Barn. There wasn't enough so-called currency in the barter agreement to connect all the buildings, but who cared? Getting plumbing into The Barn was her only priority.

For a few minutes more, Abi let the sun chase away the ache in her shoulders and the throb in her chapped fingers, then she walked across the field and into the yard.

Ben beckoned her over. "Jeffery's off to get some pasties for croust. That's lunch to you townies. I've asked him to get extras for you, Becky and the kids. Hope that's alright?"

"Hum, it's okay," she mumbled. "I've got stuff organised for later."

"My treat," Ben said.

She wanted to offer to pay for her share, but the few coins left in her purse wouldn't cut it. A Cornish pasty for lunch would really hit the spot, and, better still, she wouldn't have to find something for the kids later. They deserved something better than baked beans and fish fingers for once. She nodded and turned away as Ben handed a couple of notes to Jeffery.

Abi watched Jeffery leave through half-closed eyes. Something about the short wiry man in his mid-sixties seemed familiar, but for the life of her, she couldn't think where she'd met him before. Maybe in the local shop? Or perhaps he was one of the many grandparents who picked up kids from the school that Jacob and Eve attended in Penhellick?

"How's it going with the pump?" she asked Ben. "Do you think Jeffery will be able to fix it? He's been working on it for days now."

"The man's a wiz with machines. If he can't fix it, nobody can. The new parts arrived this morning, so I think he's getting there."

"Does he work for you full-time?"

Ben laughed. "Jeffery's not keen on being tied to any one job. Or any one boss. Several of the farmers around here use him from time to time, mainly because he can turn his hand to most things without complaint. Sign of the times too."

"How so."

"Not many farmers can afford to take on permanent staff these days." He pointed to the meadow behind The Mill. "Becky's not afraid of the chickens then?"

Abi grinned to see her sister inside a wire pen scattering grain to ten buff-coloured hens as they pecked around her feet. Two smaller houses and pens accommodating more chickens and bantams dotted the meadow.

"It seems her dad had hens and bantams when she was a kid, so she knows everything about them. I can't get a look in."

Her sister fastened the chicken run, picked up a wicker basket and made her way towards them.

"Only four eggs today," she said when she reached them. "They're still upset with the change of environment. Hopefully, they'll lay more soon."

"Especially now the days are getting longer," Ben said.

Abi frowned. "What's that got to do with it?"

"Hens lay more in the spring and summer because of the extra daylight." Becky shifted the wicker basket from one hand to the other. "That's why battery farmed hens are so productive; their houses are artificially lit to keep them laying for longer, then when they can't lay anymore, they get rid of them."

"Poor things." Abi walked towards the meadow and leaned on the gate.

Ben came up beside her. "Cute little pony."

"That's Podge." She put her fingers between her lips and whistled.

Podge lifted his head, whickered softly, and trotted towards them. Apollo ambled after him, his long white tail swishing to and fro.

Ben grabbed the top of the gate, leapt over and dropped into the meadow. He reached for Podge's head collar and spoke quietly as he examined the animal's mouth, ears and eyes. Finally, he picked up Podge's foot.

"Who's your farrier?"

"Farrier?"

Ben dropped Podge's foot to the ground and stood up, his hand on the pony's neck. "A person who takes care of horses' feet. This little guy's shod, and he either needs a new set of shoes or they need to be removed, depending on whether you're going to ride him or not. Either way, it'll cost you."

Abi's stomach churned. She should've told that woman to get lost when she turned up towing her bloody horsebox. Becky had been right all along.

She took a deep breath. "How much, and where would I find a farrier? One who doesn't mind being paid with eggs, cakes or stupid logs."

"I'll get you a couple of names. If you're going to ride Podge, he'll need new shoes every six weeks or so, at about eighty pounds for a full set of four shoes. If you take them out, like Apollo, the feet will still need to be trimmed." Ben ran a hand through his hair. "Needs to be done every eight weeks at a cost of about thirty pounds for each horse."

She looked down at her own hands and stared at the jagged nails and rough skin. "I can get by with broken nails, surely they can?"

"Not if you don't want big vet bills as well. Come closer and see for yourself."

She climbed over the gate and peered at Podge's foot, cupped again in Ben's hand.

"It smells," she said.

"That's because they've not been cleaned out. One of you needs to pick out any mud, stones or muck every day. Both animals need regular grooming. Their tails and manes are full of knots." Ben pulled out a pocketknife and gently scrapped Podge's feet, then did the same to Apollo. "There's a proper tool for this job called a hoof pick. You need to get one. Your farrier might also trim the goat's feet if you ask nicely, depends on whether they're a goat person or not."

"Not the goat as well?" Abi groaned.

"You need to properly care for them, otherwise, don't keep them." Ben's voice had an edge to it.

Abi glared at him. Damn him and his schoolmaster tone. How was she supposed to know all this? With surprise, she realised what bothered her most was feeling such an idiot in front of him.

It seemed his opinion mattered.

"Oh, the poor things, we've neglected them." Becky's plaintive voice broke the silence. "How could we have been so awful?"

"I've got enough to sort with three kids and a house not fit to live in. Why don't you get your butt over that gate and look after them?"

Her sister's lip trembled.

"Hey, come on, you two." Ben climbed back over the gate. "Your hearts are in the right place." He nodded towards Jeffery's pickup truck coming down the lane. "I'll ask Jeffery's nephew, Aaron, if he'll drop by each day for a few weeks to show you what needs to be done. Bit like his uncle, he can put his hand to most things. He's off to uni later in the year, but during the holidays and weekends he works for a few farmers around here."

Another car drove into the yard. David Penna.

"I'll get these eggs inside." Becky rushed off towards The Barn.

"Hello, Abi." David greeted her with his perfect smile, then held out his hand to Ben. "Ben. Good to see you again. I noticed the cows in the top fields, so I guess the barter agreement's working?"

David turned again to Abi. "I thought it would be a good time to undertake one of my audit checks."

Bloody hell. Why couldn't someone come with good news for once? She forced a smile.

"We're about to have lunch. Join us for a pasty, then one of us can bring you up-to-date." She grabbed a warm pasty, sat down on the grass and leaned against The Mill wall. "Jeffery, will you join us?"

"Not me, Miss, thanks all the same. Ate me pasty in the car park, and I wanta get back to that blasted pump."

He spat into his hands, rubbed them together, and made his way through the small doorway into the pump house attached to The Mill.

Abi smiled to herself as Becky walked towards them wearing clean jeans and top, her hair freshly combed. She carried a large tray filled with mugs of tea and cake.

"I believe the well that's going to provide you with fresh water was dug by Veronica Williams's father." David took a sip of tea. "Interestingly, the original well was inside The Mill. No doubt it's long gone, like the old water wheel."

"We've not touched The Mill." Ben brushed crumbs from the front of his sweatshirt. "Just connecting water supplies to The Barn."

A robin hopped across the grass and pecked at the scraps.

"My father saw Apollo's daughter race at Wadebridge Point-to-Point in January," David said. "The filly came in first, if I remember rightly."

"Jeffery," Ben yelled towards the pump house, "didn't one of Apollo's offspring race recently at Newton Abbot?"

Jeffery came outside, a greasy rag in his hand. "Came in second. Mr Henry had an eye for horses. He bred Apollo a few times. I used to look after him a lot when Mr Henry was alive."

An image flashed into Abi's mind. She got to her feet. Now she knew where she'd seen Jeffery before. He was the man who'd brought the bales of hay to the field shelter after Apollo and Dolly had been dumped at Vellangoose.

"It was you, wasn't it?" Abi said. "Watching out for Apollo and Dolly?"

"I heard on the grapevine what Veronica Williams had done." Jeffery pushed his cap back and scratched his bald head. "I couldn't leave a beauty like that to the elements. He deserved better. Besides, Mr Henry was always good to me, and with you two being his daughters ..." He cleared his throat. "I best be getting back to me job."

"Thank you," Abi said to his retreating back. A thought crossed her mind and she called out, "Jeffery, did Henry Williams organise the breeding of Apollo himself?"

"He did, Miss."

David came up beside her and grinned. "You might be onto something. Apollo could potentially bring in a good income. How stupid of me not to have thought of it. Henry Williams always boasted that Apollo was a quality horse."

Her heart thumped. "How much?"

"I'd need to check, but possibly two or three hundred pounds per horse providing the mare becomes pregnant or produces a live foal; it depends upon the contract agreed. You'd be able to charge more if his progeny continues winning."

"What about the Trust?" Becky asked.

"Apollo was left to you in the Will, not the Trust. Besides, livestock is exempt from any Trust agreements." David screwed his empty pasty wrapper into a ball. "There are a few stud farms in Cornwall. I'll check and see if one of them will have him on loan for a while. They'll take a percentage for livery, health checks, and insurance, but you'll make a profit."

Abi beamed at him.

David gathered up the mugs and placed them on the tray. "Becky, do you have time to go over a couple of things on your spreadsheet?"

Abi watched Becky and David return to The Barn, then punched a fist into the air. "Thank you, Apollo, thank you."

At that moment, the pump engine coughed and backfired. "Come on, me beauty, you can do it," Jeffery's excited voice soared over the sound.

Abi ran into the pump house with Ben close behind her. Smoke filled the air and diesel fumes clogged the back of her throat, but she didn't care. The pump chugged and throbbed into life.

"Told yer, Boss, there isn't an engine I can't fix."

"Is it pumping water?" Abi yelled.

"Reckon 'tis, Miss."

She rushed towards The Barn. The back door bounced against the wall as she barged into the kitchen. Becky jumped out of the way as Abi pushed past her and stood by the Belfast sink. Her hand hovered over the tap; she needed to wait for a few minutes for the water to work its way through the system. Finally, she twisted the cold metal and waited.

It spluttered, choked and spat out a glob of water. The pipes in the wall rattled and gurgled, then water spurted from the tap. She put her hand in the cold, clear liquid.

Becky cupped her face in her hands. "Oh, my goodness. We've got water."

"The toilet?" Abi rushed into the bathroom. Becky followed.

Abi reached out her hand, then looked at her sister. "You do it."

Becky gripped the flush handle. It worked.

A scream burst from Abi's mouth. She did a victory jig in the middle of the room.

What a day this had turned out to be. They'd got running water, a working bathroom, and Apollo was about to earn them a shedload of money. Things were on the up.

17

Becky woke with a start, sat upright and cocked her head to one side. From the darkness, Grace's usual nighttime snuffles punctured the silence. Becky exhaled and leaned back against the wall. It must've been a bad dream that woke her.

A light flashed. Momentarily, the living room lit up. Just as suddenly, blackness returned. Yellow dots and zigzags scorched the backs of her eyes.

Buddy let out a soft growl.

Becky's heart thumped.

"Shush." Abi's urgent whisper silenced the dog. "Becky? Wake up. Come with me."

Becky grabbed her mobile phone, sweater and slippers.

She came up behind Abi and peered through the kitchen window.

The moon cast an eerie light over the landscape. The large granite rock in the horses' pasture poked through the ground like a black tooth. The trees loomed on the hedge tops, the branches twisted and unfamiliar.

Suddenly, a line of dark figures appeared in the meadow. Beams of light speared the night in front of them. A man shouted. Dog barks and yelps filled the air. A few minutes later, the line moved on.

"Bastards," Abi snarled.

"Who are they?" Blood pumped in Becky's ears. "What are they doing?"

"Lampers."

"What?"

"Shits who hunt using torches." Abi spat the words out. "The light mesmerises rabbits or foxes, making them an easy target to shoot, or for the dogs to kill them."

"That's horrific. Are you sure?"

Abi nodded. "Trust me, I know."

A crack of gunfire echoed through the valley.

"Guns?" Becky automatically stepped back a pace. "They're coming nearer. What should we do?"

Abi reached for the door handle. "I'm putting a stop to this."

"No. It's utter madness to go outside." Becky grabbed her sister's arm. "You could be shot."

Abi pulled away and wrenched the door open. "Are you coming?"

Becky remained rooted to the spot. She'd never confronted anybody in her life, let alone men who kill animals for fun.

Abi ran down the steps and strode along the garden path. Every instinct told Becky to slam the kitchen door shut and lock it, but the retreating back of her sister – so determined and erect – triggered an unexpected response.

Becky stepped outside and followed Abi through the garden and into the yard. Chilly air pierced her thin nightclothes.

The gate to the meadow rattled on its hinges. Two men emerged from the dark, climbed the iron rails and dropped to the ground a few yards in front of them. Their faces were obscured with black balaclavas.

"What the fuck do you think you're doing? You're not wanted here," Abi shouted.

"That's not much of a welcome, Mrs. Here's me thinking I was doing you a favour, getting rid of them vermin an all."

The man's voice was deep and harsh, peppered with the tell-tale wheeze of a heavy smoker. A flash of colour poked from the top of his tatty dark green coat. The little strip of material appeared above his collar every time he took a breath. A tartan scarf?

"You're trespassing. Get off our land," Abi shouted again.

Tartan Scarf snorted. "I don't take orders from the likes of you."

Horrified, Becky saw Abi's fist clench, but before she had time to do anything, four more men in balaclavas clambered over the gate. Two lurchers followed on their heels. Becky fought down an urge to scream at the sight of the dogs' yellow eyes and lolling tongues. The men and dogs moved as a pack to surround her and Abi.

A scrawny man, dressed in a scruffy wax jacket, unlocked the barrel of his shotgun, inserted a cartridge and clicked it shut. His finger rested on the trigger.

Becky screamed.

"Thought that'd get yer attention," Tartan Scarf rasped. "We've been coming here for years. It's tradition."

"Stuff tradition," Abi said.

Something touched Becky's leg. A lurcher? Instinctively, she leapt forward and came eye to eye with Tartan Scarf and Scrawny Man. She forced herself not to cry out again.

"Pl ... Please leave. I ... I'll call the police if you don't go."

"Not a good idea, Mrs."

The reek of whisky and tobacco blasted her senses. In her rush to twist her face away, she stepped backwards and tripped over someone's outstretched foot. She crashed to the ground with a grunt. Earth and gravel dug into her palms and knees. The men's laughter floated above her. Any courage she might've had deserted her. She remained curled in a ball on the ground.

"Bastard." Abi launched herself at Tartan Scarf.

He grabbed her arms and shoved her away. She staggered, righted herself, and rushed at him again.

A voice in Becky's head urged her to get up, but her body wouldn't obey.

A flash of brown and white hurtled past her.

Buddy sprang at Tartan Scarf, who kicked him and said something that Becky didn't catch. In an instant, the lurchers leapt upon Buddy. In a twisted tangle, the dogs churned up the dirt. The men jeered and egged them on.

Abi ran at the lurchers and wrenched at one of their collars. "Get off. Leave him alone," she sobbed.

"Buddy!" Jacob's cries rang through the air.

The little boy tore across the yard. Abi grabbed him in mid-run. Wide-eyed, she looked at Becky, then sprinted towards the kitchen door where Eve and Grace stood sobbing.

"You never said there'd be young'uns here," one of the men said.

"Shut up," Tartan Scarf snarled.

"Frightening women is one thing, kids is another." The man let out a shrill whistle and the lurchers immediately backed off Buddy and returned to heel.

Buddy struggled to stand but collapsed, his eyes closed.

"Bastards," Abi screamed from the doorway. "You've killed my dog."

The yelling, crying, and Buddy's small whimper penetrated Becky's conscience. Something primaeval shot through her. She scrambled to her feet and picked up a stone.

"Child scarers," she yelled. "You should be ashamed of yourselves."

The four men mumbled amongst themselves. She threw the rock. It hit one of them. As a pack, they disappeared into the night. Tartan Scarf and Scrawny Man remained.

"Let this be yer warning." Tartan Scarf nodded towards The Barn. "Vellangoose isn't for the likes of you. Clear off, otherwise one of them children might end up getting hurt."

Rage wiped away her remaining fear. "You stinking cowards, you're nothing but scum."

Before Becky could say anymore, both men melted back into the darkness.

"Becky?"

"They've gone. Stay with the children," Becky shouted to her sister. "I'll see to Buddy."

Tears sprang into Becky's eyes at the sight of the brave animal. Blood poured from ragged cuts along his back. A triangular flap of skin gaped open on his side. She hesitated, then touched his head. A muscle twitched. He was alive.

Mobile phone in her hand, she ran into the kitchen where Abi sat with Grace on her lap and her arms wrapped around Jacob and Eve. Eyes red, her sister stared over the tops of their heads. "I'm so sorry I left you." Tears rolled down her cheeks. "My kids …"

Becky nodded. "Buddy needs a vet. I've already rung them to say we're on the way."

Abi let out a gasp. "He's alive?"

"You get the children into the camper van." Becky rushed to the bathroom and came back with several towels. "I'll get Buddy."

Abi remained seated. "What if those dogs had savaged Jacob? What if I'd been hurt or killed, what would've happened to my kids? I should never have brought them to Vellangoose."

Becky clutched the towels to her chest. Momentarily, she was paralysed. If Abi could be defeated, what chance did she have? Then, some inner reserve that she didn't know she had, propelled her into action. "We need to go now if you want to save Buddy."

Abi blinked, then got to her feet. "Come on, kids. Buddy needs our help."

Outside, Becky ran over to the dog. She put a towel on the ground and, with a grunt, lifted him carefully onto it. His head lolled as she staggered to the van and placed him in the back. Jacob and Eve stared at her from their child seats, their faces streaked in tears.

"You drive." Abi clamoured in next to Buddy. "I'll hold him."

"But ... I've never driven anything as big as the–"

Her sister's glare stopped her saying another word.

Moments later, she pressed the accelerator to the floor and kangarooed up the lane and onto the road to Falmouth. The wipers screeched and dragged across the windscreen, leaving frayed bits of old rubber and smear marks across the glass. She fumbled with the controls and the wipers stopped. A vein throbbed in her temple.

She looked at Abi in the rear-view mirror. "How's Buddy doing?"

"Drive faster."

Becky pushed through the streets of Falmouth, willing all the traffic lights to be green. She reached the road she wanted, swung the vehicle over the pavement and into the car park, and came to a halt outside the main entrance of an imposing granite building. Before the engine had died, she pushed the driver's door open and got out. Gravel crunched beneath her feet.

A woman in a blue uniform, and a square-set man dressed in green scrubs and white clogs, appeared from inside the property. They moved with purposeful strides down the steps to the van.

"I'm Becky Farrow," she called out to them. "I rang about a badly injured dog."

She swung the back door of the camper van open. Abi sat on the blood-soaked towels with Buddy's head in her lap.

"I'm Richard Grey, the vet on duty. This is Susannah." The man's voice was steady and controlled. "We'll take it from here." He reached into the van, lifted Buddy's eyelid and touched his eye.

Crackles and clicks from the cooling engine filled the silence.

"Is he dead?" Abi croaked.

"He's got a pulse, but it's weak. I need to get him inside." Richard Grey touched Abi's hand. "You can let go now."

He lifted Buddy from the van and hurried inside the building. The entrance door swung back and forth, then clicked shut.

Becky bent at the waist, put her hands on her knees and sucked in gulps of air. Thank God they'd got to the vets in time. Buddy had a chance now.

Beyond the gate, a car whizzed up the street. Two lads joked and laughed as they walked past. People. Voices. The sounds calmed her.

"We should go inside," she said.

Blinking in the bright lights, Becky stood in the middle of the empty reception area with Abi and the children. The smell of animals and disinfectant hung in the air. Unconsciously, they gathered into a tight group.

"Hello?" Becky called out.

Footsteps echoed in the depth of the building. The noise grew louder. Susannah came into the room and hurried towards them.

"How's Buddy?" Abi asked. "Will he be okay?"

"Buddy's currently being examined by Mr Grey. He'll be out shortly to talk to you." Susannah nodded to the waiting area. "Please make yourself comfortable."

Becky sank onto an orange plastic chair. Images batted round and round in her head: men with no faces, loaded shotguns, snarling dogs. Only a matter of months ago, her life had been uneventful, peaceful and gloriously ordinary. Now she seemed to be in a constant state of anxiety, living with people she hardly knew, and in a place where dreadful things happened. Dear God, she'd even thrown a stone at someone.

A fluorescent light flickered and creaked overhead.

She pulled the sleeves of John's old sweater down over her hands and forced herself to look around the room. A poster advised her of the dreadful consequences if she didn't get her dog regularly treated for lungworm.

The door opened in the reception area. Richard Grey stepped up to the desk, pressed the computer keyboard and turned to face them.

"Buddy has severe bites and lacerations, and I'm afraid there are internal injuries. His abdominal wall is badly ripped, consistent with being pulled apart by two dogs."

"Will he live? My kids ..." A sob escaped from Abi.

A look of sympathy flashed onto Richard Grey's face. "I've put him on a saline drip and antibiotics to help stabilise him, but he'll need immediate surgery." He paused, looked at the screen, then back at them. "I'll need consent to continue."

He swiftly entered data into the computer and scrolled down the screen. "I have a Rebecca Farrow at Rose Cottage. A guinea pig some years ago, but nothing on record for a dog."

"I have a new address. It's–"

"Buddy's my dog." Abi blurted out.

"I apologise. My mistake. I'll pull up your details. Your name?"

"He can't be operated on." Abi clutched the edge of the reception desk.

A telephone rang in the depths of the building.

"I don't think you understand the seriousness of Buddy's condition. If he's not operated on immediately, he'll most certainly die."

"I don't have any money. You'll have to put him down."

"Mum. No." Jacob stood next to Abi, his face streaked in tears.

Becky stared at her sister. "You can't have him put down. Not after all that's happened."

"What choice do I have?" Tears spilt from Abi's eyes.

Buddy deserved better. Those men couldn't win. Becky straightened her shoulders and looked at Richard Grey. "Please put Buddy's treatment on my account. I'll pay."

"You don't have any money either." Abi swiped her face dry with the sleeve of her jacket. "Besides, why would you offer to pay anyway? He's not your dog."

Becky stared at the wall behind the desk. What could she say? That her mother had never let her have a dog when she'd begged and begged for one as a child? That she'd grown fond of Buddy with his soft fur and big brown eyes? Maybe even, that they were a family, and families helped each other?

"Mr Grey, as you can see, I've always paid my bills." She rubbed her temple. "Please, can you go ahead?"

The vet moved his lips to say something, stopped, and returned his attention to the computer screen. "Your current address is?"

"The Barn, Vellangoose, Penhellick."

"Vellangoose? Henry Williams's old place?"

She nodded.

"He's our father," Abi said.

"Ah." He pressed a button on the keyboard and the printer clattered into action. "I've heard on the grapevine that Mrs Williams isn't very happy with the new arrangements."

"You could say that," Abi hissed. "She sent her lackeys to scare us. It was their dogs that attacked Buddy."

"You don't know that, Abi."

Becky's heart raced. It was one thing for them to think that Veronica Williams was responsible, but quite another thing to voice it in public. It was possible that the men had nothing to do with her, wasn't it?

Richard Grey picked up the newly printed authorisation form and held out a pen to Becky. "Please sign here."

"Really? You do know I might not be able to pay you for some time?"

The vet nodded and cleared his throat. "I was your father's vet for many years. During that time, I had a few ... dealings ... with Mrs Williams." He wiggled the pen at her.

Becky snatched it and quickly scribbled her name.

Richard Grey closed the computer screen. "For what it's worth–"

The door swung open with a bang. Susannah rushed in. "Richard, come quickly. It's Buddy."

Richard Grey disappeared into the back room again and Becky's eyes filled with tears as she watched Abi clutch her children tight to her and rock them back and forth.

Please let Buddy pull through. He's so much more than just a dog. He's ... family.

18

Abi brought the camper van to a stop outside The Barn, switched off the engine and reached across to the passenger seat. Buddy's tail thumped against the worn surface. His eyes, bright and shiny, locked onto hers. She leaned over and kissed the top of his head. If it hadn't been for Richard Grey and his wonderful veterinary skills, Buddy would've died from his injuries three weeks ago. As it was, he'd spent four days in the veterinary hospital, but today he'd had his last check-up and the final few stitches had been taken out.

Love surged through her as she felt the dog's warm breath on her cheek. "Dear Buddy, I'll never forget how you put your life on the line for me." She gave him another big hug, opened the door and lifted him onto the ground.

She glanced at The Barn. Of course, it wasn't just Richard Grey who'd saved Buddy, was it? Becky was the one who'd jumped in and taken control that night the lampers visited, and not only did she save Buddy from those monsters, she also saved him a second time by agreeing to pay the vet's fees.

Gratitude for Becky flooded through Abi along with the realisation of how much she'd come to enjoy having her sister around. It felt good to have someone she could rely on and trust, especially when that person was family.

If only Becky would say whether she was staying at Vellangoose or not. Her words said one thing but her actions – helping to make the place liveable and her dealings with Ben – indicated that her stay might be permanent. Her sister's dithering could be so frustrating. If only she would make up her mind. Truth was, Abi realised she didn't want to be alone at Vellangoose anymore.

Images from the night the lampers came dogged her thoughts. Nestled deep inside her, the smells, noises, and fear affected everything she did. What had she been trying to prove when she stomped outside to confront those brutes? She rubbed her forehead. At some point, she and Becky would need to talk about everything that had happened, but not yet. She picked up her rucksack and made her way into The Barn.

Becky stood by the kitchen sink. At the sight of Buddy, she bent down. "Hello, beautiful boy." She ran her hand over the shaved patches and scars on the animal's body. "What you need is lots of tender loving care, so that coat of yours will be nice and glossy again."

A flash of disappointment mixed with sadness rolled over Abi. How come Becky could shower Buddy with affection but she barely spoke to the kids? Oh, she was polite to them and threw them a smile now and then, but she always kept them at arm's length. Was that another sign that she was getting ready to leave?

Abi nodded at the paintbrushes soaking in the sink. "Have you finished painting the walls?"

"Come and see for yourself."

Abi let out a soft whistle. The old light-grey tiles she'd put back on the bathroom walls looked surprisingly modern against the newly painted white surfaces. Becky had added a colourful blind and a towel rail, courtesy of the local charity shop. A jar filled with pebbles stood on the windowsill next to a piece of driftwood. Abi's eyes prickled. Working as a team, they'd done a great job. The room was clean, hygienic and completely useable. Who would've thought that she'd own such a place?

She glanced at Becky. Well, half-own.

She walked back into the hallway and pushed open the door to the first bedroom. Her heart sank. Part of the ceiling hung into the room, and strips of stained paper dangled from the cracked and scarred walls.

"Oh dear," Becky said over Abi's shoulder. "The bedrooms are such a mess. Can they be sorted?"

"It already feels drier in here since Ben and Aaron fixed the roof tiles." Abi pressed her hand against one of the grey-coloured patches. "I suppose I could get the dross off the walls in readiness for the rewiring to be done." Tiredness seeped through her. Maybe if she started with this room – the smallest – the task wouldn't feel so daunting? "I think Jacob should have this one. It's just the right size for a single bed. You can have one double, and me and the girls the other."

Becky shifted from one foot to the other. "I could help clear the rubble."

Physical help would be more than welcome, but what Abi wouldn't give for a week on a beach, soaking up the sun. They lived in Cornwall; it should be easy enough. Maybe in the school holidays?

Abi opened her rucksack and pulled out two tins of sausages in baked beans. She glanced at her other food supplies on the kitchen worktop – another tin of baked beans and a few slices of bread. Enough for the kids, but she'd probably have to do without.

Becky moved over to the sink, turned on the tap and held the paintbrushes under the running water. A smile crossed her face.

"I've got some good news. You know I've been doing some catering for Sylvia Rowe, the lady with the big house in Mylor?"

Abi didn't remember but nodded anyway.

"She's having her whole kitchen renovated. Skip loads of good stuff just chucked out." With a flick of her wrist, Becky shook the brushes free of water and dropped them on the window ledge to dry. "Mrs Rowe offered me a couple of glass splashbacks I'd admired. Very pretty they are. Lime green. She said I could have a few other things as well."

"Like what?" Abi reached for her toolbox in the corner.

"How about a cooker and a fridge freezer?"

Abi jerked her head up and stared at Becky. "You've got to be kidding."

"They'll be ready for collection next week. I thought we could pick them up in the camper van?" Her sister clapped her hands together. "It would be lovely to get the kitchen sorted, then I could bake from here, rather than go to my dad's. The cooker could go here, and the fridge freezer in that corner."

"Aren't you forgetting something?"

"What?"

"Electricity."

Becky shrugged. "Ben's working on that."

Irritation nagged at Abi. One minute Becky was banging on about leaving, the next she was planning to turn the kitchen into a commercial bakery.

"I thought you said you weren't sticking around?"

The smile disappeared from Becky's lips. "I just thought I'd make the best of it while I'm here."

An uneasiness settled on Abi. There it was again: was Becky staying or going?

Abi wanted to rely on her sister but how could she? At times, it felt like they were becoming a family, but she was only kidding herself when Becky had no intention of being an aunt to her kids.

Abi grunted, picked up her toolbox and headed for the hallway.

"Abi?"

The tone of Becky's voice stopped her in her tracks. She didn't want to turn back. Instinctively, she knew what was coming. She didn't want this conversation. Not now. Not ever.

"Do you think about the lampers? About what would've happened to your children if we'd been attacked and injured?"

"We weren't. End of story."

"What if they come back?"

Abi froze, then placed the toolbox back onto the floor and faced her sister. "I think about that all the time," she said softly. "And me, acting like an idiot. Me, putting the kids in danger."

Becky nodded. "When I go into Penhellick, I look at all the men, check out their shape, the way they walk. Wonder if it was them. Stupid really."

It wasn't. Abi did the same. She'd even followed one man a few days ago because he had a scruffy dog on a piece of rope.

"I can't sleep." Becky brushed a piece of fluff from her sweater.

"I know."

"Maybe, each time one of us is anxious or can't sleep, we could talk about it?" Becky's blue eyes locked onto Abi's face.

Normally, she had no time for any sort of bare-your-soul nonsense, but this was different. This time, it seemed right that she and Becky had each other's backs.

Abi nodded, reached for the toolbox, then straightened up.

"A Detective Inspector Jack Carter rang while you were at the vets'," Becky said. "Apparently, he's taken over the case from the police constable I reported Buddy's attack to.

The detective inspector said he's spoken to Veronica Williams and several of her men. Every one of them had some sort of alibi who vouched for their whereabouts."

"Oh."

Abi clenched her fist. Damn the Williams family; their sort always got away with it. Money made the difference, allowing them to pay their way out of trouble.

"What about the lurchers? There can't be many about?"

"Lots of people around here have them, according to the detective inspector."

The metal gate to the meadow clanked on its hinges, breaking the silence.

Becky peered out the door. "Hi, Jeffery."

"Just checking on Podge, Mrs, before I go home for me tea."

She raised her hand in reply, then said to Abi, "Jeffery misses Apollo. He's such a dear man. He's been here all day with Ben and Aaron making The Mill roof safe." She picked up a cloth and wiped the sink clean. "I'm off to my dad's shortly, but I'll have a shower first."

Abi picked up her toolbox again and made her way once more towards the bedrooms.

"Abi?"

Abi sighed and turned around.

"I'll be cooking something for my dad. Would you like me to bring a meal back for us and the children?" Becky hung the cloth to dry over the side of the sink. "You'll be doing so much work in the bedrooms, I thought ..."

Abi didn't know how to reply. Relief overwhelmed her. Her kids would have nutritious food for a change. Not only that, but maybe Becky cared about them after all?

"Thank you," she said.

Abi scrutinised the small bedroom as she buttoned up her overalls, then punched the radio on full blast. She did a little dance to the music before she tapped the plaster with a claw hammer.

A noise broke into her thoughts. She spun around, her heart racing, the claw hammer clutched in front of her.

A face appeared at the window.

Abi stepped backwards. Frizzy reddish curls stuck out around a woman's rosy cheeks. The crazed person spoke louder. Cake? Did she say cake?

It must be one of Becky's customers.

Abi went to the front door with the hammer still in her hand.

"Hello, my dear. I'm Megan." The woman standing on the doorstep wore a bright green raincoat and blue wellington boots covered in red dots. "Megan Olds. I've come for my cake."

"I'll get Becky for you." She walked to the bathroom and rapped on the door.

"Becky. Megan Olds is here for her cake."

The bathroom door partly opened. "Sorry, can't come out. Could you give her the blue tin on the table?"

"And a dozen eggs, please," Megan called out. "If that's okay?"

"No problem, Megan," Becky yelled, then glared at Abi. "You know we can't sell them to her," she hissed.

Abi plodded into the kitchen, picked up the cake tin and reached for the eggs. Who cared what the Trust document said? Some cash would be handy. She stopped still, then sighed. This Megan woman might be a friend of Veronica Williams. Becky was right; she should play by the rules for once in her life.

"Can't accept money for the eggs, I'm afraid," Abi said, though it pained her.

"I've heard about your unusual arrangements. Came prepared." Megan held up a bag of potatoes. "Would these do in exchange?"

Abi smiled and took the bag. "Thanks."

"You're Jacob Pascoe's mum, aren't you?"

"Why do you want to know?"

"I look forward to seeing him on Saturday."

"Saturday?"

"Thomas's birthday party. You know, Natalie Lloyd's son." Megan's forehead creased. "All the children from his class are going. Jacob has given you the invite, hasn't he?"

"Must have slipped his mind – you know what kids are like – and I've not gone through his school bag for a few days."

Abi watched Megan leave, closed the front door and leaned against the inside.

Hurt shot through her. She'd checked Jacob's bag last night. There wasn't any fancy invite.

Natalie Lloyd. Becky's sister.

Natalie didn't like Becky living at Vellangoose, fair enough, but to take it out on a seven-year-old child was just spiteful. Jacob had been unusually quiet at breakfast and reluctant to go to school. Was this the reason?

She wanted to rage at Becky, but it wasn't her fault she had a crap sister.

In the bedroom, Abi twisted the claw hammer over and over in her hands. Investing everything in Vellangoose had its compensations, but it also had its downside. A permanent base brought the potential for grief. That was okay for her – she had a thick skin – but not the kids. Jacob had been like a new boy since he'd started at Penhellick School, until this morning. He'd put up with so much in his short life, how dare Becky's sister rip his little world apart.

The hurt turned to anger. An image of Natalie pulling into the school car park in her shiny four-by-four filled

Abi's mind. Bloody woman. She rammed the claw hammer into the wall. Bits of plaster flew across the room. Another image flashed before her eyes. Natalie in designer clothes smiling at all the mothers at the school gate. But not at her.

Why did she ever think that she and Becky would be a family when Becky's family rejected them. Natalie had been Becky's sister a long time before Abi came onto the scene. Becky would always take Natalie's side first.

Abi pulled her arm back and swung with all her might. A large clump of debris plunged to the ground in a cloud of dust. Damn them all.

Becky, wrapped in a dressing gown and hair enveloped in a towel, stepped into the room.

Abi turned towards her, claw hammer raised. "Do you know what your bloody sister has done to our Jacob?"

Becky's hand went to her neck.

"Well, I'll tell you, shall I?"

Abi's mouth twisted as she spat out what Megan Olds had said.

"What's more, you'd better tell that sister of yours to look out, because I'll be coming for her." Abi caught her breath. "And you ... you're driving me crazy with your shilly-shallying. Are you staying at Vellangoose or not? Are you with me or with Natalie? It's time you made some decisions. Time you got off the fence for once in your life."

The room fell silent.

A vivid red spot had appeared on each of Becky's pale cheeks.

"I'm so sorry. My sister is ..." Her hand flapped. "I ... I must go." Becky turned and scurried away.

Abi swung the hammer again.

19

Becky pressed Natalie's doorbell, then pressed it again and kept her finger on it. Blast. She punched a number into her mobile. Natalie's phone switched to voicemail.

"Damn you, Natalie. How could you sink so low? You might not like Abi, but Jacob's just a child." She took a deep breath. "I don't understand you anymore. Ring me. Urgent."

Half an hour later, Becky stepped into her dad's kitchen and plonked several bags of shopping and empty cake tins onto the worktop.

"Hello, love. Sorry, I'd give you a hand, but ..." Her dad tilted the frying pan towards her. Several pieces of bacon sizzled in a bubbly liquid. "Want some? I've got plenty more." He cracked two eggs into the pan alongside the bacon, and using a wooden spatula, flicked cooking oil over the tops of the orange yolks.

Her heart sank. The last thing she needed was her dad cluttering up the kitchen and getting under her feet. She leaned over the sink and pushed the window open as far as it would go.

"No time. Got to get a couple of cakes in the oven."

From the cupboards, she pulled out four sponge tins, greaseproof paper, and a large plastic storage container full of dried baking ingredients. She turned towards the cooker and stooped to the oven door.

"Oh, Dad. Please move over. I need to get on."

He grunted and stepped aside.

Metal clattered against metal as she adjusted the shelf heights and switched the temperature to one hundred and eighty degrees.

"I don't know why you're cooking when I usually make something for you," she said.

"Thought I'd save you the bother."

She'd promised Abi she'd make a meal for all of them. Trust him to be contrary, today of all days. Not that it mattered; she'd defrost and heat some meals she had in her dad's freezer.

On the corner of the worktop, she tipped sugar, butter, eggs and flour into the old-fashioned food mixer and switched it on.

"Be finished in a minute, love. Been at the allotment most of the day."

He lifted the eggs and bacon onto a plate, picked up a piece of white bread, and dropped it into the pan. Fat spat across the cooker top. The room filled with the fug of cooking oil.

"Oh, Dad. My cakes will be ruined."

"Bit of a fry-up won't hurt anything." He flicked the bread onto the plate, picked it up, and moved to the table. "Anyone would think 'twas your place, not mine."

She chucked the frying pan into the washing-up bowl, added lemon detergent, then picked up a tea towel and wafted the smell towards the window.

Back at the food mixer, she scooped some of the gloopy mixture into her mouth. The sweet, sugary goo coated her tongue. Perfect. She switched off the machine, spooned the creamy substance into the tins, and placed them in the oven.

"Want a cup of tea?" She flicked the kettle switch.

"Thanks, love." Dad squirted ketchup onto his plate and dipped a piece of fried bread into it. "The early cabbages aren't up to much this year. Think I'll get a different variety next spring. Besides, Natalie wants–"

"And what Natalie wants, Natalie gets." Becky spat the words out.

He looked across at her. "Something's rattled your cage. Get on with it, girl, speak your piece."

"Natalie."

"Might've guessed. You girls. You'll be the death of me."

"Do you know what she's done?" Before he could answer, Becky rushed on. "She's invited all of Thomas's classmates to his birthday party. Everyone, that is, except Jacob."

"Jacob?"

"Don't pretend you don't know who he is." She waved the washing-up brush in his direction.

"She can invite who she likes, can't she?"

"He's only seven. He won't understand why he's not been invited." Her temple throbbed. "She's doing it out of spite."

"What you fussing for? Don't suppose all the kids will be able to go anyway. If you ask me, 'tis best all round if you stopped sticking your nose into Natalie's business." Crumbs flew from his mouth. "She and Pete are having a hard time, and we all know why, don't we?"

She slammed the brush onto the kitchen table. "Might've known you'd take her side."

Her dad folded his arms across his chest. "Now who's being a child?"

"You never listen to me, never support me, do you?" In a flash of insight, she realised that this had always been the case. "You and Mum always put Natalie first." She dragged her fingers through her hair. "Natalie got her way all the time, while I … I just accepted it."

"What are you on about now?"

Something had been gnawing away at her for some while, but each time it came near to the surface she'd pushed it away, too afraid to face the unpalatable truth. Now, words poured from her.

"I was made to feel different. Feel second best. I always had to earn your love."

Her dad stood and chucked his half-eaten meal into the bin. "What a load of old bunkum. What's got into you? It's that woman's doing. She's changed you."

"Abi. Her name is Abi." Becky grunted. "You're right. She has made me see things differently. She cares for all three of her children equally."

"So, what's that got to do with anything?"

"I only had Jess, so I didn't realise until now." She paused and took a deep breath. "Abi would die for each one of her children. Mum wouldn't have. Not for me, anyway. If there'd been a fire, both of you would have saved Natalie first."

A fly buzzed against the windowpane.

"Dad?"

"What?"

"Admit I'm right. Please. Admit that you both treated me unfairly." A sob bubbled in her throat, but she swallowed it away. "Natalie can't be allowed to do the same thing to Jacob."

In the silence, she stared at the top of her dad's bowed head. All she wanted was for him to acknowledge that they'd favoured Natalie over her. Why couldn't he say that? Just once.

She reached over and touched his arm.

His chair scraped against the tiled floor.

She watched him leave the room and trudge down the hallway.

"This won't go away," she called after him.

His bedroom door slammed in reply.

Becky pulled into the yard at Vellangoose, got out of the car and waved to Ben, who was standing next to the tractor. Lost in thought, she made her way towards the garden.

"Becky," Ben called out. "Have you a minute to talk about the contract?"

"Is something wrong?"

"Just wondering what you wanted doing next." He wiped his hands on an oily cloth.

"How about getting electricity installed? Or the rewiring? Will the contract stretch to both?" She knew it wouldn't, but it was worth a try.

A wry smile crossed Ben's face. "It won't."

"Rewiring it has to be then."

"You'll need a qualified electrician, but I can commission the work and pay for it. I'll chat to Jennings in Helston and see what they can do now we're ready to go ahead." Ben looked up at the darkening clouds and back at the tractor. "Is that okay with you?"

Overtaken by an unexpected impulse, she gave him a big hug.

"Thanks for being such a good friend," she whispered, then spun around and walked swiftly away.

Becky glanced sideways at her sister, then immediately launched into giving her the news about the rewiring as she stacked large flasks of cooked food onto the kitchen worktop, along with a container filled with chocolate brownies.

Abi stood over the sink; her hands covered in suds. Bits of plaster from her hair dropped into the water as she nodded in response.

"You don't seem very excited?" Becky said. Please don't let Abi have another go at her about Natalie. She wouldn't know how to answer.

"I didn't think Ben would be able to start on the rewiring so soon. It's great news, but who knows how we'll get the electric connected." Abi raised her hand. "Still, who cares? Something will probably turn up."

Becky frowned. "Are you okay?"

"Why wouldn't I be?"

Becky turned away, placed five assorted plates onto the table and started talking about the first thing that came into her head.

"I dropped into the Falmouth Library on the way home. Had a disagreement with dad and needed to clear my head." She grimaced. "Did a bit of research on the library's computer to compare prices for catering and baked goods. It looks like I can charge more than I originally thought."

Abi looked up and stared at her for a few moments before she spoke.

"Apollo will also bring in some money at some point. Apparently, he's doing what all good stallions should."

"Perhaps it's time we opened a joint bank account?"

"David said much the same earlier," Abi said.

"David?"

"He called in to tell us about Apollo. I know he wanted to see you but he had to make do with me instead."

Becky fumbled with the cutlery. She kept her head down; her neck would be red and blotchy.

A small hand tucked into hers. Eve smiled up at her. Becky's heart leapt. The child was so like Jess at that age, but Becky knew if she didn't keep her emotions on a tight grip, she would be swamped with love for Jacob, Eve and Grace. That wouldn't do. She wouldn't be able to extricate herself from Vellangoose and their lives when the time came to move on.

She slowly released her hand from Eve's grip. "Food's ready."

Still bent over the sink, Abi yelled, "Jacob. Go wash your hands, and Grace's. You too, Eve."

"Goodness me." Becky jumped as Buddy crashed into the room from the hallway and ran around her legs before ducking under the table. A doll hung from his mouth. Jacob ran after him, dropped to his knees and crawled through the chairs after the dog.

"That's my dolly," yelled Eve. "Give it to me, Buddy. It's mine."

Grace joined in. "Mine. Give. Mine."

"Kids. Buddy. Be quiet." Abi raised her voice above the commotion as the children chased Buddy from under the table and back down the hallway. "Come on, guys, it's—"

A knock on the kitchen door stopped her saying anymore.

"That'll be Ben." Abi yanked the door open, flinging her arm wide in greeting.

"Welcome to the madhouse."

Natalie stepped into the kitchen, dressed in an immaculate designer trouser suit and impossibly high-heeled black shoes. Her face was immobile.

"You?" Abi glared.

"Natalie? What are you doing here?" Becky blurted out.

"You summoned me," Natalie said to Becky while ignoring Abi.

Becky glanced over at Abi, who stood in the middle of the room, back ramrod straight, arms crossed.

Becky's stomach churned.

"I think we should go outside," she said to Natalie.

Natalie thrust a yellow envelope covered in dinosaur stickers in Abi's direction. Abi didn't move. Natalie chucked it on the table.

"It's an invite for your Jacob." She turned back to Becky. "As per orders."

"You spoke to her about this?" Abi turned a puzzled face on Becky. "You did that for Jacob?"

"I … I only spoke to Natalie and Dad because–"

"Your dad as well?" Abi's cheeks reddened, then she turned away and snatched up the envelope. She brandished it in Natalie's face. "If it wasn't for my son's feelings, I would tell you where to stick this."

"Frankly, I don't care a monkey's whatsits about how your kid feels." Natalie flicked her glossy hair over one shoulder. "I did it because Thomas and Jacob are best friends. Did you know that?" Natalie looked from Becky to Abi. "I thought not. Thomas has been miserable all week. Turns out he didn't want a party without Jacob."

Silence filled the room.

"I'm so glad that's all settled." Becky let out a shaky breath. "How about a coffee?"

"Don't be stupid," Natalie snarled, then stomped out the door.

Becky ran after her. "Come back in and see the place. See what we've done."

"Why would I?" Natalie scanned the yard. "It's a tip. You must be mad to live here with that woman."

The anger from earlier in the day returned. Just like her dad, her sister was being her usual selfish self, expecting Becky to toe the line and do what Natalie wanted.

"Presumably, the mums are also invited to the party?"

"They help with the games and look after the children. Why?"

"But not Abi?"

"Not her," Natalie replied through pursed lips. "Veronica Williams is putting pressure on us because of this flaming situation. We've already lost two clients."

"That's not Abi's fault."

"In case you haven't noticed, she's Henry Williams's daughter and living at Vellangoose at huge annoyance to Veronica Williams."

"So am I. On both accounts."

A dog barked in the distance.

"Does that mean I'm excluded from the party as well?" Becky chewed her lip.

"Don't be silly. Thomas is your nephew. He'll want you there."

"You're putting me in an impossible situation. Making me choose between one sister and the other." The words came out before Becky realised what she'd said.

"My God, how could you compare me with that woman? You hardly know her." A droplet of saliva rested on Natalie's lip. "She's not a real sister."

Becky's head was full of all sorts of conflicting emotions. She wanted to scream.

"For heaven's sake, Becky. What's wrong with you?"

Becky's lips moved, but no words came out.

"Looks like you've made your choice. Don't come, if that's the way you feel." Natalie dug the car keys from her bag. "Just remember, it's not my fault that you've got yourself into this mess."

"It's not mine either," Becky finally snapped.

She watched Natalie's car disappear up the lane before she turned and walked back through the garden and into the kitchen.

At the table, Becky fiddled with the knives and forks, her head bent. What had she done? Had she really taken Abi's side against Natalie?

Abi cleared her throat. "Thanks for sticking up for Jacob. Must be hard to be stuck between two sisters. Much appreciated though."

Becky unscrewed the lid of one of the food flasks and picked up a ladle.

Abi grabbed it. "You sit down, I'll serve up. It's the least I can do as you've done all the cooking and suchlike."

Becky forced a smile. She felt odd after her fight with Natalie. They never fought. And now, Abi, who'd ripped into her earlier, was offering to help. Everything seemed topsy-turvy.

"Becky's Baps," Abi said.

"What?".

"A name for your business." Abi snatched up a tea towel and threw it at Becky. "Or maybe Becky's Buns would be better?"

Becky clutched the towel to her chest. It looked like Abi's earlier bad mood had lifted. She threw the towel back at Abi.

"That's dreadful."

"Or Becky's Bloomers." Abi snorted with laughter.

A wave of happiness unexpectedly surged over Becky. Maybe, just maybe, her stay at Vellangoose with Abi and her family would work out for the best after all.

20

Abi closed her eyes and tilted her head upwards. Sunshine caressed her face and the magic of a perfect summer's day seeped through her body. Bird song, and the rhythmic chomp of Podge eating grass next to her, added to her sense of peace. If only there were more moments like this.

Podge moved forward. Abi tightened her hold on his halter and looked down at Jacob, who stood with a grooming brush in his hand. The pink tip of his tongue poked between his lips.

"Just the two of you today?"

The sudden sound of Ben's deep voice sent an unexpected but pleasant tremor down Abi's spine.

"Grace and Eve are on a play-date with my friend, Kate, and her kids in Penryn.

Ben climbed the gate, dropped into the meadow and ran his hand over Podge's flank. "You're doing a great job, Jacob."

"Can you teach me to ride him, Uncle Ben?"

"Mr Vincent to you," Abi quickly butted in.

"Ben's fine by me." He smiled his wonderful broad smile at her. "I could give him a few lessons if you like?"

"Podge doesn't have a saddle or bridle."

"You should speak to Megan Olds. She's got a couple of ponies for her girls. She might have a spare saddle and other bits she could loan you. Jacob will need a hard hat as well."

Damn it. Wasn't there someone else other than Megan Olds, the woman who'd inadvertently alerted her to the fact that Jacob hadn't been invited to Thomas's party? Not only that, the Olds woman was clearly a friend of Natalie Lloyd. Abi couldn't ask Megan Olds, not even for Jacob.

Jacob bowed his head at her silence and dug at the dirt with the toe of his trainer. Her son already knew more about disappointment than he should in his short life. She reached out to him, but Ben beat her to it.

"Do you want a hand up?" Before Jacob could reply, he hoisted him onto Podge's broad back. Jacob grinned from ear to ear.

She studied Ben, his hand clutching Jacob's leg to steady him as he walked Podge around the meadow. When they returned, she reached out to help Jacob off. Accidentally, her hand touched Ben's. He winked. She pulled her hand away. Damn those twinkling hazel-brown eyes and that strong, tanned face. For a few moments, she fussed with Podge's halter. This was no time to be starting a new relationship.

Ben turned towards The Barn. "Is Becky about?"

"She's out to lunch with her daughter. Steve's away on business so Jess has graciously bestowed Becky with her presence."

Abi wanted to say more but bit back the words. She just hoped Eve and Grace would treat her better when they grew up. Becky didn't deserve that stuck up little madam for a daughter.

"Jennings has sent me an invoice for the rewiring work." Ben pulled a creased sheet of paper from the back pocket of his jeans. "Becky needs to check the costs and confirm that I can pay for it."

"The electrician did a brilliant job." Abi took the invoice from Ben. "I've already decorated the small bedroom for Jacob. He's moving in today."

"Mum painted the ceiling dark blue with yellow stars and a smiley half-moon. I've got a desk as well. Mum made it."

"You're a lucky boy to have such a clever mum." Ben ruffled her son's hair, waved to Abi, then leapt back over the gate.

She watched him stroll across the yard, then she turned to Jacob. "My stomach tells me it's cake time."

Ten minutes later, Jacob finished his orange juice, scooted off his chair, and ran towards his bedroom. Buddy bounced after him, tongue lolling. Abi picked up the empty muffin paper cases sucked clean by her son and chucked them into the waste bin.

She pushed their chairs back under the table and brushed the last few crumbs from its glossy red surface. She'd made good use of the tins of paint Becky had brought back from her dad's. Abi had painted each of the old garden chairs in a different colour: bright blue for Jacob, sunny yellow for Eve, and emerald-green for herself, followed by a brilliant white one for Becky, and fuchsia pink for Grace's highchair. It certainly cheered things up a bit.

Abi made her way into the hallway and peered into Jacob's room. She watched him for a moment playing with his cars on the floor. She'd bring his air bed and sleeping bag in later from the living room. A pang of frustration rolled over her. The kids needed proper beds, but the lack of electricity took priority. She and Becky had opened a joint bank account, and between them had managed to deposit a few pounds, but at the rate they were going, they'd never have enough for the connection fees, let alone pay the ongoing bills.

At least the early summer days were long and light, but what if they still hadn't got the power sorted by September when the evenings drew in? Had she the right to put her kids through a long Cornish winter with no light, heat, or hot water?

She moved into Becky's bedroom and swirled the first pot of paint with disinterest; Cotton White for three of the walls and Teal for the other. She couldn't wait to decorate the room she'd share with Eve and Grace. It would be colourful, very colourful.

The radio blared. She brushed the paint back and forth in time with the music.

"Mum. Muuum."

She flicked the radio off and twirled round to face Jacob.

"There's a lady at the door," he said, then turned and zoomed back to his bedroom.

It was Megan Olds. Now halfway down the hallway.

Megan snatched a floppy-brimmed, straw hat off her head to reveal copper-red hair twisted into one large plait. The end was tied with what appeared to be a piece of pink baler twine.

"My dear, your boy just shot off, so I let myself in." She let out a loud laugh that went on for longer than necessary.

Abi stared at her. A long, haphazardly-buttoned red cardigan fell unevenly to her knees. Unpolished riding boots peeped from under a flowered maxi skirt.

"Brought these back for Becky. Is she in?" A plastic bag swung from Megan's wrist. Cake tins poked from the top. "Delicious they were." She laughed again. "The cakes, not the tins."

"She's out. I'll take them." Abi took the tins, dropped the bag by the kitchen door and gestured towards the open front door with her arm.

Megan didn't move.

"Such a charming boy, your Jacob. Had a lovely little chat with him at Thomas's birthday bash."

"What?"

"Sat next to him during one of the games. Pass the parcel, I think." Megan beamed. "I'd hoped to speak to either you or Becky at the party. Shame neither of you were there. I thought you would be, being Natalie's sisters."

"She's not my sister."

"Oh. Of course not, silly me. Anyway, I wanted to talk to you about your old stables? And the woods, and ..." She took a deep breath, "I have a proposition for you."

"Not interested." Abi's t-shirt stuck to her back.

Megan raised one eyebrow. "It could be worth your while."

In the background, Abi heard Jacob playing with his cars. She thought of the new beds she wanted for the kids. She folded her arms.

"It's the girls. You see, they wore us down. Poppy and Rose, they're at Helston School, and Violet, Iris and Jasmine are at Penhellick School ... with Eve and Jacob. You might have seen them in the playground?" She grinned. "Can't think now why we called them all after flowers. Don't have them in the house. Flowers," another laugh boomed down the hallway, "not the children."

Eve had talked about her new best friend, Jasmine, and Abi had seen the red-haired kids waiting at the school gates, crooked pigtails dangling down their backs, but she didn't want to get into a discussion about Megan's kids. Abi shook her head.

"Never mind. You'll meet them soon, I'm sure." Megan twisted the brim of her hat between her hands. Bits of straw fell to the hallway floor.

"We've indulged them. Got two ponies. Pixie and Dixie." She paused as if waiting for Abi to comment. "Quite understandable. I was thirty-seven before I met the other half and popped out the first of my little darlings." A wicked grin crossed her face. "He's a handsome devil, my husband."

For once, Abi couldn't think of anything to say, so she gripped one red elbow and steered Megan towards the front door.

Outside, Megan's large hand covered Abi's and patted it. Mortified, Abi stepped aside.

"Where was I?" Megan's forehead creased. "Ah, yes. We don't have any land. Lost it, you know. Years ago. Silly ancestors." She flung her plait over her shoulder and yanked the hat back onto her head. "Poor Pixie and Dixie are in livery. Very costly. Saw your empty stables the other day. Thought what a jolly good place for our sweet babies." She let out a long chuckle. "The ponies, not my girls."

Every fibre of Abi's being wanted to tell her to shove off, but some instinct held her back.

Megan strode across the yard and stopped in front of one of the long, single-storey buildings. Years of grime and old cobwebs smeared the still miraculously intact, thick windowpanes. Rotten doors hung lopsided in the two entranceways.

"Yes, yes. This is it." Megan moved with big strides towards the first stable door, wrenched it open, and disappeared into the interior. Her muffled voice came from the depths of the building. "This will do nicely. Sound roof. Dry. It'll need to be cleared out, but my other half could do a lot of the work."

Abi stepped inside. Dust motes danced in the beams of sunlight. Straw bales, grey with age, towered in front of her. Megan had already clamoured to the top. Legs wide apart, she tossed several of the bales to the floor. The rotten string on one of them broke and straw burst around

Abi's legs. Her mouth and nose filled with powdery fragments. She coughed and leaned against the wall. Megan carried on, seemingly unaffected by the polluted air. More bales followed. Abi reached up to catch them and stacked them by the door.

"Good, good. Looks like the partitions are still intact. Oh, this flipping thing." Megan stopped what she was doing, grabbed the bottom of her skirt, yanked it up, and tucked the end into the top of her pants. "Hate these things. Only wore it for the other half. His birthday. He likes skirts. Me wearing them, not him."

Despite herself, Abi smiled.

Megan jumped down to the floor, stomped outside, and with a cursory flap of her hands, brushed most of the cobwebs and straw from her red cardigan. "Must be off. Meeting the other half for lunch. Already late." She looked directly into Abi's face. "That's all agreed then?"

"What?" She'd clearly missed something.

"Use of these stables." Megan gestured in a broad arc. "Use of the woods. Use of your meadows." She swung around in a circle. Her skirt pulled free from her pants and swirled about her legs. "Pixie and Dixie are biddable enough and will be able to graze with your little pony. Saw him in the field as I drove in. Pretty little thing. Looks familiar."

"Podge." Abi swiped a cobweb from her cheek.

"Ah. Know him from the gymkhana circuit. Lovely pony." Megan swung around and pointed to the woods. "A great place for the children to practice show jumping." She clapped her hands. "The Pony Club will love it."

Abi blinked.

"My dear, let me explain." Megan used her fingers to illustrate. "One – I'd like to rent the stables with shared grazing. Two – my other half will fix up the stables for dear Pixie and Dixie. Three – as Secretary of the Pony Club and ..." Megan pushed herself to her full height. "The Penhellick Country Show, I want to commandeer Vellangoose for various events. The little dears will love it." She looked at her fourth finger, forehead creased. "Four – must have insurance. Need to decide who'll pay for it." She flapped her hand. "Minor details, minor details."

"We can't accept money for any of this." Abi held her breath and waited.

"Ah, yes, I remember. Barter only. Love it. Do it all the time. My goats' milk and cheese for ... well, anything that's on offer. Shame Becky doesn't like goats' cheese. Tried to get her to take it for her wonderful cakes, but she wouldn't have it." She shook her head and smiled. "Tough business lady your sister."

Megan strode towards a battered and mud-smeared people carrier parked next to The Mill. "Hate baking. Useless at it. Where were we? Groceries? Petrol? You say what you want, my dear."

Abi stumbled after her. Her mind whirled.

"Electricity. We need it connected," she blurted out. "Need an order placed and paid for on our behalf."

"Wonderful, wonderful." Megan held out her hand. "Deal."

"Becky will need to work through the finer details with you. Otherwise ...." unable to believe what was happening, she shook the outstretched hand, "deal."

"Excellent, my dear."

A thought flashed into Abi's mind. "The Pony Club. Can any child join? My Jacob ..." She faltered, afraid to ask more in case she got an answer she didn't want.

"Can he ride?"

"He's learning. Ben Vincent's teaching him."

Megan nodded. "Good, good."

"Podge doesn't have a saddle. Truth is, I don't have any of the proper gear."

"There's loads of old stuff back at the ranch. Root through, my dear. Root through whenever you want." Megan struggled to get into the car. "Blasted skirt." She tugged at it and looked up at Abi. "All done?"

Abi couldn't let her go just yet. She had to know one more thing. She leaned her hands on the driver's open window.

"Don't you have to check with the Club members? Natalie, for instance?"

"Natalie Lloyd? No, no, I'm the Secretary."

"But Natalie ..." Why couldn't she just let it go?

"Lovely woman, lovely woman. Our children are good friends." Megan leaned out of the window and looked from side to side. "But she's a bit too ... tidy for me. Could never invite her into my house." She switched on the ignition and rammed the vehicle into gear.

"See you anon." Megan revved the engine and sped across the yard.

As the vehicle rattled up the lane, Abi let out one big yell and punched the air several times. Finally, things were coming together. The Barn would have electricity.

She couldn't wait to tell Becky.

21

Becky sat at the window of her favourite restaurant. She couldn't remember the last time she'd felt so content. On the beach below, families enjoyed the sun, and in the sea beyond, windsurfers skimmed the surface leaving crystal droplets in their wake. Waves lapped the pale sand in a slow rhythmic motion.

The hake she'd just eaten had been delicious. A knot of happiness nestled in her chest. Could the beautiful, vibrant woman in front of her really be her daughter? She was nothing like the girl who'd clung to Steve's arm when they'd visited Vellangoose recently. Today, Jess chatted and laughed freely. This was the daughter that Becky knew and loved.

Out of politeness, she knew she had to ask after Steve, but in truth, she didn't care. She took a sip of wine.

"How's Steve?"

Heads turned as Jess let out a light, joyous laugh. "Wonderful. I didn't know it was possible to love someone so much."

Becky took another mouthful of chardonnay. "Is he away on company business?"

"A problem land deal, I think. Steve doesn't bore me with work stuff." She giggled. "He's seeing a barrister. Can you believe it, they have their very own barrister? Cool or what?"

Becky's fingers tightened around the stem of her glass. "Anything to do with Vellangoose?"

"Why would it be? Steve isn't interested in that dump." Jess clamped her hand over her mouth. "Sorry, Mum. You know what I mean."

An intricate gold necklace nestled perfectly around Jess's young neck. Becky tore her gaze away and watched a yacht tacking across the bay. She couldn't bear to think what her daughter had to do to be the recipient of such an expensive gift.

"Come on, Mum, what are you having next?" Jess pointed to a particularly large, chocolatey pudding being eaten by a woman on the next table. "That's what I want."

The easy atmosphere returned as they made their choices, discussed what shops they'd visit after lunch, and what Jess might buy.

Then Jess's mobile rang, and her beautiful, happy face disappeared in the time it took her to answer the incoming call. "Darling. No. Only Mum ... Of course, right away."

Becky couldn't catch all the conversation, but what did it matter anyway? Steve was home from his trip and wanted Jess.

Her daughter hung up, picked up her handbag and rummaged inside.

"Darling, please don't go yet," Becky pleaded. "We've not even had our desserts." The high pitch was back in her voice.

"Sorry. Must go." A jumble of keys dropped onto the table with a clatter. A brown, fluffy monkey stared up at the ceiling, its glass eyes dark and shiny.

Becky sucked in a deep breath. She'd given the little animal to her daughter when she'd passed her driving test. It was a wonder that Steve hadn't forced her to bin such an immature symbol of her former life.

"Darling, don't let him dictate your life, your every move." Becky grabbed Jess's hand. "I beg you."

"Oh, Mum. Don't be silly."

"Remember, I know what a controlling relationship is like."

Jess's eyes flared. "You can't seriously be comparing Steve with Dad?"

Becky slumped against the chair. God help her, if Steve walked in now, she'd rip into him.

"Must run." Jess bent over and planted a swift, perfunctory kiss on her cheek. "Bye."

A moment later, her daughter had gone.

Becky stared at Jess's empty chair. Jess had invited her to lunch and chosen the expensive seafood restaurant, so Becky had naturally assumed her daughter would pay. She rummaged in her purse, paid the bill and made her way back to the car, all thoughts of window shopping forgotten. She stopped in the middle of the pavement. How would she pay for the ingredients she needed for tomorrow's baking? Blast Steve. The only option would be to withdraw some cash from the Vellangoose account she and Abi now shared. She took a deep breath. Oh, well, she'd had a marvellous time while it lasted.

Becky pushed the accelerator down, eased the car onto the roundabout, and joined the queue of traffic leaving Falmouth. Through the half-open window, a mixture of salty air tinged with the whiff of riverside mud drifted in on a warm breeze.

After a few minutes of stop-start progress, the line of vehicles came to a halt. She left the engine to idle and let the sounds from Classic FM wash over her. The manner of Jess's sudden departure at lunch niggled away at her thoughts. She jabbed the radio volume up to maximum. Moments later, she slapped the radio off and glanced over her shoulder. Car horns and angry voices sounded in the distance. She wasn't going anywhere. She wound up the driver's window, switched the engine off, and rested her head against the seat.

A sudden noise jolted her upright. She peered through the windscreen. The traffic remained stationary. Someone rapped on the driver's window. She twisted around and gazed into David Penna's blue eyes. He looked every inch the successful solicitor in a grey suit, white shirt and tie.

She wound the window down.

"I rapped a couple of times. You were deep in thought." He peered at her. "Are you okay?"

"Having one of those days." She waved her hand towards the stationary traffic. "And now this."

"It's an accident. Caught the tail end of the traffic news on Radio Cornwall. It's going to be a while before everything's cleared. How about a drink or a coffee?" He pointed to a cul-de-sac. "We could leave our cars over there and make our way back towards town."

As they walked, Becky's earlier happy mood returned. David took her arm, tucked it into his, and gave her hand a reassuring squeeze. She'd forgotten the feeling of togetherness that a gentle amble, arm in arm, could generate.

"What brought you into town? Thought you were up to your ears with baking?" David steered her through the Falmouth Marina car park and up the metal steps to the bar and restaurant on the first floor.

"Lunch with Jess."

Inside, David pulled out his wallet. "Drink? You looked like you needed one earlier."

"Cappuccino will be fine. Thanks."

David turned to the girl behind the bar. "Make that two, please."

"Will you be eating?"

"Not me." Becky rubbed her stomach. "Couldn't eat another thing."

"A packet of salt and vinegar crisps for me." David smiled as he handed over a ten-pound note.

They made their way outside onto the narrow veranda overlooking the yachts and boats moored in the marina below. The warmth from the sun and the gentle slap of rigging washed over Becky as she relaxed into a wicker chair.

She studied David as the girl placed the coffees and a sugar bowl onto the little glass bistro table in front of them. He had an aura of importance and authority about him, yet there was a softness to his features and a casualness to his manner that she liked.

"How are things going at Vellangoose?" David raised the coffee cup to his lips.

"Abi's re-plastered and painted a bedroom for Jacob. She's now in the process of getting mine finished."

"She's certainly clever with her hands. Is the electric sorted yet?"

"The re-wiring has been completed, so connecting the electricity is our next project."

"I take it back. You're both pretty clever."

A feeling of pleasure ran through her. Somehow it mattered that he acknowledged that they were making things work, making Vellangoose into what they wanted.

"Thought you didn't have the means to connect the electric for a while?"

"There's a lot of demand for my bakes, and I'm getting requests to cater for several dinner parties and birthdays as well. It's all bringing in quite a bit of money. Abi's also working extra hours." She realised she sounded more confident than she felt, but so what? It would be how Abi would play it. "Just need to sort the logistics to comply with the Trust." She grinned at him.

He chewed on the last few crisps and dropped the empty packet on the table. "Do you think you'll last the winter without power?"

She wasn't sure she liked the inference, from David of all people, that she and Abi would turn soft and give up on Vellangoose.

"Enough about Vellangoose," she replied. "What have you been up to?"

"Interestingly, I've acquired a couple of new clients, and one or two of the old standbys have been vying for my attention." He smiled. "Keeps me out of trouble."

"Veronica Williams?"

"You know I can't talk about individual clients, but let's just say, neither I nor the firm has seen her for some time."

"Lucky you. Lucky us."

"I would say so." He rubbed his hands together. "I'm ravenous. I missed lunch. How about joining me for a bite to eat? A dessert, maybe? Or cheese and biscuits?"

Becky tipped her wrist and looked at her watch. 3:30 p.m. She wasn't that hungry, but she didn't want to leave. Besides, she'd missed having a pudding earlier. "That would be lovely."

Ice cubes clinked against her glass as she took a sip of orange juice and soda and watched David eat his way through a plate of sea bream. Happiness rolled over her as they chatted easily together.

He placed his knife and fork onto the empty plate. "Time for dessert. I can't resist the lemon posset. I believe it's the sort of thing you make."

"One of my many superior desserts." She giggled. "If I say so myself."

"Do you truly intend setting up your own business? What if you find you can't manage everything? Orders, invoices, accounts, etc."

"Why wouldn't I be able to manage?" Becky's jaw clenched.

"Just saying, it takes a lot of hard work to run your own company. I should know."

"Really?"

She glared at him. Were his lips pinched? Dry? Like John's?

David leaned towards her. "Is everything okay? I didn't—"

The shrill ring of a mobile phone interrupted him. His brows furrowed at the sight of the caller's name.

"Got to get this."

He stood and made his way further along the veranda, out of earshot.

She picked up a napkin and pressed the cloth to her mouth. Grey clouds, weighted down with dark underbellies, had replaced the earlier sunshine.

A few minutes later, he returned and picked up his jacket. "I'm so sorry. Client problems. Must go. Stay and have your pudding. I've paid for everything."

He shrugged the jacket over his shoulders.

"I thought you said lemon posset was your favourite."

She knew her voice had an edge to it, but it was the second time that day that someone had cast her aside for another person.

"I'm afraid, this client doesn't wait." He bent over to give her a brief kiss.

She drew away from him and the kiss landed near her ear.

"I'll give you a ring," he said.

Becky watched him as he left. How dare he patronise her? She wasn't anyone's dutiful woman anymore.

The chocolate fondant she'd ordered looked delicious. The liquid centre poured onto the plate in a shiny, perfect blob. She put a spoonful to her mouth. It tasted like ashes.

She dropped the spoon onto the plate with a clang, pushed away from the table and rushed outside.

With quick, determined strides she walked to her car. David's had gone. The traffic towards Helston was still jammed, but the route into Falmouth was clear. She hooted her horn and, with hand gestures, demanded a passage through the queue, then drove back towards the town. She'd go along the seafront and follow the country lanes to Vellangoose.

The sea, dotted with boats and yachts of various shapes and sizes, calmed her. She took a deep breath of salty air. Overhead, a seagull drifted on an air current.

Neither Jess nor David had meant to upset her. Her fault. Too sensitive by far. It was just circumstances. They'd both ring her later, and she'd feel so much better. It had been a good day, she told herself.

Something caught her attention. Her brain jolted into alert mode. She recognised the stance of a man walking along the seafront with the arm of a smartly dressed woman tucked into his.

Less than two hours ago, he'd held Becky's hand in the same way.

The car bumped the curb as she pulled over, automatically switched off the engine, and stared.

The woman turned slightly, clutched David's arm with her free hand and laughed. He smiled in return.

A light breeze lifted the woman's hair away from her face. Becky moaned.

Veronica Williams.

Becky hammered the car along the narrow, single-tracked roads towards Vellangoose. The vehicle rocked over the uneven, rarely maintained tarmac. A bramble snatched at the wing mirror and dragged along the car's paintwork.

In her mind's eye, all she could see was David, arm in arm with Veronica Williams. She shook her head, but the two figures remained etched in her vision. David's face, full of warmth and laughter, swam unbidden before her. She lifted her hand and thumped the steering wheel. He'd lied to her when he said he hadn't seen that woman. Damn. She'd trusted him.

A screech of brakes whipped the images away. An oncoming car braked and swerved into a farm gateway. She didn't stop. In the rear-view mirror, the driver got out and raised his fist. She gave a two-fingered salute. She'd had enough for one day.

At the entrance to Vellangoose, a van cut into the lane ahead of her. She scowled at the big yellow letters emblazoned on the side of the vehicle - Pizza Delivery. The stupid idiot had got the wrong address. She flashed the headlights several times, waved for him to stop. An arm came out of the driver's window and gave her a thumbs-up.

She rattled down the lane after him, drew alongside the vehicle as it come to a standstill, and got out.

"You're in the wrong place," she yelled.

The man ambled towards her. He ran a finger down the delivery details. "Dough balls. Five pizzas. Variety of ice creams." He stabbed at the sheet of paper. "Abi Pascoe. Vellangoose."

Becky felt like she'd been punched. Abi had placed an expensive order for pizzas when they'd agreed not to spend any money without consulting each other first. For a brief instance, the picture of her expensive lunch flashed before her eyes. Teeth clenched, she pushed the vision away and stomped across the yard to The Barn.

Five expectant faces swivelled in her direction as she stepped into the kitchen.

Jacob leapt to his feet and rushed to peer through the doorway. "They're here. The pizzas are here."

"Party. Party." Eve shouted. "We're having a party."

Noise and laughter ricocheted around the room. Becky's head throbbed. Buddy's tail beat against her leg.

"White or red?" Ben waved a wine glass in Becky's direction.

At that moment, Abi, wrapped in a waft of alcohol, moved alongside her to speak to the delivery man.

"What do you think you're doing?" Becky spoke in a harsh whisper.

Abi came to a halt in mid-stride, one leg outstretched in front of her. "Just a second, Big Sis. I need to speak to this nice man."

The man put the brightly coloured pizza boxes into Jacob and Eve's outstretched arms. They turned, and with little steps made their way carefully to the table. The sweet smell of garlic filled the air.

Abi took the tubs of ice cream and placed them in a cool box on the worktop.

"Enjoy," the man said.

"Thanks." Abi closed the door. A box of dough balls clutched to her chest, she beamed at Becky. "You won't believe what happened today."

Becky saw her sister's mouth moving, telling her more, but her words were swallowed up in a blast of yells and screams as the various box lids were prised open.

"What? I can't hear you."

"I'll tell you later." Abi's jubilant voice rose above the noise. "Let's get this party started. Tuck in, guys."

Becky pushed her face close to Abi's. "Tell me now."

"Why don't you both go outside?" Ben placed his wine glass onto the worktop and took the box of dough balls from Abi. "I'll sort the kids' food."

Becky snatched the door open. Abi gave a nonchalant shrug, grabbed another glass of wine and sauntered out into the garden.

In the distance, a pheasant called.

Abi leaned against the wall of The Barn and giggled. "What's up?"

"You spent our money ... on pizzas. How could you?"

"Lighten up." Abi raised her glass and took a sip. "Then I'll tell you what's happened."

The words bored through Becky. Not another person telling her what to do? A knot formed in her chest. She opened her mouth to protest, but Abi cut in first.

"Megan Olds called today. You'll never–"

"Don't change the subject."

Becky flinched. That's what her mother used to say. The knot tightened. All she wanted was for Abi to answer her, and for her opinions and views to be considered first for once.

"Megan wants–"

"I don't care about Megan and her cakes. You shouldn't have spent the money on non-essentials. It's a joint account."

Abi stretched out a hand and touched Becky's arm. "Shit lunch, eh?"

Becky took a pace backwards. "What?"

A chuckle escaped from Abi's mouth. "Didn't Jess bother to turn up? Or did Stevie-boy give her a time limit?"

"How dare you?"

"Whoops. None of my business." Abi squinted at her empty glass and turned towards the kitchen.

"I haven't finished yet," Becky yelled.

Abi spun round. "Know what your problem is? You don't listen."

"At least I keep my word."

Even as the words flowed uncontrolled from her mouth, Becky realised how hypocritical she was being. After all, she'd withdrawn money from the account as well.

"Who the hell cares? If you don't like what I do, then go live somewhere else." Abi stepped up to Becky. Alcohol wafted into her face. "It's what you want anyway."

Becky straightened her shoulders and thrust her face close to Abi's. "I might just do that."

"I'm surprised you've stood it so long. I'll help you pack."

"Don't put yourself out on my account," Becky spat back.

The kitchen door swung open. Ben ran across the grass and stood between them.

"Stop it."

Abi pointed at Becky. "She's a tight-ass."

"At least I'm not a drunk."

"Piss off," Abi hissed.

"Stop this. Now." Ben veered round to Abi. "Your kids can hear everything."

On cue, Eve broke into a long wail.

Colour drained from Abi's face. She gawped at Becky, covered her mouth with her hand and rushed into the kitchen.

A shiver ran over Becky's body. What had just happened?

Ben came up beside her. "Why're you so angry with Abi? It's just a few pizzas."

"We agreed not to spend ..." It all seemed so silly, now she said it out loud.

He ran a hand through his hair. "You know how hard it is for Abi with three kids. She doesn't need this."

Becky gripped her hands together. Felt the rough skin and callouses from too much baking, washing-up detergent, and hot water.

"I work hard too." A sob escaped from her lips. "My life isn't that wonderful."

"Surely Megan's offer deserves to be celebrated?"

Becky jerked away from him. "Why does everyone keep talking about Megan? A few extra cakes aren't going to help."

"Didn't Abi tell you what happened today? The reason for the party?"

Dread coursed through her. She fought the urge to flee.

"Megan wants to rent the old stables and grazing for her kids' ponies. She was happy to barter and agreed to pay the electricity connection charge to cover all the livery costs."

"Why wasn't I consulted first?"

Her mother's words again.

Ben sighed. "Abi only accepted on the basis that you sorted all the practical details and finances with Megan."

Becky turned and ran up the lane, before veering into one of the fields where Ben had made hay the previous day. Big round bales dotted the shorn grass. She finally came to a halt. Her chest heaved in a struggle to pull in the warm evening air. She dropped to her knees and twisted around to lean against one of the bales. The course texture pricked the nape of her neck.

How could she have been so stupid and unreasonable? She'd used Abi as a scapegoat for her bruised feelings. But what had tipped her over the edge? Was it the happy scene that greeted her when she stepped into the kitchen? The easy relationship developing between Abi and Ben? The way those children loved Abi?

A single tear tracked down Becky's cheek.

Then again, when Becky had begun to think they were a team, Abi had no qualms in telling her to leave Vellangoose. Abi was just like David and Jess, telling her what to do and think. None of them had her back. Not John. Not her dad. Not Natalie.

The shrill ring of her mobile pierced the silence. She glanced at the illuminated name. David. She cut the call off.

Exhausted, she leaned her head against the bale and looked up. In the distance, the sun painted the sky pale apricot and lilac on its descent towards the sea. Her eyes fluttered. She forced them open. They fluttered again, then closed.

A noise woke her. She sat up, then scrambled to her feet and peered into the night. Across the field, The Barn was in darkness.

A gunshot rang out. Lamp lights flashed in the distance. She automatically dropped into a crouch. No. Not the lampers again? Another shot came from beyond the woods.

She clung to the bale.

Eventually, an owl called across the valley. Something small rustled through the grass stubble nearby. The lampers had gone.

She stood and walked towards The Barn.

In the living room, she slipped off her shoes and got into bed. She strained to hear a 'goodnight' or a whispered 'sorry' in the darkness. A few moments later, she tugged the duvet over her head.

She'd leave Vellangoose first thing in the morning.

22

18 June

Abi opened her eyes, then quickly closed them. Sharp pains jabbed at her temples and her mouth felt like a cesspit. She'd got the mother of all hangovers. She groaned. Only herself to blame.

Eve's small body stirred against her side. She gently moved away, rolled onto her knees and raised her head. Two solemn, electric-blue eyes studied her, before Grace's face burst into a wide grin.

Abi pushed herself to her feet, picked up her youngest daughter and whispered into her hair. "Shush, sweetheart." There was no way she was up for one of Grace's early morning, baby-babbling sessions. "Let's not wake your brother or sister just yet." Abi's head pounded; the longer everyone slept, the better. Besides, it was Sunday.

She stumbled to the bathroom. There was no need to look in the mirror, she already knew what she'd see: bloodshot eyes, blotchy skin and frizzy hair. She always looked a wreck the morning after she'd drunk too much. She splashed cold water onto her face.

Through half-closed eyes, she topped and tailed Grace using a few inches of soapy water in the bath. Her daughter clasped the wet flannel in her chubby hands, gurgled, and rubbed her face. On automatic pilot, Abi dried and dressed her. Finally, her happy daughter was ready to face the world. Shame she didn't feel the same.

In the kitchen, she lifted Grace into her highchair, and with the back of her hand made a space amid the pile of pizza boxes and dirty dishes scattered over the table.

Buddy circled her legs, then ran to the door. A soft growl came from his throat.

"Stop, Buddy. You're doing my head in." She let him out. He raced through the garden and over the hedge, his nose to the ground.

Jacob and Eve, bleary-eyed and still in their pyjamas, made their way to the table, dragged the chairs across the concrete floor and sat down.

Becky followed them into the room. Shoulders slumped, she tottered over to the worktop and gripped the edge with both hands.

Abi blinked. Pale-faced, hair stuck up in tufts, Becky still had on the white jeans she'd worn the day before, except now they were smeared with grass stains and dirt.

Something about the previous evening nagged at the edges of Abi's mind, but her head was too fuzzy to make sense of what had happened.

"Mummy, the milk's horrible," Eve whimpered.

"I'll get some more later. You'll have to eat your cereal dry for now."

Becky stared at the pile of empty boxes and ice cream cartons, then blinked. She fumbled for the roll of black rubbish bags, unfurled one, shook it open, and picked up one of the pizza boxes. For a moment, she stood with it held between her thumb and forefinger, then she let both the box and the bag drop to the floor, delved amongst the clutter on the surface, gathered up her baking equipment and tins, and returned to the living room.

Why was Becky acting so strange? Abi rubbed her temple. If only she could remember last evening. Had she let her big gob get the better of her? It wouldn't be the first time.

"I'm thirsty." A whine edged into Eve's voice. "Want something to drink."

"Have some water," Abi absentmindedly answered as she tried to piece together what she might have said or done.

Then, images bombarded her. A moan escaped from her lips. Not only had the events of the previous evening flashed through her mind in technicolour, so had the words she'd spoken. Had she truly told Becky to leave Vellangoose? She turned in the direction of the living room. Please don't let her sister be packing.

"Mummy, there are funny bits in my water."

Abi swung round. Eve held a glass of cloudy water close to her face, then tilted it towards her mouth.

"What did you put in it?" She snatched the tumbler from her daughter's hand and scowled at the murky liquid, unsure what the bits were.

"Jacob did it."

Becky returned, moved past her, and picked up more of her belongings.

"For God's sake, Jacob, stop messing around. I'm not in the mood today."

"I didn't do anything." Jacob rushed to the sink and turned the tap on. "Look. See. Bits."

At the sight of the unidentifiable fragments, fear coursed through Abi. "Did Eve swallow any of it?" She gripped his arm.

"Mum?" Jacob's voice quivered.

"Answer me."

He shook his head. "No, she didn't."

She crushed Eve to her chest and wrapped her arm around Jacob. "I'm so sorry to have shouted. It's not your fault. Mummy was scared."

Eve hiccupped and pulled away. "I only wanted to look. I wasn't going to drink it." She hiccupped again. "Why's the water smelly?"

At the sink, Becky now held the glass of water up to the light. A deep line had formed between her eyes.

Every instinct told Abi she needed to shield her kids from any more trouble. She plastered a smile onto her face, stood, and picked up a packet of coco pops.

"Finish your breakfast. There's nothing to worry about." She walked across to Becky.

"What do you think it is?"

The kids' inane chatter in the background filled the silence.

"Could there be something wrong with the water tank or the pipes?" Anxiety shot through Abi. What if it was serious? They had no spare money. "We'll need to take a look."

Becky placed the glass in the sink, stepped aside and headed for the hallway.

A knock on the front door stopped Abi from following. Ben? Please let it be Ben. He would help them.

It was Kate. She'd forgotten that Kate and her kids were coming over from Penryn for the day. Abi hadn't seen much of them since the move to Vellangoose, but the sight of her old school friend was like a miracle. If there was anybody she'd trust her kids with that morning, it was Kate.

Abi reached out and tugged her inside. "Thank God, you're here. Something's up with the water supply. I'll need to stay and sort it. Could you take the kids?" She gripped her friend's arm. "Please. I'll pick them up later."

Kate moved her lips to speak, then reached over and plucked Grace from her highchair. She turned towards Jacob and Eve with a big smile on her face.

"Hey, guys. You need to get dressed if you want to play with Alfie and George. If you're good, we'll go to the beach later and have cheesy chips for lunch."

Ten minutes later, with the kids settled in Kate's car, Abi grabbed her friend in a big bear-hug. "I'm sorry to wreck the day. I'll make it up to you. Promise."

Back in the kitchen, she sagged against the inside of the closed door.

Becky now sat at the table munching on coco pops straight from the packet.

Abi shook her head. If only she could think clearly. Was the hangover causing her to overreact? Surely Becky wasn't about to leave Vellangoose? And the problem with the water? It might just be some blip with the system or something, mightn't it? Old wells and tanks were like that.

There was only one way to find out. She pushed herself away from the support of the door and looked at Becky.

"The water tank needs to be checked."

Becky continued munching.

"Please come and look at the tank with me?"

"You can manage on your own," Becky said.

Abi's eyes unexpectedly brimmed with tears. "Please."

Finally, Becky nodded.

Outside, Buddy was already at the tank, circling the base, his tongue lolling. An acrid, rank odour permeated the air.

Abi clambered to the top of the concrete structure. Becky followed her. Without saying anything, together they reached for the metal hatch, heaved it to one side, and peered through the hatchway.

A disgusting stench rushed up into Abi's face. Her stomach contracted and bile rose into her throat.

A fox floated in the water. His once magnificent tail fanned out behind him. Sightless eyes stared into nothingness. Unthinkable stuff oozed from a hole in the animal's side and drifted in the water.

Beside her, Becky retched, stumbled to her feet and dropped onto the ground. She half-ran, half-lurched across the field, before stopping at the gate to the yard. Abi came up beside her, cleared her throat and spat on the ground. With the edge of her sweater, she rubbed her face several times. All that work and all that cleaning had been for nothing. She kicked the gate.

"Fuck it."

"The lampers did it." Becky's voice was a croak.

"That was weeks ago."

"Heard them last night. Saw their light in the woods, near Ben's land."

"Fucking Veronica Williams."

"You can't know for certain it was her," Becky said.

"She wants us out of here. I know she's behind it all."

"I don't understand why." Becky rubbed at a stain on her jeans. "Vellangoose is just a dump to them."

Abi didn't understand either. She dug at the ground with the tip of her boot. "The tank will need to be drained and cleaned again."

"You'll also need to get the water quality re-tested. Ben will help."

"Maybe not." Abi sighed. "I had an argument with him as well."

"Why?"

"He was acting a bit strange all evening. Tense. Guess I must've nagged him about his mood a bit too much."

"Oh, Abi. He's a good man."

"Best guy I've ever known. Trust me to balls it up."

"He'll come round when you tell him what's happened." Becky reached for the gate and opened it. "If all else fails, you can get him to help under the barter arrangement."

Abi grabbed her arm. "Please don't take any notice of what I said last night. I'm always a nightmare when I'm rat-faced."

"We both said silly things, but you were right. It's time for me to go." Becky walked towards The Barn. "I've been here five months now. It's more than long enough."

"If it's because of the money, I'll pay you back. I know I should've asked you first."

"I think this is the point at which I should confess that I used Vellangoose monies to pay for Jess's lunch." A smile flickered across Becky's face. "A very expensive lunch, I might add."

"So, we're evens. You'll stay then?"

"Long enough to clear out the tank, then I'll start making plans to move on. You'll have electricity soon, then you and the children will have the home you always wanted."

"I don't get it. Up until last night, you and I were doing okay, weren't we?"

"Things came to a head yesterday. Jess cut our lunch short because Steve came home early, then I saw David on the seafront walking arm in arm with Veronica Williams." Becky pushed open the kitchen door and stepped inside. "He'd told me earlier that neither he nor the firm had any recent dealings with her."

"Bloody hell."

"I've had enough of being trampled upon by everyone: my husband, Natalie, Dad. And you." Becky took a deep breath. "I'm done with being told how I ought to live my life." She picked up the crumpled rubbish bag she'd dropped earlier. "I'll clear up here and then quickly let out the chickens. You get the wheelbarrow, shovels and brushes. We've got a fox to bury and a tank to clean."

Two hours later, the body of the fox, wrapped in plastic bags, lay in the wheelbarrow. Abi and Becky had also drained the tank and scooped the awful muck onto the grass. Abi leaned on the shovel. Becky was right, they needed to bury the fox, but where? The ground was dry and solid, and any digging would be hard. Maybe the woods would be easier? Or, perhaps in the ditch where the ground was damper? Abi scanned the bottom of the hedge. Something caught her gaze. She moved over and picked up an old black glove. The ripped cuff flapped across her palm. Rage pulsed through her. Although faded and partially worn, an embossed company logo and the name could still be seen – Williams Estates and Haulage.

"That woman is responsible. Veronica–"

Abi broke off at the sound of her phone ringing. Before she'd had a chance to say hello, Kate's voice came in short gasps.

"Grace is vomiting. Started five minutes ago. Now she's got the trots."

"I'm on my way."

Kate screamed. "She's gone all stiff and jerky. I'm ringing for an ambulance. Hurry."

The phone went dead. Abi ran flat out for The Barn.

Becky caught up with her. "What's wrong?"

"Grace is sick." In the kitchen, Abi snatched up the keys to the camper van. "Kate's calling an ambulance."

"What? Grace was fine earlier."

A vision of Grace gurgling and laughing first thing came unbidden into Abi's mind, followed immediately by another image. Her legs buckled, and she flung her arm out and gripped Becky's arm.

"I washed Grace before breakfast. She likes to play with the flannel. Sometimes she sucks it. What if she swallowed some of that stinking water?"

"I'll drive you." Becky's voice was suddenly businesslike. "We'll take my car. It's quicker."

Abi stood frozen to the spot. If Grace had drunk water contaminated with muck from a dead fox, what might that do to her?

Becky's voice broke through. "Treliske or Kate's place? Abi? Abi? Where to?"

"Kate's house. She said she'll call me if the ambulance arrives before we get there. Please drive fast."

A sob rose in Abi's throat. "Please God, don't let my baby die."

The journey in the ambulance to Treliske Hospital was horrendous. Abi held Grace's small hand for every nightmare mile until the doors at last opened and a woman doctor with short-cropped dark hair and a precise, calm voice took charge of Grace.

For the next thirty minutes, all Abi could do was stare at the circle of emergency staff grouped around her daughter's bed. The air in the small side room felt too thin, too fine to draw into her lungs. Her arms folded tight across her chest, Abi dug her fingernails deep into the flesh of her biceps, the pain a welcome distraction.

"Miss Pascoe?" The doctor moved in front of her.

"Is she going to be alright?" Abi tried to push around the woman, overcome by the need to hold Grace. "Please tell me she's going to be alright."

"Please, Miss Pascoe." The doctor's arm blocked her way. "I'm Dr Roberta Smith, Consultant Paediatrician. I need you to stay here, to help me, so I can help Grace."

In the background, most of the emergency staff quietly moved away from the bed and made their way out of the room.

A lump formed in Abi's throat. She pushed it away, fought for control, but fearful words tumbled out.

"Don't let her die."

Dr Smith's face remained impassive. She bent her head and looked at the notes clutched in her hand. "I understand Grace became unresponsive at a friend's house following a violent bout of vomiting and diarrhoea." She ran her finger down the notes. "You already know she vomited again in the ambulance, and according to the paramedics, she may have suffered a small febrile seizure."

"What does that mean?"

"Nothing to be too alarmed about. It's not uncommon for young children to have a seizure or a fit when their temperature is elevated. Has Grace had any seizures before? Any family history?"

Abi shook her head. "It's all my fault. I washed her in dirty water."

"So I see from the notes. Please tell me more."

"I washed her with a wet flannel." Abi pressed a hand to her mouth. "I think she sucked in some of the water."

"Dirty water wouldn't normally cause such a reaction. At least, not so quickly. It's possible Grace had the beginnings of a stomach bug or cold, and absorbing contaminated water just accelerated matters."

Christ, she was a crap mother. If she hadn't had a hangover, she might've noticed sooner that Grace was unwell.

"It was a dead fox. The water was full of muck." She rushed on. "I didn't know until much later when my other daughter wanted a glass of water. It was then we noticed the … bits." She groaned. "Why didn't I think about Grace then? Why?"

"Please, Miss Pascoe, don't start blaming yourself. We've already started Grace on a course of antibiotics, and blood samples have been taken to give us a better picture of what's going on."

"I feel so useless. What can I do?"

Dr Smith nodded towards a woman with apple-red cheeks. "Staff Nurse Harris has been assigned to look after Grace. She'll explain everything and stay with you both. Try not to worry. I'll be back again when I have the test results."

The nurse smiled at Abi. "Call me Sue. Come over here and talk to Grace. Although she's sedated, she'll be comforted by your voice."

Abi followed Sue to the bed, leaned over and stroked Grace's face. Tubes trailed across the sheets, taking fluids to her tiny body. Monitors beeped and chirped. Grace's hand and fingers felt warm and flexible. Normal. For a moment, a rush of hope ran through Abi's body.

"Grace, sweetheart." Abi's eyes swam with tears. She blinked them away. "Everything's going to be okay. Mummy's here."

She continued to talk while staff moved in and out of the room and Sue sat like a rock on the other side of Grace's bed. Despite the nurse's presence, Abi felt so alone. Maybe, she should've asked Becky to follow the ambulance? Why hadn't she? Was it because she'd always had to cope with the kids on her own? Maybe she didn't know how to ask for help, even from her own sister? She was such a screw-up.

After a while, she rested her head on the edge of the bed and closed her eyes.

Her mobile phone vibrated in her pocket and she woke instantly. She scanned the text message on the screen.

"It's my friend," she said to Sue. "I need to ring her. It's about my other kids."

"I'll be right here with Grace all the time." Sue patted Abi's arm. "Why don't you go into the corridor and ring from there?"

Outside the door, the combination of bright strip lights running the length of the corridor, the relentless loud humdrum of staff, visitors, and trolleys moving back and forth, pounded Abi's senses. How could everything seem so normal when ... She took a breath, pulled her mobile from her pocket and with a trembling hand pressed Kate's name.

23

18 June

Becky lifted the light brown egg from the nest box. Her hand shook. The egg rolled over her fingers and dropped to the ground. She watched in horror as the mix of orange yolk and albumen seeped into the grass.

She gripped the wire of the chicken run. It was over two hours since she'd driven Abi to Kate's house in Penryn. If only the ghastly images of Grace's still body and Abi's terrified face would leave her mind. She should have gone to Treliske to support Abi. Why hadn't she?

She shook her head, stepped away from the chicken pen and forced herself to concentrate on the jobs to be done. She needed to finish collecting the eggs, then top-up the feeders and water troughs. Her stomach clenched. The fox was still in the wheelbarrow by the tank. She looked in the direction of the meadow behind The Barn, then quickly turned away. That job she would leave until later.

A vehicle hurtled down the lane. Startled, Becky jerked around as it screeched to a halt by the gate.

Dressed in a navy boiler suit and green wellies, Megan Olds got out and strode towards her. She reached Becky in a matter of seconds and stood wide-legged, with her hands on her hips. A sun-bleached baseball cap perched awkwardly on top of her red hair.

"Just the person I wanted to see. The stables, my dear. Abi told you about our …" Megan squinted at the buckets and wicker basket. "Late feeding them, aren't you? And collecting the eggs? It doesn't do to mess with their routine. Poor dears don't like it. Won't lay if ..."

Becky eyes filled with tears.

"My dear. Whatever's the matter?" Big bear arms surrounded Becky and crushed her face into the boiler suit. A mix of dog, fried bacon and expensive perfume rose from the rough material. Large hands thumped her back. "There, there, nothing's that bad. No real harm done."

Becky took in gulps of air, stepped back a pace, and pushed her uncombed curls back behind her ear. Her cheeks were hot to the touch and she knew red blotches peppered her neck.

"That's it, girl. Deep slow breathes." A whiff of garlic wafted into the space between them. "Nice and slow. Silly panic attacks. We all get them at times."

"Grace is in Treliske Hospital. She's very poorly."

"Not that sweet little girl?"

Becky blew her nose and nodded.

"What's wrong with her?"

"Fox."

"Where?" Megan spun around and scanned the meadow.

"In the water tank." A sob escaped from Becky's throat.

Megan's eyebrows disappeared under the peak of the baseball cap. "Calm down, my dear, and tell me everything from the beginning."

As Becky looked at solid, no-nonsense Megan standing in front of her, tension oozed from her body. She let out a long breath and told her about the dead fox, the contaminated water, and finally their fear that Grace had drunk some of the dreadful liquid.

When she finished, Megan grunted. "Is the fox still in the tank?"

"We got it out. It's in a wheelbarrow by the tank." Becky shuddered. She could still detect the fox scent on her hands even though she'd scrubbed them in the nearby river for ages.

"Wicked. Wicked. Lampers, not the fox." Megan straightened her shoulders and pushed out her chest. "What's done is done. Time for action. We're wasting daylight." She pulled out her mobile phone. "I'll rally the troops."

"The troops?"

"Help, my dear. Help, that's what this situation needs." Megan tapped on a name and held the mobile to her ear. It was answered immediately. "Hugh. Darling." Before she received a reply, Megan issued a list of instructions to the person on the other end, blew him a kiss, hung up, and turned her gaze onto Becky. "Let's get to work."

Becky quickly collected the rest of the eggs and topped up the containers. Megan poured river water from the bucket into the troughs. As they worked together, Megan filled her in on the details of the barter deal she'd proposed to Abi the previous evening. It only took a few minutes for the transaction to be agreed – in exchange for the use of stables for two ponies, shared grazing, and the availability of the woods for the Pony Club events, Megan would organise the installation of, and payment for, electricity at Vellangoose.

Excitement zipped through Becky despite the awfulness of the day. She couldn't stop a big grin forming on her face at the thought of hot water, instant light, and a working cooker, then her smile died. She'd be leaving Vellangoose soon.

She felt an inexplicable urge to hug Megan but restrained herself.

"Can you tell me about the Williams family?" she asked instead.

"Your father?"

"No, no." Panic rushed through Becky. She wasn't ready for that yet. "It's Veronica Williams I'm interested in. What's she like?"

"The main thing to remember about Veronica is, she always gets what she wants."

"Oh dear."

"Spit it out. Quicker I know what this is about, the quicker I can answer."

For some reason that she couldn't explain, Becky let it all pour out: the lampers, Buddy being hurt, the conditions of the Trust. She took a deep breath and rushed on to describe the black tattered glove Abi found with the Williams Estates and Haulage logo on it, and the suspicion it was Veronica Williams behind the dead fox in the tank. She even told Megan about Jess, and how worried she was. Was this what it felt like to have a mother you could talk to, or was she simply losing it?

Megan picked up a container, rinsed it out, and topped it up with water.

"I remember when Veronica and your father got married. All the villagers came out to see them as if they were royalty. I've never forgotten it." She pushed her baseball cap back and stared into the distance. "I'm not sure that they ever loved each other. Marriage of money and the merger of properties more like."

"They stayed together though."

Talk of her father made Becky feel uncomfortable. She fiddled with her hair.

"Money always does. Your father had many ..." Megan cleared her throat, "dalliances. But you know that, otherwise you and Abi wouldn't be here." She let out a loud chortle. "My, he was a handsome devil. Charming when he wanted something. All the women around here fancied him."

A small bantam rooster strutted in front of Becky. His impressive black tail feathers swirled behind him with every step. His golden mane glistened in the afternoon sun.

At that moment, Grace's still form rose unbidden in front of Becky's eyes. She rushed on.

"Vellangoose has been derelict for decades. Have you any idea who lived here last?"

"Ah, that would be Constance, Veronica's younger sister. Another beautiful woman. Moved into Vellangoose when she married Nicholas Hodges."

"Hodges? Any relation to Steven Hodges?"

"Father, my dear."

"Oh." She remembered now, during the anxiety and haze of Jess and Steve's flying visit, her daughter saying Steve had lived at Vellangoose as a child.

"Proper hoo-ha when Constance married Nicholas. He wasn't from a moneyed background and that didn't go down well. Ex-Air Force Officer. Engineer or something. He travelled a lot. His downfall. The travelling, not the engineering."

Becky broke into a trot to keep up with Megan as she strode towards the last pen. "Nice set up you have here. Very nice."

"Did Henry Williams own Vellangoose back then?" Becky poured food into one of the plastic bowls.

"You should ask Jeffery Bartlett. He worked for them. Pretty certain though it was Constance's place, or at least her side of the family." Megan rubbed her nose with the back of her hand. "Probably got transferred to Henry as a tax dodge."

"What happened to Constance and Nicholas? Why did they leave Vellangoose?"

"My dear, it was shocking. They were both killed in a car crash in Brazil. A terrible waste of young lives."

"Oh."

"There'd been a right old scandal before the accident. Kept the villagers talking for months. Nicholas found himself a new woman while he was working in Brazil and got her pregnant by all accounts. Constance fell apart."

Becky extracted a couple of eggs and put them in the basket. Poor Constance. Did all husbands do the dirty on their wives?

"The local gossips seem to think that Constance travelled to Brazil to beg Nicholas to come home. Next thing we hear, they're both dead." Megan shook her head. "Remember Mum being upset because Veronica didn't bring their bodies home. Sad, so sad."

"What about Steve? Was he involved in the crash?"

"He was in Cornwall with Veronica. She'd been looking after him for some time while Constance tried to sort herself out." Megan turned and strode towards the gate. "No time to dilly-dally. Stables to clear. Glad we reached an agreement, so glad. I'll send Hugh over to you when he arrives," she called over her shoulder.

Becky watched Megan's retreating back. She'd never met anyone quite like her. She'd said more to her in the last forty minutes than she had to her mother in a lifetime.

She picked up the buckets and egg basket. Next on her list was a call to Detective Inspector Jack Carter, the police officer who'd spoken to Veronica Williams and Steve Hodges after Buddy had been injured. Not that it had got him anywhere, but he had told her and Abi to get in touch if there was anything else they were concerned about. Well, there was something now.

Ten minutes later, she poured bleach into the kitchen sink and scoured the surface for several minutes. Later, she would need to go out and get some water from her dad's place. If only Abi would ring. She scrubbed harder.

She jumped at a knock on the door. A tall, very attractive man stood on the step. He directed his startlingly blue-green eyes onto Becky.

"Mrs Farrow. Or can I presume to call you Becky?" His blonde hair flopped across his forehead as he held one strong, well-manicured hand towards her. "Hugh. Megan's husband." He dropped a five-gallon plastic container of bottled water at her feet.

"Oh." She took his hand and gazed at him. "Thank you."

"If you would point me in the direction of the tank, we'll make a start." He indicated towards two men unloading various buckets and commercial bottles of disinfectant from the back of a battered Land Rover. "Got Jeffery and Aaron with me. I think you know them already?"

"How do, Mrs Farrow. Sorry to hear about your troubles." Jeffery nodded as he walked by, a broom over one shoulder. "'Tis this way, Mr Olds."

Becky stared at Hugh's muscled frame as he walked with easy strides towards the tank. He had to be at least ten years younger than Megan.

She watched as Megan joined the men by the tank and stood almost shoulder to shoulder with her husband. She rested her hand gently on Hugh's arm as they talked. He smiled down at her. A pang of envy forced Becky to look away.

She had to do something, and helping Megan was the more attractive option. An hour later, she stepped back and looked at the heap of old straw and other unwanted bits she and Megan had removed from the stables.

"Time for some tea, I think." Megan rubbed her hands free of debris. "Some of your marvellous cake would go down a treat."

Megan pulled various mugs from the kitchen shelves as if she lived in the place.

"They'll finish cleaning the tank today. Jeffery, bless him, brought along a strong padlock and chain to secure the hatch. We don't want a repeat of that nasty incident, do we?"

To erase another awful image of the dead fox, Becky stared through the doorway into the garden. A rambling rose, heavy with pink flowers, waved in the light breeze. Although she and Abi had cleared an area for the children to play, the main borders still consisted of brambles, straggly shrubs, and a few hardy flowers that had survived the neglect of many years. A blackbird hopped under the old apple tree in the far corner. In her mind's eye, Becky imagined the lovely garden it could become if she stayed. With a sigh, she turned back to Megan.

"I don't know how to thank you."

"Nonsense, my dear. Many hands and all that. Have you called the police?"

"The detective inspector who was involved when Buddy was hurt wasn't available, but I left a message for him." Becky bent down and stroked Buddy's ears.

"Keep on at them. Hugh's holding off burying the fox just in case the police want to see it." Megan straightened her cap. "Must go. If you'd take the men their tea, I would be grateful. Hugh left our little blighters with my mum. She'll need rescuing by now."

A shrill ring filled the air. Becky snatched at her mobile phone.

Megan stopped in the doorway.

It was Abi. Becky's heart thumped. Dear God, please let it be good news.

24

Abi's call to Becky was answered on the second ring, but when Abi opened her mouth to speak no words came out. She sobbed uncontrollably down the line.

"Abi? Abi?" Becky yelled. "Is Grace okay?"

"Oh, Becky." Abi swiped her eyes with the palm of her hand. "She looks awful. So sick. It's my fault."

"Don't think that. You weren't to know."

"I should've seen the water was polluted when I washed her."

"You washed in it as well. Why aren't you sick?"

"The doctor said adults often have immunity. Grace had an extreme reaction for some reason, and she's just a baby, so her resistance is less to start with." Abi yanked her hand through her hair. "This waiting around is awful. I can't do anything to help."

"You're with her. That counts."

Abi took a deep breath. "Have you done anything with the fox?"

She half-listened while her sister told her about Megan's visit, the tank being cleaned by Hugh, Jeffery and Aaron, and her telephone call to the police.

Down the corridor, Nurse Harris appeared at the doorway of Grace's room and beckoned another nurse inside.

"I must go. I've told Kate that you'll pick up Jacob and Eve shortly."

"Me? Wouldn't they be happier with Kate?"

"She's got an early shift tomorrow." Abi halted outside Grace's room. "Besides, the kids will be happier at home with their usual routine."

"But ... I'm not the right person to look after them. How could you–"

"For God's sake, just do it?"

There was silence at the end of the phone.

"I need them to be with family." Abi forced a bright tone into her voice. "I'll tell them to be good for their auntie."

The silence continued for a few more seconds, then Becky replied. "I'll go now."

Back in Grace's room, the machines droned on and on. Abi whispered and sang softly to her daughter, only stopping when various nurses and doctors came and undertook yet more checks and procedures.

"Miss Pascoe."

Abi looked up. Dr Smith's dark hair stuck up in spikes as if she'd run her fingers through it many times.

"Miss Pascoe, the preliminary test results are back. As we suspected, it's a virulent bacterial infection, consistent with having been in contact with contaminated water."

So, it was her fault.

Dr Smith continued. "Good news. It confirms what we thought, and Grace has already received the correct treatment very quickly."

"When will she wake up? She seems so out of it."

"Grace is under controlled sedation to allow her immune system to recover and to minimise stress. Her condition is stable. We plan to reduce her sedation later this evening. I suggest you take the opportunity to have some rest yourself."

With a start, Abi sat up, opened her eyes and looked at her watch. 7:50 p.m. She stretched her neck from side to side, her hand still firmly holding onto Grace's. Thankfully, some colour had returned to Grace's cheeks. She looked like she always did when she was asleep, except she didn't have her thumb in her mouth.

Abi got up and walked to the window. Several cars moved in and out of the staff car park. Shift changes? Nurse Harris had left a while ago, and another nurse, whose name she hadn't caught, had taken over her shift.

The nurse came up beside her. "Grace is doing fine. Why don't you get yourself a coffee and something to eat?"

Outside the main entrance to Treliske Hospital, Abi sucked in a deep gulp of fresh air, then moved to a stone wall and sat down. Rough concrete dug into her legs as she wriggled to find a flat spot to put her hot cup of vending machine coffee on. From her bag, she pulled out a large chocolate bar and tore open the wrapper.

A man walked across the car park. His long legs covered the ground in easy strides. Although dressed in a business suit, his tie was loose and half his shirt hung outside his trousers.

She stopped chewing. It was the detective inspector who'd called at Vellangoose when Buddy was hurt. She quickly got to her feet.

"Detective Inspector?"

"Carter." He stopped in front of her. "May I join you?" He indicated for her to sit again and sat down beside her. "Just the person I wanted to see."

"You got Becky's message?"

"That's what I wanted to talk to you about but, firstly, how's Grace?"

"Stable. That's all they'll say." Her voice threatened to break, but she forced herself to continue. "They hope to wake her up soon."

The detective inspector rummaged in one trouser pocket, then the other, and pulled out a pack of chewing gum sticks. "Want one?"

She shook her head.

"I popped into Vellangoose early this evening. I took a statement from Mrs Farrow and picked up the glove you found."

"It belongs to one of Veronica Williams's men. It proves she's responsible for nearly killing Grace."

He unwrapped a piece of chewing gum and popped it into his mouth. "Sorry, gave up smoking, now I'm addicted to this stuff." He shoved the remainder of the pack back into his pocket before he spoke. "There's nothing to suggest that Mrs Williams was involved in this incident. In fact, I dropped into Boswyn Manor after speaking to Mrs Farrow. I saw Mrs Williams. She'd just come back from a three-day trip to London."

"Of course she had. Covered her back again. Whether she meant that to happen or not, Grace got hurt, and she's behind it all."

"I also had a preliminary discussion with Steven Hodges, the General Manager of Williams Estates and Haulage. He couldn't identify who owned the glove. Said it came from the communal pool of protective clothing that all the men dip into as required."

"And you believed him?"

"I managed to speak to a few of his men who were working today, but they could all account for their whereabouts."

"Damn them all." Abi stood up and strode back inside.

Detective Inspector Carter fell in step next to her. "Sorry, it's not what you wanted to hear. I will continue to make inquiries."

Abi stopped. Something didn't feel right. She turned to face him. "Why are you involved in this case? A bit low level for a detective inspector, isn't it? And, why so quick off the mark with your ... preliminary discussions?"

He scratched the side of his nose. "A child's life has been put at risk."

"But you were involved before, when only my dog was hurt." For a moment, she still couldn't figure out what nagged her, and then it came to her. "Veronica Williams has done this before, hasn't she?"

"That's not something I'm able to answer." He cleared his throat. "I'll keep you informed of any changes."

"I'll kill that woman."

"Miss Pascoe, don't take the law into your own hands. I'm warning you, keep away from Mrs Williams."

"Stuff your warning." She tried to shove past him.

He stepped in front of her. "I'm dealing with this." His lips tightened into a hard line. "Do you understand?"

For a few moments, she glared at him, then nodded.

Back in the room with Grace, Abi returned to her bedside vigil. A single tear ran down her cheek. Didn't Veronica Williams realise that a dead fox dumped in a water tank would hurt someone?

Of course she did.

Dr Smith came into the room, her face tired and pale. "We're about to take Grace off sedation."

"What if she doesn't wake up? What if she's brain-damaged?" Panic ran through Abi. The encounter with Detective Inspector Carter had pushed her over the edge.

"Miss Pascoe, there's no reason to suppose any of those things." Dr Smith walked up to the bed and adjusted one of the tubes. "It's 10:05 p.m. and Grace has been taken off controlled sedation. It'll take an hour or so before she wakes. I'll come back then."

Grace's chest rose and fell. Her eyes fluttered but remained shut.

Abi found herself praying. To whom or what, she didn't know.

The monitors continued to bleep and chirp.

"Grace, it's Mummy. Open your eyes, sweetheart."

Grace stirred but her eyes remained closed.

Dr Smith returned to the room, spoke to the nurse and checked the notes again. She moved to the bed, removed a pen from her pocket and ran it along the sole of Grace's foot. The foot jerked away. Dr Smith repeated the action.

Grace's eyelids flew open and two electric-blue eyes fixed onto Abi's face. A chubby hand flew up into the air and Grace plugged a thumb into her mouth.

An overwhelming surge of love engulfed Abi. She covered her daughter's face with kisses.

Nothing in the world felt better than this.

25

Becky stood at the kitchen window and stared out into the darkness. It was the early hours of Monday morning and she couldn't sleep. Jacob and Eve had gone to bed ages ago, Jacob in his room and Eve by the fireplace in the living room, in the space she normally shared with Abi and Grace. The children had been sullen and quiet on the journey back to Vellangoose, hardly ate anything for their evening meal and more-or-less ignored her.

Which was just how Becky had wanted it – no emotional ties.

So why did she feel so desolate, especially as Abi had rung late last evening to say Grace had regained consciousness?

Something touched Becky's leg. Startled, she looked down. Eve clung to her thigh.

With the girl's tousled hair, tear-stained face, and mouth turned down at the edges, Becky had to fight her maternal instinct to pick Eve up and hug her tight. Instead, she unfurled Eve's arms from her leg and took her by the hand.

"Let's get you tucked back into bed. You've got school tomorrow."

Ten minutes later, Becky crawled under her duvet at the other end of the living room, picked up her book and read a few pages by torchlight.

Suddenly, she sat bolt upright. Her book toppled to the floor. What had woken her? She got to her feet and peered through the window. Nothing. She cocked her head. Buddy's snores reassured her. It was 4:30 a.m. She returned to her bed, switched off the torch, and rolled onto her side. It was then she heard the sobs.

Eve hadn't even bothered to come to her for comfort this time.

Becky's hand covered her mouth. What sort of person had she become, letting a child suffer to protect her own emotions? She shoved the duvet aside, hurried across the living room and took Eve into her arms.

"Mummy. I want Mummy." Eve clung to her chest and sobbed. "Why doesn't she come home?"

"Shush. Don't cry. She and Grace will be back soon."

The hinge on the living room door squeaked. Jacob stood in the doorway. "My daddy never came back. Nor did Grace and Eve's. What if Mum …" His bottom lip trembled.

Becky patted the bed next to her. Jacob ran over and pulled the mix of sleeping bags, blankets and duvets over his skinny body. She tucked one arm around him and stroked Eve's hair with the other.

"Why don't we think about something nice we could get Grace, for when she comes home?"

"She likes chocolate buttons," piped up Eve.

Jacob frowned and in the early morning light he looked like some old man pondering on the worries of the world.

"Grace likes rabbits," he said. "We could get her a toy one."

"Can I help choose it?" Eve pushed away from Becky's chest and fixed her gaze onto her, then her tired little face crumpled. "I'd like one as well."

"Let's decide in the morning. It's school, remember. Time for sleep."

They nestled against her. She was trapped between them.

Eve reached up and kissed her, then snuggled down with her arm across Becky's stomach. "Night, night, Auntie Becky. You're nice. Love you."

Jacob turned his solemn eyes onto her again. "Night, Auntie Becky."

Becky stared at the two small bodies as they slept next to her. Their long, dark eyelashes fluttered over soft, perfect checks. She kissed the top of Eve's head, then Jacob's. They wriggled closer. It was at that moment that something snapped inside her. She had used all her willpower over the past few months to fight off feelings for these children, but now, despite all her efforts, love surged through her.

She always knew she had enough love for more than one child. It was John who'd said he only wanted Jess. Maybe if he'd been less interested in his nights out with his pals, his unsuccessful business ventures, and the other women, things might have been different? Becky pushed her head back against the pillow. Who was she kidding? Their marriage had been a farce. To compensate, she'd put all her energies into raising Jess and making Rose Cottage into the perfect home. John had jettisoned it all with no regard for her feelings.

Well, she was no longer the Becky Farrow who'd done what John wanted. She'd changed.

She hugged Jacob and Eve again. She hadn't just been renovating The Barn because it would add value to the property in some distant future. Neither had she probed Megan the previous day for information on Veronica Williams just to help Abi.

The Pascoe family were now her family, and Vellangoose had become her home.

Becky stood somewhat self-consciously outside the school gates. It had been many years since she'd waited for Jess, but things hadn't changed much; parents still gathered in little groups and clogged the area with cars.

Lisa normally collected Jacob and Eve from school and was happy for the arrangement to continue with Becky picking them up later from her, but Becky told Lisa over the phone that she would do the school run herself until Abi came home. Truth was, she didn't want to get into a face-to-face meeting with Lisa because she was David's sister, and though he'd left several voicemail and text messages for Becky since he'd cut their lunch short on Saturday, she hadn't replied.

"Thought your school run days were over?"

Becky turned to face Natalie. "Taking a bit of a risk talking to me, aren't you? What if Veronica Williams sees you?"

The smile on her sister's face died. "That's not funny. I heard what happened to you and that woman–"

"Abi."

"Everyone's talking about it. Is it true you found a dead fox in your water tank? And that the kid–"

"Grace."

"Alright. Alright." Natalie glared at her. "Well, is Grace in Treliske Hospital?"

"By courtesy of Veronica Williams."

"Surely not, Veronica wouldn't ..." Natalie's voice trailed off.

"If it wasn't for the skills of the wonderful staff at Treliske Hospital, I don't think Grace would be here now."

"Oh." Natalie stared into the distance. "Veronica is not someone to cross for sure. We've lost four clients because of her."

"You should speak to Detective Inspector Jack Carter. He's investigating the incidents. I'm sure he'd be interested in what you've just said."

Natalie looked quickly from side to side. "Don't be stupid. We can't afford any more trouble. And you ..." her voice dropped to a whisper, "you should leave that place before you get hurt."

With a quick nod of her head, her sister stepped away, then turned back, and squeezed Becky's hand. "If you need help with the children, you know where I am." Then with a toss of her immaculate hair, she was gone.

Back at Vellangoose an hour later, when the children were in the garden playing fetch with Buddy, her phone rang. Abi. Becky held her breath and pressed answer.

Her sister launched into a burst of animated conversation. Becky pulled out one of the kitchen chairs and sagged into it. Thank goodness, Grace was getting better by the minute.

"Is that Mum?" Jacob rushed up the steps from the garden. Eve and Buddy followed close behind.

"Mummy, Mummy," Eve yelled.

Becky studied Jacob and Eve as they talked to their mother in turns. So different from the two very subdued children she'd picked up at Kate's the evening before. How things had changed. How she'd changed.

"Auntie Becky," Jacob's voice broke into her thoughts, "Mum wants to speak to you."

He shoved the phone into her hand, grabbed the ball from the floor and shot out of the door. Eve and Buddy chased after him.

"How's it going?" Abi said. "Hope they're behaving themselves as I told them?"

"They've been great. Is Grace being discharged soon?"

"Dr Smith thinks it's unlikely that Grace has caught anything long-lasting, but she wants to keep her in for a bit longer for a few precautionary tests."

"Should I bring Jacob and Eve in to see you both?"

"Let them play. Hospital is not the place for kids."

Becky hesitated before speaking again. "Would it be alright if I took them to my dad's later?" She rushed on before Abi could respond. "I've got a load of orders for this week, and a dinner party to cater for. I need to check what ingredients I have."

"Will your dad be okay having my kids in his house?"

"He'll be fine. He's come to terms with the situation now."

What was a little white lie between them?

In truth, she and her dad hadn't discussed the subject of Vellangoose, or Abi, since the big argument. Still, if her dad wanted her to bake and cook for him, he'd have to put up with her and the children for a half-hour.

"Do what you think's best. Got to go." Abi paused. "Becky?"

"Yes."

"Thanks," Abi whispered, then hung up.

Becky moved to the doorway and called out. "I've got to go to my dad's. Do you want to come with me, or shall I ring Kate and see if you could go there and play?"

"We'll come with you," Jacob said.

"Good, come in now and get ready to go."

Eve sat on the kitchen floor with one leg in the air. Becky knelt and helped her fasten the sparkly plastic sandals she'd chosen to wear. Her niece had a puzzled look on her face.

"Do you honestly have a daddy? He must be so old."

"Not that old."

"My mummy doesn't have a daddy, does she?"

"Not anymore." One day Eve needed to know the truth about Henry Williams, but not from her.

"We have a gran," Jacob said.

"I want to see Gran." Eve's lower lip quivered.

"You can't, silly. She's in Aus … Australia."

Jacob glanced at Becky. "Mum and Gran had a fight. Do you think that's why Gran left because Mum was so angry?"

Becky was astonished at the child's perception.

"I'm sure that's not the case. People fight sometimes but it doesn't mean that they don't love each other."

She busied herself with the buckle of Eve's sandal. Best that she kept her nose out of this. Her track record with family relationships wasn't that good. Maybe one day, she and Abi would be able to talk about their father and their respective mothers.

"All done." She stood up. "Dad's got an allotment with lots of vegetables and fruit trees. If you're very good, he might have some fresh strawberries."

As she said the words, she prayed that her dad would be kind to them. She was taking a risk, she knew that, but it had to be faced at some point.

She reached for her bag and car keys. "OK, guys. Let's go."

Becky opened the door.

David stood on the step.

26

Abi longed to be free from the overheated room and the constant bleep-bleep of monitors. She couldn't wait to take Grace home, to hug Jacob and Eve, and to feel the fresh air at Vellangoose on her face.

She leant over the metal safety rails and ran a finger lightly over her daughter's soft, dimpled cheek. It felt warm, healthy, and wonderfully normal. A blanket of gratitude wrapped around Abi. She might have another day or so of this stupefying boredom and inactivity, but she'd put up with anything to ensure her daughter was fit and well again.

"Abi?"

She jerked around, looked at Nurse Sue Harris, and back down at Grace.

"Don't worry, Grace is fine." Sue smiled. "There's a young man outside asking to see you. Ben Vincent?"

Abi's heart thumped. Pleasure? Or embarrassment following their argument at the ill-fated party less than forty-eight hours ago?

Sue put a hand on her arm. "Go and see him. I'll keep an eye on Grace. If she wakes up and needs you, I've got your mobile number."

Abi stepped from Grace's room.

Ben stood in a pool of sunshine looking out of the window with his hands pushed into the pockets of his sand-coloured chinos. He wore a light blue t-shirt. He certainly scrubbed up well: no farm jeans or old shirts today.

He turned in her direction. His eyes opened wide in recognition, then he strode quickly towards her.

"How's Grace?" The words tumbled from him. "I only heard this afternoon." He took her into his arms. "Sorry," he whispered into her hair. "I'm so sorry about what's happened."

Abi leaned against his muscled chest. The comforting smell of shampoo and soap filled her nostrils. She waited for the relief of having someone to rely on to flood through her, but she didn't feel anything.

She stepped away from him.

"It's Veronica Williams. She's responsible."

"How do you know it's her?"

"I just do."

Ben shifted from one foot to the other. "Sorry about my mood on Saturday evening. I care a lot for you. You know that, don't you?"

"The argument was partly my fault, I suppose. Hadn't had any alcohol for ages." Abi grinned. "Not a good thing as it turned out."

"Don't be so hard on yourself." An impish smile played on his lips as he brushed her cheek with the tip of his thumb. "You were quite endearing to start with."

All sorts of unexpected emotions and thoughts ran through her. If she let it, the situation between her and Ben could turn into something good, and if it didn't, well, she'd survive anyway. She always did. Why should she hold back?

She took a step away from him. The time wasn't right.

A family group walked down the corridor and split to pass either side of them.

Ben hunched his shoulders and pointed towards the exit. "Fancy a coffee? We could walk over to the business park, to Costa Coffee."

"Sounds good to me. I'll just get my bag and tell the nurse where I'll be."

Abi took a seat by the window while Ben joined the queue for drinks. Not a great view, just rows of parked cars, but at least she could see the sky dotted with small puffball clouds. The rich aroma of fresh coffee, the chatter and laughter from the other customers, made her feel like she was part of the real world again.

She looked up as Ben placed a tray filled with steaming cups of coffee onto the table; a strong double expresso for him and a milky latté for her. Two oblong pieces of flapjack lay on a white plate.

"Thought you might fancy something other than hospital food."

She picked up a flapjack and took a bite. The sweet taste of butter, treacle and oats melted onto her tongue. Just what she needed. She took another bite and chewed slowly.

"Do you have much to do with the Williams family?"

Ben's seat creaked under his weight. "Nothing, apart from renting the fields at Vellangoose before you and Becky came along. Why?"

Abi used the tip of her tongue to lick a crumb from the corner of her mouth.

"Veronica Williams nearly killed Grace. I need to know why she wants Vellangoose so much. Becky said something about a sister who lived there years ago. Constance? Steve's mum?" Abi pushed the plate to one side. "She and her husband were killed? Is that right?"

"I was just a kid when it all happened. I only know what my parents said at different times." He dropped a sugar cube into his expresso, picked up a teaspoon, and stirred. "Mum worked for both Veronica and Henry Williams at Boswyn, and Constance and Nicholas Hodges at Vellangoose. Mainly cleaning, but also some basic cooking or waitress work when the need arose. Mum liked Constance a lot more than she did Veronica. They were both especially beautiful women, but Constance had no airs or graces, and always had a kind word. The best of the bunch, Dad said."

Ben took a sip of his coffee. "Constance lost the plot when Nicholas confessed to having a bit of nookie on the side in Brazil. Mum tried to help her, but it made no difference. In the end, Constance rejected all offers of friendship. Had some sort of breakdown."

"Breakdown? What with all that money?" Abi shook her head. "She should've coped. For Steve's sake."

"Apparently, Constance took to drink – and men – after Nicholas left." He cleared his throat. "Henry Williams was a regular caller by all accounts."

Silence hung in the air. What was there to say? Maybe she and Becky were lucky there were only the two of them to inherit Vellangoose.

"It upset Mum when Constance upped sticks without a word and went to Brazil. She thought Constance would've said goodbye, despite the difference in their status. I remember Mum crying when Veronica broke the news that they'd both been killed."

"Steve must have been a kid when they died?"

"It was thirty years ago, so he was about six or seven. He attended Penhellick Village School like the rest of us, but Veronica moved him to a private school in Truro soon after his parents died. I always felt sorry for the poor kid having to live with Veronica Williams, but he seemed happy enough on the few occasions I saw him at some country show or other."

The shrill ring of Abi's mobile pierced the air. She flicked it open.

"Is Grace okay?" Her chair scraped across the tiled floor as she stood up.

"She's fine," Sue said. "Just woken up and needs her mummy."

Grace's cries floated down the phone line.

"I'm coming." Abi closed her mobile and turned to Ben. "Must go."

"I'll walk you back."

"No need."

"To the hospital entrance at least." He fell into step beside her. "I'm sorry we didn't have a chance to talk about us."

"Forget it. We're fine. Friends, like we were before."

Abi jogged back towards the hospital. Ben's long strides kept pace. She stopped as they neared the entrance and stood on tiptoe to give him a perfunctory goodbye kiss. As she reached up, he crushed her into his arms and kissed her with a fierce passion.

All the feelings she'd pushed deep down broke free. She may not want any involvement now, but her body was telling her something else. Wrapping her arms around him, she eagerly kissed him back. She couldn't fight this. Like always, she was lost. Once again, her heart ruled her head.

"Wow." He grinned at her as he held her at arm's length and looked into her eyes.

She wriggled free from his grip. "Grace needs me."

"Yes. Of course."

"Sorry."

"Go."

She turned and ran through the main entrance. The double doors closed behind her with the all-to-familiar swoosh-clunk.

27

Becky crossed the yard, opened the gate and stood aside to let Jacob and Eve into the garden. David followed. Without a word, she shut the gate behind them, walked back to the steps by the kitchen door and came to a halt.

"Thanks for taking the time to show me the tank and where the glove was found," David said. "It's useful to have a complete picture of events. It might help you and Abi if the opportunity arises at any point to contest the conditions of your father's Trust."

"Eve, Jacob, don't get dirty. We're off to dad's when David leaves."

"Sorry for calling without warning." David rubbed his temple. "You didn't answer any of my messages and I couldn't risk you doing a runner if you knew I was coming."

Already psyched up about the visit to her dad's place, a confrontation with David was the last thing she needed. Her hand went to her neck. She opened her mouth to issue an apology, but an image of David walking on the Falmouth seafront, arm in arm with Veronica Williams, swam into her head.

She strode over to a rickety, plastic garden table she'd found amongst the overgrown shrubs and brambles, and picked up her old secateurs and a pair of thick gardening gloves.

"You don't believe Veronica Williams is behind all this, do you?" she said.

"I know she's made her position clear and wants Vellangoose, but–"

"But what?" Becky glared at him. "She's above having a fox put into our water tank?"

"I find it hard to imagine she'd resort to such low-handed tactics."

"Really? You'd rather think Veronica Williams is a good person than believe I'm telling you the truth? Explain then, how a glove with the Williams Estates and Haulage logo was found next to the tank?"

Becky yanked a long bramble stem from the hedge, snipped it at the root, and threw it to the ground. It snaked across the grass. The thorns caught on David's trousers. He stood on the long stalk with his booted foot and stepped away. She grabbed another long stem. He moved back a couple of paces.

"Have I upset you?"

She clipped another piece.

"I thought we were getting on very well." He sighed. "If you don't want to see me again, just say. Not answering my calls or talking to me seems a bit childish."

"Childish?"

The word stung. With a jolt, she realised he was right. Rather than face a problem and tackle it head-on, she'd done what she always did; she ignored it in the hope it would go away. It was how she behaved with John and the rest of her family. Not anymore.

Feet wide apart, she placed her gloved hands on her hips and positioned herself in front of David.

"I saw you with Veronica Williams after you cut our lunch short."

He flinched.

"Walking arm in arm. Very cosy. Less than an hour after you told me you hadn't been in contact with her."

"Oh, Becky. I don't know what you think you saw, but–"

"I know what I saw. I saw two people, obviously very comfortable in each other's company. Veronica laughing and you smiling. Tell me I didn't see that."

Tears threatened. She blinked, reached down and lifted a stone from the long grass, and placed it on top of the garden hedge.

"Stop. Please," David pleaded. "We need to talk."

She swung around and glowered at him. "You said you hadn't seen or heard from her."

"It was a pure coincidence that she rang. She hadn't been in touch for some while."

Becky snorted, grabbed a long-handled garden fork she'd used earlier, rammed it into the earth beneath the root of the bramble and rocked it back and forth.

"I believed in you and assumed all you've said was true. Now I have doubts about everything, even what you told us about the Trust and its conditions."

The bramble root snapped. She wrenched it free and tossed it onto the growing pile of bramble stalks. "How can I be sure you're on our side? She's one of your firm's biggest clients. For all I know, you could be advising me and Abi and, at the same time, telling her everything."

He groaned. "How could you think that about me? I thought we had an understanding. Thought our friendship was heading somewhere special?"

"So did I."

"If it helps, I'll arrange for another solicitor to go through the Trust documents with you? You'll know then I'm telling the truth." He reached out to her, then dropped his hand to his side. "I swear Veronica Williams won't influence my dealings with you. You need to believe me. Please."

Becky turned towards a rambling rose entwined amongst the brambles. Laden with tight white flowers, she inhaled their wonderful, sweet scent. She glanced over at Jacob and Eve looking in the border for worms and other creepy crawlies. Unlike Jess, they might like gardening and growing flowers and vegetables. She would get them each a trowel and fork.

"Becky?" He cleared his throat. "I'll give up Veronica Williams as a client if that's what it'll take to convince you how I feel about you."

"Don't be ridiculous. We're adults. We can sort this out without being that extreme."

She walked across the garden to the old apple tree. Its gnarled and twisted branches, doggedly covered with fruitlets, touched the ground in places. She ran her hand over the rough, scarred bough and patted it. This tree was a survivor. She'd never chop it down.

"Beautiful, isn't it?" David said.

She turned and looked at him. Dark circles had formed under his eyes since she'd last seen him, and the sun highlighted a few strands of grey in his light-brown hair.

"Why don't you want me to set up my own business?" she said.

"What?"

"At our lunch, you tried to put me off the idea of setting up a baking and catering business. Why?"

"I was worried for you. Veronica's a hard woman. Determined. I didn't want her destroying you and what you're doing." He dug at the grass with the tip of his boot. "She'll break you and Abi in the end. You know that, don't you?"

"Not us. This time, we'll win. I need you to believe that." She watched a red and black spotted ladybird crawl along the pitted branch, its wings flexed, ready to take flight. "I can't have you telling me what to do, how to run my life. Not after John. I'm done with that."

"What happened to the scared, timid woman I first met?" A smile spread across David's face. "The one who ran from my office when I tried to tell her about her father and the Trust?"

"She's gone. Too much has happened."

"I'm glad." He removed a bramble leaf from her hair. "Do you think we could start again?"

For a few moments, she studied the half-opened door to the walled garden. It hung on one hinge. A few flecks of green paint clung onto the rotten, splintered wood. Beyond the door, she'd glimpsed brambles and weeds, but also bushes and trees struggling to bear fruit. She itched to push the door wide open, to go through and clear away the rubbish, to allow the fruit trees and shrubs to breathe. Another job to add to her 'to-do' list.

She turned towards him. "Perhaps we can."

He let out a deep breath, took her into his arms and kissed her.

A soft moan escaped from her lips. She let the secateurs drop onto the grass, wrapped her arms around him and luxuriated in the feelings that flooded through her. It was the first time she'd kissed a man since John, and for a moment, she was lost.

"Yuck," yelled Jacob from the other side of the garden.

Eve giggled.

The spell broken, Becky stepped away from David.

A flush of heat rushed across her face as she grinned at the children.

"Hey, guys, how about a trip to the beach for a swim and ice cream? Maybe even a burger and chips on the way back?"

Their yells of delight rang through the air.

"OK, go get your swimming stuff and a couple of towels."

The children raced towards the kitchen.

She looked at David and carefully considered him. "Want to join us?"

"Love to." The fine lines around his eyes crinkled.

"I need to stop at my dad's place on the way." She picked up the secateurs and put it back on the plastic table, along with her gloves. "Could you sit in the car with the children while I go inside and sort my baking ingredients for this week? I'll be quick."

"No problem."

"Good."

She ought to question him about Veronica Williams; about what had made her into a hard, determined woman, and about how friendly she and David were. She also ought to introduce the children to her dad. But she knew she wouldn't do either – not today.

David took her into his arms again. Waves of desire ran up and down her body. She'd waited so long to feel like this. To be loved.

She let her heart and flesh succumb to the wonderful sensations, but her head remained clear.

This relationship would be strictly on her terms.

28

Abi lifted her foot free from the warm, soapy water and admired the bright red nail polish she'd nicked from Becky, who was out for the day. What were sisters for if you couldn't 'borrow' their stuff now and again?

One of the kids' plastic ducks floated on the surface of the coconut-scented foam. Abi slid down the bath and disappeared under the bubbles, then came back up, pushed the hair from her eyes and leaned back against the smooth enamel. She couldn't remember the last time she'd felt so relaxed. Home alone on a weekday, she'd taken the opportunity to pamper herself. Besides, Ben was coming over at lunchtime and hopefully there would be time for a bit of fun.

Hair wrapped in a towel, she tugged on her old dressing gown and made her way down the hallway to the kitchen. She flicked the kettle on, and the novelty and excitement still made her want to punch the air with joy. She'd never take electricity for granted again.

In the past month, everything had gone right. Grace had been deemed hundred per cent fit and discharged from hospital, and they finally had electricity, courtesy of Megan, whose ponies, Pixie and Dixie, were now grazing in the Vellangoose fields and using the overhauled stables.

Abi opened the fridge door. Fresh milk. Another thing she'd never take for granted again. The second-hand fridge-freezer and cooker Becky had got from her client in Mylor a couple of months ago looked great.

During the last few weeks, her sister had certainly been making herself at home. Every time she came back from her dad's place, she brought more of her stuff from his garage. The kitchen shelves were now full of saucepans, casserole pots, and colour co-ordinated bowls. Cookery and baking books, including well-thumbed notebooks full of handwritten recipes, took up one shelf entirely. Becky had even started to bake some of her cakes at Vellangoose, rather than travel to her dad's bungalow every day.

In the living room, Abi pulled on a pair of denim shorts and a white t-shirt. She and the girls were moving into the third bedroom at the weekend. She looked around the room. It would need to be decorated at some point, but not yet. She wanted to make a couple of beds first. Using pieces of seasoned wood from The Mill, she was determined to make timber-framed beds for Jacob and Eve, then later, two more for herself and Grace. Becky had talked about bringing Jess's single bed to Vellangoose, but it hadn't appeared yet. Abi was glad. It wouldn't feel right for her sister to have a bed when the kids were still sleeping on the floor.

Her mobile phone rang. She didn't recognise the number.

"Hello?"

"Good morning, Miss Pascoe, it's Detective Inspector Jack Carter. I just wanted to–"

"Please tell me you've finally nailed that woman for something. And that she's going to get her comeuppance for what she did to Grace?"

"I'm sorry, Miss Pascoe, nothing has changed since our conversation at Treliske Hospital. Same with the various inquiries afterwards, which you already know about." He cleared his throat. "I just wanted to check that all was well with you and your family. And Mrs Farrow."

For a moment, Abi's good mood took a dive, but she pushed her shoulders back. It was what she expected.

Sweet F.A. Veronica Williams knew how to cover her tracks.

When the telephone call finished, Abi smiled to herself. That detective inspector had a lovely voice. Not bad looking either, for a copper. And kind-hearted, if the follow-up call was anything to go by, even if he was only fishing for more evidence against that old cow.

She looked at her watch. 11:00 a.m. Ben wouldn't be over for a couple of hours, and she had an urge to cook the Spaghetti Bolognese already planned for that evening by Becky. Her sister had gradually taken on cooking the main meal for all of them on most days, even though her baking-cum-catering business had really taken off and she often arrived home knackered. It gave Abi extra time to push on with the renovation work. They made a good team. Having pampered herself that morning, Abi felt it was only right that Becky should put her feet up when she got home tonight.

Abi lifted a heavy-bottomed pan onto the cooker top and tipped in a big dollop of olive oil. Quickly, she chopped an onion and dropped it into the oil to soften, followed a few minutes later by a clove of crushed garlic. From the fridge, she took out a pack of minced beef and stirred it into the sizzling mixture, together with a twist of black pepper and a pinch of salt.

From memory, she checked off the other ingredients she needed: a tin of tomatoes, ketchup, and herbs. Her fingers ran along Becky's herb and spice jars, now stored neatly in a cream wooden rack fixed to the wall. The jar of oregano was empty. No basil either.

She had time to go to the village shop. Dragging the pan from the heat, she switched the cooker off and grabbed her purse and keys.

A bell tinkled overhead as Abi pushed the shop door open. An open/closed sign hung on a piece of string.

An elderly lady, almost hidden behind the racks of magazines, daily newspapers, chocolate bars and sweets in front of her, was dusting a large metal till.

"Good morning."

Abi gave the woman her own best smile in return and moved over to the fresh produce displayed in various wooden boxes. Mushrooms, that's what she wanted. Becky didn't always add them to her recipe, but nowadays Abi liked to include thinly diced mushrooms and a finely grated carrot or two, so the kids got their veggies in disguise. She tore off two paper bags from a bundle tied to a nail and rooted through the small supply of mushrooms and knobbly, earth-covered carrots.

A few minutes later she made her way towards the back of the shop, dropped a bottle of tomato sauce into her wire basket, then reached over to the fridge and picked up two packs of cheese and ham for lunch.

In the next aisle, she passed a young mother with a toddler in a pushchair, then stopped in front of the herbs and spices. As she reached for a jar of basil, a large man wheezed and pushed past her. A waft of stale tobacco breath filled her nostrils.

She froze, her hand in the air. Her heart raced. She would never forget that sound or that smell.

Tartan Scarf.

The wire basket hit the tiled floor with a crack as Abi rushed after him. Her breath came in gasps.

Tartan Scarf stood next to the display of warm pasties and pre-wrapped sausage rolls. He wore the same tattered, dark green coat and tartan scarf he had on the night he and the other lampers had called at Vellangoose. There was one difference. Today he was bare headed, his face free from the black balaclava.

He had his back to her. She came up behind him and thumped him between the shoulder blades.

"Oi, you. Turn around so I can see your ugly face."

Tartan Scarf grunted and lumbered around to face her. "What the …" He stopped in mid-sentence.

"Recognise me, eh? You should, you fucking coward."

She winced as he grabbed her arm in a fierce grip and pushed his red-veined face close to hers.

"Keep your trap shut or you'll regret it." He jabbed her ribs with the fingers of his free hand and shoved her away.

She fell against the shelf. Several boxes of cereals toppled to the ground with a thud.

"Is there a problem? Can I help?" The assistant stood wide-eyed.

"Nothing for ya to worry about, Mrs Mudge. Me and this lady were just having a bit of a chat, that's all." He uttered a guttural laugh, picked up two pasties and made his way to the counter.

Abi clutched the shelf for support and struggled to breathe. His laughter penetrated her senses. She flung herself after him and pushed herself between him and the counter.

Mrs Mudge let out a small cry. The mother with the pushchair stood open-mouthed next to a box of cauliflowers.

"I said tell me your name."

"Best ya don't know. Best for your family if you get me drift," he wheezed.

Mrs Mudge placed her hands on the counter and stammered to Abi. "I … I think you should leave. I don't want any trouble."

"Mrs Mudge?" Abi looked from the woman to Tartan Scarf and back again. "You know him, don't you? Tell me his name."

Tartan Scarf fixed his blood-shot eyes onto the trembling Mrs Mudge.

"Wouldn't do that if I were you," he said.

With her hand clutched to her chest, Mrs Mudge asked Abi once more to leave.

"I'm not going anywhere until I know his name." Abi pulled out her phone and looked the woman in the eye. "You either tell me, or you tell the police."

Mrs Mudge gulped. "Ken ... Kenneth Dunstan. He works for Williams Estates ... and Haulage."

Tartan Scarf pointed his finger at Mrs Mudge. "You'll regret that, ya will."

"Picking on old ladies now as well as kids and dogs. You piece of shit," Abi snarled.

Tartan Scarf moved surprisingly quickly. He grabbed her fingers, twisted her hand backwards, and forced her to her knees.

The mother yanked her child from the pushchair and disappeared into the back of the shop.

Mrs Mudge plucked a mobile phone from under the counter. "I'm calling the police."

As quickly as he'd grabbed Abi, Tartan Scarf let her go, tossed some money onto the counter, picked up his pasties and crashed out of the shop.

"Expect a visit from the police soon," Abi shouted as the door slammed and the open/closed sign dropped to the floor.

She turned to Mrs Mudge. "No need to ring the police. I'll speak to them, now I know who he is."

"Goodness me, I feel a bit wobbly." Mrs Mudge collapsed into a chair behind the counter.

Abi rubbed her wrist. "You're not the only one."

A few minutes later, Abi moved back down the aisle to finish her shopping. A smile crept across her face.

The kids were asleep when Abi sat at the kitchen table and told Becky again about the encounter with Tartan Scarf and the conversation that took place afterwards with Detective Inspector Carter.

"Plays his cards close to his chest does that man. Despite his so-called check-in call earlier in the day, he didn't let on that my information would be of any use to him. Still, having the name of one of the lampers is bound to help his investigations." Abi swirled the dregs of her coffee as she spoke.

"Let's hope so." Her sister yawned and stood up. "Definitely my bedtime. It's been a long day. Thanks for making the Spaghetti Bolognese. You must give me your recipe."

A happy glow flooded through Abi. All in all, it had been a good day: she'd got the name of one of the lampers, spent some quality time with Ben after lunch, and Becky had praised her cooking. Things were definitely on the up.

At the Belfast sink, she washed up and emptied the rubbish bin. Outside, she dropped the bag by the back gate and covered it with an old curtain to keep the seagulls and crows from tearing it open.

Something rustled in the hedge a few feet away. She turned towards the sound and came face-to-face with a figure clad completely in black.

Veronica Williams.

Abi's heart thumped. It was the first time she'd seen her in the flesh. The newspaper pictures she'd seen hadn't done her justice. Still beautiful, the slim, honed woman in front of her oozed power and wealth.

Although Abi towered over Veronica Williams by several inches, a stab of fear shot through her. Everything people said about the woman was true; even her stance told the world she expected to get what she wanted.

To her surprise, Abi found herself stuttering when she spoke. "Wh … What are you doing here?"

The slim figure moved closer. Too close. Should she shout for Becky? No, it would wake the kids.

For a moment, Veronica Williams's face broke into a smile showing perfect teeth, and Abi caught a whiff of peppermint. Then the smile quickly disappeared, and the thin lips twisted into a snarl.

Abi stepped back. Her hand touched something – the long handle of Becky's digging fork stuck upright in the ground. She gripped it behind her back. If Tartan Scarf and his mates were also here, she would put up a good fight, and Veronica Williams would be the first to get it.

"I understand you had a regrettable encounter with one of my men today." The cultured voice pierced the stillness of the night. "Very unfortunate that other people witnessed our little problem."

"Problem? You nearly killed my daughter. That wasn't a problem," rage shot through Abi, "that was nearly murder."

Veronica Williams stood erect, shoulders back. "I think it's time you clearly understood the situation from my point of view."

Abi tightened her hand on the wooden handle and waited.

"I want Vellangoose. It's mine by right." Veronica Williams's chin jutted upwards. "And I will have it. Following this morning's charade, I would like to quickly expedite a solution agreeable to all parties."

"What the hell are you on about?"

"We can do this the easy way. Or, we can do it the hard way." She pushed a loose strand of blonde hair back under her black hat. "I am willing to give you, and Mrs Farrow, shall we call it, an advance. In cash. Solely on the condition that you both leave Vellangoose immediately. When the Trust period expires, I will purchase Vellangoose at the market price."

Abi sucked in her breath. Did Veronica Williams genuinely think she'd be able to buy them off, after what she and the lampers had put them through? After what she'd done to Grace? She was mad.

"You can stick your money." Abi spat the words out. "We're staying put."

"I would warn … No, I would advise you, that I will be instigating legal action against you both if we can't resolve this matter to my satisfaction. My source has reliably informed me that you have already broken the conditions of the Trust."

"That's a lie." Abi forced her voice to sound strong, but a kernel of doubt formed in her mind. Had they become a bit too relaxed and slipped up?

"I'm sure you wouldn't want this matter to go to court." Veronica Williams tugged at the cuff of her black leather glove. "You would lose, and that would leave you with absolutely nothing."

Words poured out of Abi's mouth. "Get off our property. Now." She grabbed the garden fork and held it out in front of her, the prongs facing upwards.

"Fifty thousand pounds."

The fork wobbled. Did she say fifty thousand pounds?

"Twenty-five thousand each. Don't take too long to decide. I'm not a patient person."

Before Abi could react, Veronica Williams turned and vanished into the night.

The shrill call of a vixen echoed through the darkness.

Abi let out a puff of air.

She wasn't sure if her day had just got worse, or better?

29

18 July

Becky's dream vanished. Something had woken her. In an instant, she sat up.

"Shush. Don't wake the kids." Abi was kneeling on the floor next to her. "Get up. We need to talk."

"It can't be morning already?"

Becky squinted at her clock. 12.05 a.m. She flopped back onto the bed. Her eyelids fluttered.

Abi shook her again. "Veronica Williams has just been here."

The words penetrated Becky's sleep-addled brain like spears of ice. She struggled to her feet and padded after her sister into the kitchen.

Becky blinked at the sudden brightness, then blinked again at the mix of emotions on her sister's pale face. Disbelief? Fear? Excitement? Before Becky could speak, words tumbled from Abi's mouth.

"Veronica Williams has offered to pay us to leave Vellangoose."

Becky opened her mouth to speak but Abi held up a hand to silence her.

"That's not all. When the Trust expires, she'll buy the property at market value." Abi paced the room. "The bloody woman scared the life out of me. Dressed in black from head to toe, she was, like some old witch." Her face became more animated. "We could be rolling in money. We–"

"How much?" A cold ball of anxiety unfurled in Becky's stomach.

"Fifty thousand pounds. To share."

The words hung in the air. The amount took Becky's breath away. Veronica Williams certainly meant business.

"I don't get it. Why?"

"Twenty-five grand. Each. Cash." Abi stared at her. "Can you believe it?"

"What's so special about Vellangoose? The land is peanuts compared to what she already has. Most of the buildings are old and decrepit, including The Mill, and The Barn is only just habitable."

"Who cares what the reason is?" Her sister pulled her hair back and twisted it into a knot. "It's megabucks for us each to do what we want."

Becky's thoughts were all over the place. What did she want? What would she do with the money? She picked up a pen and piece of paper from the windowsill and began writing her shopping list for the morning.

"Henry Williams owned Vellangoose for over thirty years; why didn't Veronica Williams buy it from him if she wanted it so badly?"

Abi snatched a handful of clean clothes from the laundry basket on the unit top and yanked one of Jacob's school polo shirts into shape. "It's probably like Megan said, tax avoidance or some such rubbish. Or maybe, he just didn't want to sell it to her."

"It's got to be more complicated." Becky tapped her chin with the pen. "I wish I could find some information about Constance and Nicholas. There's nothing on Google about them or the car crash."

"No wonder there's nothing on Google. It wasn't invented when they died."

"Even so, it's the Williams family; you'd think there would be a record of Constance's death."

Abi picked up another shirt and clicked her tongue. "You're not getting it, are you? Veronica Williams will pay us twenty-five thousand grand. Each."

"I heard you the first time." Becky scrawled furiously on her shopping list: chicken, carrots, King Edward potatoes. "You trust her to keep her word?"

"I trust her to do what she threatened to do, to sue us and take us to court."

"Why pay us if she's got some sort of evidence to legally force us out of here?"

"Cheaper? Less hassle?"

"Fifty thousand pounds' worth of less hassle? Come on."

Abi turned away from her, scrunched the half-folded shirt into a ball and chucked it back into the basket.

"Maybe you should ask your boyfriend," she said. "Or is David too busy advising Veronica Williams on what legal action she should take?"

Becky's hand trembled as she peered at her baking supplies, returned to her sheet of paper and scribbled: plain flour, sultanas, nutmeg. She'd got to know David pretty well in the last few weeks. She couldn't believe he'd hurt her. Or Abi.

"David wouldn't betray us," she snapped. "He's confident we're sticking to the conditions of the Trust."

"So how come Veronica Williams knows all about what we're doing?"

"What about Ben? It could be him." Becky hurriedly wrote down: apples, bananas, biscuits. "My God, this is just what she wants; for us to fall out and then go our separate ways. She probably hasn't got anything on us."

Abi reached back into the laundry basket, picked up a pair of Grace's pink leggings and stroked the soft material.

"I've never been able to treat my kids to the stuff others have. You wouldn't know about that, so you can't understand what this money would mean to me and my kids."

The icy ball in Becky's stomach grew. Her sister was right. Jess had been spoilt, and neither she nor her daughter had ever known what it was like to live from hand to mouth. But Abi couldn't give up on Vellangoose, it was unthinkable. She'd started it all. She was the driving force.

"You can't be serious?" Becky said with strength. "You can't leave."

"I'm thinking about it. And you'd be a fool if you didn't do the same. You could get your own baking premises or use the money for a deposit on another Rose Cottage. Go back to the lifestyle you once had; the nice house and all that stuff."

The impact of what Abi said shook Becky. Not long ago she would have jumped at the chance of going back to her old life. Now, she was lost for words at the realisation of how much the idea appalled her.

"Sleep on it." Abi picked up the folded laundry. "We'll talk more in the morning." The door closed softly behind her as she left the room.

Becky glanced towards the sink, and with fierce strokes that tore through the paper, she added washing-up liquid to her list.

It was late afternoon when Becky parked her car outside The Barn. The children's happy, excited voices floated over the hedge from the garden. Radio One blasted from the kitchen. The briefest whiff of curried meat drifted in the air. Abi was cooking the evening meal.

Becky rubbed her eyes. She hadn't been able to get back to sleep last night after the depressing talk with her sister. Kidding herself she needed to shop early before a long day of baking at her dad's, she'd crept out of bed at 6:00 a.m. It hadn't achieved anything. Avoiding Abi had only delayed the potentially life-changing discussion.

The blanket of anxiety that had nipped at Becky's heels all day turned to panic at the impending confrontation. She hadn't felt like this since the first month or so at Vellangoose.

Swiftly, she turned, walked across the yard and into the meadow leading to the ponds.

A large dragonfly, its wings an iridescent quiver of blue-green, danced over the water. Small groups of hedge sparrows chattered amongst the branches of the hawthorn trees that bordered the path. These timeless images soothed her, and the final trace of her angst dispersed.

She knew with absolute certainty she could never take Veronica Williams's offer. The money would be tainted, and anything built or created with it would never feel right.

A twig snapped nearby.

Abi walked towards her. In silence, they fell in step and made their way back to the yard and the noise of the children still playing in the garden.

As Becky removed a couple of shopping bags from the boot of her car, her sister broke the silence.

"Have you decided about the money?"

A dry lump formed in Becky's throat. The conversation had begun even before they'd got inside. She swallowed and put the bags onto the ground.

Abi hurried on. "You must understand, I have to take it. It's what's best for the kids."

"Best for them? In what way?" Anger surged through Becky. "By the time the Trust expires, and we've done all the repairs and changes, Vellangoose will be worth at least ten, twenty times, what Veronica Williams is offering us."

"But we'd have the money immediately. A bonus, she said. And we'd get the total market value in four and a half years."

"You mean her idea of the market value. She'd ensure that all the estate agents in the area would quote the figure she wanted to pay. Besides, she'd run the place down even more by then. It won't be the property you and I are going to make it in that time."

"It's too long to wait. I want my kids to have a better life now. I could rent a half-decent house with that money."

"Enough for four and a half years? Come on, do the maths. At best, you'd only get some crummy flat in Penryn, and only then if you kept working at Asda."

"What's wrong with Penryn? I grew up there."

Dear God, why couldn't her sister see the longer term, when this place would be something special?

"Look at your children, see how happy they are. You could never find them what they've already got here: the garden, Podge to ride, the fields. Besides, you'd have the same problem as before finding somewhere that'll take Buddy."

"I'm taking the money." Abi glared at her, eyes wide with defiance.

"Have you forgotten what Veronica Williams did to Grace? What she did to Buddy?"

"Damn it, Becky. It's because of what she did to Grace that I have to take the money. Veronica Williams isn't going to stop. What if next time one of my kids is killed?"

Becky's hand flew to her mouth. Why hadn't she realised how scared Abi was? Her sister's tough, strong persona had fooled her.

She let out a sigh. How could she fight Abi's fears for her children's safety? They had to come first. Her shoulders slumped, but then … She grabbed Abi's forearm.

"You're not on your own anymore. You have me. I'll help you keep the children safe. Please, just think about what we've already done. What you did."

She turned Abi's hand palm upwards and ran her fingertips over the rough calloused patches. "You got these working hard for Jacob, for Eve, for Grace. Only yesterday you talked about making beds for them using wood from The Mill."

She manoeuvred Abi around to face the large, still derelict building, with the mismatch of new and old tiles.

"See that roof. You made that happen. Remember? It was one of the first jobs you had completed, so the children would be safe. Are you going to let all your efforts go for a miserable twenty-five thousand pounds?"

"I'm not sure I've any fight left in me." Abi sagged against the car. "When I'd no choice, I could keep going, but the money …" She paused and shook her head. "What else can we barter?"

"Loads. I've been thinking about this ever since I agreed to stay at Vellangoose." Renewed energy swept over Becky. "Come with me."

She steered Abi towards the piggery, to the building that once housed their first 'bathroom' in the form of two portable toilets and plastic bowls to wash in.

"This would make a great carpentry shop for you. It's a fantastic space to make your beds." Becky swung around. "There're so many other things you could make from the old timber and stuff in The Mill. And, what about our woods, must be tons of material there?"

"What's the point, we can't sell any of it?"

"But we can barter in exchange for household supplies, groceries, and food for the animals. I've been thinking that the old dairy and the milk house would make a fantastic commercial kitchen at some point, which would enable me to produce more goods for barter." Excitement bubbled through her. "We also have the buildings and the fields. Maybe Megan knows of others wanting stables or grazing?"

"You're mad. How can just the two of us do all that?"

"This, from the woman who single-handedly cleared, re-plastered and painted The Barn, and at the same time chopped piles of logs, fed the animals, and raised three children."

"There's not enough stuff to barter with for four years or so." Abi kicked the floor of the piggery with the end of her trainer.

"You've been blinded by the thought of instant money. Look around. We've got the ponds, wildlife, and animals. We could offer nature walks and trails, set up a bird-watching shelter. We've already got Megan holding the Penhellick Country Show in the meadow at the end of August." Becky took a deep breath. "And don't forget, Apollo will be back tomorrow. David said we can take any earnings from Apollo in cash, as livestock is exempt from the constraints of the Trust. You'd have money for school uniforms, shoes, clothes. Perhaps a TV? Or–"

"Stop. Once you get started there's no stopping you. I'm beginning to have some sympathy for John at this rate." A grin appeared on Abi's face. "Okay. Okay. I'll think about the offer some more."

Abi picked up the shopping bags and made her way through the garden into the kitchen. The children ran up the steps after her. Voices asking for biscuits and juice floated through the air.

Becky stood for a few minutes. A wave of happiness rushed over her. Veronica Williams could stick her money.

She and Abi would be staying at Vellangoose, come what may.

30

20 July

Abi swung the camper van into the tree-lined lay-by and slammed on the brakes. Brambles dragged against the passenger door as the vehicle shuddered to a halt. With an angry shake of her head, she switched off the ignition and leaned back against the seat. A short distance along the road, she could see the entrance to Veronica Williams's place.

It had been two days since she had materialised out of the darkness to offer Abi and Becky a fortune to leave Vellangoose. For two evenings, Abi had paced the garden, or sat in the shadows, waiting for her to return. When Abi eventually went to bed, she spent the rest of the night listening out for some signal or sign. What did she expect? A knock on the door? A pebble dashed at the living room window?

What she got was silence.

Now, Abi was parked just a few yards from Boswyn Manor. Surely, a quick visit would solve the problem? She pinched the bridge of her nose. It had already been a bad day, with grumpy kids recovering from colds and even grumpier customers at Asda.

A tractor and trailer lumbered by on the road. Should she go on, or go home?

An image of Becky with one of her disapproving looks flitted into her head. Her sister would go ballistic if she knew what Abi planned to do, arguing it would only make a bad situation worse. Maybe she was right?

Abi reached for the ignition and switched on the engine. Right, towards home? Left, towards trouble? At the edge of the lay-by, she inched the van onto the road. Her head told her to turn the steering wheel towards home, but before she knew what she was doing, she'd yanked the wheel to the left.

Jaw clenched, she drove through two granite pillars leading to Boswyn Manor and made her way down a long tarmac drive, bordered on each side by grassland. Cows and half-grown calves contentedly chewed their cud under the large oak and sycamore trees dotted throughout the open landscape. For a few seconds, she slowed to take in the spread of patchwork fields rolling away to the sea in the distance. The afternoon sun beat down. A trickle of sweat rolled down her neck.

She urged the camper van onwards and through another set of stone posts. The van swayed and bumped over a cattle grid, into a different landscape. The track narrowed, and on both sides the open fields were replaced by high banks of rhododendron, camellia and hebe shrubs. Tall trees, set further back, darkened the area and cooled the air, then without warning, the vehicle broke free of the gloom and into brilliant sunshine. She gasped. A huge expanse of well-manicured lawns stretched towards a large, very grand, white house.

Boswyn Manor.

She braked at the edge of a gravelled drive which curved either side of a large fountain. Steps ran up to a porch, supported by two white pillars. Pots holding perfectly trimmed shrubs lined the route. The house filled her vision. From the number of windows she guessed the property had a dozen or more bedrooms. Fifty thousand pounds was just loose change to Veronica Williams.

Abi jumped out of the camper van, ran up the steps two at a time, then across the stone terrace. She pressed the bell and waited. A few moments later, she heard footsteps clattering in her direction and the thick wooden door swung open.

Jess stood there, open-mouthed, her face perfectly made up and her hair tied back in a French knot. She was dressed in an immaculate navy suit and an old woman's blouse.

"Jess. What a pleasure to see you. Hostess with the mostess. Your mum will be so pleased to know how you've gone up in the world."

Before Jess could reply, Abi stepped quickly around her and moved into the hallway. Numerous doors led off the reception area. A highly polished, mahogany floor flowed towards a formidable staircase. An enormous arrangement of chrysanthemums sat on a half-moon table.

Voices floated through a partially opened door and Abi hurried towards them.

"You can't go in." Jess ran in front of her, arms open wide, attempting to block her way. "You must leave."

Abi shoved past her and barged into the room.

Regency red and white flock wallpaper coated the top half of the panelled walls. Three olive green floral sofas were arranged around an unlit fire. A low table stood in the middle. Over the marble fireplace, a stern-faced man with a beard stared out from a life-size portrait.

At the far end of the room, six women sat in matching chairs around a dark wood table. A tall silver coffee pot, white bone china cups, and a well-stocked plate of cakes stood amongst the papers scattered in front of them.

Veronica Williams, in tailored slacks and a silk blouse, rose from the table and made her way towards Abi.

Jess rushed up to her. "I'm so sorry, she–"

"Miss Pascoe. What a surprise. I was not aware you would be calling today." Veronica Williams's voice was calm and controlled.

"I've come about your offer."

Veronica Williams inclined her head. "It might be best to discuss our business in my study." She swept her arm towards the door. "This way."

One of the women in the window looked in Abi's direction then turned to whisper to her neighbour. A string of pearls lifted and fell on her pale green cashmere sweater as she spoke.

Veronica Williams shifted from one foot to the other. "Miss Pascoe, if you would please follow me." Two red spots had appeared on her cheeks.

A surge of joy shot through Abi. For once, Veronica Williams would know what it felt like to be wrong-footed. It was even better considering it was on her home turf, in front of her old cronies.

Abi turned towards the group at the table, a big smile on her face.

"Ladies, did you know that the lovely Veronica Williams came to my house in the dark of night and offered me and my sister a load of cash to leave our home, or else she'd sue us? Is that the actions of an upright citizen?"

One of the women rose from her chair and strode quickly towards them. "Veronica, my dear, is everything alright?"

"Of course, Celia. Would you be so kind as to chair the meeting while I talk to Miss Pascoe? I will arrange for a fresh pot of coffee to be brought in."

Celia hesitated, looked Abi slowly up and down, then nodded. "Of course."

Veronica Williams turned her gaze back to Abi. "Follow me."

"We can chat here." Abi smiled again. "I've nothing to hide."

Veronica Williams nodded to Jess, who hurried from the room.

The group around the table resumed muttering in hushed voices.

Veronica Williams's eyes flicked from the women, then back to Abi. "I must insist."

"Really?"

The door opened. Steve Hodges stepped into the room.

"Steven, please show Miss Pascoe out. I believe we have concluded our meeting."

Steve grasped Abi by the arm, pinching her flesh, and forced her to walk towards the door.

She struggled and shouted back over her shoulder. "Don't you want to know our answer then? Well, you're going to hear it anyway. It's no. N. O. Fucking no."

The words hung in the air.

Celia tutted.

Abi twisted free from Steve's grip and swung around to face Veronica Williams.

"What's the big secret? Why are you freaking out about us being at Vellangoose?"

Veronica Williams stiffened, her lips a thin line.

Steve regained his hold, and with extra force he propelled her out of the door, through the hallway and onto the terrace.

Jess tottered after them.

They stopped at the top of the steps.

"Piss off. Don't come back, or you and that brood of yours will regret it." His lip curled as he spoke. "Same applies to your idiot sister."

"Don't talk about Mum like that," Jess said.

"Shut up," he snarled.

A flash of heat coursed through Abi. She'd seen men like this before, been on the end of their violence and cruel words. She fixed her eyes on Becky's daughter. Her niece.

"What are you doing with this piece of shit? He's a bully. Come with me before he hurts you."

Steve scowled at Jess and gave her a dismissive wave. Jess flinched, turned, and ran back inside.

Abi's heartbeat throbbed in her ears. She swung her hand towards Steve's face, but he grabbed her wrist and shoved her. She stumbled down the steps. Pain shot through her ankle.

"Fuck you," she yelled.

Veronica Williams stood erect in the doorway. "Steven, come inside."

Abi's earlier triumphant mood ebbed away as a slight smile tugged at the corners of the woman's lips.

"Miss Pascoe. Thank you for calling. You can expect to hear from my solicitor in due course."

The heavy door of Boswyn Manor banged shut.

Abi limped to the camper van, yanked the door open and hopped on one foot into the driver's seat.

She thumped the steering wheel. Why hadn't she gone straight home after her shift finished at Asda?

She pulled to a halt outside The Barn. Ben waved to her. He stood with Jeffery by the meadow gate. Apollo hung his head over the top bar as the older man scratched behind the animal's ear.

What a disaster the visit to Boswyn Manor had turned out to be. Her fault for being so cocky. Becky would go mad when she found out, and how could she tell her sister that she'd witnessed Steve's abusive attitude to Jess?

Abi eased herself out of the van and dragged her rucksack onto her shoulder. Her ankle throbbed. Forcing a smile, she attempted to walk without limping to The Barn. The last thing she needed was to explain or make up a lie about her injury.

Ben rushed over, wrapped an arm around her waist and took her weight. "Hey, what's up with you? Customers got a bit rough?"

"Ha. Ha. Very funny."

Before she could protest, Ben lifted her into his arms, carried her across the garden into the kitchen, and gently placed her on one of the chairs.

"You need to keep that foot elevated. I'll get some ice."

A tear slowly tracked down her cheek. She hadn't the strength to wipe it away.

"Are you okay, Miss?" Jeffery stood on the doorstep.

She blurted out a story about tripping in the Asda car park in her rush to get home.

"Honestly, Jeffery. I don't know why I'm being such a baby."

Ben leaned down and hugged her. "Looks like you've had a bad day?"

She nodded. Why didn't she tell him the truth? Come to that, why hadn't she told him about Veronica Williams's nighttime visit and her offer of money? From their conversation over breakfast, Becky hadn't told David either. Why?

Ben got to his feet and plucked three mugs from the shelf, then turned to Jeffery and asked him what he wanted to drink.

"Can't stay. The missus has me tea on the table at five o'clock prompt. If I'm late, she'll have me guts for garters." He tipped his head towards Abi. "Hope you're feeling a lot better soon, Miss."

He made his way out of the door and down a couple of steps, then stopped. Fumbling in his jacket pocket, he came back into the kitchen.

"I'd forget my head if it wasn't screwed on. Could you give this to Mrs Farrow?" He handed Abi a yellow envelope, creased and wrinkled with age. "Inside is the name and address of the company that Nicholas Hodges used to work for in Brazil. Becky asked about him, and me missus remembered she had this Christmas card from Nicholas, sent all them years ago."

A smile crossed Jeffery's face. "He thanked her for helping out with Constance and the boy while he was abroad. The missus was so proud like, she kept it. Only thought about it the other evening when we were remembering the old days." He scratched his head. "Anyway, enough of me blabbering on. Me tea's waiting."

"Thanks, Jeffery," Abi said as he raised a hand in farewell and made his way outside.

Ben tipped a tray of ice cubes in the middle of a tea towel, twisted the ends together and placed it onto her ankle.

She fingered the yellowed envelope. At least Becky had a choice now. Good news first, or bad?

31

4 August

Becky dropped her handbag onto the kitchen table and made her way down the hallway to Jacob's bedroom. In the doorway, she stared at the piles of wood in various shapes and sizes, and the sheets of do-it-yourself instructions scattered across the floor.

"Oh dear."

"Damn it." Abi scrambled to her feet, tossed a hammer onto the floor and pushed the tip of her thumb into her mouth.

"Sorry to startle you." Becky twisted a curl around her finger. "Will Jacob be able to sleep in his bed tonight?"

"It's the blasted sides." Abi bent down and picked up the hammer. "I can't fix them to the frame on my own."

"I can give you a hand."

"Thanks." Her sister smiled. "Some coffee would also help?"

Five minutes later, dressed in old jeans and a faded top, Becky put two steaming cups of coffee onto the windowsill.

"Tell me what to do."

"If you could hold one of the sides in position, I'll screw it to the headboard and then the footboard, so they're joined together."

Becky eyed the bed ends leaning against the wall, each section made with three planks of wood fixed together with additional pieces for the legs. She shook her head.

Her sister was so clever at this stuff, yet at other times she didn't have the sense she was born with.

It was over two weeks since Abi had visited Boswyn Manor and arrived back at Vellangoose with a sprained ankle and a badly dented ego. Not that Abi had immediately told Becky what she'd done, but when she'd finally admitted the truth, Becky had been justifiably angry at her sister for putting herself in such danger and, at the same time, so fearful that she'd made the conflict between them and Veronica Williams worse.

Later still, when Abi told Becky how Steve had treated Jess, it was Abi who'd stopped Becky from storming to Boswyn Manor. Becky had texted Jess and left several messages on her mobile, but her daughter hadn't called back. Worryingly, they hadn't heard from Veronica Williams either.

"Hey, daydreamer, hold this." Abi waved a piece of wood. "Just here." She indicated the exact spot where the side part would fix to the headboard, and began to screw the two bits together.

"Any luck at the Records Office?"

"I found an obituary notice for Nicholas and Constance in the *Western Morning News*. Short and low key. Just said they'd been killed in a tragic accident in Brazil. I thought there might've been something in *The Times* or the other tabloids, but I couldn't find anything." Becky gripped the wood tighter. She didn't want to wreck Abi's beautiful handiwork because her mind was elsewhere. "Couldn't find copies of their death certificates either."

"As they died in Brazil, would there be any in this country?" Abi moved to the bottom of the bed and screwed the piece to the footboard.

"The bodies weren't brought home so, you're right, they didn't need to register the deaths in the UK. Still, it seems odd to me, considering there would've been custody issues and suchlike to sort, regarding Steve." Becky shifted the position of her hand. "I'll keep checking when I can."

"Did anything come of the address Jeffery gave you? The one for the company Nicholas worked for?"

"The company's still operating. I've emailed their headquarters in Rio de Janeiro, asking a few questions about Nicholas. I don't expect they'll reply, but I included my contact details, just in case."

"That's one side done." Abi got to her feet. "Now the other one."

"I still haven't got a clue why Constance went to Brazil. Whether she went on her own accord, or if Nicholas invited her."

"If Veronica Williams were my sister, I'd shoot off to Brazil after I came out of rehab as well. Either that or I'd be back on the booze mighty quick. Hey, Becky, hold it still or you'll drag the screws out."

For a few minutes, Becky concentrated on keeping the wood level. "I've even less of a clue as to why she left Steve behind. Perhaps it was because Veronica Williams had been looking after him for so long?"

"Whatever. Who can fathom anything about that family?"

"Both Megan and Jeffery said what a good and loving mum Constance was, so she must have thought it was best for him." Becky sat back on her haunches.

"Not that Mums always get it right," Abi said.

Becky got to her feet. Wasn't that the truth? Both their mums had lied to them, keeping their secrets close to their chests.

Abi straightened and rubbed her back. "That's the tricky bit over." She sipped her coffee. "Would you pass me those four pieces of wood in the corner?"

"What are they for?"

Becky picked up the four flat, thinner items: two the same length as the head and footboards and the others the length of the bed.

"These are the cleats or, in simple terms, my dear sister, they sit inside the frame and provide a ledge for the base slats or boards to rest on. Once I've fitted these, the bed frame is almost sorted."

Abi picked up the spirit level and one piece of wood, then got down on her knees to position the shorter bit.

"Are you seeing David tonight?"

"He's cooking me a meal at his house."

"Oh yeah? Chance to stay over?"

Becky's heart raced. "I'll probably come home."

"You're not sleeping with him yet?" Abi glanced at her. "Why not? Great looking guy like that."

Becky felt her cheeks grow hot. She forced herself not to put a hand to her throat.

"Nothing like a night of great sex to relax you." Abi twisted the last screw into place, tested the frame and nodded. She sat and leaned back against the wall. "David would take your mind off everything, including Jess and Steve. And Veronica Williams."

"You talk about sex and sleeping with someone as if it's an easy thing to do. You and Ben make it seem so … uncomplicated."

"It is. Just do it. You only live once."

"I'm not like you." Becky sat next to her sister, stretched out her legs and jabbed at her bare knee poking through a tear in her jeans. "I feel flabby and old. What if I can't … you know … do it anymore?"

Abi burst into laughter. "What are you on about? You look fantastic, not like the scrawny person I first met. A bit of weight suits you."

"Gee, thanks." Becky continued to poke at her knee.

"What's really bothering you?"

This conversation was embarrassing. Becky moved to stand up but her sister gripped her arm and stopped her.

"Talk to me."

Becky looked down and stared at the wedding ring she still wore. She wound it around her finger a few times.

"I've only ever slept with John."

"You what?"

Becky lightly punched Abi on the arm. "For goodness sake, put your jaw back in place. I did get married at eighteen. John was my first proper boyfriend."

"But he treated so badly. Surely you had other men?"

"I loved John. It was never in me to just use a man and walk away. That would be too awful." She bowed her head. "Besides, I don't know if I could bear it if another bloke let me down."

"David wouldn't do that. He's one of the good guys. I've had enough slimeballs to tell the difference."

A surge of warmth ran through Becky. She and Abi were so different, but it didn't matter. She'd grown to love her and to rely on her.

"I admire you. You know that, don't you?" Becky whispered.

"Why? I'm nothing special."

"You never give in. You fight for your children, and they adore you. I envy your ability to generate such absolute love."

If only Jess loved her half as much.

Becky pulled her knees up and hugged them to her chest.

She knew she was being oversensitive. Her daughter had loved her unconditionally when she was a child, and now she had her own life to lead. It was normal for her not to keep in touch. She probably didn't see her dad much either.

Abi got to her feet and picked up a slat of wood from the pile in the corner and a ruler from the windowsill. She placed the loose slats crossways on the bed base and glanced at the sheet of instructions on the floor.

"Looks like a gap of four centimetres between each slat." She pulled a pencil from behind her ear and began to mark the spots. "You love children. Why only Jess?"

"I wanted a larger family but …" She sucked in a deep breath. "I had to get married. Looking back, I realise how ignorant and naïve I was. My mother never told me about contraception, and John said he'd take responsibility for it." She shrugged. "Well, John being John."

Her heart was thumping. Why was she raking over ancient history? But she couldn't stop; she wanted to talk.

"Now I can see that if I hadn't got pregnant, John and I wouldn't have got married. We would've broken up like young people do. Don't get me wrong, I did love him, and I know he loved me once."

"So, Jess was a mistake?"

"I had a miscarriage a month after the wedding. My mother said it was a pity it hadn't happened sooner, as it would've saved the expense of a wedding."

"Nice."

"I didn't cope very well after the miscarriage." Becky flicked some dust from her jeans. "Became depressed and stayed home all the time. John went out with his mates. We still made love now and then. Thank goodness, otherwise we wouldn't have had Jess. For a while after her birth, we were happy. The three of us in our little world." Becky sighed. "Then, well, you know the rest."

"Yeah, the cheating slimeball walked all over you."

Becky felt an urge to argue with Abi but stayed quiet.

Abi was right. David deserved better. Why was she holding out on him? Misguided loyalty to John? Frightened of what her dead mother would think? Or maybe because she was aware that her feelings for him were growing stronger each day, despite her determination to ensure this relationship remained entirely on her terms.

Abi's voice broke into her thoughts. "Wow, not bad if I say so myself."

Becky stared at the fully functional bed. "Jacob will love it."

She got to her feet.

"He better had," Abi said.

"I've still got Jess's single mattress. It's almost new and in perfect condition. Jacob could have it. What do you think?"

Tears welled in Abi's eyes. She blinked and looked quickly away, then nodded.

"It's in Dad's garage. There's plenty of time to get there and back in the camper van before I go to David's." A giggle rolled from Becky's throat. "Also, plenty of time for me to pack my overnight bag. Just in case."

32

Abi wiped the beads of sweat from her forehead, readjusted her gloves, and continued to rummage amongst the debris and timber in The Mill. Eve had been banging on for over two weeks about having a bed like Jacob's, except she wanted a white unicorn on the headboard, rather than the racing car Becky had stencilled onto Jacob's.

She ran her fingers along a section of timber. It would make a good side for the bed frame. She placed it by the door. Other piles of wood stood to the left and right of her; one pile to be chopped into logs, and the other for burning in the living room fire during the winter. She was making inroads into clearing The Mill and could now see what looked like old furniture stacked against the wall at the back. With luck, it might be good enough to be exchanged for something she and Becky wanted.

Half an hour later, Abi rubbed her lower back. She'd had enough of lugging stuff around for one day. Just one more piece and that would be it.

Dragging a long plank from the rubble, she walked backwards.

"Whoa," Ben said. "Let me help before you injure yourself."

He took the wood from her and added it to the pile, then turned and took her into his arms.

"Hi, there." He planted a kiss on the tip of her nose. "Missed you."

His hands ran up and down her back before resting on her bottom. She giggled and curled her arms around him. He pulled her closer and began to nibble her ear. How she loved the feel of his strong, muscled body. Maybe there was time for a little break? She placed a hand in the middle of his chest and gently pushed him away.

"Don't even think about it. I've only got this morning to find the wood I need and get working on it, otherwise, I'm going to be totally in Eve's bad books."

Ben dropped his arms. "Her bed?"

"Got it in one."

He glanced around. "You're certainly sorting through the rubbish now."

"I want to get to the old furniture against the far wall. Might be something of value."

"I don't reckon anyone's touched those pieces for years." Ben squinted at the pile of junk. "You need to be careful. It looks precarious."

Leaning down, she tugged at a large sheet of wood on the floor. "Can you give me a hand? I tried to lift this earlier, but it seems to be stuck or nailed down. It would make a great headboard."

Ben grabbed one end and she gripped the other. They both heaved. Nothing happened.

"I'll lever the edges to release it." Abi picked up a crowbar. "Hopefully in one block."

She worked the end of the metal bar under the wood and pushed downwards. After a few attempts, the timber sprang free with a loud crack – still intact.

Ben hauled it upright and leaned it against the wall.

Abi stared down into the darkness. A damp, musty smell rose from the depths. She coughed. "What the hell's that?"

"Come away." Ben grabbed her arm and pulled her back. "I think it's the original well. It looks really deep."

A shiver ran over Abi. The stench stung the back of her throat.

"I remember Jeffery saying something about an old well when he first came to Vellangoose to fix the water pump," she said. "I wasn't really listening, but Becky seemed interested. I'll ask her later."

"If you're considering using The Mill for anything, you'll need a structural engineer to check it out."

"Well, I can't afford one." She grabbed the sheet of wood. "I need to get on."

"Don't you ever stop?" Ben clutched the other end of the wood and together they lifted it and took it outside. "I'll cover the hole before–"

"Coo-eee."

Abi jerked around.

Megan rushed up to her.

"My dears, so lovely to see you both."

She tugged a faded denim hat off her head and wiped her forehead with it. At the same time, she fumbled in the pocket of her dungarees and pulled out a crumpled leaflet. Then another.

"One for each of you."

"What is it?" Ben asked.

"The schedule for the Penhellick Country Show including details of the various show jumping classes, the gymkhana and the fun dog show. My little darlings are so excited about next Saturday." A smile crossed her face. "My dear Abi, you and Becky will be fed up seeing Poppy and Rose around the stables. They've got lots to do to get Pixie and Dixie in show condition."

She turned to Ben. "Young man, I need someone strong to help erect the show jumps on Friday. My darling Hugh will be in the meadow, along with Jeffery, young Aaron and several others. Many hands make light work, you know."

"Wouldn't dare miss it." Ben grinned.

"Good, good. Must go. Schedules don't distribute themselves."

Megan stepped away, then swung back to face Abi.

"There's still lots of gossip around the village about your little foray to Boswyn Manor last month, you know. Like I said at the time, very brave, my dear, but terribly foolhardy. Veronica wouldn't have liked being made to feel like a chump in front of friends and business associates."

"I didn't think any of those old witches had the guts to gossip about the revered Veronica Williams."

"Walls have ears, or at least, the staff at Boswyn Manor do. Some of them rather enjoyed the spectacle." Megan squeezed one of Abi's hands. "You must be careful, extremely careful. Veronica is out for revenge. You can bet she's gathering information and evidence against you and Becky as we speak." Megan shoved her hat onto her head. "Enough said. Cheery bye, my dears. See you both anon."

"You need to heed Megan's advice." Ben stepped closer to Abi. "I should've said something before."

"How long have you known?"

His face reddened. "A few days after your visit. The usual busybodies with nothing better to do."

"Why didn't you say something then?"

"Thought it best if you told me first."

Abi stared at Ben. Why had he kept quiet? They saw each other most days, he could easily have raised the incident with her.

But then, she hadn't told him either, had she?

Suddenly, her earlier good mood disappeared.

Later in the afternoon, Abi worked alongside Becky preparing the living room for decorating. Words tumbled from her as she updated her sister on Megan's warning.

"I don't know whether to be scared or relieved that we've heard nothing from Veronica Williams since your hot-headed visit." Becky pulled a bucket of soapy water closer, wrung out a damp cloth and wiped the paintwork on the door with fierce strokes.

"It's because the old witch doesn't have anything on us. I believe my confrontation, in front of witnesses, has made Veronica Williams think twice about what she's doing."

"If you say so."

Abi watched Becky for a few moments, then sighed. It was wishful thinking to believe Veronica Williams had given up on her quest to get them out of Vellangoose. Still, a girl could dream, couldn't she?

"Have you found out any more about Constance or Nicholas?"

"Nothing." Becky scrunched her lips. "I'll keep looking though. Might get lucky."

Why was everything to do with Veronica Williams so complicated? It was doing her head in. She wanted answers now, not more of Becky's drip-drip research. It took Abi all her strength not to jump in the van, drive to Boswyn Manor and shake the truth out of the old bat.

She jabbed at the rough patches on the wall with the scraper, then stopped.

"Hey, I should've said earlier, but I found the old well in The Mill this morning. It stunk like hell. Didn't Jeffery rabbit on about it once?"

"He said it was used when The Mill was up and running, but when the business came to an end, the stream was diverted, and the old millstone and other items were sold. I'll see if I can find out some more about it."

Not more research? Abi took a deep breath, turned away and looked around the living room. It would be a doddle to sort out compared to the bedrooms. Scrape and smooth the rough spots on the walls, wipe everything down, a few coats of paint and the room would look brilliant.

"Did you get your decorating skills from your mum?"

Abi jerked her head up. "What?"

"Your mum, did she teach you how to decorate and all the other stuff?"

A laugh burst from Abi's chest. "She'd struggle to open a tin of paint, let alone know what to do with a paintbrush."

"She's in Australia, isn't she?"

"Who told you?"

"Jacob said."

"At what point do kids learn to keep their mouths shut?"

"He said you fell out. I know it's not my business, but don't you miss her?"

Becky quickly bowed her head and dunked the cloth back into the bucket.

A flash of sadness rushed over Abi. She hadn't spoken to her mum since she'd left for Australia, but then neither had her mum tried to contact her.

"She lied to me. Lied. All my life."

"Oh?"

"Fair enough, she did tell me Henry Williams was my father, but forgot to mention she continued to see him, right up until he died." Abi waved the paint scraper at Becky. "He came to our home when I wasn't around, and she never told me."

"Oh dear."

"What thanks did she get? The piece of shit left the property she lived in for decades to Veronica Williams." Abi spat the words out. "When it came down to it, his wife mattered more to him than my mum. There wasn't a formal agreement for the sort of service she provided for our father, so she was out on her ear."

"She was probably only doing what she thought was best for you."

"I can't forgive her. He was my father, yet I wasn't allowed any contact with him. Does that seem fair to you? How could she permit him to use her like that?"

"Under his spell perhaps? Or was she simply in love with him?"

"That's not my idea of love." Abi prodded the wall. "What about your mum? Was she under Henry Williams's spell?"

Droplets of water splashed from the bucket as Becky wrung out the cloth again. "I've no idea. At least you could ask your mum if you wanted to."

Abi grunted.

Becky turned toward her. "I sometimes dream I'm chatting to my mother about Henry Williams, asking her whether I was born out of love, or just some one-night stand."

"Does it matter?"

"It would be nice to know, but my mum wouldn't be the sort to talk about love or sex, even if she was alive."

"Who can talk about love with any confidence?" Abi ran her hand over the patch of wall she'd just scraped. "I would've crawled on my hands and knees to stay with Jacob's father, but he had no interest in me. Or his son. With Eve and Grace's dad, I fell for his good looks and stayed with him the longest." She snorted. "He'd disappear for weeks, then he'd slither back as if nothing had happened. After I left him, I mainly used other guys for what I wanted, and didn't give a damn for their feelings." She paused. "Until Ben, that is."

"John used me. Thank God, David's different." Becky giggled. "I think I'm falling in love with him."

"Good on you." Abi placed the scraper on the floor and hugged Becky. "Go for it. Love's the best feeling in the world, even if it comes to nothing later." Abi stepped away from her sister. "I know I'm going to have the best time ever with Ben." She grinned.

Reaching for the scraper again she stopped suddenly and pulled her hand back.

"We've done enough for today. How about another cuppa and a piece of your walnut and coffee cake?"

Becky chucked her cloth into the bucket.

Abi rushed to the doorway.

"Bagsy the first slice."

33

Becky gently touched the golden crust of one of the six Cornish pasties cooling on a wire tray. Still warm; just the right temperature to be wrapped and packed.

She glanced out of the window. Small puffs of cloud drifted lazily across a perfect summer sky. They'd chosen the right evening for a picnic on Long Rock Beach. Not her favourite place – she preferred Falmouth's Gyllyngvase Beach or Maenporth – but Long Rock was one of the few dog-friendly beaches during the peak holiday season. Still, the view of St Michael's Mount was amazing. She never tired of it, no matter the weather or the time of year.

A tap on the kitchen door broke into her thoughts. It was probably Jeffery back again to fuss over Apollo, or Megan sorting out last-minute arrangements for the show.

"It's open," she called out.

Jess stepped into the kitchen.

Becky's heart thumped. It took all her willpower not to rush over and embrace her daughter. Steve didn't seem to be with her. Thank goodness. Although something must be up for Jess to come to Vellangoose without him.

"What a surprise," she said, relieved it came out sounding almost normal.

"I was just passing and ..." Jess shrugged.

"About time." Becky smiled at her daughter. "You look well. Very smart."

What she wanted to say was that Jess looked middle-aged in her dark trouser suit and over made-up face: a clone of Veronica Williams. Becky hadn't enjoyed Jess's teenage tantrums and arguments but anything was better than this soulless frump in front of her.

Jess kicked off her court shoes and walked barefoot over to the table. Thankfully, some things hadn't changed; her daughter had spent most of her life at Rose Cottage without shoes or socks on.

"They're so cute." Jess pointed at Grace's tiny pasty, and the one with a pastry bone on top for Buddy.

"We're having a picnic on Long Rock Beach. There's enough food if you want to join us."

In the silence, Becky ripped a sheet of greaseproof paper from the roll and a similar-sized piece of aluminium foil. She wrapped one pasty, first in the greaseproof, followed by the foil, then she reached for the next pasty.

"Put the kettle on, darling," she said. "I'm desperate for a cup of tea. There's a chocolate and orange tray-bake in the white bin on the shelf. Have some, it's your favourite."

"Steve doesn't like me to eat too much." Jess glanced sideways at her, then reached for the kettle.

"Trust me, I won't tell him." Becky's nails tore a hole in the aluminium foil as she struggled to wrap the last pasty.

Jess moved over to the cake bin, took out a square piece of cake and broke off a piece. A few crumbs fell to the floor. It didn't matter; Buddy would find them later.

She had to ask. "How's Steve?"

"He's okay."

Becky turned away to hide a quiet smile. Only okay? Not wonderful or brilliant? Perhaps her daughter was coming to her senses, at last?

She put all the wrapped pasties into a shopping bag and added bags of crisps, cake, and biscuits. More than they would normally eat, but everyone always ate extra on a picnic, especially one by the sea.

"You and Steve must come over one afternoon or evening," she said, her voice casual.

Getting no response, she moved to the fridge, picked up two large cartons of orange juice and put them into another bag, together with mugs and a roll of paper towel. Coffee next. She reached for the flask.

"I saw Apollo in the field." Jess washed her hands in the sink. "He looks so handsome." She dried her hands, walked over to the worktop and made two mugs of tea.

"He's only recently come back," Becky said. "He's been out to stud."

"Several of Steve's men were well chuffed when Apollo's offspring won some point-to-point in Devon and put them in the money. Not that Veronica or Steve were very happy when they heard the news."

Becky flinched at Jess's use of Veronica Williams's first name. Not unexpected under the circumstances, but it was still a bit of a shock.

Jess adjusted the collar of her cream blouse. "I look a dork, don't I?"

"Truthfully?" Becky held Jess's gaze. "Yes, you do."

"Veronica expects me to dress like this when I help out at Boswyn Manor or when I'm in the offices. Steve thinks the same."

"You don't have to do what they say. You're not twenty-one yet. You should enjoy being young."

"She's not a woman to be crossed. You should've seen her after … you know who … gate-crashed Boswyn."

"Her name's Abi. Your aunt."

"Whatever. After the guests left, Veronica went ballistic. She threw stuff at the walls: her valuable china cups and the silver coffee pot. Honestly, Mum, she scared me at first, then I had to leave the room to stop myself from cracking up in front of her." A giggle escaped from Jess, then she burst into laughter.

Becky joined in. "Wish I could've seen it."

The wonderful sound of Jess's laughter released something inside of Becky, and she moved over to her daughter and took her into her arms.

"I love you. You know that don't you?"

"I love you too, Mum." Jess returned the hug.

"What's up?" Becky looked at Jess. "Why the visit?"

"Veronica and Steve are up to something, and I'm scared for you. Trust me, they're working flat out to get you both out of this place, lining up so-called witnesses and other serious stuff. Their solicitor is at Boswyn nearly every day."

Becky stiffened. "David Penna?"

"Sounds right. Anyway, some old guy. Bald."

Becky grinned to herself. Jess might consider David to be 'some old guy' but he most definitely wasn't bald. He'd promised he wouldn't have anything further to do with Veronica Williams, so it must be either his father or another partner in the firm.

"The people providing evidence, do you know who they are?"

"Most of them are tenants or people who work for Williams Estates and Haulage." Jess picked up another piece of cake. "Mind you, a few refused to help Veronica, which made her even angrier."

"Oh?"

"Everything about Boswyn Manor is crazy. The staff gossip all the time about the Williams family, even when

I'm in the room. They must think I'm deaf, or daft, or something."

Becky casually added a bottle of ketchup to the picnic ingredients, then took a deep breath. "Do they ever talk about Steve's mother, Constance?"

"Well, the old dear who helps out in the kitchen kept banging on one day about how convenient it was that Constance died, seeing as how Veronica had always wanted to get her hands on Steve."

Becky busied herself filling a flask with hot coffee. "Anything else?"

"I've tried asking Steve, but he won't talk about his parents much. He thinks they'd still be alive if his mum hadn't gone to Brazil. He blames his Uncle Henry for some reason." A red flush crossed Jess's face. "Sorry, Mum, but Steve's got it into his head that Henry Williams scammed his mother out of Vellangoose. Feels it would be his now, if–"

Jess jerked, snatched at her pocket, and pulled out her mobile phone.

"Hello. I'm in Falmouth, shopping. Oh, do I have to? Okay. I'll leave right away."

Jess finished the call, pushed her feet into her shoes and reached for the door handle.

"Have some more tea? Or coffee?" Becky didn't want to lose her daughter again.

"It's Steve." Jess made a face. "He needs me."

Becky raised her eyebrows and glared at Jess. "Really?"

"Oh, Mum. Don't."

"Okay … but come and see me again. Soon."

"They keep me pretty busy. I'm not sure when–"

"It wasn't a request," Becky said in an authoritative voice. "I'm here most afternoons. Right?"

Jess blinked, then nodded.

"Next visit, I'll show you what we've done to the place."
Jess stared at her. "You've changed."

"Dead right, I have." Becky hugged her daughter again.

"Abi's pretty awesome as well," Jess whispered into her ear, then stepped away and rushed out of the door.

Happiness flooded through Becky as she packed towels, jelly shoes and sweaters. She stood for a moment and did a mental recce: food, drinks, clothes, picnic rug. Whoops, she nearly forgot Buddy. She reached for his lead and water bowl, then filled a bottle with tap water. Everything was ready to go. Only needed Abi and the children now.

She picked up her book and sat in the chair – time for a few pages?

A chapter later, her mobile phone burst into life. The connection crackled before a man's voice came over the line.

"Rebecca Farrow?"

"Yes."

"Nicholas Hodges. I'm calling from Rio de Janeiro."

"Nicholas Hodges?"

"You've been asking after me."

"Constance's husband, from Vellangoose in Cornwall?" Becky's heart raced.

"Well, you know who I am. Who are you? Why are you asking after me?"

"But you're dead," she blurted out.

A startled grunt came over the phone. "News to me."

Becky's head spun. She took a deep breath and told the man who claimed to be Nicholas Hodges about Henry Williams's death and how she and Abi had inherited Vellangoose.

"Well, well. Henry's still up to his old tricks, even in death. He liked to stir things up where he could. Bet Veronica's none too pleased?"

"You could say that." She shook her head. "Everyone was told you died in a car crash thirty years ago. There was even an obituary announcement in the local paper."

"Well, there was a car crash. I was so seriously injured I spent nearly two months in a coma and another three months in hospital. What I don't understand is, why hasn't Constance told you all of this?"

"But Constance died in the crash with you."

In the ensuing silence, Becky grasped the absurdity of the words she'd just said.

When he finally spoke, Nicholas's voice had an edge to it. "Is this some kind of sick joke? Constance is in Cornwall."

"Constance was included in the obituary notice."

"Steve?" Nicholas shouted over the phone. "Where's Steve? My son."

"Steve's fine. He's been living at Boswyn Manor with Veronica Williams for the last thirty years."

Nicholas groaned. "Is this for fucking real?"

"It would be helpful if you could tell me what you know? Nicholas? Nicholas, are you still there?"

"What the hell's going on?" he said. He sounded like he was crying.

"I don't know," she said gently. "That's why I need you to tell me everything."

Becky held her breath in the silence that followed. She could hear him taking deep gulps of air, steadying himself.

Finally, he spoke again.

"Constance didn't cope well after our marriage broke down. When I found out about her drinking, I immediately came back to Cornwall to see her and Steve. Before I returned to Brazil, Constance agreed to start a rehab course in London." He sighed. "She wanted to get better for Steve, so she could look after him again. In the meantime, he was happy with his Aunt Veronica. It seemed the logical solution then."

"So, you just deserted your son? You just left him?"

"It wasn't like that. A month after I got back to Brazil, I was involved in that terrible car accident. When I eventually come out of the coma, I tried to contact Constance, but Veronica said she didn't want to speak to me. She reassured me that Constance was making great progress on the rehab programme and would be returning to Cornwall soon. Veronica also told me that Constance wanted a clean split on the grounds I wouldn't be around for her or Steve. I even had a few words with my son. He sounded okay."

"He was your child, how could you ..." Becky clamped a hand over her mouth.

"I did what I thought Constance wanted," Nicholas snapped. "You need to understand, it was an awful time for me and my partner."

"I'm sorry. It's so good of you to talk so freely with me."

Silence.

"Please?" she pleaded.

He cleared his throat. "After the phone call, Veronica transferred a large sum of money into my bank account on the condition that I never got back in contact with any of them again. To be honest, I was still so ill and too sick to work. My partner was pregnant and we had hardly any income. In the end, I took what I thought to be a final settlement. In fairness, I was happy in the knowledge that Constance was about to go home to care for Steve."

"If she did return to Cornwall, it was only briefly, before she was supposed to have gone to Brazil."

"What a mess. I should've kept in contact after that last telephone conversation with her. She rang me from the rehab clinic about three or four weeks after she'd been admitted. It was just before the car crash. She seemed so much better. We had quite a long talk and finished the call on good terms. So, when I received the financial settlement from Veronica after my accident, I took her word for it that all was well with Constance and that she, Steve and the baby would be okay. Over the years, I had more children and ... What the hell has happened to Constance? Where is she?"

One word had hit Becky like a bullet.

"Baby?"

"Constance was pregnant. She told me during that last phone call."

"Pregnant?"

"It wasn't mine, if that's what you're asking?"

Becky could barely breathe. "Do you know who the father was?"

"Only one person I'm aware of. Always sniffing around, even when Constance and I were together."

She knew what the answer would be before the two words came down the line.

"Henry Williams."

34

Normally, Abi loved the sea, whether it was the gentle waves on their endless journey back and forth or huge crashing breakers. Today, the vast stretch of water made her feel small and helpless.

She stared across the sand, a partly eaten pasty in her hand. On the water's edge, Jacob played with a boy he'd met fifteen minutes ago, their dark heads bent over a clump of seaweed, no doubt in the hope that some poor crab or other unfortunate creature would crawl out. Eve and Grace paddled hand in hand in the small pools of seawater dotted across the long stretch of sand. Buddy ran from one group to the other and back again.

Unconsciously, she called out, "Jacob, don't go into the water again. You've just eaten. Eve, don't go any further, and don't let go of Grace's hand."

Out of the corner of her eye, she saw Becky clearing up the remains of the food and drink. Not that there was much; the kids had devoured most of it like a pack of wolves.

"Coffee?" Becky sat on her heels, flask in one hand, mug in the other.

Abi nodded, pulled off another bit of her by now cold pasty, and popped it into her mouth. It tasted like sawdust; any food would have done. Ever since they'd arrived at the beach, she'd been mulling over the news that Nicholas Hodges was alive. How could she eat, when everything she thought she knew about the Williams family had been thrown up in the air?

"I can't get my head around it. How could he not know what's been going on with his son for the past thirty years?"

"Veronica Williams effectively ensured that all contact between Nicholas, his family, and Cornwall, were severed when she paid him off." Becky reached over to the pile of wet swimsuits, picked them up and pushed them into a plastic carrier bag. "Nicholas thought he was doing what Constance wanted."

"Then where the hell is Constance? If she didn't die in Brazil, and she isn't in Cornwall, where is she?" Abi shook her head. "And why would she leave Steve with Veronica Williams? No sane person would, let alone a mother."

She sat bolt upright.

"What's wrong?"

"She did away with Constance."

"She what?"

"Veronica Williams knocked Constance off. Think about it." Abi shoved her pasty back into its wrapping.

"It's the only logical explanation."

"Oh, come on, you're certainly letting your imagination run away now. I know Veronica Williams is a nasty woman but ... murder?"

Abi picked up a pebble and threw it with force across the beach. "I think that woman's capable of anything. Look at what she did to Grace."

"Isn't it more likely she paid off Constance like she did Nicholas, enough to start a new life somewhere else with her baby? It would've prevented the inevitable gossip about the baby, and who its father was."

"So would killing her." Abi gulped her coffee.

"But with both of them paid off and out of the way, all Veronica Williams had to do was to tell everyone they'd both been killed in Brazil."

"Risky. What if Constance came back?" Abi picked up another pebble and tossed it from one hand to the other. "She's such a liar. Clever though. She got what she wanted. She got Steve."

"I can't stop thinking about Constance being pregnant." Becky reached for her sweater and shrugged it over her shoulders. "You know that means we have a brother or sister out there somewhere?"

"Well, let's hope when all this gets out, he, or she, doesn't want to get their hands on a share of Vellangoose." Abi chucked the dregs of her coffee into the sand.

"It helps that Nicholas said he'd keep schtum until I get back to him. He wants to see Veronica Williams get her comeuppance as much as we do."

Abi watched two kite surfers scudding across the bay. The sight of the brilliant red and yellow kites and the sheer exuberance of people having fun usually calmed her but today her heart raced. She couldn't remember the last time she'd felt so anxious. Maybe because there was so much at stake? In the past, if things got difficult or some guy got on her nerves, she just upped and left. Not this time. This time she had Vellangoose. She couldn't walk away; it had become too precious to her and her kids.

Abi parked the camper van next to The Mill. She smiled to herself as Jacob and Eve burst from the vehicle and hurtled towards the garden.

Becky got out and gathered up an armful of picnic stuff. "Looks like Megan's busy again."

Abi hoisted Grace onto her hip and waved to Megan, who stood in the middle of the meadow bellowing instructions to several people working on various tasks. Then Megan bent down, picked up a mallet and thumped a metal stake into the ground.

"Where she gets her energy from, I don't know."

Thirty minutes later, Abi flopped into one of the kitchen chairs. "That's Eve and Grace asleep. Jacob's playing with his racing cars but his eyelids are drooping. The sea air always does it. Brilliant stuff. If only we could bottle and sell it."

Becky yawned. "There's more cake left. Do you want some?"

"Please. Just what I–"

Startled by a loud knock on the door, Abi swivelled around to see a large man in the open doorway. Dressed in black leathers and knee-high boots, he stepped into the kitchen. A dark motorcycle helmet covered his face.

Abi's heart thumped. She got slowly to her feet.

The man flicked the visor up and his dark eyes looked in her direction.

"Abi Pascoe?"

"What of it?"

He turned towards Becky.

"Rebecca Farrow?"

Her sister nodded.

He handed a large envelope to each of them.

"Consider yourself formally served. Good evening, ladies." With that, the man turned and walked outside.

The door slammed behind him.

With trembling fingers, Abi opened her envelope and pulled out the papers; court papers that duly notified her of proceedings to declare the Trust Agreement null and void on the grounds that the conditions of the said Trust had been broken. Her vision blurred. Only a few words filtered into her brain: use of ... said property ... commercial purposes ...

A glance at her sister and Abi knew instantly that Becky's pale face and wide eyes reflected her own.

Finally, Becky spoke the words that Abi was afraid to voice. "If Veronica Williams wins this case, we'll lose Vellangoose. Our beautiful home." A tear tracked down her cheek. "We'll lose everything."

Abi gripped the back of the chair, her knuckles white. Her lips moved but no words came out.

"I've baked several cakes at Vellangoose." Becky's voice was unusually soft. "Only for friends, and I was careful not to take any money, but how can I prove that if Veronica Williams wants to challenge it? That woman has the wealth to buy the best legal advice to fight her claim." She shoved the lid back on the remainder of the cake and returned it to the shelf. "You've chopped sack loads of logs for barter. Did you ever take cash instead?"

Abi stiffened. "Jeffery slipped me some notes a few times. Twenty pounds when he knew I needed diesel. Ben did the same another time." A knot of dread formed in her stomach. "But they're friends. They don't count."

"Don't they? Jess said that Veronica Williams knows everything we're doing at Vellangoose. How? Someone close to us must be providing her with information."

"Do you seriously think one of our friends has dumped us in it?"

Abi couldn't believe that, not of the people she'd grown to like ... and love.

"Think about it."

"Bloody hell." Abi glared at her sister. "Who do you think it is? Not Ben, surely? Or David? Who else is there?"

"It can only be someone who visits Vellangoose regularly."

"Jeffery? He's always coming over to see Apollo. And, what about that nephew of his, Aaron? Now I think about it, what eighteen-year-old hangs around with an old man?"

"You'll be accusing Megan next."

"Megan?"

Damn it, Megan came to Vellangoose every day to check on Pixie and Dixie, and to clean out their stables. But she couldn't be the grass; she was like family.

"The Penhellick Country Show on Saturday," Becky gasped. "Lots of people are coming. People paying an entry fee to come to Vellangoose. Megan has organised an ice cream van, fast food tents, and the village shop to provide a stall. The owners will be selling their produce for money. Veronica Williams could rip us apart in court."

"You've baked cakes for the raffle stall, and I made some wood keyrings and other little bits." Abi ran her fingers through her hair. "What a mess."

"Then there's the insurance. What if our names are on the policy document?"

Abi remembered now how keen Megan had been to arrange and pay for the insurance. It was part of the original deal to offset the cost of stabling and grazing and to provide The Barn with electricity. The acidic taste of bile rose in Abi's mouth. She swiped her lips and quickly moved across the kitchen.

"Where are you going?"

"We need to find out if Megan's the snitch," Abi snarled.

"Oh dear." Becky's hand rested for a moment on her neck, then she pushed her shoulders back. "You're right, we need to know while there's still time to cancel the show."

"We'll stop people at the entrance gate if necessary. It's our place, and I'm keeping it that way."

Abi opened the kitchen door, grabbed Becky's hand and, with their heads held high, they stepped outside.

As they approached her, Megan dropped the mallet on the ground, and with a big grin on her face advanced towards them.

"My dears, I'm so pleased to see you. I could do with some extra help."

"We need to talk."

A rush of sadness came over Abi. Never in her life had she wished so hard to be somewhere else.

"No time for any chit-chatting." Megan waved her arms towards the mountain of red and white poles, metal stakes and rope laid out at various spots on the grass.

"Make time," Abi snapped.

Megan took off her straw hat, pulled a man's handkerchief from her pocket and wiped her brow.

"I'm all ears."

"Have you set us up?" Abi stepped closer to Megan.

"Yes, yes. Everything's all set up for Saturday."

"Not that. Have *you* set *us* up?"

Megan stopped in mid-wipe. "You've obviously got something on your minds." She shoved the handkerchief back into her dungarees. "Come on, spit it out."

"We think we should cancel the show." Becky rushed in. "You see–"

"Cancel? What are you talking about? Some of the young ones are already polishing their saddles and grooming their ponies as we speak. The poor dears are so excited, the children that is, not the ponies. Mind you, some of the mothers are so awful, it might be worth cancelling it all to avoid them." Megan slapped her hat back onto her head. "What's going on, ladies? Tell me."

"Veronica Williams is taking us to court," Abi glared at Megan. "Says she has evidence we've been taking cash for goods. It's not true, but her solicitor could manipulate anything, so we–"

"We're worried that the show will be seen as a money-making venture for us," Becky butted in. "We could lose Vellangoose."

"Nonsense. I've arranged everything in either my name or on behalf of the committee. Rest assured, there's no come back on either of you."

"We need to see the documents."

"I guess I can understand that." Megan held Abi's stare. "Follow me. Quick. Quick."

Megan stomped over to her battered people carrier, yanked open a mud-splattered door, and reached inside to rummage in a box on the passenger seat. It overflowed with papers, packs of colourful rosettes and shiny prize-winner trophies.

"Ah, here it is." She flipped open a battered vanilla folder, pulled out sheets of paper, thrust some into Becky's hand and some into Abi's. "See for yourselves. Everything's above board. Only the stallholders, the committee, and Cancer Research running the tombola stall will receive any monies."

"What about the insurance?" Becky asked.

"All completed in my name. See, right there, and there." Abi followed Megan's finger as she prodded at various sections on the crumpled document. "My dears, I have to say, I'm finding this most irregular. Most irregular."

Abi placed her documents onto the bonnet of the people carrier and read them. Becky did the same. When Abi had finished, she glanced at Becky. Her sister nodded.

Abi cleared her throat and looked at Megan. "It all seems okay, nothing to suggest we'd be making any money from the show."

"Quite."

"I'm sorry we had to put you through that," Abi said.

Megan grabbed the documents, shoved them back into the folder and tossed it into the vehicle.

"I have to say, your lack of trust has shaken me a bit. It would be untrue for me to say otherwise. I do understand it's a very difficult situation for you both, but I thought you knew I'm on your side."

Abi dug the tip of her trainer into the yard's rocky surface.

"Well … what's done is done." A smile suddenly flashed across Megan's face. "I adore Vellangoose, and so do our precious Pixie and Dixie. And, my girls, they love the place as well. They're in the stable now, grooming those poor animals to within an inch of their lives and practising how to plait their manes. They might just get the hang of it by Saturday."

Megan marched to the stable door and leaned inside. "Poppy. Rose. Leave those poor creatures alone. They need some rest. Come on, it's time we were on our way home." She turned back to Abi and Becky. "Keep your chins up, my dears. We're all rooting for you."

Tears pricked Abi's eyes as she watched Megan's vehicle rattle and sway up the lane. Now familiar waves of fear and panic washed over her. What if Veronica Williams won the court case? How could she tell Jacob, Eve and Grace they had to leave the home they loved, and once again be dragged from one temporary dump to another?

Becky linked her arm through Abi's. For a few minutes, Abi and her sister looked around the yard. The sun, on its journey westwards, had painted The Mill in a soft apricot colour. In the waning light, the glassless windows appeared like black, empty eye sockets.

Suddenly it hit Abi.

"Constance's body is in the well," she said, her voice hoarse. "That's what Veronica Williams is hiding. That's why she wants Vellangoose."

Becky put a hand to her mouth. "No. It can't be."

"Well, there's only one way to find out." Abi glanced at her sister, then turned and headed towards The Mill.

Becky caught up with her and grabbed her wrist. "We should call Detective Inspector Jack Carter. It's his job to–"

"I'll call him after I've found the body."

Minutes later, Abi stared into the deep, black hole. Round in structure, stones jutted from the rough surface. She let out a long breath; at least it was narrow enough for her to stretch her arms out and touch the opposite sides at the same time. If she couldn't get a good grip, she could lever herself downwards using her feet, arms and back.

"Jeffery said that the well had dried up years ago when Veronica Williams's father diverted the stream."

"Thanks for that, Becky. At least if I fall, I won't drown."

"Oh." Becky tugged at Abi's arm. "Please don't do this."

A bead of sweat ran down Abi's forehead. She swiped it away, snatched up a long piece of rope coiled at her feet, walked outside and fastened one end to the towing eye on the camper van, then returned, looped the rope around her waist and tossed the remainder down the well. She tucked a torch into the waistband of her jeans, took a gulp of air, then eased her body into the hole, threading the rope through her hands as she descended.

A cough bubbled from her mouth as an earthy, dank smell overwhelmed her and dust coated her throat. Her trainer slipped against the uneven surface. She fought to find a grip on the granite walls. A fingernail ripped. She steadied herself, breathed deeply, then inched downwards until darkness closed over her.

"Are you okay? Abi?" Becky's muffled voice floated down to her. "Abi?"

"I'm … I'm alright," she yelled.

The rope bit into her waist. She wedged herself across the hole, feet against one side and back against the other, and shook her hands. Her bloodied fingertip throbbed.

She looked down and shone the torch beam into the darkness. It was only a well; the bottom couldn't be that far away.

A stone came loose in her hand, sending dust and gravel crashing beneath her. Her heart pounded against her ribs. What if the walls caved in around her? Crushed her? Her breath came in gasps. At the thought of her kids, she forced herself to count to ten, then continued her descent.

After what seemed like forever, her foot touched something. A crack ricocheted around the enclosed space.

A scream burst from her mouth. Constance?

Abi shone the torch into the darkness. The beam wobbled. Please let this be the answer to all their problems. Sweat ran into her half-closed eyes as she gazed down. A laugh-cum-sob escaped from her throat.

An old tree branch lay broken in two at her feet.

For a while, wedged across the hole, she let the disappointment flow over her, then she twisted back and forth and once again probed the shadows with the weak shaft of light from her torch.

At first, she prodded the surface with the toe of her trainer, then falling to her knees, she plunged her hands into the dirt and mulch collected over the years. Constance had to be here. Abi jabbed and burrowed into the putrid mess. Worms slithered through her fingers.

Eventually, she leaned her forehead against the wall.

A tear rolled down her face.

She grabbed the rope and began to climb.

It felt like an eternity before Becky clutched Abi's hand and hauled until she collapsed onto the floor of The Mill. Involuntary tremors ran up and down the muscles in her arms and legs.

"Abi? Abi, are you okay? Did you find anything?"

She scrambled to her knees. Dust clogged her throat. She spat on the ground.

"Nothing. A big, fat, nothing."

Which was exactly what she and Becky would have if Veronica Williams won the court case.

35

Becky checked the food laid out on the kitchen table: cold ham, chicken, potato salad and freshly baked bread. From her dad's fridge she took out coleslaw, a big bowl of salad and various homemade, pickled vegetables and relishes. A large sherry trifle and strawberry cheesecake stood on the shelf for later. It was her dad's birthday and she wanted him to have his favourite food.

Her phone pinged. A text from Natalie saying she was running late and for Becky and her dad to start lunch without her. Typical Natalie. A ball of nerves coiled in the pit of Becky's stomach. Surely, her sister would come, if only for their dad's sake? It would be the first time the three of them had dined together since Henry Williams's death.

Becky moved to the open window and called out. "Dad. Time to come in. Food's ready."

Her dad pushed open the kitchen door, wiped his shoes on the mat and stepped inside. A fragrant waft of sweet peas flowed into the room.

"My word, love, 'tis some lovely spread you've got there."

"Happy Birthday, Dad." She hugged him. "What have you been doing with the pots?"

"Just a bit of a tidy up for now. Cleared out several of the old plants. I'll replace them when I've a few minutes." He walked to the sink, pumped liquid soap into his palm and washed his hands under the running water. "It's the allotment that's taking my time now. Everything's starting to fruit and the veg is ready for eating. Too much for me."

Becky picked up three plates, knives, and forks, and arranged them on the table. She cleared her throat.

"I've been working on getting the gardens at Vellangoose back to their former glory."

"Ah." He slowly wiped his hands on a towel, then dropped it in a ball on the worktop. "Suppose they're a right old mess?"

Tears welled in her eyes. Would she get the chance now to put all her plans for the gardens into action? Not if Veronica Williams won the court case. Becky turned her back on her dad and surreptitiously wiped her eyes.

"Surprisingly, several flowers and shrubs have survived in the main garden. In the autumn, I'm going to plant hundreds of bulbs. I want a mat of colour in the spring with masses of daffodils, crocuses and grape hyacinths."

Her hand fluttered to her neck. For goodness sake, she needed to pull herself together. She had to believe that she and Abi would be able to stay at Vellangoose.

"Anything left in the walled garden?" her dad asked. "I remember when me and the kids from the village used to sneak in after school. 'Twas fun pinching handfuls of strawberries and eating them down by the ponds."

"There's a plentiful source of weeds, dead branches and gorse. I've cleared a lot of it and found three or four raspberry canes in the process. Also, a gooseberry bush and a couple of shaggy blackcurrants." She pulled out a chair and sat. "Looks like I'll get a small number of apples and pears from the old trees. Might even be enough fruit to make a few jars of jelly or preserves."

Her dad sat across the table and rested his elbows on the red and white oilcloth. "Them raspberries and blackcurrants can't be anything special now. Past it, after all this time." He reached for a bread roll and the butter dish. "Best to start again with new plants."

"What about the brambles? Are they okay to keep? There's a lot of blackberries on them."

"Them things will grow anywhere. Need to be trimmed right back later, if you want to get the most out of them."

"I don't know a lot about cultivating fruit, so any advice you could give me would be welcome. I also want to produce my own vegetables next year."

"It'll take a lot of hard work. 'Tisn't as easy as going to the supermarket."

"Oh, Dad, I know that, but I want fresh ingredients for my cooking." She put two slices of chicken breast and a portion of ham onto her plate and passed the platter to him. "What I need is expert guidance and any practical help I can get."

Silence stretched between them before he spoke. "Sorry, I've not always been the greatest of dads."

Becky wanted to say to him that he was being silly, that it wasn't true. Instead, she said, "It doesn't matter now, Dad. What's past is past. You're my father in every way that matters."

He grunted and shook his head. "'Tis hard for me to admit I was wrong, but I need you to know how proud I am of what you've done. I never thought you'd stick it at Vellangoose."

Becky forced a watery smile at the mention of Vellangoose.

"Didn't think you had it in you. Now, love, don't go tearing up. You've certainly shown them old gossips what strong stuff you're made of." He scratched the back of his head. "And you've even set up your own business. I don't know where you got the guts from to do it all, but I know for sure it didn't come from me."

"I've never really had a chance to do what I wanted before. I let Mum ... John ..." She twisted a strand of hair around her finger. "I thought it made for an easier life to do what everyone told me to. Meeting Abi and her family, and living at Vellangoose, has been one of the best things that's ever happened to me." She reached for her dad's hand. "You should come over and meet them."

He squeezed her hand, then reached for his knife and fork. She didn't need him to say or do any more. He hadn't refused outright, and that was enough for now.

"Now come on, love, what's this I hear about you getting yourself a new fella? Natalie says he's a solicitor. Isn't it about time I met him?"

Becky glanced at the rapidly fading mark on her finger where her wedding ring used to be, and smiled.

For a while, the conversation flipped between David, the allotment, and what Becky would like to achieve with the gardens at Vellangoose. They'd just finished their main course when the kitchen door flew open and Natalie swanned in, red shoulder bag banging against her hip and a large, brightly wrapped potted shrub in her arms.

"Happy Birthday, Dad." She kissed him on the cheek and presented him with the gift.

"Thanks, love. Just the job for one of the pots I emptied earlier."

"You won't believe the morning I've had." Natalie dropped a brief kiss onto Becky's cheek. "Lily woke up grumpy and refused to go to pre-school. By the time I cuddled her and talked her around I hardly made it to the salon for a manicure." She held her hand up and admired her red nails. "Then to top it all, the traffic coming into Falmouth was horrendous."

"Grab yourself a pew, girl. Our Becky has done a handsome job with the food."

"We've had our main course." Becky waved to the chair next to her. "There's plenty left."

"Thanks. I'm ravenous. Only had a meal replacement shake for breakfast. Banana flavoured. Disgusting. Never again."

Becky stood, walked to the fridge and reached in for a block of Cornish Yarg, Natalie's favourite go-to food when she wasn't on a diet.

"Wasn't certain you'd make it, love."

"Couldn't miss seeing you on your birthday, Dad."

A bubble of happiness rose in Becky's chest. The three of them were together again, at last, chatting like a normal family over lunch.

"I can't stay too long. Got to buy a new uniform for Thomas." Natalie chuckled. "He's sprouting up so fast, and the new term starts next week."

"Jacob's grown out of most of his school clothes as well. Abi's doing a recce on costs and whether she can get it second-hand."

Natalie cut a large chunk of Yarg. "I shouldn't be eating this. Still, you only live once." She buttered a chunk of bread, then looked at Becky. "If she's stuck, Abi can have Thomas's old stuff. Jacob's not so tall, so the clothes should fit him for a term or two. She'd be doing me a favour, save me a trip to the charity shop."

Becky gave her sister a wry smile. "Thanks. I'll mention it to her."

"Well, I have to admit that Jacob's a delightful boy. Bright." Natalie tossed her shiny hair over her shoulder. "He's been a good influence on Thomas. Made him pull his socks up at school."

Becky removed the empty plates from the table and dropped them into the sink. A smile tugged at her lips. Nice one, Jacob.

"How are things going with David?" Natalie selected a chicken thigh and dropped it onto her plate. "I hear on the grapevine that's he's no longer working for Veronica Williams. Good on him. She's evil." She yanked off the skin and bit into the cooked meat.

"She certainly made Lloyd Accountancy suffer when you moved into that place. Several of our clients took their business elsewhere, which left us with one massive financial problem."

The mention of Veronica Williams's name, and the thought of the impending court case, flooded Becky with a wave of fear and panic.

"Is it very bad, love?"

For a moment, Becky thought her dad was asking her, that he knew about the court case. But he was speaking to Natalie.

Her sister grabbed a paper napkin and wiped the corner of her mouth. "Thankfully, several of the clients have seen sense and come back to us. They were fed up with Veronica Williams telling them what to do. If it wasn't so very unprofessional, I would hug them all."

Unbidden, an image of Abi scrabbling out of the well flashed into Becky's mind. Her hand trembled as she reached inside the fridge, lifted out the trifle and cheesecake and placed them on the table.

Natalie nicked a fresh strawberry from the top of the cheesecake and popped it into her mouth. "So, what's been going on with the both of you?"

"The allotment's doing alright this year. You can take some strawberries with you when you go. And lettuce."

"And I was telling Dad about the gardens and fruit trees at Vellangoose," Becky rushed in.

"Oh, yeah." Natalie drew a compact from her handbag and flipped it open.

"It's going to look great when I eventually finish everything I plan to do. I'm trying to persuade Dad to visit."

"Good luck with that." Natalie ran her tongue over her teeth.

"You could come as well."

Natalie snapped the compact shut. "Very funny."

Becky tried again. "You could visit together and–"

Natalie suddenly sat upright and clapped her hands, stopping Becky in mid-sentence.

"I've got something to tell you both. I'm going back to work at Lloyd Accountancy." She laughed.

"What brought this on, love? Veronica Williams, I suppose?"

"Her actions have taken their toll on Pete, for sure. The drop in income is also a major inconvenience. So, I'm re-joining the world of the employed." She laughed again, a bit too loudly. "If Pete and I work together, I know we can build up the client base again."

"Pulling together like some old married couple." Becky grinned at Natalie. "That's quite a surprise."

Her sister poked her tongue out at her.

"About time, girl. That man of yours has been working like a horse for a long time."

"Well, for once, Dad, you're right." Natalie looked at Becky. "What Veronica Williams did to you and Abi and Grace, made me think about the important things in life." Before Becky could reply, her sister reached for a wedge of quiche and took a bite. "Mmm. Delicious. Can I have the recipe?"

"Good grief." Becky pretended to search around the kitchen. "What's happened to my sister?"

"I can cook, you know. Just didn't see the point when I could get it from Waitrose or I had you to cook and bake for me." Natalie grinned at her. "Now you're so busy with your own business, I don't get a look in."

Becky giggled and picked up the dessert knife. "Who's for cheesecake?"

"Me, please," Natalie said. "A big piece."

"Only if you promise you'll visit Vellangoose soon. I've been there eight months now, and it's time you saw what Abi and I have done to the place." She checked herself from adding that if she didn't visit soon, she might never get to see it.

Natalie took the desert bowl from her, deftly scooped her finger across the top of the cheesecake and popped the soft mixture into her mouth.

"That's so good. Any chance of taking back three portions for Pete and the children?"

"Natalie, don't change the subject."

Her sister reached for a spoon and held it poised over the dish. "I'll come … when I'm ready and the time's right. That's all I can promise for now."

Becky gave her sister a small nod, then turned to face her dad. "Trifle?"

"Thanks, love." He pulled a handkerchief from his pocket and blew his nose. "'Tis some lovely birthday I'm having. Both of you being here has made my day."

"Aw," Becky said.

"Bless," Natalie added.

Half an hour later, Becky handed her sister a plastic storage bin containing the remainder of the cheesecake.

"Thanks." Natalie hugged her. "I had such a good time. We must catch up again soon."

On the doorstep, Becky waved until Natalie's immaculate four-by-four disappeared around the corner at the end of the road, the horn tooting the whole while.

She cleared the table, tore off a piece of clingfilm and covered the remainder of the trifle.

"Why don't you take that home with you, love? My stomach's like a drum. I won't eat more trifle today."

"Are you sure?"

"Take the rest of the chicken and ham as well." Her dad cleared his throat. "I ... I could bring some fresh fruit and veg over tomorrow afternoon if you like? Maybe you could show me them fruit trees you want pruning?" His eyes searched her face. "What do you think?"

She rushed to her dad, flung her arms around him and kissed his cheek several times.

"Enough of that, you daft thing, otherwise I might change my mind."

Becky laughed.

"Oh, Dad. I do love you."

36

Abi came to a halt and tilted her face towards the sun. The warmth felt wonderful. Everything about the day so far had gone like a dream, and the walk to the top of Godolphin Hill was the icing on the cake. The wild, rough terrain topped with gorse bushes and bramble and dotted with large masses of granite boulders filled her with joy. Above her, only a few white puffs of cloud scudded across a clear blue sky.

Ahead of her, Jacob played with Buddy while Eve picked blackberries. Abi grinned to herself as her daughter stuffed every other berry into her mouth rather than into the plastic bag she gripped in her hand. She was gathering them for Auntie Becky, who'd promised to show her how to make a blackberry and apple crumble. Maybe there would soon be another cook in the family?

"Gee-up. Gee-up," yelled Grace.

Further along the track, Abi's youngest child clung to Ben's back. Grace's chubby legs urged him to go faster.

"Slow down, little one. Horsey needs a rest." Ben reduced his pace until Abi caught up with him. "Fantastic spot, isn't it?"

She nodded.

"I'll take you to the top of Tregonning Hill at some point. Lots of landmarks and historical stuff, and the scenery is even more spectacular."

"It's a date." She tucked her hand into his arm and stroked Grace's leg.

"Gee-up."

"Whoops, the mistress has spoken. Must go." Ben laughed, did a mock buck, and trotted up the hill.

High above Abi's head, a buzzard lazily surfed the thermals, letting out a plaintive peep-peep sound as it circled over the valley.

Ben jogged back towards her. "I'm surprised Megan let you off so lightly. I thought she would've roped you in to help with the last bits for the show tomorrow?"

"I did my stint this morning. Seriously, I never knew how much work went into organising these things. It's Becky's turn this afternoon."

"Did Becky's old man turn up yesterday? When I saw her in the morning, she was pretty anxious in case he changed his mind."

"He came with a load of produce and freshly picked strawberries. We even had a chat for several minutes before Becky took him to see the walled garden." Abi pushed a lock of hair behind her ear. "Looks like he'll be a regular visitor, pruning the trees and suchlike. Made Becky's day."

"What about Natalie? You won't want her to be a regular visitor, will you?"

"I can handle her if that happens. Besides, what choice do I have? She is my sister's sister, and our sons are best friends."

"Mummy, can I have a ride, like Grace? Please, Mummy."

Eve's round face, complete with purple lips, beamed up at Abi. She smiled and reached for Grace.

"You know, I think it is your turn just about ... now."

Ben scooped Eve quickly onto his back and galloped once again up the path.

Holding Grace's hand, Abi stopped for a while to watch the scene in front of her. Jacob, with his sun-tanned limbs and sturdy frame, now had the look of a child who spent a lot of time outside in the open air. His pale, sallow complexion, which had marked him out as somebody who lacked a nutritious diet, and the solemn, angry look shaped by too many 'uncles' and so-called 'homes', had gone.

Her son loved living at Vellangoose. He'd already been busy that morning, working with Jeffery getting Apollo ready for the show, and he and Ben had groomed Podge. A warm feeling ran through her. For once, it seemed that Jacob might get the father figure he deserved. Veronica Williams couldn't take it all away. She just couldn't.

"Mummy, when are we going to make the fancy dresses?" Eve called out.

Abi groaned inwardly. Courtesy of Megan, that was a job for later.

"We'll sort it as soon as we get home."

Abi looked at her eldest daughter with her arms tight around Ben's neck. Rosy-cheeked, her eyes were as bright as the strands of plastic beads that hung around her neck. On her feet, she wore her favourite sparkly sandals. Totally unsuitable for today's adventure, but her feisty daughter was playing at being a lady rather than being the tomboy she usually was.

"Ber ... berries." Grace tugged at Abi's shorts. "For Auntie Becky."

She looked down. "Thank you, sweetheart. That's so helpful." She took the squashed blackberries from Grace's outstretched hand and dropped them into the partly filled plastic bag she was holding for Eve, then she scooped Grace into her arms.

Head down, Abi marched onwards, over the rocks and large tufts of grass.

"Hurry up, Mum," called Jacob. "We're hungry."

She glanced up at the sound of her son's voice and came to an abrupt stop. She placed Grace onto the ground and stood open-mouthed. The terrain had levelled out and she could see for miles. St Michael's Mount. St Ives. Penzance. She did a hundred-and-eighty-degree turn. Carn Brea Castle. St Agnes Beacon, and much more.

Ben came up beside her and put his arm around her waist. "What do you think? Worth the trudge?"

"It's amazing. Magical."

She tugged off her rucksack, opened it and pulled out a picnic lunch: various sandwiches and rolls wrapped in tin foil, packets of crisps, pizza slices, and cans of cola.

"Can we have cake at the café later?" Jacob peered at her as he munched on a ham and tomato roll. "And hot chocolate?"

"Can we, Mummy?" Eve hopped on the spot. "Can we?"

Abi looked from Jacob to Eve, then to Grace, and burst into a big grin. She was so lucky to have such fantastic kids. At least, Veronica Williams would never be able to take that feeling of love away from her.

"Today, guys, you can have anything you like."

The kids' excited chatter filled the air, mixing with the crunch of crisps and Ben opening cans of coke.

Abi laid on her back and studied the buzzard still gently sweeping back and forth. Veronica Williams and the court case tugged once again at the edges of her mind, but she forced herself to feel the sun on her face and to listen to the bird song until the threat temporarily ebbed away.

"It's so good to leave it all behind, isn't it?" Ben flopped onto his stomach next to her. "Maybe, we should stay up here forever?"

She rolled towards him, rested a hand on his chest and kissed him gently on the lips. If only they could.

"Have you found out anything further about Constance and Nicholas?"

A knot formed in her stomach and she moved once more onto her back, away from him.

"Nothing, since we spoke last."

Why had Becky made that deal with Nicholas? Okay, she knew it was great that he had agreed not to contact Veronica Williams or Steve yet. This gave her and Becky some time to figure out how Nicholas being alive might help them in the impending court case. But why did she make Abi promise they would keep it secret too? Even though Becky hadn't told David about Nicholas either, the whole secrecy thing with Ben left Abi feeling like a fraud.

"Are you worried about the court case?" Ben moved a strand of hair from her face and curled it around his finger.

"Only an idiot wouldn't be. Mind you, don't know why you're concerned. You'll be better off if Veronica Williams wins."

He jerked his head up and stared at her. "Why do you say that?"

"Only joking." She elbowed him in the ribs. "I only meant you could rent the fields again for money. No more barter contracts for the next four and a half years. No more Becky following you around with a checklist."

"Oh, yeah." Ben sat up and reached for a sandwich but didn't take a bite.

"Oh, yeah?" Abi grabbed a handful of dried grass and chucked it at him. "If Veronica Williams wins, you won't get the special perks you get from me."

"You're such a tease." Ben chucked the sandwich back onto the food pile and reached out for her.

"No, you don't." Abi laughed, scrambled to her feet and began to run across the grass.

She'd only gone three or four paces when his strong arms closed around her waist and pulled her to his chest. He kissed her. A giggle formed in her throat at the serious look in his eyes as he took her face between his callused hands.

"Marry me."

Abi's heart raced. "What?"

"Marry me."

"Don't be daft. Why would you want me? I've got three kids."

"I love you. I love those kids. You mean everything to me."

No one had ever spoken such words to her before unless they were out for sex or money. She stared at him and saw the love in his eyes.

"Please," he pleaded.

Love for him surged through her. "Yes," she whispered.

"Thank God." He hugged her, then held her at arm's length. "I so want to take care of you and the kids."

"Hey, you know, I'm pretty good at both of those things myself." She reached up and smoothed down a tuft of hair that stuck up from the back of his head, then looked him straight in the eyes. "Don't cheat on me. Or lie. That's all I ask of you."

He kissed her lips, then each cheek and the tip of her nose before he whispered, "I won't let you down. I promise."

"Mummy, are we having chocolate cake soon?" Eve tugged at her arm.

Abi burst into laughter. Nothing like kids to puncture the moment.

"Since you've asked so nicely, I reckon it's time for loads and loads of cake."

She held Ben's hand tight in hers. She'd tell the kids about the proposal later when the time was right. For now, she wanted to keep Ben's amazing words to herself.

"Well, what's everyone waiting for?" she said.

Ben bent down and hoisted Grace onto his shoulders. "Let's get going. Last to the café is a sissy."

Abi pushed the remaining bits of food and rubbish into her rucksack, lifted it onto her back and picked up Eve's plastic bag. She snatched a few blackberries from a nearby bramble, then turned and ran after her family. A whoop of joy rolled from her chest.

She'd never been so happy.

37

Becky couldn't believe what a beautiful day it was. Not only was the cloudless sky and light summer breeze a rarity for a bank holiday, it was also perfect for the Penhellick Country Show. Cars and lorries had rumbled down the lane to Vellangoose from eight o'clock that morning, and in the two hours since, the meadow had filled up with children, doting parents and general sightseers. Horses, ponies and dogs in all shapes and sizes added to the happy crowd.

She ambled around the meadow, one hand gently wrapped in David's and the other clutched around a battered biscuit tin. Megan had allocated them the task of selling raffle tickets, and as Becky and David made their way through the people, they stopped to sell strips of the numbered chits and to catch up on the news with friends and neighbours.

The meadow had been transformed. Two show-rings were filled with brightly coloured hurdles: a big ring for show jumping and another one for the gymkhana. In the far corner of the field, a small area had been roped off for the dog show. Various tents and food vans dotted around the edges.

Excited children's voices vied with the crackle and fuzz of the ancient loudspeaker system. Depending upon the success or otherwise of the horse-human combination in the show jumping ring at the time, smatterings of applause or groans rang out intermittently. The place hummed with activity.

Children with a motley selection of dogs lined up to take part in the Penhellick Dog Show, although Becky decided that the word 'show' added an element of grandeur to the event that was quickly dispelled when she read the list of classes: 'Puppy with the Most Appealing Eyes', 'Dog with the Waggiest Tail', 'Dog that Looked Most Like its Owner' for starters. Good luck to the person judging.

David had let go of Becky's hand and now stood with a group of women outside the WI tent. Laughter and giggles floated in the air as he tore off strips of blue raffle tickets, placed them in out-stretched hands, and collected the money.

For a moment, she stood and gazed at the man who made her feel so special and so very happy. She knew her face glowed with the love she felt for him.

Her stomach rumbled. She, Abi and the children had all had an early breakfast and the rich, beefy smell of burgers, bacon rolls, and other food made her mouth water.

A pony whickered in the distance. A few feet away from her, another one answered.

"Selling raffle tickets? Baking? Is there no end to your talents?" The light-hearted voice in her ear made Becky jump.

She turned around to see a square-set man with a big grin on his face. Richard Grey leaned forward and kissed her on the cheek. She smiled and returned his embrace. It was always a pleasure to meet the vet who'd saved Buddy's life that dreadful night when he'd nearly been killed by the lampers' dogs.

"What a turnout." Richard held his arms out to encompass the meadow and the field beyond, where all the cars and lorries were parked. "You and Abi have done an amazing job."

"Megan Olds has been the real driving force behind it all." She glanced towards the main ring, where Megan issued instructions to all and sundry.

"Dear Megan. A truly remarkable woman." Richard turned his gaze back to Becky. "Your success today will be a bitter pill for Veronica Williams to swallow, that's for sure. I know Boswyn Manor has been the usual venue, but I for one would vote for Vellangoose again next year."

"Your support is really appreciated." She tucked her arm into his. "Several people have said the same to us."

Richard pointed at the line of wriggly puppies and equally excited owners making their way into the ring. "Megan's roped me in to help with the judging. I'm the vet on duty as well, so I'm effectively her captive for the day, so to speak."

"I know what you mean." Becky jiggled the raffle tin in front of him. "Let's be having your money."

He reached into his pocket. "Talking of money, your bill for Buddy's treatment is now settled, though it puts the crew at the surgery in a bit of a fix. They're desperate for the barter scheme to continue. Any suggestions?"

"I'd like it very much if we could continue with a running account and the barter arrangements. Buddy will need his annual vaccinations soon. Then there's Podge, Apollo, and Dolly. And I've seen a stray cat around the yard in the last couple of days. No doubt, he or she will be a permanent resident soon, needing jabs and worm tablets. Eve has already named it Fluffy."

"Talking of strays, I know someone who's got a couple of llamas that he wants to find a good home for. What do you think? They're free."

"Oh dear. When Abi and the children hear that, the llamas will be installed at Vellangoose in a flash." Becky laughed. "We'll have a zoo soon."

The loudspeaker system crackled into life. "Calling for veterinary assistance in the main ring. Calling for veterinary assistance in the main ring."

"Duty calls." He kissed her cheek again, then whispered in her ear. "Keep up the fight. Lots of people are on your side, you know."

Richard rushed away with a wave, just as Abi and the children arrived. Jacob, bare-chested and wearing a much-used headdress of synthetic feathers, sat on Podge. Eve and Grace, dressed as American Indian squaws, walked alongside.

"Wow, everyone. You look great." Becky grinned at Abi. "Looks like Megan got her way after all?"

"What chance did I have? Have you seen her? I don't know what she's on but as I've said before, I want some of it."

When Megan turned up the previous evening, she'd reminded Abi – using her fingers to illustrate the importance of the information – that a) Jacob and Podge had been entered for the fancy dress competition for children aged seven and under, b) Abi would have to lead Podge around the ring, and c) she expected Eve and Grace to join in.

Message delivered, Megan had dragged a large, tattered cardboard box out of her people carrier and handed it over to Abi. It contained various old clothes, hats, and party outfits that Megan and Hugh's 'tribe' had used over the years. "Make what you can out of that lot, my dears," Megan said before she marched off to feed the ponies, leaving Becky and Abi staring at her back.

"Come and see what we did." Eve grabbed Becky's hand and pointed at three yellow handprints painted onto Podge's flank, along with various red zigzags and circles. "Mummy helped us. We used lots of her make-up, and the stuff you use to decorate cakes."

"It was my idea, Auntie Becky." Jacob butted in. "American Indians put war paint on their ponies before going into battle. They paint their own faces as well. Did you know that?"

She did know but pretended she didn't.

"We'd better get over to the gymkhana ring. Hugh's judging the fancy dress class. Maybe, he'll be kind to us?" Abi made to move, then stopped. "Hey, look who's here."

Jeffery and Aaron came towards them, one on either side of a splendidly groomed and very lively Apollo. Wide-eyed and with his nose in the air, the horse swung his head from side to side, ears flicking back and forth. When he came to a halt next to Podge, Apollo pawed the ground and snorted.

Becky reached out and patted Apollo's muscular neck. The animal no longer frightened her like he did when she first arrived at Vellangoose. She'd probably never ride him or be confident enough to clean the insides of his enormous hooves, but she often fed him bits of apple and helped to groom him.

"Miss Pascoe. Mrs Farrow." Jeffery doffed his cap, then quickly rammed it back on as Apollo stepped to one side and dropped a big hoof onto Aaron's foot.

"Ouch." Aaron shoved the horse away with his shoulder. "Get off, you big lump."

"Serves yer right." Jeffery burst out laughing. "You'd better pay more attention at that posh university of yours next week."

Becky had almost forgotten about Aaron leaving for university. That would be one person off her list of potential suspects telling Veronica Williams about events at Vellangoose.

"Apollo's looking very handsome," Abi said.

"Me and Aaron are taking him into the ring soon. For a bit of a parade around. Folks want to see him."

"Why a solo parade?" Becky moved the raffle tin from one hand to the other.

"Well now, Apollo's a bit special around here. That is to them people who put their money where their mouths are at the local races and point-to-points. Then there's the curiosity factor of Apollo, him being Mr Henry's horse."

Jeffery pushed his cap back further on his head and looked around. "Good crowd here. More than normal. Guess the nosy whatsits want to see you two and what you've done to the place."

"Curiosity factor?" Abi grinned. "Us being Henry's offspring."

"Reckon you're right, Miss."

The loudspeaker crackled again.

"We're in the ring next." Jeffery tightened his hold on the horse's reins. "Come on, Apollo. Look your best now."

David came up beside Becky and slipped his arm around her waist. They stood for a moment as Jeffery and Aaron moved off, and Abi and the children made their way to the fancy dress class.

Henry's offspring, indeed. Well, let everyone have a look. Becky felt invincible with David next to her. Besides, The Barn and yard looked smart, and the animals were happy and content in the fields. Most of all, she hoped people could see what a united family she, Abi and the children were.

"I think we've done the raffle now. I'll whip the ticket stubs and money over to the main tent. You want to come?" David took the biscuit tin from her and stacked it on top of his equally battered tea caddy.

"I'm going to watch Apollo, then grab a bacon roll and wander over to the dog show for a bit. I'll see you by the gymkhana ring in about forty minutes for the fancy dress?"

The dogs and their owners were such a delight. She smiled to herself as Richard, in the middle of the ring, tried to control an over-enthusiastic black Labrador in the 'Puppy with the Waggiest Tail' class. She sat on a bale of hay for the 'Scruffiest Dog' category, then looked at her watch. Less than ten minutes before the fancy dress class was due to start.

She weaved quickly around people and small groups of bystanders in her rush to get to the gymkhana ring. A group in front of her parted to let her through. She thanked them, looked ahead, then came to an abrupt stop. She gasped.

Veronica Williams, dressed in an immaculate red linen suit and matching blouse, walked towards her. A blue and gold Penhellick Country Show badge, lifted by a light breeze, fluttered from her lapel.

For a moment, Becky couldn't move or speak. How did that woman have the nerve to be at Vellangoose, as if nothing had happened between them?

She stepped forwards.

"You're not welcome here. Please leave. Now."

"I am afraid that is not possible. As President of the show, I am duty-bound to be here. To mingle, present the trophies to the winners, and so forth." A smile flickered across her face. "I am assuming Megan forgot to tell you?"

Becky's heart raced. Had Megan played her and Abi for fools after all?

"As the show's President, I had grave misgivings when the committee out-voted me for the first time and agreed to move the venue from Boswyn Manor to Vellangoose. I—"

"I said leave. I won't tell you again."

A few people had stopped to watch the little tableau of two. Becky could hear the hushed whispers.

"Mrs Farrow, please compose yourself." Veronica Williams brushed a blonde strand of hair away from her cheek. "I just wanted to say, I think you have done a marvellous job. In fact, I cannot wait to tell the committee members they can hold the show here again next year. By then, the court will have found in my favour, and Vellangoose will be back in my rightful ownership."

Blood pounded in Becky's ears. It was time that this conceited, self-important, stuck-up madam was put in her place. Time she was made aware that she and Abi knew she was a barefaced liar, with a host of dirty little secrets to hide.

Becky opened her mouth to speak.

38

Abi looked up. The long, white hen's feather she'd been threading into Podge's mane drifted to the ground. Her gaze darted from one side of the meadow to the other, scanning the groups of people scattered around the showground.

Ben touched her arm. "You okay?"

"Something doesn't feel right."

While Ben tied two more white feathers into the coarse hair of Podge's mane, she rubbed the spot between the animal's ears and scoured the meadow for signs of something wrong. In the main ring, on the far side of the meadow, David handed a couple of old battered tins to Megan, and a clearly overexcited Apollo headed back to the stables after his parade of honour. The sight of the magnificent horse, and the huge grin on Jeffery's face calmed her.

Jacob, Eve and Grace took it in turns to fiddle with their outfits and fuss over Podge. Everything was fine. Her kids really ought to win the fancy dress prize if they were judged on the effort they'd put in. Just then, a child-sized Lancelot rode by in a clatter of mock chain mail, followed by Guinevere in a long flowing gown perched elegantly on a stunning palomino-coloured pony. Abi let out a sigh. Oh well, all the entrants would get a rosette just for entering, so the kids would be pleased anyway.

David hurried through the main ring. Megan took big, purposeful strides behind him. Abi tracked the direction they were headed. A horse pranced sideways and blocked her line of sight. A bluebottle buzzed against her cheek. She swatted it away. At that moment, the horse shifted to one side, and, in an instance, Abi had a clear view of the meadow.

Bloody hell.

Becky and Veronica Williams stood toe-to-toe.

Abi thrust Podge's reins into Ben's hand and sprinted flat-out over the rough ground. She reached Becky's side at the same time as David and Megan.

Red-faced, Becky was shouting. "And, what's more, I've had enough of your vile, underhand attempts to take Vellangoose away from us. It's time everyone knew you for the liar you are. Time, they knew the truth about Constance and–"

Abi pushed herself between the two women, forcing Becky to stop talking and to step back several paces.

"Not here, you idiot. Come away," Abi spoke in a harsh whisper.

"She needs to be told." Becky shoved past Abi. "That woman's deliberately taunting us by coming here today. I'll–"

David wrapped his arm around Becky. Holding her in a firm grip, he steered her in the direction of the yard.

Her sister safely out of the way, Abi turned to Veronica Williams, but before she could speak, Megan came forward and kissed the old witch on the cheek.

"Veronica, how lovely to see you. I wasn't expecting you. Thought you were otherwise engaged today?"

Veronica Williams offered Megan her cheek, but her eyes remained fixed on Abi's face.

"I changed my plans. Felt it was expected of me to attend." She patted Megan's arm. "As President, I needed to be reassured that everything is being run to my exacting standards. I cannot have inexperienced hands ruining the show's reputation."

"My dear, it's all going marvellously well." Megan let out a guttural laugh. "Although, I have to say, the role of Acting President has gone to darling Hugh's head. Gone a little bit overboard, between you and me. Men and power, men and power."

A smile flickered across Veronica Williams's face. "Quite."

Enough was enough. Abi couldn't stomach to hear anymore. She moved closer to Veronica Williams and hissed at her through clenched teeth.

"You're trespassing."

"Really?" Veronica Williams held one hand in front of her and casually inspected her well-manicured fingernails. "Like you did when you barged into my home at Boswyn Manor?"

Abi shifted her weight from one foot to the other. A dried-out bramble stalk jabbed at her ankle. "Screw Boswyn Manor. Your husband left Vellangoose to us, not you. It's time you got used to it."

"That will not be necessary." She turned away, then swung back to face Abi. "My source has been so helpful in providing the evidence I needed. I will now have my day in court when all the world will witness an injustice put right."

A mix of fear and red-hot anger raced through Abi as those words sank in. For the millionth time, she wondered who the squealer could be.

Megan, who now stood at Abi's elbow, opened her mouth to speak, but Abi cut in with a harsh whisper.

"Get this woman out of my sight before I do something I might regret. You promised us she wouldn't be here today."

The loudspeaker burst into life. A crackly voice proclaimed that all fancy dress entrants should make their way to the gymkhana ring. She had to go; the kids would be waiting.

Abi bumped Veronica Williams's shoulder as she walked past her. "Stick your so-called source, you've got nothing on us."

A hand grabbed Abi's forearm. She looked down at the long, bony fingers with distaste. A large diamond ring glinted in the sun.

"Miss Pascoe. Give my sincere best wishes to Benjamin. Tell him, I am so sorry I missed him today." A triumphant smile formed on Veronica Williams's lips. "It is always such a pleasure when he and I have our little discussions."

Abi blinked.

In the next field, a lorry tooted its horn twice, accelerated amid shouts of farewell, then rattled up the lane. A couple of kids ran by, waving red and blue rosettes in the air. The ribbons tugged and twirled in the wind.

Veronica Williams removed her hand and walked briskly away.

A wide-eyed Megan stared at Abi for a moment, then ran towards the ring, where Pixie had unseated one of Megan's daughters.

Abi blinked again, then stumbled a few yards to the boundary hedge and reached out for support. Jagged granite rock bit into the palm of her hand and drew blood.

No. Not Ben. Not her Ben.

Pain streaked across her chest as she attempted to control her breathing. She loved him. For Christ's sake, he'd asked her to marry him, and she'd accepted. She bent over, gripped her knees with her hands and drew in quick gasps. Not again? She was so sure that this time she'd found the right man. He loved her. She knew he did.

Jacob's shouts penetrated the fuzz in her head. Panting, he ran up to her. "Mum ... quick ... in the ring ..."

She remained hunched over. It couldn't be true. Veronica Williams was a liar and a manipulator. She'd used Ben's name to bait her, to stir things up, and to drive a wedge between them. That was it.

Relief surged through Abi. She shoved all doubts away. They loved each other. That was all that mattered.

Jacob tugged at her sleeve. Abi straightened up, pushed her shoulders back and looked down at him.

"Mum. Come on. We've got to go into the ring. Now."

They hurried back to Podge, Eve and Grace. Everything would be fine; she chanted the words over and over as she ran.

She had no idea how she got through the fancy dress event. Veronica Williams's words banged around in her head as the ponies' hooves drummed over the hard, sun-dried ground. Round and round in one big circle. Podge was tetchy and even nipped her thigh when all the entrants stopped in a straggly line while Judge Hugh inspected each entry in turn.

Her kids being presented with the third prize rosette briefly pushed all bad thoughts away, and she joined in with their whoops of delight.

She plastered a smile onto her face when they left the gymkhana ring and Ben fell in step next to her.

"You okay?" he whispered.

She stared ahead and kept on walking. "Veronica Williams told me everything."

Ben came to an abrupt halt. "What?"

She brought Podge to a stop, and for the first time since Veronica Williams had uttered her dreadful words, Abi looked at Ben. His face was pale. His eyes, dark and pleading, locked onto hers.

In the fraction of a second it took to let out the breath she hadn't realised she'd been holding, her love for him wilted and died.

39

Becky leaned against the wall of The Barn, closed her eyes and inhaled a deep lungful of air. Every nerve in her body fizzed with anger: at Veronica Williams's unshakable arrogance and nerve in attending the Penhellick Country Show, at Abi who had pushed her nose in where it wasn't wanted, at David for treating her like a child in the middle of a tantrum. How could he? She clenched her fists and let out a long, low growl.

"Sorry," David said.

"Sorry?" she shouted. "Sorry isn't enough. How could you do that to me?"

"I thought …" David pushed his hand through his hair and gazed at her from under dark eyelashes.

"I don't need you to think for me. You'd no right to interfere."

"Please." He reached out his hand towards her. "I didn't want you saying something you might regret later. That would play right into Veronica Williams's hands."

She moved away from the wall; away from him. "You're missing the point. You're the person who's upset me the most. I've told you before, I won't allow another man to tell me what I can or can't do."

David's shoulders slumped. He searched her face with imploring eyes.

She held his gaze. Deep down she knew he'd only acted in her best interests and that it wasn't the right time or place to have it out with Veronica Williams. But he'd behaved like John, taking control. She wasn't that person anymore. Why couldn't he see what he'd done with his interfering?

"I need some space," she said.

David grunted, walked a few paces towards the meadow, then turned back. "I really am very sorry."

Weariness surged through her. "Maybe you could find out what happened in the fancy dress competition? One of us ought to be there for Abi and the children." She sighed. "I'm going to freshen up. I'll catch up with you in a bit."

In the bathroom, Becky brushed her hair, applied fresh lipstick and sprayed a puff of perfume into the air. She walked through the fine mist, then rubbed her arms. It was getting a bit chilly. She ambled into her bedroom and blindly grabbed a jumper from one of her storage boxes. Her hand froze. It was John's old sweater, the one she'd worn for comfort during those first months at Vellangoose. For a few moments, she pressed it against her cheek, then returned to the kitchen, flipped the bin lid open and dropped the sweater inside.

Desperate for a cup of coffee, she reached for the kettle and automatically looked out of the window. She stiffened.

Veronica Williams, hand shielding her eyes, was peering through the doorway into The Mill.

Fury swept over Becky. She rushed to the door, through the garden to the yard, and stepped up behind the intruder.

"Just what do you think you're doing?"

Veronica Williams spun around. For a moment, Becky caught a flicker of panic in those piercing eyes. Then, jaw jutting upwards, the woman navigated her way around a pile of old timber and debris that Abi had stacked outside of The Mill.

Drawing near to Becky, she held her hands, palms upwards in front of her.

"I am waiting for my nephew."

"What were you snooping for? Nothing here belongs to you."

Becky waited for the vitriolic outburst.

"My great-grandfather built The Mill," she said, and her voice was unexpectedly soft. "My grandfather and father continued to farm the land for many years, so my sister and I often played here when we were children." She scanned the outside of the building. "Our memories, our very existence, are etched into the fabric of this place. Nobody can take that away from me."

Becky watched small beads of perspiration form on Veronica Williams's upper lip, then found herself asking: "How did your husband come to own Vellangoose when it had been in your family's possession for generations?"

"My father gave it to Constance, as a wedding present." She shook her head. "Unfortunately, my sister often lacked clear judgement. During a low point in her life, after her husband left, she sold Vellangoose to my husband. Why she did not come to me, I ...?" She shook her head again. "My husband was a fool. If he had refused to buy Vellangoose, we would not be in this appalling situation now, where the products of his sordid affairs own what rightfully belongs to me and Steven."

The words slapped Becky in the face. She pushed her shoulders back and faced her adversary head-on.

"What happened to Constance? Where is she now?"

"She died in Brazil, over thirty years ago, as well you know."

"That's not what Nicholas told me."

Veronica Williams paled and stepped backwards, her back pressed against The Mill.

Becky pushed on. "Oh, yes, I had a long telephone chat with your brother-in-law. He was quite informative, considering I was talking to a dead man."

"Nicholas?" Bony fingers gripped the stone wall for support.

"Does Steve know his parents didn't die in Brazil?" Becky asked.

"You cannot for one moment think of tell–"

"Of what? Telling him that his father's alive, and his mother is ..." Becky held her hands up in a questioning posture, "where?"

Veronica Williams straightened and patted her hair. "My sister wanted a new beginning abroad. I helped to facilitate that." She glared at Becky. "I felt it best that Steven remained unaware that his parents deserted him. If you inform him, I tell you, I–"

"I don't think you're in a position to tell me anything. You've too much at stake to threaten me. Too many old secrets and lies you still want to be kept hidden."

In the meadow, the loudspeaker briefly sputtered into life, then fell silent.

Becky smoothed down the front of her skirt and glared at Veronica Williams. "Let me just get this clear. You told everyone for years that Constance and Nicholas had been killed. I know Nicholas is alive but now, according to you, Constance is alive as well. And your beloved nephew, who you're supposed to care so much about, is totally unaware of these facts." She plastered a large grin onto her face. "I think this might be an appropriate moment to mention the court case. I might even suggest that you speak to your solicitor about your... what shall we call it? ... Your sudden lack of evidence?"

Veronica Williams moved away from the wall, her fist clenched. "How dare you? If you mention so much as one word of our conversation to anyone, I will deny it all. You will live to regret it." Her eyes flickered sideways.

Becky tracked her gaze. David was walking towards them.

Veronica Williams rushed over to him and clutched his arm. "David, please take me home."

David frowned at Becky. "What happened?"

"We were discussing her withdrawal of all legal action against us. Weren't we, Mrs Williams?"

"Please, David. Get me away from this woman."

David shook his head at them both. "Don't you think it's time all this animosity stopped?"

Without waiting for an answer, he took Veronica Williams by the elbow and walked towards his car.

Becky scrutinised their retreating backs. "If you go with her, don't bother coming back."

David stopped in mid-stride, then turned, his lips pressed tightly together.

She locked eyes with him. Her heart thumped. Please let him do this for her. Please let him love her more than his business.

Anger etched lines into David's face. "Who's telling who what to do now?"

Becky gasped as her own words were thrown back at her. Unable to offer a reasoned reply, she waited.

David held her gaze for a few moments, then unfurled Veronica Williams's arm from his own, and stepped to one side.

"Veronica, I'm sorry, but I'm unable to drive you home. Can I arrange for someone else to take you?"

"You will regret this," she hissed. "Solicitors' practices survive on goodwill, and we all know how easily reputations can be damaged."

David looked from Veronica Williams to Becky and back again. "Quite frankly, I've had enough of both of you."

He stomped to his car and drove away.

Another car pulled into the yard and came quickly to a halt. From the passenger seat, Jess flashed Becky a smile.

"Aunt Veronica." Steve jumped out of the vehicle and hurried to his aunt's side. "I got your call. Is everything alright?"

Jess got out and took a step towards Becky.

"Get back in. I need to take Aunt Veronica home." Steve's voice was loud and sharp.

"I want to speak to Mum."

"I said get in."

"Stay here, darling." Becky moved towards her daughter. "You don't need to put up with this."

"It'll only take a minute." Jess glared at Steve.

"Now," he shouted.

Becky's heart felt like it would shatter as her beautiful daughter bowed her head and got back into the rear seat. Veronica Williams had settled herself into the front.

Head high, Becky stepped up to the passenger door window and rapped on the glass. Veronica Williams turned her face away. She rapped harder. Jess wound the back window down. Becky leaned through the gap and gazed at each of the occupants in turn: Veronica Williams, tight-lipped, stared ahead. Steve, in the driver's seat, pulling on his seat belt. Jess with her jaw clenched and eyes fixed onto the back of Steve's head.

Becky's gaze lingered on her daughter, and she smiled. She recognised that look of defiance – she'd seen it many times in the past.

In a clear voice, Becky spoke loud enough for all in the car to hear. "Mrs Williams, there's lots more you and I need to discuss, or would you prefer I talked to Steve about his parents instead?"

"What?" Steve scowled at her.

"Drive." Veronica Williams commanded.

"What's she on about? Tell me."

"Nothing. Go."

Gravel and stones flew from the car's wheels as Steve revved the engine and headed for the lane, passing Abi, who was alone and had her head down. Her eyes widened as the car roared past her. She rushed up to Becky.

"I thought that woman had gone ages ago. What happened?"

"We've had a nice chat, that's all." A wry grin formed on Becky's lips.

Abi stared at her. "Come on. Spill."

Becky kept her eyes on Steve's car until it reached the end of the lane and disappeared onto the main road.

"I told her about my conversation with Nicholas."

"What? Everything?"

"Most of it."

Abi blew out her cheeks. "Bloody hellfire. What now?"

40

Abi reached over and picked up her mobile phone by the bed. In the darkness, the tiny patch of light displayed the time. 3:30 a.m. She rubbed her gritty eyes and sighed. Ever since she'd crawled, exhausted, into bed at midnight, the events of the day had gone round and round in her head. Was it only yesterday that the show was held at Vellangoose, and Ben had …? No, she refused to lie there and think about him.

With a savage thrust of her arm, she yanked the duvet to one side and stood up.

Buddy, curled up at the end of the bed, got to his feet and stretched as she pulled on her jeans and a hooded sweatshirt.

"Stay, Buddy. I can't have you chasing and barking at Fluffy again, it'll set the chickens off and wake Becky." She rubbed his ears. "I know what you're like, you rascal."

The dog lay down, rested his head on his paws and watched her every movement until she patted his head and left the room.

She closed the kitchen door quietly behind her and stepped out into the garden. The chilled air whipped around her face. She shivered. Autumn would be here soon. She pulled the hood over her uncombed hair and tugged the sleeves of her sweatshirt down over her hands.

Apollo's white head bobbed up and down in the stable doorway. A soft nicker of welcome rolled from his throat.

In the watery moonlight, she walked over to him and drew back the bolt on the half-door, stepped inside and fastened it behind her. In the far corner, Dolly stood chest-high in straw, her jaw rhythmically moving from side to side.

"Hey, Apollo, couldn't you sleep either? No wonder, considering the time you had. What with the grand parade and everyone wanting to say hello to you. You certainly made Jeffery a very happy man."

A sob escaped from her throat and she rested her forehead against the animal's smooth neck. "At least someone had a great time."

Apollo nuzzled her thigh.

Abi wiped her nose on her sleeve. She knew she should be relieved that Becky had got one over on Veronica Williams, but all she could think about was Ben.

When she'd seen that look of guilt on his face, she'd tried to hurry Podge and the kids away, but Ben had grabbed her elbow, forcing her to look at him. Tears had stung the backs of her eyes, but, grim lipped, she'd refused to let any droplets fall. Thank God Megan had rushed up and offered to take Podge and the kids for another circuit around the meadow. "So, everyone can see your rosettes," Megan had said, with a smile that hadn't reached her eyes.

As Megan walked away, Abi had snatched her arm from Ben's grasp.

"Please, Abi. Let me explain," he'd begged.

"Fuck off," she'd hissed before walking away from him.

Apollo snuffled warm air into Abi's hair.

"It's alright, big fella, I'll be okay." She rubbed his velvety nose and swallowed back another sob. Luckily, the kids hadn't been here this evening to see how upset she was. Megan was a saint for taking them home with her for the night.

Apollo pushed his nose harder against her hand. "What do you want? Shall I take the fancy whatsits out of your mane?"

She reached up to the arch of the horse's neck, fingered the first tight knot of coarse hair, located an elastic band, tugged it free and put it into her pocket for safekeeping. Jeffery had insisted that Apollo looked his best and had spent an hour or so plaiting his mane. He planned to take them out in the morning, but it gave Abi something to do now. It helped with the awful loneliness that gnawed at her insides.

"You've been a clever boy. We've had a bucket load of money from the breeder, and it's all your doing."

Neither she nor Becky had seen the crisp white envelope on the hallway floor until after the show. When Abi opened it, something fluttered to the ground. A brief, handwritten note told them that scans had revealed that Apollo had successfully served six mares, and because it was likely that all the foals would be born alive, a cheque was enclosed for the first half of the stud fees.

She pocketed another elastic band and ran her fingers through the crinkled ringlets. "I think your pal Jeffery had something to do with us getting the money early," she said softly, "but we're not complaining. And you had fun, didn't you, big fella?" She let out another sob. So many people were going out of their way to help them.

Abi leaned in against Apollo's warm body and hugged him. This beautiful animal had solved their immediate financial worries. In the wider scheme of things, it wasn't that much dosh, but it meant they could get some of the stuff they wanted: sofas for the living room, winter foodstuff for the animals. What's more, another cheque would arrive after the foals had been born.

Her luck had altered beyond all recognition in the last eight months. So many wonderful changes had happened:

Vellangoose, Becky, the kids settled and thriving, money. So why didn't she feel happy?

"Damn you, Ben. Damn you. Why did you go and ruin everything? We would've been so good together."

Apollo tossed his head upwards and stepped back a pace.

"Whoa. It's not your fault. It's my inability to pick a decent man."

At some point, she'd confront Ben. She needed to know why he did it. His betrayal couldn't just be because he wanted the land, could it? She had to be worth more than fifty acres of scraggy fields and a few overgrown ponds.

Apollo's ears flickered back and forth and he padded from one foot to the other.

"Settle down, big fella. Sorry for upsetting you."

Absentmindedly, she continued to talk to him in a low, smooth voice and became lost once again in the thoughts that tumbled around in her head: Ben's mind-blowing kisses, his gentleness in bed, the unmistakable look of love in his eyes. Surely that hadn't been faked?

She shook her head. Enough. Though she'd put up with many men before who'd double-crossed her or treated her like shit, she knew she would never forgive Ben. It was all different now; she would never be treated like dirt again.

Apollo snorted and swung sideways.

"Watch it." She patted his neck to steady him. "You nearly stepped on my foot."

The horse stared through the door in the direction of The Mill. She followed his gaze.

A beam of light flashed once, then again. Abi froze. In the semi-darkness of the approaching dawn, a black-clad figure paused outside The Mill, then disappeared into its depths.

Abi scanned the yard. There didn't appear to be anyone else around. Quietly, she drew back the bolt on the half-door and slipped outside. A five-prong muck-fork stood against the wall. She picked it up, and, in the shadow of the outbuildings, edged towards The Mill. A voice in her head nagged her to wake Becky. She stopped, looked towards The Barn and back again to The Mill. By the time she woke Becky, the intruder might have bolted.

She pushed onwards.

She reached The Mill door and stepped inside.

At the end of the room, the figure shone a torch into the remaining pile of old furniture and other rubbish stacked against the far wall.

Rubble shifted under Abi's foot. The clatter echoed around the cavernous space.

The figure jerked, and their torch dropped to the floor. The beam flickered and went out, plunging the room into darkness. The intruder let out a muffled grunt.

Panic shot through Abi. Had the person moved? She stepped back to the doorway and reached for the old, roughened wood.

Slowly, her eyes became accustomed to the darkness. The black-clad figure turned towards her.

"You," Abi snarled.

"Get out of my way," Veronica Williams said. "I am leaving."

"You're not going anywhere until you tell me what the hell you're doing here."

"Move."

"No." Abi waved the muck-fork at her.

Veronica Williams's eyes blazed with fury. She pushed a loose strand of hair back under her black hat. "If you must know, when I saw all that rubble piled up outside yesterday, I wondered whether there were any items left in The Mill that rightly belonged to my family."

Over Abi's shoulder, a soft-orange glow marked the imminent birth of a new sunrise. In the meadow, the cockerel let out a loud triumphant welcome to a new day. A hen clucked in response.

The face before Abi was now illuminated a ghastly yellow-grey.

"Pull the other one. There's nothing but junk in here."

"The old dresser, and the writing bureau my father used," Veronica Williams rubbed her temple. "I wanted to see them. I was going to ask you if I could have the pieces … for sentimental reasons."

"Come off it, lady." Abi shook the muck-fork. "You've had thirty years to sort that. Yet here you are, sneaking around in the dark."

"I do not have to explain myself to you, you silly creature."

"What were you really looking for? Constance's body, maybe?"

Veronica Williams flinched and took a gulp of air. "My sister moved overseas years ago."

"Crap." Abi stepped closer. "No mum would leave her child with you."

The woman shifted from one foot to the other, her lips in a tight line.

"What was the final straw? Was it your husband getting your sister up the duff?" Abi leaned on the muck-fork. "Oh, yeah, we know all about Constance being pregnant. Must've been quite a shock? Another one of Henry's bastards for you to cope with."

Veronica Williams raised one bejewelled hand to her throat.

A ball of bright orange pushed up from behind the horizon and flooded through the windows and doorway, covering The Mill and everything inside in a blood-red hue.

"What a right old stain that would've been on the Williams's oh-so-perfect reputation. The gossips would've had a field day. Easier all around for you to do away with your sister and the offending baby. Problem solved."

"You are being quite hysterical." Veronica Williams pursed her lips. "You know nothing."

"Where is Constance? She's not down the well. I've looked."

"You did what?" Veronica Williams gawped at her, her eyes wide and mouth open.

"I knew it, that look says it all." Abi looked around. "Come on. Spill. Where is she?"

Veronica drew in a sharp breath. "Nonsense, utter nonsense. I have had enough of this." She took a couple of paces towards the door. "Get out of my way."

Abi jabbed the muck-fork at Veronica Williams once again. "Detective Inspector Carter needs to sort this out. I'm going to call him right now."

A loud metallic click filled the silence. The clear, sharp sound ricocheted around the room.

"That wouldn't be a good idea."

Abi spun around.

Steve stood in the doorway, his rifle pointed straight at her.

41

Becky woke from a deep sleep, groaned, and pulled the duvet over her head. What was wrong with Buddy? In Abi's bedroom, the dog's whining grew louder, then he started to scratch the door. She sighed, rolled off her mattress and got to her feet.

Becky scanned Abi's room. The bed was empty. Becky yawned. As far as she was concerned it was still the middle of the night and all she wanted to do was crawl back under her duvet and sleep for a hundred years. She yawned again, but she needed to check that Abi was okay.

In the kitchen, Becky grabbed a sweater from the back of one of the chairs and pulled it over her pyjamas.

"Stay, Buddy. You've hassled that poor cat enough for one day. Eve will never forgive you if it leaves Vellangoose for a dog-free place." She gave Buddy a handful of biscuits. "You and Fluffy will be good friends soon, I'm sure."

She stepped out into the garden.

A vixen screeched. The trees loomed dark and menacing in the half-light. She folded her arms in a hug and moved further into the yard.

In the stable, Apollo tossed his head up and down over the half-door, snorted and pawed the ground.

What was wrong with the animals this morning?

"Abi?"

The single word echoed around the buildings.

"Where are you? It's blooming cold out here. Come inside. I'll make us some coffee."

Becky straightened up and squinted towards the meadow. Her sleep-addled brain suddenly cleared. What was that?

Voices?

She strained to listen. Blood pulsed through her ears, but silence settled around her. Silly. There was no one else out there.

"Abi, I'm getting worried now. Where are you?"

"I'm in The Mill."

There was a tremor in her sister's voice. Had Abi been crying?

Becky rubbed her hands together and walked into The Mill. "You could've found a better ..."

Her heart thudded. She locked her eyes onto the dark hole of a rifle barrel, dimly aware that there were two other people in The Mill with Abi.

"Get over there," Steve yelled.

Her instinct was to run, but Steve waved the gun at her and she moved to stand next to Abi. They huddled close together, shoulders touching, and reached for each other's hands.

"Sorry," Abi whispered.

"Shut up." The lines around Steve's mouth deepened as he spoke. "I'm the one doing all the talking here."

Becky couldn't take in what was happening. Why were Steve and Veronica Williams in The Mill?

"Steven, this is madness. Put that weapon down," Veronica Williams begged her nephew.

Dear God, Steve was holding Veronica Williams at gunpoint as well.

"I've already told you to shut up." Steve swung the barrel towards his aunt, glanced from her to Abi and

Becky, then back again to his aunt. "I followed you. Something's going on. I want answers."

"It's nothing. I wanted to check out the old furniture. Your grandfather's old bureau and dresser, I would like them for sentimental reasons."

"Bullshit." Steve turned and growled at Becky. "You, there. Tell me what you wanted to say earlier about my parents."

Becky's tongue stuck to the roof of her mouth. She and Abi needed help. Very carefully, she fingered the rear pocket of her jeans. She gave an inward groan. She was wearing pyjamas, and her phone was on the floor by her bed.

"Steven. Please, stop this before you do something stupid." Veronica Williams's arms hung limply by her side.

He glared at his aunt in reply, then nodded at Becky. "Get on with it."

In her heart, Becky knew the truth had to come out at some point. She just hadn't expected to be the person to tell him.

Apollo banged his chest against the stable door and pawed the granite floor with a clunk-clunk of metal shoes.

"Can't that stupid horse be quiet?" Steve stared in the direction of the stables, then switched his gaze back to Becky. "I'm waiting."

She took a deep breath and fixed her eyes on his. "Your parents are still alive," she said, her voice surprisingly clear and controlled.

Steve sneered. "Rubbish."

"Your father's living in Brazil. Your mother–"

"No," Abi shouted. "Constance is–"

"Shut your mouth." Steve yanked the rifle towards Abi's head. "I want to hear what she's got to say." He swung the weapon back towards Becky. "My father died

332

in Brazil, in the same car crash that killed my mother. Sure, he worked there for a while, but he's dead."

Becky held his gaze. "Your mother was never in a car crash in Brazil. Your father was, but he recovered."

Steve shook his head. "No. That's not true. They both died in Brazil. Tell her, Aunt Veronica. They're both dead. Tell her."

Veronica Williams looked at Becky then Abi. The woman seemed to shrink before Becky's eyes. She almost felt sorry for her.

"My darling. I'm so sorry, I just wanted to shield you from the horrible truth." Veronica Williams moved towards her nephew, then stopped as he raised the rifle to her chest, a wild look in his eyes.

"Steven, the truth is, your mother took my money and left for a new life. To be frank, she didn't want you."

"You liar." Abi stepped forward.

Becky grabbed her sister's sweatshirt and pulled her back.

Abi's feet skidded on the loose rubble as she shrugged Becky's hand away.

"She's lying. Your–"

"Shut up," Steve snarled. "I can't think straight."

Hand on his forehead, he paced back and forth.

Becky's heart thumped against her ribs. Maybe she could make him understand. She took another deep breath.

"Steve. Please listen to me. Let me finish."

He stopped and looked at her. "Go on.

"I wanted to find out all I could about Vellangoose and why your aunt wanted the place so much. I contacted the company your father used to work for, in the hope they could tell me something about your parents and how they died." A dry lump rose in her throat. "Your father rang me."

"What? No." A muscle in his cheek twitched.

"Yes. A few days ago. From Brazil. He wants to see you."

"Are you mad?" Steve dragged his hand through his hair so hard it stood up on end.

"It suited your aunt for you, and others, to believe that both of your parents were dead. She took advantage of your mother when she was in rehab, and your father when he was incapacitated following a terrible car accident." Becky ran the tip of her tongue over her lips. "Your aunt manipulated them so she could keep you."

Steve stared coldly at his aunt. "Is this true?" His voice was frighteningly normal.

His aunt shrank away from him, her hand clutched to her throat. "I did what was best for you. I thought–"

"What? You loved me more than my mother or father could?" His words came out in a cold, ugly snarl. Spittle clung to his lip. "No. No. My parents can't be alive. They would never have left me with you."

Apollo snorted and thumped his chest against the stable door again.

Steve turned and yelled into the yard. "That bloody horse is doing my head in."

"He's just frightened," Abi said.

"Frightened? It's that beast's fault my Uncle Henry is dead, not mine."

"Yours?" Becky asked. "Why would it be your fault?"

Steve blinked, shook his head. He looked confused. "I only wanted to talk to him."

Veronica Williams cried out. "You killed Henry?"

"No. No. It was an accident. I waited by the roadside; the silly fool took the same route every day. I knew he'd changed his Will. I wanted to know ... Well, he never liked me."

Steve's gaze tracked between Abi and Becky. "He laughed and said he was leaving Vellangoose to you two.

How could he? It was my mother's home." Steve's face hardened. "He sneered at me. Said he could do what he wanted. I lunged forward to grab him. He raised his crop and urged that beast straight at me. That animal was going to trample me. I thumped it on the nose. It reared, then bolted." He stared at his aunt, a bewildered look on his face. "Uncle Henry fell off. He never fell off."

"How could you?" His aunt croaked. "How could you leave him there? On the road. On his own?"

"He was alive when I left, I swear."

"But you–"

"Stop." He shook his head again. "Shut up. Just shut up." He let out a moan, like an animal in pain. "Fucking women. You're all the same, out for what you can get. All bloody liars." He pointed the rifle at Becky and Abi. "You two are nothing but parasites, accepting this place from a father you never knew. And you, Aunt Veronica, are a liar, and a fraud."

A tremble rolled over Becky's body. She knew, with a mother's instinct, what was coming next.

"Even Jess turned against me." He frowned. "She got too big for her boots. I gave her everything: money, clothes, a lovely home." He started pacing again. "She packed her rucksack. Said she'd had enough of me telling her what to do. But no one dumps me, so I put her straight."

Becky clenched her fists and made a move towards him. Abi grabbed her arm. Becky stopped and spoke through gritted teeth.

"If you've hurt my daughter, I'll–"

"It was only a few slaps." Steve glared at Becky. "I locked her in the cellar to cool off." He let out a high-pitched laugh. "She'll stay there until she comes to her senses."

Something unfurled in Becky's chest. In a rush of primitive emotions and fury, she leapt through the air. Her world shrunk to the cruel, sneering face in front of her. Her hand touched flesh, then gripped metal, and she kicked out. Steve grunted, doubled over, yanking the gun from her grasp.

She heard the click, then the ear-splitting explosion which blasted through the room. A woman screamed. The noise went on and on.

Becky opened her mouth, but nothing came out. Abi stood a few feet away looking down at her torn and bloodied sweatshirt, bewilderment etched on her face. In slow motion, Abi's legs buckled, and she dropped to the ground.

Her eyes fluttered, then closed.

42

Pain ripped through Abi's body. In an instant, she was pitched from darkness into consciousness. Seconds later, a confused jumble of voices floated into her head.

"Abi. Abi, are you okay? Can you hear me? She needs help. Please let me go to her."

"I said, don't move."

"Steven, what have you done?"

"Shut up. I wouldn't be here if it wasn't for you."

"Abi. Please. Speak to me."

In amongst the mishmash of sounds, a horse neighed. Somewhere, far away, something banged, banged, banged.

Tremors swept through Abi. A groan escaped from her lips. She gingerly rolled onto her side, curled into a foetal position and sucked in gulps of air.

Steve grunted. "Told you she'd be alright."

Eyes closed, Abi breathed through the agony and, with all the effort she could muster, struggled to gather her thoughts, work out what had happened, where she was. Nearby came the sound of rubble moving under someone's foot.

"I have to check on her."

Becky?

"Don't move." Steve shouted. "Kneel. You too, Aunt Veronica. Now."

Abi's side felt like someone was prodding her with a red-hot poker. She clutched her waist. A large wet patch spread out beneath her hand. Panic rose in her throat.

She took short, juddery breathes, slowly breathed in, breathed out, then partially raised one eyelid and peered into the room.

Becky knelt a few feet away, her hands linked together at the back of her head.

Veronica Williams squatted in the same position on the other side of Steve, her head bowed.

"Stop this now, Steven," she whispered. "You could have killed her."

"What does it matter? She's nothing to you."

"I don't want you arrested for murder."

Steve stopped pacing and turned to his aunt. "You started it with your lies."

"Steven, please. Let's go back to Boswyn and talk in comfort. I promise to tell you everything."

Random bits of the conversation churned around in Abi's head. She pulled in a lungful of air. Her mind cleared. People and events clicked into place. Veronica Williams. Steve. Christ, they were both insane. She and Becky had to get away.

Another thought rushed into her head. Steve needed to know the truth – all of it.

"Are you stupid?" Steve yelled at his aunt. "We've got to do something with these two first, or they'll have the Police on us."

The words pulsed into Abi's ears. She opened her mouth. "Your mother's dead."

Becky turned her head towards her and said, "Don't try to speak. Save your strength."

Shit. Nobody had understood her.

The faces of Jacob, Eve and Grace swam before Abi's eyes. Love drove her on. She tried to talk again, but the words wouldn't form in her dry, claggy mouth, and for a moment the world around her tipped and rocked from the effort.

"Are you okay?" Becky whispered.

"Constance … dead." Abi rolled her eyes towards Veronica Williams.

A deep furrow formed between Becky's eyes, then her head snapped back.

Through rubbery lips, Abi whispered, "Tell … him."

Becky hesitated, gave a small nod and slowly lowered her arms. "Steve, let me …" She quickly put her hands back onto her head when Steve pointed the gun directly at her. "Please. Let me tell you what your father said."

"I don't care what he said. He didn't want me either."

"That's not true. Your mum promised him she would look after you and the baby. He genuinely believed you were all happily settled as a family."

"Baby?"

Abi stiffened. Steve could explode at the news that his mother was having a baby. Becky clearly thought so too because she glanced at Abi.

"Go on," she rasped.

Becky turned back to face Steve.

"Your mum was pregnant. Your father said she was pleased about it and very eager for a new start with you and the baby."

Steve rushed up to Becky and poked her hard in the chest with the tip of the gun barrel. The force pushed her over onto her side.

"Liar!" he roared.

Becky spat out dust and grit, then eased herself warily onto her knees. Hands positioned on her thighs, she nodded towards Veronica Williams.

"Ask her."

Steve whirled around to face his aunt. "Did you know about a baby?"

"It is all utter nonsense." Veronica Williams straightened her back and looked him in the eye. "Mrs Farrow is saying these things to upset you. It is one of the reasons I want them off the property."

Abi gritted her teeth against the pain, forced herself to a sitting position, and slumped against a pile of rubbish. Darkness circled the edge of her vision.

"Your mother's dead," she rasped. "Your aunt murdered her."

Everyone in the room froze.

Steve stared at her.

Veronica Williams broke the silence first.

"She is becoming delirious. Steven, we need to go. The Police will understand that this was all a ghastly accident."

Steve locked his eyes onto Abi. "Talk."

Her mouth was dry, and her whole body ached from her neck to her toes. Broken bricks and shards of rubble cut into her thighs. She licked her lips, but before she could speak, Becky rushed in.

"The baby was your Uncle Henry's child. Your aunt couldn't have your mother making that information public, so she killed her."

"Enough," Veronica Williams shrieked. "We are leaving. Now."

"Stay where you are." Steve jabbed his forehead with his fingers. "I need to know the truth."

"Your mother was coming back for you, but something happened." Abi gasped for air. "We know things about ... your aunt ... her secrets." Bile rose in her throat. Her voice dwindled to a whisper.

"What? I can't hear you." Steve moved closer to Abi. "Say that again."

In the stable, Apollo let out a high-pitched squeal, and the sound of splintering wood echoed across the yard and into The Mill.

Steve swung around to face the door. "What the–"

Becky's eyes flashed a signal at Abi, who kicked out with all her remaining strength. Her feet connected with hard bone. Pain rocketed through her. She screamed. Steve staggered backwards. Black spots danced in her eyes, and her vision dimmed. She lost sight of him. Where was he?

Through the hazy gloom, his silhouetted figure rose in front of her. She screamed again.

Then, Becky was there. The whack of something against flesh rang in Abi's ears. Light returned. Steve lay flat out on the ground, his eyes closed. Her sister stood over him, a large plank of wood in her hand. Tears streamed down her face.

"You hurt my Jess. How could you?" Becky raised the plank again.

"Becky, don't," Abi cried out.

Her sister let the piece of wood drop to the ground with a thump.

Movement caught Abi's eye. "Becky," she moaned.

Her sister grabbed the discarded rifle and pointed it at Veronica Williams, who had edged her way towards the door. "Don't even think about it. Move over there. Sit down. Now," Becky shouted. "That's right, in the dirt, where you belong."

Becky squatted next to Abi. "My God, you look terrible. You're bleeding badly."

Abi lifted the front of her sweatshirt. A long red channel gouged through the flesh from her abdomen up to the middle of her ribcage. She bit down on her lower lip, tentatively touched the bloody track and examined the area around it. No broken ribs. No hole. A flesh wound. How lucky was she?

"I'll tie him up." Becky squeezed her arm. "Then I'll go and get help."

Abi grabbed Becky's sleeve. "We need to finish this first."

"But Jess ..." Becky scrambled to her feet. "I need to go to her."

"Please," Abi whispered. "For all our kids' sakes."

Becky hesitated, then reached out a hand and helped Abi to her feet.

Abi staggered to the wall and leaned against the cold rough granite and watched, helpless, as Becky tugged pieces of twine from the rubble, swiftly tied Steve's hands behind his back, bound his feet and secured his trussed-up body to a large, heavy plank of wood. When she finished, she stepped away from the unconscious figure, nodded at Abi and picked up the rifle from the floor.

Abi jabbed her finger in Veronica Williams's direction. "Talk or ..." Abi pointed to the rifle in Becky's hand, "I'll make you."

"I have already told you everything."

"Like hell you have," Abi rasped.

Veronica Williams folded her arms and stared towards the door.

"What happened when Constance came back to Cornwall? Did she demand to have Steve back?" Abi winced but carried on. "Did she blab about her affair with your husband? Maybe how easily he gave in to her charms?" She took a breath and urged herself to string the words together. "Were you afraid she'd take your husband as well as Steve, leaving you with nothing but a cold bed in that big, barren house?"

"Lies. All lies."

"Did she say Henry was going with her? Precious, beautiful Constance was going off with all the prizes. Again." Abi shifted position. Blood seeped through her fingers. "For God's sake, the game's over. Just tell us what happened to Constance. The police will soon find out the truth anyway."

Veronica Williams's back hunched.

"Everyone thought she was the most wonderful and adorable creature," she tugged at the sleeve of her jacket, "but she was a slut. Several people could have been that baby's father. Constance was our father's favourite child, so she was used to having everything her way. Even expected me to give up my son." Veronica Williams suddenly snapped her fingers. "Just like that."

"Steve was her child," Becky said. "She'd every right to take him."

Veronica Williams snorted. "She was not fit to be a mother to Steven. Drugs, drink, men; she'd never give them up, no matter what those misguided people at the rehab clinic said." Her mouth twisted into a sneer. "I had to make her understand that Steven was mine and that I was his mother."

"What happened?" Abi asked.

"We had an argument. A fight." Veronica Williams let out an abrupt laugh. "In the end, her little accident turned out rather fortunate for me."

"Accident?" Becky said.

"It was her own fault." Veronica Williams's jaw tilted upwards. "She taunted me about the pregnancy. Took delight in telling me it was Henry's baby." She tugged her beautifully manicured fingers roughly through her hair. "I could not have children. She rubbed my nose in it, like she always did. I already had the humiliation of knowing that my husband had at least one illegitimate child." Her gaze flickered towards Becky. "Enough was enough." She let out another savage grunt, then fell silent.

"How did she die?" Abi forced herself to ask.

"My sister had this dreadful smirk on her face, then she laughed. I hit her on the nose. She punched me and scratched my cheek. I shoved her away and made for the door. We fought a lot as children, and I suddenly realised she was not worth the bother. When I looked back, she'd disappeared. Gone."

"Gone where?" Becky asked.

Abi shook her head in the effort to remember everything. She looked at her sister for help.

Becky's face had paled.

It all fell into place. "Oh," Abi said.

Becky drew in a deep breath. "Constance is here. In The Mill. That's why Vellangoose was abandoned for all those years, and why you want to get rid of us." Becky put a hand to chest. "Where though?"

Abi rubbed her temple. Something nagged at the edges of her mind. She couldn't think clearly. Her head was thick with tiredness. Her gaze fell on the square piece of wood covering the well.

"The well. She fell down the well when you shoved her." Abi shivered. "But she's not there now."

A jolt of pain shot through her. Her strength ebbed away and she lowered herself to the floor. Her thoughts were slipping away from her again.

Becky knelt beside her and grasped her hands. "When you found Veronica Williams earlier, where was she standing? What was she doing?"

"In the corner. Over there … looking at that old pile of stuff. Her father's old furniture or some such shite."

Becky stepped up to Veronica Williams. "What's behind the furniture?"

Abi struggled to her feet once more and came up beside her sister.

Becky put her arm around her, then glared at Veronica Williams. "Stand up. I think you should finish your search."

"I cannot do that."

"Oh, I think you can," Becky growled.

Sweat glistened on Veronica Williams's forehead as she pulled wood and other detritus away from the walls leading into the corner. The legs of her father's old writing bureau collapsed. The whole unit crumbled into a heap of dust and rubble onto the floor.

Finally, the rubbish was cleared.

Abi, arm squeezed tight across her abdomen, hobbled unsteadily to the cleared corner. She and Becky stared into the empty space. The furniture had hidden sweet F.A.

"Told you there was nothing to see." Veronica Williams's lips twisted into an ugly pout. "I was looking for the furniture, nothing else."

Abi leaned against her sister. What a mess.

Then, she saw it. The bricks. Some of them were a tad lighter and mismatched, as though they'd been added at a different time.

Becky had noticed them too and had already reached down and picked up a metal rod from amongst the debris. She walked to the wall. Her arm swung back and then forward; the rod hit the brick with a loud clunk. The sound filled the room.

Clunk. Clunk. Clunk.

The brick crumbled.

Veronica Williams gasped, stumbled backwards, and collapsed back onto the floor.

Becky thrust her hand into the exposed hole and tugged at the roughened edges. Abi moved closer. Another brick gave up its long-held position and dropped to the ground.

Becky stood rigid; her hand suspended in the air. Abi's heart pounded. They both stared into the cavity.

A skeleton stared back at them.

43

Becky tucked the aluminium foil around the partly cooked turkey, picked up the roasting pan, and placed it back into the oven. Another ninety minutes should do it. Their guests would arrive in about an hour. By the time Christmas greetings had been exchanged, drinks poured and all the presents opened, the turkey would be ready. If it wasn't, who cared? Nothing was going to spoil this day.

The smell of roast turkey and the spicy tang of mulled wine on the cooker top filled her nostrils. She took a deep breath and smiled. How different from last year when she'd spent most of Christmas Day alone at Rose Cottage. John and Jess had both hurried off after lunch, leaving her to wash up and tidy her cream co-ordinated kitchen in gut-wrenching silence.

Laughter floated through the open kitchen window. Jacob, Eve and Grace were helping Abi to feed and muck out the animals. Earlier, when the children's over-excited voices had rocketed to an ear busting level, Abi had yelled, "Time to run off all that chocolate you had for breakfast and give the animals their Christmas treats."

The children had rushed into the kitchen to carry a large bowl of chopped apples and carrots outside.

Becky pulled open the cutlery draw and scooped out all the knives, forks and spoons she could find, dropped them onto a tray, added a large pack of paper napkins and a set of red reindeer salt and pepper pots. She made her way to the living room and laid the tray on a makeshift table that temporarily filled half the room.

The kitchen door banged open, and the children charged down the hallway to their bedrooms, Buddy yapping at their heels. Within seconds, the noise of play resumed.

"I said wash your hands and put on your new clothes before everyone arrives. Now. Or there'll be no more presents." Abi fired off the instructions as she backed through the doorway, dragging a large wicker basket full of logs. Becky seized the other handle and together they wriggled it into a spot next to the fireplace. Abi immediately chucked two more logs onto the flames that flickered and flared in the granite fireplace.

"I should've told everyone to come dressed in t-shirts and shorts." Becky couldn't stop the giggle in her voice as she leaned over and flipped a switch.

The seven-foot-tall Christmas tree stood next to the fireplace, flooded with tiny lights. Becky's treasured baubles and glass decorations – saved from her life at Rose Cottage – sparkled amidst the hand-made paper chains, tinsel and other ornaments the children had added. Grace's favourite doll tilted precariously on the top of the tree. A pile of unopened presents tumbled around the base.

Abi stood back, hands on her hips, and stared. "I imagined this the very first time I saw this room."

Becky grinned as she moved back to the table and folded the red and green napkins. Her sister was at it again.

"You were the first to light the fire. Remember? You were a wet, stinking mess, scared rigid after Apollo had chased you." Abi reached out and touched one of the baubles. "You'd lit a fire to dry your clothes. The room was full of smoke, and you'd used Jacob's sleeping bag to keep warm. I could've throttled you. But all this. The tree. The fire. I saw it then."

Becky hadn't been able to see anything but the dreadful presence of Abi towering over her – angry, rude, and foul-mouthed – the younger half-sister she'd never known about or wanted. Thank goodness they'd made the decision that day to live together at Vellangoose.

Grace let out a loud shout. "Mummy. I want Mummy."

"I'm coming, sweetheart. Kids, eh. Who'd have 'em?"

Becky raised her eyebrows. Who indeed?

She smoothed a crease from the bedsheet-cum-tablecloth. Eve and Grace had decorated the white surface with multi-coloured stars and gold glitter. Christmas crackers and party hats in different shapes and sizes were heaped in the middle. It would be cosy for sixteen people, but no one would mind.

A few minutes later, a smartly dressed Eve, hair combed and pinned with new hair clips, rushed up to Becky and shoved a bundle of coloured cards and pieces of paper into her hand.

"Me and Grace made these for the table. Jacob helped. He wrote the names. Bye."

Becky scanned the homemade place names, decorated with stickers of flowers, hearts and tinsel, and fingered the ones for Auntie Natalie, Uncle Pete, Thomas and Lily – her sister and family. Nowadays, the relationship between Becky and Natalie couldn't be better. It would take a bit longer for Abi and Natalie to warm to each other, but they were getting there.

"I'm off to pick up Grandad." Jess slammed the front door behind her before Becky had a chance to reply.

Where did her daughter get her energy from? She was always in a hurry, off here and there and visiting friends. She would miss Jess when she moved out in the New Year to share a flat with a girlfriend, but that was just as it ought to be. Thank goodness she'd put the whole affair with Steve behind her.

Jess had recently spent a week in Devon with her dad, and Leanne, the barmaid, who John had left Becky for. They now ran a pub together, but only Leanne's name was on the licence. Sensible woman. Becky and John's divorce had been granted without him seeking any money from her, nor had he asked for a share of Vellangoose. Maybe he had a conscience after all?

She picked up two yellow cards: Gran and Grandad – her dad and Abi's mum, Fran. Dad spent a lot of time at Vellangoose. The pruned fruit trees and the newly dug vegetable patch in the walled garden were all his work. The children followed him around like puppies. The day they first called him Grandad, he couldn't stop grinning.

Fran had returned from Australia immediately she heard the news that Abi had been shot. She now lived nearby and would join them for lunch.

Abi half leaned through the doorway. "Shall I get the sausages, bacon, and the other food bits from your new bolthole?"

"There's lots of stuff, I'll come with you."

"Any excuse to admire your dream kitchen again." Abi nudged her as they entered what used to be the old dairy and milk house.

The two buildings had been knocked into one big room and were now fitted out with stainless steel worktops, and clean-lined, white units. Becky couldn't wait for the new commercial oven to be delivered in January, then she would no longer need to cook at her dad's.

Fifteen minutes later, with all the food now cooking in the oven, Becky headed back to the living room and picked up another handful of place names: Abi, Jacob, Eve and

Grace (no card for Ben). She seated them together, but wondered whether all the children might want to sit in a group? She shrugged. Someone would sort it out.

Abi bounced into the room, numerous wine glasses threaded through her fingers. She put the glasses on the table and picked up one of the remaining cards – Jack – and put it next to her place setting.

Detective Inspector Jack Carter had been a frequent visitor to Vellangoose in the last few months. He supervised the crime scene, took the initial statements, and provided updates on Veronica Williams and Steve. During that time, Abi had gathered some data of her own on the detective inspector: single parent, amicable divorce, co-parent of two sons.

The Coroner's Hearing concluded Constance had died from a fractured skull. Jack said there hadn't been enough forensic evidence to confirm whether it had been sustained as a result of an accident or an act of violence.

Veronica Williams had yet to come to trial for the various charges she faced.

"The bloody woman's faking it," Abi said when Jack told them that Veronica Williams had suffered a nervous breakdown and was now housed in a mental health facility.

Becky wasn't so sure. Maybe the woman's conscience had finally caught up with her and the breakdown was retribution for covering up the truth, whatever that was, for all those years?

Steve was given a suspended sentence for his involvement in events. Back in sole charge of Williams Estates and Haulage, he now lived alone at Boswyn Manor. Maybe the business would prove to be his true love?

The little bones of Constance's baby, wrapped inside its mother's skeleton, were unable to reveal whether its father was Henry Williams or not. Maybe, that was just as well.

Now and then, Becky and Abi talked about Henry Williams and tried to second guess why he'd left them Vellangoose and Apollo. Perhaps he regretted he'd had nothing to do with them when he was alive? Or maybe it was simply an act of revenge on Veronica Williams and their toxic marriage? Becky and Abi concluded they would never know why. It didn't matter; they were their own people and at ease with who they were.

During the fog of the days after the shooting, Megan, Hugh, Jeffery, and many of the villagers, silently came back and forth to feed the animals and muck out, only exchanging a brief hello, or a nod of the head as they went about their business.

When the police and forensics had finished, Hugh and Jeffery had led a team of volunteers to clear out The Mill. They filled in the well, re-plastered the walls, and concreted the floor. For several weeks, neither Becky nor Abi would go near the place, until one day, hand in hand, they went inside.

"It feels so sinister in here. That poor woman and her baby. Maybe I'd feel better if we had some sort of ceremony?" Abi tightened her grip on Becky's arm. "You know … to cleanse the place."

Shortly after, Jeffery and his wife, and a small group of friends and family, attended a service of blessing led by the local vicar for Constance and her baby. The children used The Mill now as a playroom. There would be time enough to make further decisions on what to do with it.

Becky picked up the final card and studied the large purple writing on an orange background. David. One hand on her stomach, she smiled to herself. She'd got a second chance with this amazing man. With Veronica Williams out of the picture, he'd made an application to have the restrictive conditions of the Trust document declared null and void. No counterclaim was presented to the court, and the submission was granted. Becky and Abi's money worries were over.

"So, when are you going to tell him?" Becky jumped at Abi's voice.

"What?"

"The baby." Abi leaned against the door frame, a stupid grin on her face.

Becky put a hand to her neck. She knew the silly red blotches would have already appeared.

"How did you know?"

"I can spot a pregnant woman a mile away. How far are you gone?"

"Ten weeks."

Becky straightened a couple of knives and forks. She felt so stupid. Who had an unplanned pregnancy at her age? She would be forty next year, for God's sake.

"You need to put him out of his misery. The poor beggar has asked you to marry him, or to move in with him, or whatever you want. You know he'll be over the moon at the news."

She did know. That wasn't what held her back.

"I'm going to tell him later. And Jess. Good heavens, what do I say to her? She'll be so embarrassed."

"She's guessed already. Waylaid me last week and banged on about it, wanting to know what I knew. Your daughter's all grown up. And for your information, she's okay with it."

"Oh."

Abi moved towards her. "So, what's the real problem?"

For a moment Becky didn't want to confess, but it needed to be said.

"I don't want to leave Vellangoose."

"Then, don't. Nothing needs to change. David could

visit whenever he likes if he doesn't want to live here, or he could move in."

"Where?"

"Come on, Becky, have you got pregnant woman brain or something? Think about it, we've already fixed up the old dairy and the piggery for our work premises, but we could expand into the other buildings. Farms around here have set a precedent, converting out-buildings into houses and holiday homes." Abi picked up a red party hat and arranged it at a jaunty angle on her head. "I reckon we should make a planning application to convert the old cows' house and the hayloft above it into a two-storey residence. Maybe, that would be for me and the kids, and you and David could have The Barn?"

Becky's head spun. Where had this sensible businesslike Abi come from?

"Perhaps later, we might think about doing something with The Mill? Tea rooms? Holiday flats? Vellangoose has so much potential, what with the ponds, woodland, and the land. There's nothing to restrict us."

"We must keep the stables for Megan for as long as she wants them."

Abi nodded. "Agreed."

A car pulled into the yard and the driver hooted the horn.

David. First to arrive, like he promised, so he could organise the drinks. Becky moved into the kitchen to greet him.

Behind him, Jess's old mini rattled down the lane, followed by Fran's car. Natalie's four-by-four brought up the rear.

David rushed into the kitchen, hugged and kissed her, then grabbed an armful of bottles from the fridge and hurried into the living room. How she loved him. Maybe she would tell him about the baby after he'd poured the champagne? Or maybe when the brandy flames engulfed the Christmas puddings? Or later when they were snuggled up together by the fire? Maybe, just maybe, she'd accept the diamond solitaire she knew he'd present to her again at some point during the day? On the other hand, she didn't need the so-called security of marriage to make her happy.

A flood of emotion overcame her as each family member burst into the kitchen and filled her home with food, presents and love.

David's voice floated from the living room. "Happy Christmas. Happy Christmas. In here everyone. Drinks."

The kitchen emptied. Abi came back into the room and handed her a small glass of champagne.

"To family," Abi said.

"Family." Becky took a small sip of the bubbly liquid.

They both looked at each other, smiled, and clinked their glasses. "To Vellangoose," they said together.

Another car pulled into the yard. The final guests had arrived. Abi put her drink on the worktop and made her way outside.

Through the open door, Becky watched Jack as he eased his long legs out of the vehicle, bent down and kissed Abi on the cheek. Her sister's smile reached her eyes, and she leaned against his chest. Maybe something would come of this friendship. Or maybe, it wouldn't. It didn't matter anymore. Abi seemed content with her life without a man, now that she'd finally acquired the home she'd always craved for her children.

Jack's boys tumbled from the car. He held the hand of the youngest one and wrapped his other arm lightly around Abi's waist as they made their way through the garden towards the kitchen.

Down the valley, the sun punched a thin slot through the blanket of grey cloud. Wintry light tinged the treetops and hedges in a soft glow. Becky savoured it all – the voices and laughter coming from the living room, the wonderful smells, the love – and tucked it all away someplace deep within her heart.

The oven timer pinged. She tugged on her oven gloves, lifted the turkey onto the worktop, then pulled the foil aside.

"Perfect."

Acknowledgements

Thank you to Grosvenor House Publishing Ltd for helping me bring this book to print.

Special heartfelt thanks to Kath Morgan (mentor and editor) and Wendy Mason (fellow writer). Without their help, advice and constructive criticism, Sisters of Vellangoose would never have been written. A big hug to Liz Wever for reading an early draft and for her enthusiastic encouragement along the way.

Thank you also to Sarah Bourguignon for the legal advice on Trusts and Wills. Any errors or misinterpretations are entirely mine.

My biggest thank you must go to my husband, Adrian, for always being there on the good writing days and the bad. Love you.

Lightning Source UK Ltd.
Milton Keynes UK
UKHW011156151222
413978UK00006B/647